Power Lies

By Jerry Allen

Published by Island Dog Publishing

Copyright © Gerald N. Allen
July, 2015

ISBN-13: 978-1514830918
ISBN-10: 1514830914

Also by Jerry Allen

Bad Habit

Break a Bad Habit

Cast and Blast

For those that love the land.

This story is the result of an overly active imagination and any resemblance to people either alive or dead is purely coincidental.

1

The knock startled Wilson Northrop. His German wirehaired pointer jumped up barking wildly, charging at the door. Nobody ever came to the front of the house.

Will put down the book he had been reading, then walked silently across the thick braided rug to peek out a window. A man wearing a gray blazer and khaki slacks stood at the door. "Duchess, sit, quiet," said Will.

He opened the door, asking, "Can I help you?"

"Hi," said the man, "I'm Frank Atkins, with Northern Land Investments." He offered a hand. "It's quite a nice place you have here." A briefcase sat on the steps beside him.

Will ignored the offered hand and said, "I don't think you drove all the way out here to compliment my property. What are you selling?"

"You must have heard about the power line that United Eastern Power is planning. It will bring clean renewable energy to our country."

"Yeah, I've heard of it, and I've been wondering where the hell it was going to go."

The original plan called for the huge power line to run down the other side of Hawk Hill, but, to the surprise of United Easter Power, many landowners would not sell. Speculation on a new route had filled the local newspapers.

"My company is acquiring land for the project and we would like to buy your piece, all four hundred and seventy-five acres of it, and we're willing to pay you twice what you paid for it only one short year ago."

"You must be getting desperate," laughed Will. "This property isn't for sale. I'm planning to stay here for the rest of my life." He turned and swung the heavy paneled door shut, its thud ending the conversation.

"So they think they're going to come this way," said Will, looking at Duchess. "I thought they might." The dog looked puzzled.

From a living room window he watched Frank Atkins walk down the drive and climb into a silver Range Rover. "He must have stopped over to Barbara's place too," he continued. "Her piece is smaller and would have cost them less money." Shaking his head and walking toward the kitchen, he added, "City people and their damned money, trying to walk all over us."

He grabbed a light jacket from a hook by the door and glanced in a mirror hanging next to it. For fifty-two, he didn't look too bad, with no extra weight and few gray hairs. Stepping out the back door, Duchess darted ahead and around the side of the house to dance beside a Ford F150 pickup truck. Will opened the truck's door and she jumped in. Together, they started out the long straight driveway.

The Range Rover had already disappeared.

A large tabletop flat pasture stretched off in every direction. At the end of the drive they turned right onto asphalt, and soon the road bent to the right and they started the climb up Hawk Hill, passing through patches of hardwoods broken up by sloping pastures. High up, where the road crossed the height of the land, cows grazed still higher up in a field to the right and near the edge of the dark woods. Above them, the spruce and fir trees of Hawk Hill formed a rounded peak.

Up on the flat shoulder of the hill they could see to the rolling hills and small mountains stretching out into the next state. A few camps or second homes had been built around a small round lake. Large level pastures stretched off to the south, all of them owned by Charlie and Agnes Hammond.

The Hammonds had stubbornly refused to sell their property to United Eastern Power, which turned them into homegrown heroes. Very few of the locals wanted to look at a string of tall towers stretching across the countryside. Rumor had it that the Hammonds had turned down over two million dollars for just an easement across the corner of their land.

Rounding a bend, the Hammond's home came into view.

"Oh my God," said Wilson, with his foot settling on the truck's brake.

2

Three State Police cars and a half dozen fire trucks sat beside the smoldering charred remains of what had once been the Hammond's home. Several cars parked along the roadside, where people wearing blank expressions stood and watched.

Will slowed.

Charlie Hammond's blackened truck sat in the driveway, next to Agnes's burned SUV. Stopping beside two male bystanders, Will put down the truck's passenger side window.

"Were they at home?"

Duchess stood on the seat, trying to sniff the bystander.

"Nobody knows," said one of the men. "It don't look good." He spit a wad of tobacco juice onto the grass. "It don't look good," he repeated.

The State Police officers stood by one of the cruisers, wearing serious expressions and talking. One of them pointed at the wreckage and then down the street. The firemen continued to pour water onto the rubble. Gray steam drifted upwards. One of the fire trucks whined as it started across the lawn then onto the road. Will guessed they were going to the lake to refill with water.

He eased his truck ahead and started down the hill. "Well, that sucks," he said, glancing at Duchess. "I hope they weren't home."

The rolling road took them downhill past longstanding farms and patches of woodlands. Coming into town, old Victorian homes sat behind bright green lawns. Wilson slowed and stopped in front of Big Bear's Restaurant as a logging truck rumbled through town. After making sure the truck's windows were open a couple of inches for air, Will told Duchess to stay as he stepped out.

Only two couples sat at tables inside. He walked by and slid onto a stool at the counter.

"You're back again," said the waitress. "This makes six days in a row." She smiled. "You must like the food here."

"It's good," said Will, a bit nervously. "And I like the company. Don't you ever get a night off?"

Smiling, she ignored the question. "Meatloaf is the special, with mashed potatoes, gravy, and green beans."

Will ordered it and she disappeared into the kitchen. Only two weeks before he had noticed Kim working there. She was in her mid-thirties, he guessed, stood about up to his shoulder, with auburn hair in a ponytail that bounced when she talked, and very dark brown eyes. Quick with a smile, he found her easy to talk with and started coming nightly for dinner, timing it when he hoped so she wouldn't be too busy.

He picked up the local paper and started to read a front page story about United Eastern Power. Kim reappeared carrying his dinner.

"So, do you ever get a night off?" he asked again.

"Usually I work two or three nights a week, and open a couple of mornings," she said. "I prefer the mornings, five until one. This week I'm filling in for somebody."

"What do you do when you're not working?" asked Will.

"I like to hike and fish. I'm trying to get my guide's license."

Outdoorsy, that didn't surprise Will. Something about her spelled tomboy. "Really? To take people fishing?" He realized that was a dumb question and felt foolish.

"Yes, excuse me," she said, departing to tend a couple preparing to leave.

A knot tightened in Will's stomach. In the six years since a tractor trailer flattened his wife's car, instantly killing her, he had not dated. He picked up the newspaper again, but his mind wouldn't focus. Part of him still felt like he was cheating on his wife, even if he had only thought about asking another woman out.

When Kim returned, he asked, "So do you have a boyfriend?"

"Not at the moment," she smiled. "There aren't a lot of candidates to choose from around here."

"Do you want to go fishing sometime?" He had planned to ask her out to dinner, but fishing sounded like a safer idea. "You could show me some local spots."

"Ha!" she laughed. "You're trying to get me to guide for free."

"No, and you don't have a guide's license yet."

She grinned. "Yeah, I'd like that. So, where are you from?"

Will explained how he had moved from Massachusetts and bought the old Stanley farm a little over the year before. He skipped the part about his wife dying and the money from the trucking company's insurance. The house came with a small barn and big fields. He spent most of the first year putting in a new kitchen, bath, and painting the inside walls.

"There's good fishing in the Mooslikamoosuc River," said Kim. "Particularly in the stretch you own. The water slows there and there's some deep holes. Every once in a while there's a big brown trout."

Tires chirping on asphalt caused them both to look out the window. A State Police car rounded the corner and headed out of town.

"I wonder where he is going?" said Kim.

Will recounted what he had seen on the way to town.

"The Hammonds are local heroes," she said. "I hope they weren't home."

"Their property blocked United Power's first proposed route," said Will. "I wonder what happens to their land if they died."

"They have a daughter," said Kim, wiping the counter. "She's about my age and works down country as a nurse practioner somewhere."

"The people on either side of the Hammond's place made an agreement with United Power," said Will. "The way I understand it, they received ten percent of the selling price when they signed, and will get the balance when the project is permitted."

"That's right. The people up in this country don't have much," said Kim, "except the land. Some of them have had tough times, with the paper mill closing and now the hotel. I can't fault anyone for selling, but it hurts when they do."

"I love the country up here, it's an undiscovered beauty," said Will.

Kim leaned on the counter across from Will, and said, "Those huge towers carrying power lines would be an eyesore. You'll be able to see them from all over the place. And there is some concern about health hazards from the radiation they emit."

Will shook his head. "This area has suffered economically, but the people are tough."

Kim laughed and started to wipe the counter again. "Wait until you've spent a few more winters here. You'll be tough too, or gone."

She excused herself and went to take money from the last customers, who were waiting next to the register. Will finished up his dinner.

"I love it this time of the year," she said, returning. "Look at how light it still is."

The clock on the wall said eight-thirty. Outside, the sun had set, but daylight lingered.

"So when shall we go fishing?" asked Will.

"I'm off tomorrow. We could try in the evening. There may still be some alderflies hatching."

"Where shall we meet?"

"How about at your place, say at five," said Kim. "We can fish the river along your property."

Will loved the smile she gave him, before she turned and disappeared into the kitchen. He put money on the counter and left.

On the way home he passed the fire trucks and police cars that still surrounded the blackened remains of the Hammond's home. A Fish and Game Department truck had parked there too, and Will recognized John Johansson talking with a police officer. Steam and smoke still floated up from the rubble. Most of the gawkers had left. A wide yellow police tape, attached to the tops of skinny wooden stakes, corralled the mess.

Only a few houses sat on the top of the hill and then the road started down. Will loved the view of the rolling mountains that stretched off into miles of timberland. An enormous pasture, with black and white cows standing in it, climbed off to the left. Where the road dropped faster, thick trees lined either side with only a few dirt driveways leading to hidden homes.

At the bottom of the hill he turned left. Pastures opened up again on both sides. Another left took him onto his long driveway. His small house, tucked among a cluster of white pines, stood on a small knoll.

The first time he saw that house the place reminded him of a ranger's camp, with a steep green metal roof and a farmer's porch across the front. A short distance beyond, a weathered brown barn stood where the pines met the field. At the far edge of the pasture, the hardwoods of Hawk Hill climbed upward.

Duchess beat him to the door. Inside, he walked into the living room to turn his laptop computer on. While it started, he removed his boots and set them on the hearth of the stone fireplace. An oil painting of a ruffed grouse flying over a tumbled down rock wall hung above the thick mantel. A picture of Maggie, his deceased wife, holding their new puppy Duchess, sat next to a pewter candle holder on the mantel and he stopped to look at it.

A touch of guilt poked him. "I love you Maggie, and will forever," he said. He knew she would want him to move on, but it didn't stop the painful emotion.

He looked out the window over a desk made of cherry. Dark purples and traces of red colored the sky, and a lone star glowed over the hill to the south. "Hi Maggie," he said, smiling at the star. "I know you are there and that you understand." He sat to open his laptop.

Duchess stopped to rest her chin on his thigh, which brought him back to the moment. Opening up email, the first came from his daughter, Amy.

Will worried about Amy. Since her husband died, serving his country in Afghanistan, life had been tough. Her five year old son, Ethan, was a handful, having inherited his father's recklessness. The previous summer the boy managed to break an arm by falling out of a tree, and then proceeded to damage the cast so badly it needed to be replaced. Twice. Amy had her mother's independent streak and always refused Will's offers to help, but at least her job as a nurse practitioner paid well.

Hoping for pictures of his grandson, he clicked on the email.

Dad,
We are coming up tomorrow.
Love, Amy

"Well, I wonder what that's about," he said, scratching the dog's ear.

3

Frank Atkins sat at a table with Robert Henderson in the restaurant of the inn known as The Fenton House. Two other male patrons at the mahogany bar watched the Red Sox on a television over the bartender's head, and two women sipped wine at table next to a darkly paneled wall. The waiter set a beer in front of Frank and a tumbler of amber liquid by Robert. The thick carpet silenced his steps when he left.

"So you don't know anything about it?" asked Frank.

"I didn't, until you called," said Robert, picking up the whiskey. "It could be a stroke of luck for us."

"We don't know who will get the property," said Frank, wondering if Robert told the truth.

"Oh, that's good," said Robert, after tasting the 15 year old Macallan. "I'll have my people look into it. Did you have any luck with Wilson Northrop?"

"No. Even though he's a newcomer, he's just as enamored with the damned land as the people that grew up here. I don't think he'll sell, at any price."

"Let's wait a bit and see what pans out with the Hammond property. We already own the land on either side of them. If we bought Northrop's we'd have to buy two of his neighbors' places too."

Frank sipped his beer, wondering what exactly went on in Robert's head. The man spent money like water, buying expensive whiskey and even more expensive hookers. A shared business trip to Florida had been one long party. How the man ever landed a job overseeing the construction of an expensive high power line was beyond Frank.

Robert seldom talked about his personal life, except to periodically complain about his wife. Days would go by without any word from him, and then all hell would break loose and everything had to be done in a hurry. Frank often feared he was about to be fired, but it hadn't happened, yet.

Talking the locals into selling their land proved to be a difficult task. Neither of them had ever imagined the people up there would love the land the way that they did. With the area's tough economic history, they thought buying up a corridor for the high tension lines would be a snap. Already, they had spent many times the original estimated amount and were nowhere near done.

The only reason Frank didn't think that Robert had the Hammonds killed and then their house burned was because it was too obvious. United Power had too much to gain by their death and would most likely be a suspect. This stroke of luck might work out in their favor, unless a relative showed up as stubborn as they had been.

"Did you notice those two broads at the table over there?" asked Robert, tilting his head in their direction.

Frank nodded silently.

Robert grinned and said, "I'll have the bartender send them over some drinks. Maybe they'll join us.

*

The air smelled of charred wood, not the sweet smell of a campfire, but the stale musty odor of smoldering dreams that had burned beyond recognition. Flashlights poked through the darkness, their feeble beams sucked into the black debris. Part of the first floor had fallen into the basement, so the firemen and police moved cautiously. Several vehicles were parked around the perimeter with their headlights illuminating the remains of the home.

John Johansson noticed the charred hand with its curled fingers, as if grasping for the unseen. It poked out from under a fallen section of blackened wall. "We have a body here," he said, shining a flashlight on it.

A tall state cop walked over and stopped by John's side. "That makes two."

"Damn it. They were both home."

"The chief already has an arson squad coming up in the morning. They'll be sending along a pile of homicide detectives now too."

"I'm calling it a night," said John. "This stuff isn't part of my jurisdiction anyway."

The cop patted him on the shoulder. "Thanks for the help."

*

Will climbed out from under the blanket, flicked on a light, and then slipped on a bathrobe. Duchess lifted her head, but didn't get off her bed in the corner of the room. Her bushy eyebrows cast an enquiring look.

"I can't sleep," he said, looking at the dog. "I'm going to dig out my fly fishing stuff." He started down the stairs.

In the kitchen he found a bottle of scotch and poured an inch in a glass, then continued down to the basement. Duchess followed, but without enthusiasm.

Will hadn't fished since he moved into the house. From boxes he pulled waders and reels and containers of flies. Cased rods leaned against a corner of the wall. He started sorting, picking a nine foot rod for a four weight line, an Orvis CFO reel, and a nine foot leader for the next day. Stuffed into the pockets of his fishing vest were the fly boxes he had carried the last time he fished, and he opened each one to see what it contained.

When the scotch had disappeared, he carried an armload of gear up to the living room, before going upstairs and back to bed.

4

Will started coffee. Outside, the gray light of morning illuminated the field. Soon the sun would peak over distant hills and paint the pasture in the various shades of green. Duchess stood patiently by the door, asking to go out. When Will opened it the air smelled sweet, of growing grass and summer.

"It's going to be a great day," he said to no one, watching Duchess trot across the back yard and along the side of the barn.

While the coffee perked, Will pulled on his boots and then fell into the usual morning routine of breakfast for the dog, bacon and eggs for himself, and a second cup of coffee while reading at the dining table. As usual, he read the newspaper from the day before. United Eastern Power was on the front page again, accusing a local conservation group that opposed their project of distorting facts. It felt like the same story had been on the front page a couple of weeks before.

"It's the same old shit," he said to Duchess, who lay by the door. "The battles never end."

Duchess raised her head as tires crunched on the gravel in the driveway.

"It's Burt," said Will, standing from the table.

Boots clunked up the back steps and the door swung in. Will handed a second cup of coffee to Burt and said, "Good morning."

"That it is," said Burt, shuffling toward the table. "The Hammond's place is quite a mess."

Burt didn't stand as tall as Will's shoulder, but his shoulders were half again as wide as Will's. With his bright blue eyes and scuffling walk, he appeared more like a dwarf than a human. Will wasn't certain how old Bart was, but the local stories put him around eighty years old.

"It sure is."

They both sat. "There's a state cop car there," said Burt. "Do you think United Power tried to burn them out?" He pulled a flask out of his back pocket to pour a dab of golden liquid into his coffee.

"Their bodies might be in the rubble," said Will. "Both of their cars were there."

Not long after he first had hired Burt, the flask appeared and caused concern. Will really didn't want a drunk working for him. Soon he learned that the flask contained locally made maple syrup.

"Both of them were pretty spry," said Burt. "I don't think they would have been trapped inside, unless they'd been asleep, and from what I hear that fire happened in the afternoon."

Wanting the change the subject, Will said, "So we're going to mark out another cut today?"

"Yeah. That patch of fir up above the stream." Burt picked up the newspaper, pulled a pair of drugstore reading glasses from a shirt pocket, and looked at the front page.

A lifelong dream of Will's had been to own a woodlot and actively manage it. The reason he had bought the property that he did was because mature timber covered much of it. The owner of the local hardware store had recommended Burt, who lived in town and was a semi-retired forester. It turned out Burt, who loved to work, would do anything, from mowing the fields and tilling the gardens, to developing woodlot management plans and helping with the firewood. Soon, the two of them had become fast friends and they spent many days bird hunting together the previous fall.

Setting down the paper, Burt said, "I talked to a young guy last night about cutting the timber for you. You'll like him."

"Well, let's go mark out some wood," said Will, standing from the table.

*

The aromas of cooking strawberries filled Barbara Hawkins old farmhouse. She chased her cat out of the kitchen, for the third time that morning, and set a kettle on the stove to simmer. Two dozen sterilized jars waited on the counter to be filled with the jam.

After the jam was poured, she went outside to feed her chickens and see what they had laid the night before. Heading back inside, she carried an even dozen eggs. The girls certainly had been earning their keep.

The tea had steeped by then and the cat returned, brushing against her leg. "Oh Tabby, you are relentless," she said. Using a smaller copper watering pot that sat beside the sink, Barbara watered a philodendron hanging in front of a window. "That bread dough needs to rise," she reminded the cat. "You leave it alone."

For over a week, a nice man named Frank Atkins had stopped by her house. The first time happened just as cookies she had made had just come out of the oven for a church bake sale, and she insisted he come in for a cup of tea and a cookie or two. He obliged and they sat and talked for almost two hours. It had been years since she had spent that much time talking with a man and Barbara found it fun.

He seemed to like the rural countryside and explained to her Eastern United Power's plans. It all sounded good, the way he explained it, and his interest in her wellbeing she found pleasing. Frank explained the economic gains the community would share when the power lines were built. Once he mentioned that they might need her land and said that if they did she would then be a rich woman.

Barbara was no fool though. Since a skidder rolled over in a logging accident, crushing her husband of only two short years to death, she had managed to keep their little farm going for over a decade. Life was work and Barbara enjoyed the rewards. She had been brought up to believe that anything easy in life should be suspect. Never ever would she sell the property, but she did not mention that to Frank.

She also knew those jobs that Frank mentioned would only last as long as the construction, and once the power line was completed the jobs would go away. But still, his visits had been nice, and each day she sent him away with cookies or bread or vegetables from her garden. The last two days, when he didn't show up, she missed chatting with him.

That day Barbara wondered about her new neighbor, Wilson Northrop, the one everyone referred to as Will. Later, she would stop by his house to drop off fresh strawberries, a jar of jam, and a loaf of still warm bread.

*

From the house Will rode in the old International Scout with Burt barely looking over the steering wheel. Duchess sat in the center of the back seat, peering through the middle of the windshield. They followed a gravel road across the vast flat field to the river, where they crossed on a timber bridge into a stand of hardwoods. The old road soon withered to a pair of wheel ruts. Burt shifted into four-wheel drive and they continued to the north, up along the side of the hill. Striped maple and occasional alders crowded the edges of the trail. Where the land flattened out, Burt pulled the rig between a fat rock maple and an old ash, then shut it off.

Duchess ran ahead as Burt led Will on foot up another long slope. The logging road had long since grown in until only moose kept a single path open. Ten minutes later, they could hear the sound of rushing water off to their left and the forest changed from hardwoods to spruce and fir as big around as a man's waist.

Burt explained how the fir trees were old and starting to decay. The trees would never be worth more, so it was time to cut them. And, with the economy improving, the price for spruce and fir had gone way up.

Together they hung surveyor's ribbons, marking the edge of the area to harvest. The road up the hill would have to be improved and that would also open up other areas to cut in the years to come. Along the stream they left a wide buffer, to keep the water shaded and cool for trout, as well as to prevent silt from running in and smothering the aquatic insects along the stream's bottom.

Hanging the ribbons, they noticed the scattered birch and poplar trees among the softwoods. Both knew the poplars would root sprout and grow quickly to provide excellent cover for both ruffed grouse and woodcock. When Will first hired Burt to come up with a forestry management plan, he mentioned providing early successional forest for ruffed grouse and woodcock. That was when Burt said, "You're my kind of young fellow."

They walked a circuitous route back to the truck, discussing other areas to cut. Burt seemed to float through the woods, never moving fast, but with a steady even pace, regardless of what the ground was like. Someday soon they would come back to mark an area of mature poplar they found. Will still had yet to see every corner of his own land, and loved following the old timer through the trees.

Heading back toward the Scout, they discovered an acre sized alder patch around a dried up beaver pond. Duchess got all birdy, sniffing and wagging her tail, frantically searching, and then soon froze like a statue. The sight of his motionless dog gave Will goose bumps. He walked ahead of Duchess and a woodcock tweetered up through the foliage to fly away.

"I love that," said Will.

"We'll have to come back here next fall," said Burt.

*

Cindy Hammond stood beside the Fish and Game Department truck, looking at what remained of her parents' home. A phone call from a longtime family friend woke her during the night, bringing the news.

Her two college-aged sons were both working on the island of Martha's Vineyard for the summer, and she left them voicemail with a brief account of what had transpired and where she was headed. Approaching the town of Fenton, she called the only person she knew in law enforcement, John Johansson, a Fish and Game Officer. They had both gone through the local school system and then on to college. She hadn't seen him since then.

"When will we know how they died?" asked Cindy.

"It may be days," said John.

Her phone call had woken him just before dawn. In the twenty-six years since he had last seen her, Cindy hadn't changed too much. She still wore her dark hair short and the big dark eyes were as expressive as ever, but tears had streaked her cheeks. From a mutual friend, at a class reunion years before, he learned she was married with two kids, but knew little more of her life than that. He couldn't imagine the things going through her head.

"The police want to ask you some questions later," said John. "There's nothing to do here. Can I talk you into breakfast?"

She nodded. "Yeah. Some coffee would be good."

He opened the door of his truck and she climbed in. Her car was parked in front of his home on a side street back in town.

"When did you see them last?" he asked, sliding onto the driver's seat.

"Only a week ago, over the fourth of July."

She looked as if tears might flow at any second. He dug paper napkins out of the glove compartment and handed them to her, then said, "Their names have been in the newspaper a lot lately, because they blocked United Eastern Power."

Sniffling, she said, "I know. They were really upset about that power line coming through."

"To a lot of us they were heroes."

She didn't say anything on the way to Main Street, and John didn't try to force a conversation. At the restaurant, he held the door as she walked in and suggested a table by the window, where the day felt a little bit brighter.

"So how long are you staying?" he asked, sitting across from her.

"I haven't thought about it," she said. Forcing a smile, she added, "I did grab a few things before leaving home."

He asked where home was and she told him Westchester County, just outside New York. Her two grown boys were on their own for the summer and she had loads of vacation time accumulated from her job in the financial district.

"I've often thought about relocating up here," she said, trying to look very brave

John smiled. "This country gets under your skin. I never dreamed of living anywhere else."

"You always wanted to be a Fish and Game officer, even back in high school," said Cindy. "I guess you made your dream come true. I miss the small town, where everybody knows everyone."

"What does your husband think of the idea?" asked John.

"I'm divorced," she said. "We split up not long after my second son was born." Turning toward the window, she wiped an errant tear. "I'm sorry. My emotions are…shredded I guess."

A waitress came and they ordered. The place filled with the going to work crowd. A few people recognized Cindy and stopped to offer condolences. After eating, she and John stood to leave.

"There's an extra bedroom in my house," offered John. "You're welcome to use it."

"You never married, did you?" said Cindy, trying to smile. "This is a small town. We'd create a lot of gossip."

"Hey, neither of us are married. This isn't the backwoods like it used to be. And I keep a pretty clean house. You're welcome to it if you want. It beats hiding out in some motel. I can drop you off and show you around, and then I have to go to work."

She nodded. "All right."

5

Duchess stood when she heard the tires on the driveway. Will looked out the window to see his daughter's Camry in the driveway.

"Amy's here," he said.

Duchess dashed to the back door and danced in circles until Will let her outside. Five year old Ethan already ran toward them. Duchess pranced about as hugs were exchanged. Ethan started throwing a stick for the dog to retrieve.

"So what brings you up here?" said Will, opening the back door.

"We needed a break," said Amy.

Will knew his daughter well enough to know there had to be more than that, arriving on such short notice. "Is it Ethan?"

Amy hugged her dad again. "That's part of it."

She hadn't mentioned dating since her husband had been killed in Afghanistan, but he asked, "A guy?"

With her arms still wrapped around her father's chest, she nodded her head.

"What did he do?" he asked.

"He was married."

Will said, "He's an asshole. Forget about him." Amy felt small in his arms. "How long do you want to stay?"

"I have four weeks of accumulated vacation time coming," she said, breaking off the hug. "Can you put up with us that long?"

"Of course. The two guest bedrooms are just like you left them." Her eyes were edged with tears. The guy must have really hurt her.

"Ethan has been so excited, since I told him we were coming to see you."

"I'm glad you both are back," he said. "The house felt too quiet after you left last time. But I made plans to go fishing with a friend later and we're supposed to get a bite to eat afterward, so make yourselves at home. You know where all the food is." She looked slightly put out, so he added, "I won't be late."

The back door opened and Ethan chased Duchess inside. Will stepped outside to fetch the luggage and Duchess followed. A red CJ5 turned in the end of the drive.

Coming back inside with the suitcases, Will said, "Kim's here."

"Kim, as in Kimberly?" said Amy, peaking out the window. "You didn't tell me you were fishing with a woman. Is it like a date?" She grinned.

"I just met her," said Will, rather apologetically. "And I don't know if it's a date. We're just going fishing."

"And then out to dinner," said Amy, smiling. "It sounds like a date to me."

Duchess bounded around the red CJ5 like Indians circling a wagon train.

"Wow, a German wirehair pointer," said Kim, stepping out and reaching to pat the dog. "What's her name?" Dark aviator glasses hid her eyes and a ponytail stuck out over the sizing strap of her cap.

"That's Duchess. And that's a great Jeep," said Will. "I always loved those."

"It's a 1968," she said. "It's got a v-6, and I have a hardtop for the winters."

Peeking inside, he asked, "Do you take off the top often?" The seats looked brand new.

"Sometimes. If there's a drought it guarantees rain," she laughed, still rubbing the dog's ears. "Is Duchess coming with us?"

"She's come fishing with me before. She just sits on the bank and watches."

"Well, get your stuff. Is the Camry yours too?"

"No. It belongs to my daughter. She's visiting for a while."

Kim insisted on taking her Jeep and Will didn't protest. Duchess sat on the floor between the two bucket seats, as they bounced down the road across the field. Will wondered how much older Kim was than his daughter…maybe six or eight years. She parked on the right side of the timber bridge where it crossed a narrow spot in the river. Her legs looked longer in jeans than the skirt she wore in the restaurant.

They followed the shore upstream, wearing waders and carrying their gear. The limbs of tall silver maples and elms spread over the stream, providing protection from the summer sun. Where a long riffle tumbled into a pool, she insisted on sitting to watch the water for a while.

Small mayflies mated in the air above the fast moving water. Two or three moth-like caddis flies bounced on the slower water. Kim pointed out the feeble alder flies fluttering around foliage that crowded the stream's edges.

"Start down the bottom of this pool," she said. "It's not deep, at least along the edges. Fish close to the banks. The trout will be feeding there. It's mostly brookies, but some of them are good size." Grinning, she added, "Once in a while a big brown will come up from downstream and surprise the hell out of you.

"Here," she continued, handing him a couple of flies. "Tie one of these on. If you're not snagging a branch once in a while, you're not fishing close enough to the banks." The flies looked like elk hair caddis, about a size 12.

"What are you going to do?" asked Will.

"I'm going to go upstream a bit and fish there."

Will walked down to the foot of the pool, where there was plenty of room for casting. He sat on the bank to tie on one of Kim's flies, realizing he could still smell her scent. Was it the insect repellant she was wearing? Or perfume? Whatever it was, he liked it.

Fly fishing was a solitary sport, he decided. Even when you went with someone else, you ended up spending most of the time living with your own thoughts. He wondered how far upstream Kim had gone. Did she think he was a fool for not knowing anything about alder flies?

Working out a length of fly line, he picked a likely spot halfway up the pool and let it go. The fly landed inches from leaves that arched out over the water. Patiently, he retrieved line as it drifted back. Three times he repeated the act, each time casting further along the bank, and then he worked the far shore.

Cooler air wafted out from the woods on the far side. More and more alder flies swarmed among the thick streamside foliage. A trout rose not a dozen feet from his legs.

For the next hour, the fishing became crazy, with trout sometimes jumping clear out of the water to catch the alder flies in the air. Will lost count of how many he caught and released. The biggest brook trout came to fourteen inches, which he thought was pretty big for that small river.

Things finally slowed when the shadows disappeared. Duchess looked anxious, sitting on the bank. Will decided he should have fed her before they went fishing. Flicking the line back into the air, he wondered where Kim was. The cast placed the fly where the tongue of the riffle flowed into the pool.

The tiny tuft of hair and fur drifted back, a white speck on the slick of black water. And then the surface dimpled. His reflexes snapped the rod back, setting the hook. The line vibrated and then sliced through the water downstream. He dropped the slack from his free hand, trying desperately to keep tension with his rod hand, and attempted to wind in the loose line. The taut line snapped back at him like a withering serpent.

"Shit!"

"I told you there might be some big browns in here," said Kim, standing on the bank and laughing. The dark glasses were up on her head and the hat was stuffed in a pocket. Kim's hair hung loose on her shoulders.

"How long have you been there?"

"Since the fly landed on that last cast."

Even in the twilight, he could see a sparkle in her eyes. "How about we drop the dog off at the house and I buy you dinner in town?" he said, wading toward the shore.

*

Will's car was in the driveway, along with a Toyota Camry. Barbara hoped he didn't have guests, but knocked anyway. A young woman answering the door surprised her.

"I'm Barbara Hawkins, from next door. Is Will at home?" she asked.

"No. He's gone fishing. I'm his daughter," said Amy. "Can I help you with anything?"

Barbara smiled, recognizing Will's eyes in his daughter's face. "I brought him a few things," she said, holding up a basket.

"Come in," said Amy, stepping back from the door. "Can I make you some tea? Or maybe you'd a glass of wine?"

"Is it late enough in the day for wine?" said Barbara.

"I'm having one," said Amy. "We just got here." She introduce Ethan as he came pounding down the stairs.

They sat at the dining table and exchanged stories, filling each other in on their lives. Ethan disappeared into the bedroom he used when visiting. Barbara asked dozens of questions about Will and his life. Into their second glass of wine, a car door thumped outside.

"That must be my dad," said Amy, standing to look out the window. "Do you know the woman he is with?"

"He's with a woman?" said Barbara, looking too. "Oh, that's Kim. She works as a waitress in town."

Amy noticed the disappointed look on Barbara's face, so then said, "I think it's the first time he's gone fishing with her."

The back door opened and Duchess charged in, followed by Will. "Hi," he said. "Barbara, I haven't seen you in ages. What brings you here?"

"I brought over a few things from my garden," she answered. "And I made an extra loaf of bread for you."

"That's nice of you," said Will, stopping to peek in the basket. "I wish I could stay and talk, but we're supposed to be heading to town." Turning to Amy, he asked, "Can you have Ethan feed Duchess?"

"Of course. Don't stay out too late."

Will noticed Amy's eyes...his own daughter was laughing at him and he wondered what that was about. "I won't."

After the door closed, Barbara asked, "So...are they dating?"

"I don't know," said Amy. "Ethan and I just got here a couple of hours ago, and he's never mentioned her. We were up here visiting just a few weeks ago and her name never came up." It was obvious that Barbara was interested in her dad. Amy added, "She looks a little young for him."

"Some men like them that way," said Barbara, looking flustered. "I should be going."

Amy said, "I found hamburger in the refrigerator and the makings for spaghetti. Why don't you join us?"

Barbara hesitated, but then said, "I'd like that. There's lettuce and a tomato in the basket. I can make us a salad. And there's fresh bread that still might be warm."

"My dad doesn't know what he's missing," said Amy.

He sure doesn't, thought Barbara.

6

Will woke and listened. Neither Amy nor Ethan were up. He rolled to look out the window. It would be another hot day.

Settling back into the pillow, he sorted through the previous night. It wasn't at all like he remembered dating…how many years ago was that?

Dinner had been fun. After fishing, they took two vehicles from his house and dropped the Jeep at her home, then drove to the restaurant at the Big Spruce Lodge. The hostess sat them at a table for two beside a big stone fireplace. Deer heads and trout hung on the pine paneled walls, along with paintings of ruffed grouse and fish. An ancient double barrel shotgun lay across iron pegs over the mantel of the fireplace.

While they looked over the menu, Will sipped Glenfiddich and Kim drank a Long Trail Ale and conversation flowed easily. The food had tasted excellent and they shared a bottle of Parallel 45 Cotes du Rhone. Kim told stories of growing up in the north woods and fishing with her father in the wilderness ponds. The conversation drifted to bird dogs and hunting, and Will promised to take her bird hunting in the fall. After splitting a molten lava cake for dessert, he led her out to his truck.

He had opened the truck's door for her, she turned and they slipped into each other's arms for a frantic kiss.

Will fluffed up his pillow and smiled, remembering how that kiss didn't stop. When it finally did, she had asked if he wanted to spend the night at her place.

Sitting up on the side of his bed, Will placed his feet on the floor and tried to remember just how big an idiot he must have sounded.

He had stammered…it was the last thing he had expected, to spend the night at her place on their first date. If Amy wasn't visiting, he might have, hell, *would* have, but he couldn't let his little girl wake up to find her father not home, even if she were all grown up.

Will hoped he hadn't made a fool of himself and scared Kim off. Duchess walked over and placed her chin on his thigh.

He stepped from the bed to pull on jeans and a shirt, then went downstairs to start coffee and let the dog out.

"Well, aren't you the popular man," said Amy, walking into the kitchen. "I didn't know you had such an active social life up here." A big grin spread across her face. "So, did you get lucky? I'm surprised she didn't keep you for the night."

Will laughed. "That's not a thing to ask your dad. And we've only had one date."

Amy giggled. "It happens on the first date sometimes. You're a good looking man. I bet she wanted to jump your bones." She poured coffee into two mugs.

"Jump my bones?" laughed Will. "Is that what they call it these days?"

"Practice safe sex, Dad," teased Amy. "You do remember how to do it, don't you?"

Smiling and shaking his head, Will said, "I can't believe you are talking like this to your father." Even though she had been off on her own for years, it was still hard to think of his daughter as an adult.

Amy sipped the hot coffee. "Well, I hope you call her up and let her know you had a good time, that's if you want to see her again."

"I will. It's early yet."

"Oh, and by the way…Barbara seems to be interested in you too. I think she'll be bringing you more goodies."

"What was in that basket she brought?"

"Oh, we ate most of it," said Amy, still mocking. "She stayed and had dinner with Ethan and me. It seemed like all she wanted to talk about was you."

"She's just a nice neighbor," protested Will.

"If you say so," laughed Amy.

Duchess barked to come back in.

*

"I don't like them," said John Johansson, standing by the stove. "United Eastern will make huge money at the expense of the people that live here." Using a fork, he picked bacon from the frying pan and set it on a plate.

Cindy sipped her coffee. "Do you think they would kill my folks?"

"I don't know. Somebody wanted them dead," said John. The night before he told her that he thought the parents had been murdered and then the house burned to destroy any evidence. The official State Police report wouldn't be out for days.

"Who else would gain from their death?"

"Other property owners who wanted to sell. Your parents blocked the preferred path, and there were a few people along its course that were anxious to cash-out." He flipped eggs in the pan.

"I'm not going to sell the land," said Cindy. "Ever. I want to put a conservation restriction on it, so it won't ever be used for anything but a farm."

"There's people that can help you with that." John set a plate of eggs, bacon, potatoes, and toast in front of Cindy. "Eat. You hardly ate anything last night."

"I know. Thank you for all this." She picked up a piece of bacon with her fingers and bit off half of it. "It's good. I haven't eaten a breakfast like this in years."

"I try to eat a good breakfast every morning," said John, sitting across from her. "I'm going to talk to some of your parents' neighbors. Do you want to come along for the ride?"

She didn't answer for a moment, so he added, "You don't have to get out of the truck and talk to any of them, if you don't want."

When he came home the day before, Cindy looked terrible, as if she'd spent most of the day crying. He cooked up pork chops for dinner, but she ate almost nothing and retired to the guest room. At least she turned the television on in there, rather than sulk in silence, and it was still playing when he went to bed in the middle of the night. He guessed she had fallen asleep with it on.

He had stayed up for hours, looking over maps and trying to figure who stood to gain with the Hammonds dead. Someone who didn't know they had family to pass the farm on to would be the most likely candidate. But maybe the killer wasn't thinking that far ahead. From the internet he reread articles about United Eastern Power, and googled both Frank Atkins and Robert Henderson.

Henderson had been involved in all sorts of construction projects. During the Boston Big Dig project, he was investigated for fraud, but charges were eventually dropped. In Florida, he started a company that buried a wetland to create a golf course and built high-end retirement homes. A Dade County building inspector had mysteriously disappeared during the project and fingers were pointed at Henderson, but nothing was ever proved.

Frank Atkins had worked in the North Country selling real estate for over a decade. Before that he sold cars down country and dabbled in investment counseling. He left investments after being brought before a state ethics board. His present company, Northern Land Investment, LLC, appeared to only work for United Eastern Power.

Around midnight, John had poured a dab of Maker's Mark into a glass, opened a book, and settled into a favorite chair, hoping to calm his mind down enough for sleep. An hour later he woke up and went to bed.

"I'll go with you," said Cindy, picking up the last piece of bacon. "I'd like to see some of the country up here."

All of her adult life, she had come north to visit her folks regularly, usually staying a long weekend. Most of the time was spent around their farm and sometimes she took them out to eat somewhere. It had been years since she'd done much more than that.

She went upstairs to change while he cleaned up the kitchen. When Cindy came down, he noticed she wore hiking boots with her jeans. It was going to be another hot day and the jeans would be sticky, but he didn't know what she had brought for clothes, so said nothing.

Out in the driveway, he opened the truck door for her and she liked that. In the years since the marriage fell apart, she had only dated a few times. Most men bored her, chatting away about their own lives, as if they were the center of the universe. The only one she had found interesting didn't like kids, and her two boys were still living at home then. Sliding onto the truck's seat, she realized just how nice a guy John Johansson was.

Walking around the front of the truck, he looked tall, easily over six feet, with broad shoulders inside his neatly pressed green uniform. His home had surprised her with its tidiness inside and the manicured yard. For a big man, there had to be a soft spot.

"So how many of your neighbors are watching us?" she joked, as he climbed in. Along the street, neat old houses stood behind the maples that lined the street.

"Probably all of them," he said, smiling.

"You don't have women staying over often?"

"No. I was seeing a woman over in East Sheldon, but that was going nowhere."

They headed north and out of town.
*

Frank Atkins stepped from his silver Range Rover. The air stunk of wet charred wood. Around the remains of the Hammond's home, a wide yellow ribbon prevented anyone from getting close. Two State Police SUVs and a van parked in the driveway. He didn't recognize the approaching officer, so he guessed he came from downstate.

"Can I help you?" asked the officer.

"I'm with the press," lied Frank. "I wanted a picture or two."

"Pretty fancy car for a reporter," said the cop.

Frank glanced back at his immaculate Rover, realizing it probably cost more than double what a newspaper reporter made in a year. "I work freelance, for a publication down state."

The officer said, "Just stay outside the ribbons."

"Do you know if the Hammonds had family?"

"There's a daughter somewhere. There will be a statement from the department later today."

Frank thanked him and pulled a small camera from his pocket. If the officer thought it was a tiny camera for a professional, he didn't say anything. Frank took two pictures from the driveway, and then walked around the ribbon to the far end of the house. Coming back, he noticed the Fish and Game Department truck pulling into the driveway.

Shit, he thought, it's that asshole John Johansson. A woman stepped from the other side of the truck. Frank knew Johansson's opinion of the power line project. Johansson's calm soothing manner had convinced many of the locals not to sell their land, sometimes when Frank had been close to having them sign.

Twice, when Frank had parked along wooded roads to survey possible power line routes, Johansson had stopped to ask if he was fishing or hunting, and of course he was doing neither. But then Johansson would tediously check Frank's identification and drag the process out, and Frank knew it was only to annoy him.

"Good morning Frank," said John, approaching. "Taking pictures of your handy work?" The dark haired woman walked beside him.

"I didn't have anything to do with this," said Frank. "I'll have you in court if you say that again."

John smiled. "That would be fun, watching you answer questions under oath." Motioning toward Cindy, he added, "Have you met Cynthia Hammond?"

Frank's eyes opened wide. "You're the daughter?"

John felt Cindy move closer to his side, as she answered, "Yes."

"I'm sorry for your loss," said Frank, shifting into his salesman mode. "If there is anything that I can do to help you." His face melted from stone-like to soft and friendly. "I don't suppose they left you much except the land."

"Cut the crap," said John. "She is not selling."

"She should know her options," said Frank. "I was just trying to help."

"Go back down country," said John, "and climb back under whatever rock you used to live under."

The police officer that had greeted Frank when he arrived walked their direction. Frank said, "I have to be going."

John and Cindy talked with the police officer for a few minutes. As the silver Range Rover disappeared down the hill, John told the officer who the driver really was. The officer mentioned the department's statement that was promised for the afternoon and agreed to send them a copy as an attachment to an email.

7

Will set another log onto the hydraulic splitter and pushed the control handle aft, causing the ram to press the wood against the steel wedge. Even over the purr of the motor, the crackling protests of the log could be heard. When the wood fell to the ground he tossed it into the pile next to the barn. An old International Scout drove across the back yard and stopped in front of the barn's large open door.

"You're at it early," said Burt, stepping from the Scout and adjusting a suspender strap.

"I try to do a little each day, before it gets warm," said Will, straightening up. "I'd still like to have one more cord for the coming winter."

"You can't have too much. A big woodpile brings peace of mind." Burt's florescent orange Jones-style cap pushed the tops of his ears out and his baggy jeans sagged, only the suspenders kept them from landing at his ankles. "Let's go down and check where your property runs behind Barbara Hawkins' place. There's softwoods mixed in the hardwoods on the far side of the river that ought to be cut soon."

Will wondered how Burt knew that. The man had to spend all his free time out wandering around in the woods. The stories about Burt's overbearing wife might explain it. To make things worse, Agnes couldn't hear a cannon shot right under her nose and she spoke as if everyone else were just as deaf as she. The story around town was he spent as little time at home as possible.

*

Barbara Hawkins walked to the house carrying a basket of string beans, freshly picked from the garden beside her barn. It was such a nice time of the year. The day would be a hot one, but the chores were finished. Before the sun had even climbed above the treetops, she had the horse stall shoveled out. Then, as first rays of sunshine struck the barn, Barbara picked the garden's produce. She walked inside and set the basket on the counter in the kitchen. From the refrigerator, she pulled a pitcher of iced tea.

Dinner the night before had been such fun, with Will Northrop's daughter and grandson. She learned about the loss of his wife and where he came from. The fact that he went out to dinner with Kimberly Norton, that hussy from the restaurant, caused a knot in Barbara's stomach, so she tried not to think about it. How could he be serious about a woman that young?

She stopped to look at a mirror in the hallway. For fifty-one, she looked pretty darn good. The face was tanned and her active life kept the extra pounds away. Maybe a trip to the hair salon was due, but the thick sandy-blonde hair looked healthy pulled back into a ponytail. Taking a deep breath, she smiled. Her figure looked as good as ever.

Upstairs in her bedroom, she sat at a desk and turned on her computer. She started searching for clothes, looking for something that she might wear if she were actually to go out on a date with Will. Most of the things looked great on skinny twenty-something models, but she couldn't imagine wearing most of those clothes. An hour slipped away while she sat there, and Barbara scolded herself for wasting such a nice day.

She went downstairs and walked out the back door. On the slamming of the screen door, her horse, an eighteen year old Trakehner, looked up from grazing in the pasture. The shaggy white goat keeping it company never stopped munching the grass.

Walking toward the pasture, the gray horse meandered over to meet her at the gate, with its dark eyes asking for food. Barbara stepped inside the paddock and then handed her a carrot. "How's my Martha this morning?"

The carrot disappeared inside Martha's mouth amid much crunching.

"Shall we go for jaunt?" said Barbara, slipping a bridal over Martha's head. "We really need to get out more."

The goat never looked up. "Hey Ram," said Barbara. Ram ignored her and continued to eat.

"He's not the most sociable, is he?" she said, leading Martha towards the barn.

Martha had been part of Barbara's life for seven years. As she cinched up the saddle, she talked to Martha about Will, rambling on about his family and house. The horse listened patiently.

They followed a worn footpath across the yard and into the woods. The air under the hardwood trees felt thick from the humidity, but the leaves overhead reflected the heat of the sun. The trail rounded a gentle knoll, where bright green ferns grew beneath the trees, and then descended on its back side, following logging roads carved decades before by men with strong backs. Where the land became steep, a long switchback made the traveling easier. The track led down into a valley where the ferns grew taller, turning the path into a shallow green canyon. Ahead, she heard the rumble of the Mooslikamoosuc River.

A row of painted red blazes on the trees marked her property line. She crossed onto land owned by Will Northrop, wondering if he had ever been to that far corner of his property. The trees looked the same and, for a moment, she imagined him riding a horse beside her.

The air cooled where the path leveled next to the river, and the rushing water drowned out all other sound. Deer and moose tracks covered a soft long-abandoned road that ran parallel to the water's course. A tiny pasture opened up beneath an ancient white pine that climbed to the heavens. On that little flat shelf near the river, where the soil was perpetually damp, the grass grew green and lush. Barbara climbed off Martha onto the soft ground.

"It's your favorite place," said Barbara, stroking the side of Martha's nose.

A small spring trickled from beneath softwood trees at the far edge of the little opening. Deer and moose had bedded there, matting the grass, but there was no sign of other human visitors. Tall pines shaded much of the opening, yet sunlight warmed where they stood. She slipped the saddle from Martha's back and set in on a fallen pine trunk that had turned silvery from years of bleaching in the sun. Martha would be there when she returned.

Barbara stepped between a crowd of Christmas sized fir trees and out onto a granite ledge, worn smooth by eons of water running over its surface. Big rocks pinched the river together before it tumbled over a precipice into a pool, where millions of bubbles swirled to the surface, creating a natural Jacuzzi. Across the river, spruce and fir trees crowded together and she could smell their sweet heavy scent.

Out from the shade of the forest, blue sky stretched overhead and the sun warmed her skin. She pulled the tie from her ponytail and shook her hair loose. It felt so free to be out in the woods and alone under the expansive blue sky.

Barbara sat and pried off her riding boots. The smooth granite felt warm beneath her feet. She pulled her jersey off over her head, letting the sun caress her shoulders. A gentle breeze funneled up the valley, just strong enough to move away any insects that might bother, yet not cool the sun warmed air. She wrestled out of her jeans and stretched out naked on the flat warm granite.

The river sang one long song, a harmony that emptied her mind. The place brought on the most relaxing sensations she had ever experienced. For years, on warm summer days, she had been riding Martha down to that favorite piece of paradise.

Under that embracing sun, she reminded herself to not get too much of a good thing. To be tanned all over would be nice, but pink or burned wouldn't do.

*

John Johansson turned the Fish and Game Department truck up the driveway next to the mailbox marked with the name Toll. It gradually curved to the right to where he and Cindy could see the carcasses of two rusted trucks and a mottled yellow skidder that obviously hadn't moved in years, because a six inch diameter tree had grown between its blade and the front axle. A sagging half-shingled home, with torn black felt paper hanging where shingles had never been, sat just beyond the end of the driveway. On the porch a rusted washing machine sat open next to a bicycle that missed its front wheel. A mangy rust-colored mutt barked and growled near the front door, restrained by a stout chain.

"Do you know these people?" asked Cindy, her eyes wide, taking in the mess. A second washing machine lay on its side by the edge of the lawn with beer cans spilling out of its open top.

"They signed with United Eastern Power," said John, "and were pretty upset when your parents wouldn't."

"Do you think they would kill my folks?"

"I don't know. Probably not. They had about a million dollar motive though." He parked near the front of the house.

John stepped from the truck, but Cindy decided to wait inside. The dog worked itself into a frenzy when it noticed John clear of the truck.

He walked toward the front door as a gangly man in tattered clothes and needing a shave, stepped out.

"You are not welcome here," said the man. He spewed a mouthful of tobacco juice on the ground.

"Is Brian home?" asked John, still approaching.

"It's none of your damned business," said the man.

John stopped in front of the man and Cindy couldn't hear what they said. The man's eyes looked full of hate, or desperation, much like a cornered animal. Soon, John turned and walked back toward the truck. The dog never stopped.

"What's going on?" asked Cindy.

John started the truck and backed it up. "Their son, Brian, has been poaching game since not long after he could walk."

"Have you ever caught him?"

"Lots of times. His father used to do the same thing, but his legs are bad and he can't get out in the woods to do much damage anymore. There's a sister too, and she's been arrested for shop lifting and drugs." Turning onto the road, John added, "It's a wonderful family."

"Where are we going?"

"The next house along the power line route. I want everyone to know that power line is not going to happen."

*

Senator Greggory Grogg sat in the air conditioned pub across from Robert Henderson, watching the sweat dribble down the side of his gin and tonic. A few patrons sat at the bar, but all of the other booths were empty. In spite of it being a tourist town on the edge of the mountains, the hot weather kept things pretty quiet.

Henderson sipped his beer and said, "So we're prepared to give three hundred and fifty thousand dollars to your campaign."

That was more than Grogg spent on his last two elections, combined, but he kept his face emotionless, a trick he had learned long before as a car salesman. Instead, he slowly turned his glass on the table, as if thinking.

"All we want you to do is talk with the press," said Henderson, "tell people how good this is for them. You're a popular guy up in this neck of the woods."

Grogg still stared at his glass and said nothing.

"United Eastern owns a villa down in the Caymans, sort of an executive retreat. How would you and your wife like a couple of weeks down there in February, when the people up in this country are buried up to their assholes in ice? We can fly you down on our company jet."

Henderson swallowed another mouthful of beer and set the glass down with a thud. Greggory Grogg's continued silence unnerved him. Maybe he had met his wheeler-and-dealer equal. "I can arrange for an account in a Cayman's Island bank, with your name on it, with a half million in it waiting for you," he said. "Nobody needs to know." If Grogg bit on that one, he was in their pocket. The amount was pocket change, compared to what they'd already spent on land.

The corner of Grogg's mouth twitched, as if repressing a smile. Henderson held up his empty glass for the bartender to see. "I'll buy us another round to celebrate."

"The money would be helpful," said Grogg, relaxing and sitting back. "But how about a trip to the Cayman's without my wife."

Henderson leaned in, this was even better. "You got a girlfriend you want to bring?"

"It's my campaign manager," smiled Grogg. "She works hard and deserves a vacation."

"I bet she does," said Henderson.

8

Burt led Will through the woods, following an old grown-in logging road along the side of the river, kept open by traveling moose, deer, and bear. They sidetracked places where the ground became soft mud and twice they detoured around softwood trees that had fallen across the path.

Will's mind wandered, his thoughts shifting between his daughter and grandson and the date with Kim the night before. Remembering her kiss brought a pleasant shiver, but he tried to think about it the things they had talked about. That kiss though....

A ruffed grouse exploded into the sky, startling them both.

Laughing it off, they trudged on. Not a whisper of wind found its way down into the trees and the humid air felt thick.

Soon, the hardwoods gave way to spruce and fir. Near the bank of the river an occasional white pine or hemlock stood above the other trees, usually with a trunk that two men together couldn't put their arms around. Spent needles on the ground muffled their steps, but an occasional unseen red squirrel would chatter nearby, alerting the forest of their presence.

Will had never walked down that side of the river. The soundless woods felt surreal, almost eerie, with soft brown needles or moss muffling sounds beneath the hundreds of dark straight trunks. An occasional dead twig reached out to snag at his clothes, often snapping with a pop that seemed uncannily loud. Even their voices felt muted when they spoke.

Burt was right. The fir trees would soon start to decline and cutting the large old pines would be a bonus. He guessed most of the pines contained over fifteen hundred board feet, and maybe of them some twice that.

He followed Burt to the left and they stopped by the river next to a huge white pine. Burt dug his flask out of a pocket and screwed off the cap, then offered it to Will, who shook his head. Burt took a long pull, and then put the flask away. Will wondered how the man's body dealt with all the sugar.

"It's hot," said Will, wishing he were back at the house.

"Yeah," answered Burt. "Do you see what I mean, about the wood?"

They talked for a few minutes about what would need to be done to get machinery in there. It would be easiest in the winter, when the ground would be frozen. That would also minimize ground disturbance.

"Do you hear that fast water?" asked Burt, pointing downstream. "The river tumbles over a bunch of rocks, like a small waterfall. It's another half mile down. We used to swim there in a big pool when I was a kid."

"I never knew it was there."

"Most people don't." Burt grinned. "In high school we used to take the girls down there skinny dipping." He laughed and shook his head. "That was almost seventy years ago."

"I'll have to check it out sometime."

"The easiest way to go in is behind Barbara Hawkins' place."

They headed back toward the Scout, with Will again following Burt. Almost to the truck, they intercepted young Brian Toll, who carried a bucket full of small trout.

"Well, Brian, that's quite a mess of fish you got there," said Burt, scratching at his chin.

The lanky kid just smiled. Five fish or five pounds, whichever was reached first, was the limit, and it looked like he had sixty little fish totaling six pounds.

"If you're going to take fish like that," said Will, "you are not welcome on my property."

"Fuck you," said Brain. "I'll fish wherever I want." He turned and strutted across the field.

"When I was young," said Burt, shaking he head and watching the arrogant kid march away, "we'd take guys like him, strip 'em down bare-ass, and tie them to a tree out in the woods during blackfly season."

Will said, "If I see him here again, I'll call John Johansson."

*

Seventeen year old Suzy Toll sat on the couch watching television. Her twenty-seven year old boyfriend, Jake, had gone to the store for cigarettes and beer. At the rumble of his Dodge Ram Charger in the driveway, she shut off the TV. It was hotter than hell inside the little house, but the boredom of outdoors was worse.

She glanced in a mirror before stepping outside. The tiny shorts didn't quite cover the cheeks of her ass and she knew Jake would notice the way her breasts bulged over the bikini top. The skimpy clothing of summertime was the only thing Suzy liked about the hot weather, because it allowed her to flaunt her shapely body.

"Hi honey," she said, stepping out the door to meet him.

Three plastic lawn chairs sat on the deck, beside a rusted gas grill. A beagle, attached to a metal chain, lifted its head, but otherwise didn't move. Jake opened a white plastic cooler and tossed a bag of ice and two twelve-packs of beer in.

"We got to get a fucking fridge," he said. "It really sucks having the thing busted in this weather."

"I know," said Suzy, bending over to open the cooler and take a beer. She lingered and hoped he noticed her breasts.

"Aw, gimme another one of those," said Jake, disappointing Suzy by reaching for a beer. "Let's go down to the lake and have a swim."

"Oh no," said Suzy, shaking her head. "No way. The last time I got a fucking leech on my leg."

"They don't hurt you," said Jake. "We'll bring along a salt shaker. The salt makes 'em drop off."

Suzy tilted her head back and swallowed a mouthful of cold beer. "Fuck that, I ain't going," she said, then belched. After another swallow, she asked, "Did you find out about a job?"

"I'll worry about the money," said Jake. "You just worry about keeping me happy." He put his arm around her bare waist and pulled her close. "How about we go down to the river?"

There was a secluded sandbar that they had visited before that jutted out into the river like a thumb. The water meandered lazily through the flat valley, but at least no leeches had attached to her skin there.

"We could bring the little cooler," she said, pressing her hip against his. "Fill it with beer," she added, licking her lips and trying to look sultry, "so we have something to suck on." She pulled his mouth down to hers for a kiss, then added, "And we could bring a blanket to fuck on."

Jake grinned and said, "Now you're talking."

"Goody," she laughed, breaking from his side and dashing inside.

"Have you heard any more about the fire?" he asked, sitting in one of the plastic chairs and waiting for her to return with towels and a blanket.

"Nope," she answered through the doorway. "I haven't talked to my folks."

"They must have been pissed when the Hammonds wouldn't sell."

"I'll say. Dad went on a three day bender. He thought he was going to be rich."

"You'd have been rich too," said Jake. "Think about it. Your old man would a got two mil for that place of his. Easy. Those power line people been spreading cash like butter on toast."

Suzy came out carrying towels and a blanket under one arm, and a bright red cooler with the other hand. "I don't know if I'd a seen any of it," she said. "Pop's pretty tight with his money."

"Not when he's got that much, he wouldn't be. I bet he can't even count that high," said Jake, laughing.

Suzy opened the big cooler to put beer in the smaller one. "I'm sure he'd keep pretty close tabs on it."

"Well, with that fire at the Hammond's, maybe his luck has changed," said Jake, scratching at his crotch. "Have you ever thought about getting married?"

Suzy smiled. Jake thought she was eighteen and would panic if he found out she was only seventeen, as in "jailbait material". Getting married at seventeen would require parental approval and that was iffy. A lot of days her old man would have given permission for a hundred bucks, but other times he just might refuse, or hold out for something unrealistic, like a thousand.

"Maybe someday," she said.

*

Frank Atkins sat in his Range Rover with the engine and air conditioning running, and daydreamed about being at the coast. For the previous half hour, he had sorted through property maps, trying to find alternative routes past the uncooperative land owners.

His cell phone rang, which surprised him. It seldom worked up in that sparsely populated country. The screen said the call came from Robert Henderson.

"Hey, what's up?"

"We've found some leverage," said Robert. It sounded like he was chewing food. "That bitch, Cindy Hammond, she's got two sons in college. She makes good money, but they are barely squeaking by with tuition and all. I think we can sweeten the deal and make her come around."

Frank's impression, during his brief meeting with Cindy Hammond, was a stubborn and idealistic woman, not the flexible type. "Do you really think so?"

"Yeah, everybody has their price. Listen, how would you like a few days down on Martha's Vineyard?"

Frank had never been there, but it sounded like fun. "Can I take my wife?"

"What the fuck do you want to do that for? Make it a pleasure trip and leave her home." Henderson laughed at his own sorry joke. "I booked you a room at the Harborview Hotel. It's the classiest place on the island. You lucked out, because they had a cancelation, or else I'd never have got you in. You've got a ferry reservation for tomorrow at one. Bring cash, twenty grand from the business stash. Call me when you get to your room."

The phone went dead.

Twenty grand? Frank wondered how deep he was getting in. The "business stash" was an account that he and Henderson used for all sorts of lavish perks when they were wining and dining landowners. Henderson had said not to talk to anyone about that account, because corporate didn't know of its existence. Frank had never asked where the money came from, but its existence made him feel uneasy.

9

"So how long are you going to stay?" asked John, sitting at the table in his dining room.

"At least until the funeral," said Cindy. "Do you mind?"

"No. I like having you around. It's not a big house, but it feels that way when I'm here alone."

The entire day had been spent stopping at people's homes along the proposed power line route. They talked with them about the things going on and watched closely their reaction to the news of the Hammond's fire and Cindy's plans to put her parents land in conservation. John felt either United Eastern Power or the Tolls were the most likely suspects, and probably the latter.

It all seemed like a wild goose chase to Cindy. Back at the house, she called the funeral home to check on the arrangements, and then they cleaned up before starting dinner. While she was still upstairs, John opened a bottle of red wine. Steaks thawed in the sink.

"I should call my boys on Martha's Vineyard," said Cindy, coming down the stairs, "to fill them in on everything. They'll want to come up for the funeral."

"There's room for them to stay here too," said John. Cindy looked nice in shorts, sandals, and a tank top. "I apologize for not having air conditioning. Almost nobody has it up here. This weather doesn't happen often." He passed her a glass of wine. "To new found old friends," he said, holding his glass up.

She smiled and sipped the wine. "Is it cooler outside?"

"Probably, and I should light the grill," said John. "The potatoes are in the oven already. And I made a salad." He held the screen door open for her.

The night insects sang one long chorus. Beyond the lawn a strip of woods separated the yard from the neighbor's. John lit the charcoal and flames danced over the grill. "Sit," he said, motioning toward a cedar loveseat.

"Thanks," she said. "I'm exhausted. I guess it's the events of the last couple of days."

He sat beside her and asked how she liked her steak done. Then they talked about high school and grammar school, and tried to remember where all of their old friends had gone. Only a handful still lived in the area.

"I had quite a crush on you," said John. "I think it was in the fourth grade."

"I never knew that."

"I was rather shy, and you were one of the smart ones. When we got older you started dating that guy who was a year ahead of us in school."

"I always thought you were sweet," said Cindy.

John laughed. "Sweet? That's just what a guy loves to hear. I was chicken."

She smiled and sipped her wine. "We're both single now."

Summoning his courage, John asked, "Would you like to go out on an honest-to-goodness date with me tomorrow night? I'll take you to the nicest restaurant around."

Cindy's eyes lit up. "I would love that."

*

Amy came down the stairs.

"Is he asleep?" asked Will.

"Not yet, but he won't last long. He had a full day. Thanks for taking him fishing."

He and Ethan had dug worms after lunch, before going down to the river to fish some of the deep holes where the water cut under the river's banks. The fishing turned out to be slow, but the time spent together had been fun. Ethan had ended up swimming in his underwear.

Later, they ate pork chops cooked on the grill for dinner. Afterward, while Amy and Will cleaned up the dishes while Ethan played fetch with Duchess until it was time for him to go to bed.

"Would you like another glass of wine?" asked Will, starting the dishwasher.

"Sure. Let's sit out on the farmer's porch. It might be cooler."

"We'll try it. The mosquitoes might chase us into the screened porch."

"So when's you next date?" asked Amy, sitting in a wood rocker.

Even in the dim light on the farmer's porch, he could see her teasing smile. "Tomorrow afternoon. We're hiking up Roger's Dome." Duchess lay at his feet. A breath of air kept any annoying insects at bay.

"A hike? She must be the outdoors type."

He told her how Kim wanted to be a guide and that he hoped to take her bird hunting in the fall.

Amy swallowed a mouthful of wine, then asked, "How old is she?"

"I don't know, in her thirties I guess."

"I think she's a lot closer to my age than yours," teased Amy. She leaned over and patted her father's knee. "I hope she doesn't wear you out."

"Tell me about the asshole you were dating," said Will, trying to change the subject.

Amy shrugged her shoulders. "He was a jerk and I was stupid." Nervously, she toyed with the ends of her hair. "I should have paid more attention to details and I would have known he was married. All too often we only see what we want to see."

Settling back in her chair, she said, "I stopped by the hospital today. They have a job opening for a nurse practitioner."

The comment caught Will by surprise. "Are you going to take it?"

"Would you mind if we moved up here?"

"Mind? I'd love it." Will sat up straight. "You can stay here until you find a place of your own."

"I'm thinking about it," said Amy. "I'd love Ethan to see you regularly, but the schools back home offer so much."

"I'd love for him to be around. And the schools up here are good. A big percentage go on to college."

"I'm just thinking about it," she reminded him, glad to see her father's enthusiasm.

Will sipped his wine and looked out across the field. The black silhouette of distant hills stood against a dark sky. Only a few stars poked through the humid night sky and no moon shown. The air smelled sweet of grass and green things. A loud cricket chirped near the edge of the porch. Fireflies momentarily glowed out over the field before disappearing as another started to shine.

"So tell me," he said, "when people date today…how fast do things…usually move along?"

Amy giggled. "Do you mean, how soon can you expect to sleep with her?"

"It's been over thirty years since I dated anybody, other than your mother," said Will, feeling defensive.

"There's no rules, Dad. Everybody is different. Just go with what feels right." Amy sipped her wine, trying to read her father's face. "Did she drag you to bed on your first date?" The look on his face made her laugh. "She did, didn't she? You are a hot catch."

Will wished he hadn't brought the subject up. "She wanted me to spend the night."

"And you didn't? You are a *rare* one. I saw enough to know she's pretty attractive, and most men wouldn't have refused the chance."

"I wanted to be home when you woke up."

Smiling and shaking her head, Amy said, "My Dad, there's nobody else like him.

"Don't forget Barbara Hawkins," she continued. "Those strawberries that I made the shortcake out of came from her garden. She's got her eye on you too."

"No she doesn't."

"She's attractive and closer to your age. I bet you two have a lot in common. She loves the outdoors too."

The sound of a distant gunshot rolled off the hills.

"What was that?" asked Amy, looking out into the night.

"Maybe someone jacking deer."

*

Jerome Toll shut off the truck and killed the headlights. The night looked dreadfully dark. The rusted hinges on the truck's door moaned as it swung open. Cautiously, he stepped out, testing his equilibrium. "Christ," he said to no one, "how fucking much did I drink?"

For four hours he had played pool at the local bar, sucking down beer and chasing it with Canadian whiskey. Luck had been on his side and he had come home a few dollars richer than when he went out.

The front door was open and a light was on inside.

"Kathy?" he said, stepping in and shutting it. "Dumb bitch, letting all the bugs in."

The house was silent. He walked into the kitchen, where moths bounced off the overhead light with audible clicks, and opened the refrigerator to take out a beer. In the living room, he flopped onto the couch and took a long pull from the brown bottle.

"Shit," he said, "I forgotta piss."

Standing, he staggered out onto the deck to pee off the side. As the pressure flowed away, a lone mosquito whined in his ear. He tried to swat it with his free hand, causing him to wet all over his right leg.

"What the fuck?" he said.

He unbuckled his pants and they dropped to the deck. Stepping out of them, he said, "I need a beer."

Dressed in stained baggy boxers and a worn tee shirt, he staggered back into the kitchen, having forgotten the already open beer. Walking back into the living room and seeing the waiting bottle, he said, "That dumb cunt, she left a beer out."

He flopped into the sofa again and passed out.

10

Jerome Toll woke up on the couch, wondering where his pants went. Scratching where his gut poked out below his tee shirt, he tried to recall the previous night, but finally gave up. Two nearly full bottles of beer sat on the coffee table, and he reached for the nearest.

"Uhg, warm beer," said Jerome, sitting up. He picked up a pack of Marlboro's and shook one out. Matches sat next to an ashtray heaped with burned cigarettes. The nicotine improved the day's outlook.

Wondering why he couldn't smell coffee brewing, he waddled toward the kitchen. Evidently the wife wasn't up. He walked to the bedroom, mumbling to himself about how she should straighten up her act, but found the room empty.

"Well, what the fuck?" he whined.

He walked down the hall, passing his daughter's room. Suzy hadn't been in there since she ran off with that smart ass Jake. At least he wasn't having to feed her. Jerome pushed the door to his son's room open. The kid's eyes blinked.

"What's up?" said Brian.

"Where's your mom?"

"I don't know," said the kid. "I didn't see her when I came in." He pulled the blankets up over his head. "Go away."

"Useless kid," muttered Jerome, walking back down the hall.

He passed through the kitchen and opened the back door.

His wife's body lay splayed over the back step, with the back of her skull busted open to expose what looked like bloodied gray tofu. A pool of blood oozed down the stairs. In her lap lay a pistol.

Jerome turned back inside, dropped to his knees, and vomited, spewing warm beer and puke, then collapsed into the foul puddle. He sobbed like a child, clutching at the rug.

"What is it?" said Brian, walking into the room. "Oh Christ, that stinks." He backed out of the room, grabbing his nose. "You shouldn't drink so fucking much."

Brian had never seen his father cry and wondered what it was about. He walked through the house and out the front door. Maybe it was time to run away.

Jerome's tears eventually stopped. He stood up with the vomit soaked tee shirt sticking to his skin. Peeling off the clothing, he headed for the shower. Cleaned up and before dressing, he dialed 911.

*

"How did you hear about it?" asked Frank, talking on his cell phone.

"I got friends inside the police force," said Robert. "They're saying apparent suicide. Where are you?"

"I got to Woods Hole early and I'm in the standby line for the ferry. So who am I meeting on the Vineyard?"

"Like I said, call me when you get to your room. I'll tell you then." The phone went dead.

Dead people made Frank nervous. He doubted anyone from United Eastern Power would actually kill anyone, but just the thought of it caused a knot in his stomach. Serious prison time was something Frank never wanted to experience. The Hammonds both dying in a fire could turn out to be a very convenient coincidence, and he hoped it truly was a coincidence. It didn't seem that Kathy Toll's death could possibly benefit the power company, but the goings on of the higher ups often baffled him.

The next ferry was almost an hour away, so he left the Range Rover in the Steamship Authority staging area and walked up the hill to buy a coffee at a tiny restaurant where the road forked. The southwest breeze blowing up Buzzards Bay and Vineyard Sound had to be fifteen degrees cooler than the air inland.

*

Will followed Kim, noticing her long stride. Every step stretched to the fullest and each footfall landed securely. It took effort to keep up.

Far ahead, Duchess trotted through the trees, forever hunting.

Kim carried a small knapsack, wore short shorts, a tank top, and hiking boots. With every step, her wavy auburn ponytail swung from side to side. He wondered if her heart pounded like his. She certainly was in good shape to keep up that pace all the way to the top. Maybe it was because she was so much younger than he.

The small mountain known as Roger's Dome had once been forested, but lightning started a fire early in the previous century, and then the topsoil of the burned-over crown eroded away to nearly bare ledge. In August people often hiked up there to pick wild blueberries that grew where enough soil lingered, but it would be weeks before the berries were ripe. Will had never been up there, but had heard the views were spectacular.

He carried a fanny pack and had stuffed his shirt into it not long after starting. A bead of sweat trickled down his ribs and another dripped from his brow. Almost no wind found its way down into the forest, but the treetops twitched from a light breeze.

Switchbacks cut into the side of the hill, creating a gentle climb up between the rocks and ferns. Tall yellow birch and rock maples provided shade, but the air around them felt thick as cotton. Will's feet were hot inside his hiking boots and his untanned legs looked pale compared to Kim's.

She stopped where a spring bubbled out beneath a rock. "Would you like a drink?" It didn't look like she had even worked up a sweat. Duchess drank where the water puddled near their feet.

Will inhaled deeply. "Sure." Saying more would have been difficult until he caught his breath.

Kim passed him a tin cup of water. As he drank, she said, "We're almost out of the trees. The open ledge starts over the next hump."

He nodded and handed her the cup. She drank, then poured another cupful over her head, laughing. Will laughed, so she offered him the cup again and he did the same.

The cold water revived him. Soon, they stepped from the trees into the open sunlight where they stopped to look into the valley.

"There's your place," said Kim, pointing at a series of flat fields against the side of a hill.

"What a view," said Will, looking to the west. "You can see where the Mooslikamoosuc flows into the Connecticut."

A few white puffy clouds hung motionless in the sky. Beyond the valley, rolling green hills ran off into the next state.

"Come on," said Kim, turning to trek on.

They followed a worn path marked by cairns up the nearly bare ledges of Roger's Dome. Free of the forest, a breeze blew from the west and cooled their sweaty skin. Clusters of low-bush blueberries grew where soil clung to hollows or collected in cracks. Lichens and moss struggled to grow on the rock. Soon they reached the top where Kim dropped her backpack and sat against a barrel sized boulder. Will slid down next to her.

"You can see where United Power's lines would go," she said, pointing. "It would come up along the river and then over the east side of the hill to head south through that gap into the next valley. I hope it never happens. This view wouldn't be the same."

A puff of wind tugged at a strand of her hair and Kim pushed it back behind an ear. Her dark brown eyes darted over Will's face.

Will leaned in to kiss her and Kim's arms wrapped around his bare shoulders. They tumbled into a soft bed of moss. Far away, a raven cawed and the sound echoed off the hills. Overhead, a red tail hawk made lazy circles in the sky.

The kissing stopped when Duchess nudged their sides.

"Duchess, no. Down," said Will.

The dog obeyed.

Kim, laying on her back and breathing deeply for the first time that day, said, "Did you bring a condom?"

He shook his head and mumbled, "No."

Kim grinned. "I did."

*

The knock of the door startled Amy. Through the kitchen window she could see Ethan playing on the swing under the pine trees. In the driveway sat a big pickup truck that she did not recognize and reflexes, learned living in the city, brought on concern.

She felt better when she recognized Burt Bertram at the back door. Opening it, Amy said, "Hi Burt, come on in." A second man taller stood beside him.

"Is Will around?" he asked, stepping in out of the sun.

"No, he's off hiking with Kim."

"From the restaurant? Good for him," said Burt. "This is Shawn Ash," he added, without turning. "He owns a logging company and I wanted him to meet your dad. Do you think he'd mind if we took a look at the wood across the river?"

Shawn looked to be six feet tall, with short sandy hair and broad shoulders and abs that rippled the front of his snug tee shirt...Amy loved the way his gray eyes smiled so easily.

"Heck no," said Amy. "I just made a huge jug of lemonade. Would you like some?" She smiled at Shawn, hoping the flirting wasn't too blatant.

"You can talk me into anything," he answered, chuckling.

Those eyes...Amy felt herself blush. "Go sit on the porch," she said. "There's shade and a bit of a breeze there. I'll bring it out."

As Amy collected glasses and the lemonade, Ethan dashed in the back door. "Who's here?" he wanted to know.

"Your buddy Burt, with a logger to meet Grandpa."

"A logger, cool," said Ethan. He dashed out the front door to the porch.

Amy followed, carrying a tray with glasses and a pitcher. Ice cubes rattled inside the lemonade. Ethan and Shawn stood on the lawn beyond the porch, tossing a ball back and forth.

"I thought it was too hot for playing in the sun," said Amy.

"They're having fun," said Burt.

"I can see that."

Shawn threw the ball to Ethan and headed for the porch. "He's a great kid," he said.

"Thanks. He loves it up here."

They talked about where she was from and how long her father lived there. She learned that Shawn lived in a small log home, just over the hill on County Road, and had started his own logging company six years before.

Burt mentioned Shawn had five men working for him, using modern mechanized machinery for harvesting timber.

Ethan, who had been listening and not saying anything, cut in, "Can we go see the loggers?"

"Of course," said Shawn. "I'll even let you cut a tree or two."

Ethan's eyes lit up. "Wow. I can't wait."

"It's safe," said Shawn, turning to Amy. "We'll be inside an enclosed cab when we cut the trees. He can sit in my lap and I'll have him push the levers."

There was that smile of his again. She wondered if there was a wife somewhere. "We'll look forward to it," she said.

"We should get going," said Burt, standing. "It's a fair hike ahead of us."

Shawn towered over him. Turning to Amy, he said, "I hope to see you again."

"Me too," she said, flustered that they were leaving. "If you're thirsty on the way back there's still more lemonade."

He smiled and said, "We might take you up on that."

11

Frank Atkins sat in Henry's, the plush bar at the Harborview Hotel, and sipped a Sam Adams Lager. Beside his left knee, a large briefcase sat on the floor beneath the table. Four attractive women in tennis whites shared a bottle of wine at the nearest table. A paunchy silver-haired man, sitting at the bar, tried desperately to impress the much younger woman who sat beside him. The bartender mindlessly polished glasses, ignoring the cleavage bulging from the woman's skimpy black dress. At a round table in the far corner of the room, a couple, who were obviously tourists, picked at a plate of grilled oysters.

Frank waited for a man known as Jimmy Deluga. Robert Henderson had assured Frank that Jimmy would arrange for the changing of Cindy Hammond's mind. She would suddenly need money, and lots of it. Frank wondered what magic this man from New York City might work.

A short man strolled in, impeccably dressed in a pale blue blazer and white pants with a sharp crease down their front. "Frank?" he said.

"Yes." It had to be Jimmy Deluga. "Can I buy you a drink?"

"Thanks. Hendricks with a dash of tonic," he said, sitting to Frank's left.

There wasn't a waitress, so Frank went to the bar, ordered the drink and returned. "When did you get to the island?"

"This morning," said Jimmy. "Do you have the payment?"

"In the briefcase." Nothing about the little man inspired confidence. "What are you going to do?"

"It's done."

The bartender stopped at the table to set down their drinks. Jimmy Deluga said something to him that Frank could not hear.

As he left, Frank asked, "Already? What did you do?"

"I've worked for Robert Henderson before, I knew the money would arrive."

It was obvious Jimmy Deluga wasn't about to say *what* he had done. "How long are you staying on the island?" asked Frank.

"I'll fly back to New York later tonight," said Jimmy. "United Eastern Power's jet is at the airport. What about you?"

"I've never been here before," said Frank. "I might try to see some of the island tomorrow, but I should head back tomorrow night."

The tennis women laughed loudly about something as the bartender opened another bottle of wine for them.

"This is from the gentlemen sitting there," the bartender told them, motioning toward Frank and Jimmy.

There were lots of smiles and raised glasses.

"Maybe we'll have some fun," said Jimmy, sliding his chair closer to the other table.

Frank glanced nervously at the briefcase full of money. It wasn't his worry anymore. He really would have rather gone to eat somewhere and then back to his room to call his wife, but he slid his chair over to the women's table too.

*

Two Town of Tisbury police cars and one State Police SUV pulled into the parking lot of Wild Wind Watersports, where Cindy Hammond's two sons worked for the summer. Two State Officers, leading an enthusiastic German shepherd, strode in the front door of the business while one of local cops stood by the back door. The last cop waited outside the front, so no one else would enter. A few minutes later the State Police led her two sons, Justin and Warren, out and walked them over to the rusted Toyota Corolla the brother's shared. The dog barked and pawed at the trunk.

Warren opened the trunk. Brick size packages, each wrapped in plain brown paper, filled the trunk.

*

John Johansson opened a Long Trail IPA and stepped out onto the back porch. Cindy had left a few minutes before, not a half hour after getting the call from her son Warren. John wished that he could have gone with her, because she was extremely distraught and he worried about her driving the three hundred miles to the Martha's Vineyard Steamship Authority terminal in Woods Hole.

Cindy claimed her sons had never done drugs and that they were good kids. Both sons swore they had never seen the heroin before and that somebody had set them up. John wished he had met the kids, judging any young man on their mother's opinion was sketchy at best. He squirted lighter fluid onto a pile of charcoal in the grill and tossed in a match. After the initial whoomffff, the dancing flames sent out ripples of light that lit the yard.

If Cindy is right, who would benefit from this? Did the kids have enemies? John didn't know much about Martha's Vineyard, except that it was the summer playground of the rich and famous. What sort of things went on there? Did the two boys get caught up in something stupid?

And what would their bail would be set at? Big money for sure. And lawyers…those assholes could sure chew up money fast. Cindy had mentioned once that they lived comfortably, but also said she hadn't been able to save enough for the sons' colleges, so there were huge student loans. This would put them all in a big bind. Could the kids have been trying to make a big score to help things out?

He sipped the beer and watched the flames settle down.

Or did someone actually set the two boys up? United Eastern Power would certainly love to see Cindy sell her parent's land.

*

Amy picked up the phone, "Hello?"

"Amy, it's Shawn Ash, the logger. How are you?"

"Fine." She suddenly felt incredibly nervous.

"Would you and Ethan like to go out for an ice cream cone," he said.

Oh my God, she thought. "Now?" She immediately hoped that didn't sound like what-do-you-mean-now.

There was laughter. "I know it's short notice. The weather is hot and nothing is better than ice cream on a night like this."

"Sure. Ethan would love it. He's just watching TV."

"How soon can you be ready?"

"I guess anytime."

"I'll be over in fifteen minutes to pick you up."

*

Will asked, "So what happened to the Hammonds?"

Kim stabbed at a chunk of hot Italian sausage and said, "They were killed because they wouldn't sell their land. I'm not sure who did it though. It may have been a neighbor that was counting on selling out or someone connected with United Eastern Power." She swirled the meat in the marinara sauce.

"Any ideas who?" He picked up his wine glass.

"There's a hundred and sixty-five miles of power lines, so there are lots of possibilities."

"Say someone nearby?"

Two candles sat on the small table between them. The sliding door of Kim's home was open wide and the sounds of the night insects drifted in over the back deck.

"The nearest neighbor who wanted to sell was Jerome Toll, and that family is a bunch of whack jobs," said Kim. "I think they all were bred a bit too close to home. The kids have been in and out of trouble since the day they were born."

"Are they capable of murder?"

"Oh yeah. It wouldn't bother them." Kim filled Will's wineglass again.

"So how do we prove it?"

"We? Isn't that the job of the police?"

"You're from up here," he said. "You must have noticed that we don't get much attention up in this corner of the state. What makes you think the State Police are going to make this a priority?"

"You're right," said Kim. "And there might be some money changing hands to make sure their deaths get lost in the paper shuffle."

"Let's drop in on them tomorrow," said Will.

"You like to live dangerously. They're liable to shoot us," said Kim. She smiled and added, "So let's try it."

They talked about other landowners that might have wanted to sell, but concluded there weren't any nearby. Most people in favor of the power line lived down state, where they tended to be less attached to the beauty of the land.

Kim poured the last of the wine into Will's glass. "I've got strawberry shortcake for desert," she offered. "Do you want it now or would you like to wait a bit?"

"Oh," said Will, settling back in his chair. "I'm stuffed and need a break." In the dim candlelight Kim looked gorgeous.

After their earlier hike, she had showered and changed into a light little jersey and short white shorts. He wished that he had brought a change of clothes too. While the sun settled in the western sky, they drank beer and munched on shrimp out on the deck. The wine bottle they shared over dinner had emptied as if by magic.

"Shall I open another bottle? Or maybe you'd like a drop of single malt scotch. I have a bottle of 15 year old Dalwhinnie."

"My, you are perfect," he said, reaching across the table to touch her hand. "That sounds great, I'd love a drop."

12

Will let Duchess out, then fumbled around under the counter, looking for another bag of coffee. By the time the coffee started dripping, Duchess scratched at the door to come back in. After feeding the dog, Will grabbed a frying pan, set it on the stove, and pulled a pound of bacon from the refrigerator. He needed coffee and protein to face the day.

Duchess nudged her stainless steel water bow, making it ring like a bell. Will picked it up to set it in the sink and started the water running.

"It's going to be another hot one," he said to Duchess, who waited patiently. "Kim was a lot of fun last night. I think she likes you." The dog started to drink when Will set the bowl on the floor.

Outside, the hot weather insects were already singing their songs, even though the sun had barely climbed over the hills. Stretching the bacon out in the frying pan, he wondered if the State Police had found anything at the Hammond's. Every time he drove by, the police cars were still there, and a couple of times the press had been there too.

Kim had to open the restaurant that morning, which meant she had at least an hour less sleep than he did. Will wondered how she was doing as he lowered the flame on the stove.

Their evening had ended with strawberry shortcake in bed, along with creative uses for the whipped cream topping. He chuckled remembering the details. Before he climbed into bed at home, he showered to clean off the sticky residue.

"Kim's got a wild streak," he said to Duchess, who had curled up on the floor near the dining table. Will poked at the bacon, not really sure how comfortable he was with her craziness. It had been fun the night before and up on the mountain, but on the long term?

Will wondered about the Tolls, who he knew little about except where they lived. He had heard stories about the family and there were a lot of jokes told at their expense. If half the stories were true, the Tolls were a bunch of hellions.

Jerome Toll had a motive, particularly with the way United Power bought up the land. The ten percent he had received up front was only a tease, compared to the balance to be paid when the project was fully permitted. Will shook his head…people like the Tolls would blow through their money and be broke again in no time, and then without their land beneath them.

"Hi." It was Amy, wearing a wrinkled tee shirt that went down over her hips. "How was your date?" A sleepy smile covered her face.

"Fine. What did you do last night?"

"We went out for ice cream with Shawn Ash." She poured coffee and went on to tell how she met him and his phone call to take her and Ethan out for ice cream.

"Have him come over tonight for dinner," said Will. "We'll invite Burt too, but I'm not sure if he'll come. I'll call Kim. She'd love to meet you."

This was more than Amy's sleepy brain could absorb. "So what did you do all day?" she asked.

He went through the high points, skipping past the mountaintop intimacy and the shortcake episode.

Amy blinked her eyes open, trying to force away the cobwebs. "Shawn's a nice guy, you'll like him."

Will went out to the woodpile next to the barn and started up the hydraulic splitter. The mindless work of turning round wood into split firewood emptied his mind, much like meditating. Too many things were happening at once and he needed a mental break. Life up there was supposed to be simpler.

His daughter and grandson had showed up, which made him smile. That they might actually stay in the area was good too. But she had met a guy already? Will never had been comfortable with his daughter dating and had immediately disliked every young man that she had ever brought home.

Will wasn't sure what he expected, dating someone Kim's age. Things moved along a little slower when he dated his wife so many years before. Were all women Kim's age so sexually active? Rolling another log up onto the splitter, he smiled. It certainly had been fun. The log groaned, popped in two, and fell to the ground. Did Amy do those same things?

Eastern United Power had been arrogant, the way they showed up in town and tried to buy up property. They started only two days after he closed on his own land. For the past year, the town had been in turmoil, with most of the residents against the outsiders coming in. Yet a few people willingly cashed out. He shook his head and set another log on the splitter.

The big gnarly maple log crackled and creaked and cracked in two.

If the power lines had gone in along the first proposed route, Will would have driven under the wires almost daily. Why would anyone want to turn the north woods into an industrial park? Couldn't they just bury the wires out of sight? The company complained about the cost…spread that over a trillion kilowatt hours and it was pennies.

The splitter's engine growled under another load. A stubborn chunk of yellow birch with a big ratty knot in it slowed the ram. Reluctantly the wood snapped and opened up.

Will had met the Hammonds only a couple of times. They definitely didn't deserve to die like they did. And murdered? Both of them seemed quite spry, making it hard to imagine them trapped inside a burning home, plus their bodies had been found on the ground floor. Couldn't they have climbed out a window? Someone had to have killed them.

Will straightened up to watch the Fish and Game Department's truck coming up his driveway. John Johansson stopped next to the barn and stepped out.

"Good morning," said Will. Glancing at his watch. "What brings you out this way so early?" It wasn't even seven o'clock yet.

"I wanted to drive by the Hammond's. The State Police are keeping an officer there around the clock, and I brought out coffee for the morning shift."

"I noticed the cruiser there when I came home last night," said Will. "Have they decided how the Hammonds died?"

"Both from a blow to the head," said John. "So it's now a crime scene." He went on to fill Will in on the events at the Toll's house.

"Murder?"

"There was a note," said John. "It just said, "life sucks", nothing more. It wasn't your typical suicide note."

"Who would want her dead?"

John shrugged his shoulders.

"There's coffee inside," said Will. "Want one?" John looked like he needed to talk to somebody.

"Sure."

"What brought you out this far?" They started toward the house.

"There was a truck registered to United Eastern Power parked on the other side of the hill yesterday, so I drove by and it was there again this morning. I think they're walking in on the back side of your property, scouting for a route around the Hammond's place. It has to be your land or Barbara Hawkins next door."

"Fred Atkins stopped by here the other day," said Will, "and I shut the door in his face."

John smiled for the first time. Inside the house, he then went on about the events surrounding Cindy Hammond while Will filled two mugs with coffee.

"What's your gut feeling?" asked Will. "About Cindy's sons."

"I think they've been set up to get her out of here and to create a need for money."

"That could be."

"Did you see our Senator Grogg on the news last night? Somebody is putting money in his pocket. Suddenly he's touting about how many jobs the power lines are going to create and all the money it's going to bring in. Does he think the people up here are stupid? The jobs are short term and those power lines are going to be an eyesore forever. People's property values are going to go down. And it has to hurt tourism.

"Cindy doesn't deserve any of this," continued John. "I'd love to get to the bottom of this mess."

Will had never seen John so upset. He wondered what his sudden attachment to the Hammond's daughter was.

Amy came in the room wearing shorts and a tee shirt. Will introduced her and they talked about the continued hot weather.

"I'm going to walk outback," said John, standing to leave. "Maybe I can find whoever came in that truck."

"I'll go with you," said Will. "My property isn't posted, so there's no law against them walking on my land and you can't kick them off, but I can."

13

Where the water piled up knee deep before squeezing under the bridge, Ethan sat up to his armpits, giggling at Duchess who tried to find a stone he had just tossed.

"He doesn't get tired of swimming," said Amy.

"That's good. It's too hot to do much else today," said Will.

Both of them were still wet, having taken a dunking in the deeper pool on the downstream side of the bridge. A lone elm tree provided shade and they had brought towels and a cooler, as if going to a beach. The fine streamside pebbles felt like laying on a beanbag and a faint southwest breeze cooled their dampened skin.

Will tossed a short fat stick that landed with a splash only a foot from Duchess's nose. The dog snapped it up and pranced proudly to the shore. Ethan giggled and tried to catch her short tail.

"The Game Warden seems like a nice guy," said Amy.

"He is. I like him. We went bird hunting together last fall."

Earlier, Will and John hadn't found anyone from United Eastern Power on his property, but they did find flagging that marked a path across the corner of his and Barbara Hawkins's land. He and John pulled down every piece of the orange ribbon and stuck it in their pockets.

"Is he married?" asked Amy.

Will felt an eyebrow involuntarily rise, daughters were such a worry, even grown ones. "I thought you were interested in Shawn, the logger." Amy had turned out to be a beautiful woman, just like her mother, and he guessed she could snag any single guy that she set her sights on.

She smiled. "I was just wondering."

"He isn't, but I think he's a little old for you."

Amy grinned and said, "I think the age difference would be about like yours and Kim's."

Touché, thought Will, taking a deep breath. She was probably right.

"They both are coming over for burgers tonight," he said, playfully, and added, "You can make side by side comparisons."

Amy stood and walked down to join Ethan in the water. Will lay back, feeling the soft pebbles beneath the towel, and shut his eyes. His plans to drop in on the Tolls vanished when Kim called to say she would be working a long shift to cover someone who wasn't coming in. That was probably just as well. The Tolls did sound crazy enough to be dangerous. Kim had agreed to come over for burgers on the grill that night.

Will wondered when someone would miss all those ribbons he had pulled down.

*

Cindy sat in the small office of the only lawyer on Martha's Vineyard who had returned her phone call. The night before she had arrived at Woods Hole too late to catch the last boat to the island, so Cindy ended up spending a restless night at a hotel in Falmouth. Any hope of bringing her car to the island the next morning vanished when she tried to book a crossing. It was summer on the Vineyard and a weekend, which meant no standby line, and the next available space for an automobile was over three days away.

So she left her car in one of the Steamship Authority's parking lots, walked aboard the ferry, and then rented a car in Vineyard Haven. On the drive down the day before, she had called three lawyers on the island, and only one of them returned her call, a young man named Brian Carney, who had a new law practice. He promised to see her two sons that afternoon, which at least made her feel a little better.

The drive from Vineyard Haven to Carney's office felt like it took forever, with the traffic entering Edgartown backed up for over two miles. When Cindy reached his office she learned that the police had also found a pistol under the back seat of her son's car and traced it to an unsolved double homicide that happened four months earlier in New York City.

"The boys were in school, not New York," she repeated. "I'm sure they have friends who can vouch for them." With his fiery red hair and gangly frame, Brain Carney looked like a big kid and didn't inspire confidence.

"I believe you," said Carney. "Now what about the drugs?"

"Neither of them have ever done drugs."

"Usually the parents are the last to know."

"I know my boys. Someone hid those drugs in the trunk of their car and then called the police."

Carney shuffled papers on his desk. "Who would want to set them up? Do they have any enemies?"

"I do," said Cindy. She recounted the entire story, from United Eastern Power attempting to buy her parent's property, to their suspicious deaths, and then her determination to put a conservation easement on the land.

Carney turned and looked out the window. A row of stopped cars waited to sift through a stop sign. Closer, at the edge of the asphalt, a heron gull picked at a flattened gray squirrel.

"That may well explain a motif," he said. "It might be a stretch though, and tough to prove. But the state's case against your sons is a weak one, maybe even more so with the appearance of the weapon.

"The two unsolved murders involved a well-known drug distributor and a promising young district attorney. The killings were particularly gruesome, with both of the men tortured before they were killed execution style." He leaned back and shook his head. "I'm sure the New York police will want to talk to your two sons.

"If their alibis hold up," he continued, "and with their clean records, it should be easy to have the charges dropped. I mean, why would they still have a gun that was used in a crime months ago? There were no fingerprints on it."

"What about bail?" said Cindy.

"New York is pressing for first degree murder charges and no bail. They claim the risk of flight is too great."

Cindy stood and walked to the window. They had already discussed his fee, which was most of what she had ever managed to save.

"The Feds are interested too," said Carney. "The DEA will be on the island this afternoon."

*

Barbara Hawkins's RAV4 sat in Will's driveway, its backup lights indicating it about to leave. The lights went out when Barbara looked in the rearview mirror and noticed Will's pickup truck coming up the drive.

"Hi," he said, stepping out.

"Hi," said Barbara. "I brought you more vegetables. The garden is producing faster than I can use everything, and I know you have guests." She pointed at a basket on the steps.

"Hi Barbara," said Amy, walking from the passenger side of the truck. The screen door slammed as Ethan ran inside.

"You look like you've been having fun," said Barbara, noticing the wet swimsuits.

"Ethan loves to swim," said Amy. "It felt good to cool off. You should join us sometime."

"Oh, I haven't put on a bathing suit in years," she answered.

Will tried to imagine her in a bathing suit as he let Duchess out of the back of the truck. "Well, thanks for the vegetables." He wondered if his daughter might be right and she did have her sights set on him. She looked very attractive in shorts and tank top.

"We're cooking burgers on the grill tonight," said Amy. "Please join us."

"Oh," said Barbara, hesitating. "What can I bring?"

"Make a salad," said Amy. "You have great lettuce. There will be six or eight people."

Will noticed the impish grin on his daughter's face. Was she trying to play cupid? Kim was going to be there too. Might things get awkward?

14

Will carried the mug of black coffee out onto the porch and dropped into a chair. Haze hung in the humid air, softening the dark forest beyond the field. Somewhere, an unseen raven squawked once and then went silent. A moment later its raspy call echoed off a hill. The summer insects had not started their daytime songs yet and the soft faint rumble of the river carried across the pasture.

The night before was something of a blur. Everyone had showed up, even Burt had brought along his wife, Agnes. She hadn't seemed nearly as bad as the stories around town had made her out to be. John Johansson arrived last, but spent much of the evening on the telephone talking to the Hammond's daughter down on the island of Martha's Vineyard, and then was the first to leave. Amy had spent some time chatting with John, but the logger, Shawn Ash, had kept pretty close to her side.

Shawn seemed like a great guy. Will had made a point of chatting with him and later Shawn joined him at the barbecue grill. Will learned he was a local boy who dreamed big, worked hard, and loved the outdoors. When Will stepped away from the grill for a moment, Shawn stepped right in to take over.

Kim melted easily into the group, with most knowing her from the restaurant. Both Barbara and Kim helped Amy in the kitchen at different times. Ethan bounced between all the adults and enjoyed the attention that one child gets in a group of grownups. It wasn't long after dinner before he fell asleep on the couch in the living room.

Barbara had been the biggest surprise. She looked beautiful in jeans and a white jersey, and her hair pulled back into a thick ponytail. She brought a huge salad with a dressing she had made, and homemade hamburger buns. Who had ever heard of someone making hamburger buns from scratch? They were delicious.

At one point, while Kim was in the kitchen with Amy, Will found himself on the porch talking with Barbara. Her zest for life was infectious, and they talked about horses and dogs and critters in the wild. She loved her horse and spoke of riding in the woods that their properties shared on the backside of Hawk Hill. Will didn't know a lot about horses, but had found her enthusiasm contagious.

Will looked at the rising red sun and glanced at his watch, ten o'clock was still over four hours away.

The night before, Barbara mentioned a hinge on the door of her barn that the fasteners had pulled out of. She used to hire Charlie Hammond to help with odd tasks around her farm and, with him gone, asked Will if he knew anyone else she could hire. When he offered to help with the door, a sparkle lit up her eyes.

Will smiled...either that door was very important to her or Amy was right. Ten o'clock was when he promised to be there.

Kim had stayed until everyone else had left. They ended up in the loveseat on the porch and things got rather heated. She suggested going up to his bed, but it felt awkward, with his daughter and grandson in the house. Will knew that might be old fashioned, but it was hard to change the way he felt. Trying to explain it to Kim, he felt like an idiot.

But Kim knew enough about men though to know that once she got them to a certain point, their willpower wilted. After a few more minutes of kissing and fondling, they pulled the cushions off the seat and made love on the deck.

She lingered, probably waiting for an invitation up to his bedroom, which was never offered. It was almost two in the morning when she finally had left.

Will sipped his coffee and smiled, remembering how they lay on their backs afterward, looking up at the stars that poked through the humid haze. That girl was something.

Why did he feel so guilty about her spending the night? Having his daughter around was like living with his parents again. Some of the old Puritan blood must still run in his veins.

*

John Johansson woke with a start when a Massachusetts State Police officer rapped on the window. As the window of his fifteen year old Chevy Blazer went down, a large tractor trailer grumbled down the hill toward the ferry dock.

"Can I see your license?" said the officer.

"Sure," said John, trying to force the cobwebs out of his brain. The sun hadn't poked over the horizon behind him. A herring gull squawked overhead and several more sat on top of the Steamship Authority's terminal building. The officer took the license and walked back to his cruiser.

When he had arrived the night before, the Woods Hole Terminal of the Martha's Vineyard Steamship Authority looked deserted. Floodlights on tall poles illuminated the parking lot with an orange glow and nobody was around. He had pulled to the side of the entrance road, where he promptly fell asleep after the five hour drive.

Glancing at his watch, it had only been three hours before. Three long rows of cars already sat in the enormous parking lot, along with another row that was separated from the others. At least a dozen large trucks waited along the road ahead of him.

"What brings you here?" said the officer, handing back the driver's license.

"I have a friend in trouble on the Vineyard," said John, guessing the officer knew by then he was a Fish and Game officer from out of state.

"Good luck," said the officer. "Go into the office and get a ticket. You might be able to get on standby this morning. Believe it or not, this place is pretty quiet for a summer morning."

John thanked him and drove down to the main building. A half hour later the first ferry left, and he still sat in the parking lot, but his Blazer had moved up to the front of the standby line. An hour and fifteen minutes later, he drove his Blazer into the next ferry.

Two decks up, he bought a cup of mediocre coffee and wished he had left Will Northrop's barbecue earlier. He had talked to Cindy on the phone from there and she sounded extremely upset, even breaking down and crying on the phone. His heart had ached for her, so he left a phone message in the Fish and Game office for his boss and then drove south.

The Vineyard Sound sparkled on the crossing to the island. It had been years since he had seen the ocean and he counted three white sails along the low flat coast of Cape Cod. The unloading of the ferry felt like it took forever, and then the traffic getting out of Vineyard Haven moved with the speed of a slug. John had no idea where Cindy was, but wanted desperately to get out of the congestion. At the first intersection he turned left. Soon he crossed a draw bridge and then was out of the business section of town.

Stopping in a wide spot on the side of the road, he dug out his phone and called Cindy.

She answered on the second ring. "Hi."

"Good morning," said John. "How are you feeling?"

"Better."

"I'm on Martha's Vineyard. Can I take you out for breakfast?" It was quarter past eight.

"You're here?" She sounded relieved or excited, either were good. "I'd love that. I'm at the Westerly Hotel in Oak Bluffs."

Cindy gave him directions and forty-five minutes later they walked up Lake Ave past the boat filled harbor. Circuit Ave, with its touristy stores, already had dozens of people on the sidewalks. John led her into Linda Jean's Restaurant where they sat at the only table available, one by the window. During Cindy's long explanation of all that she had learned the day before, they never once stopped holding hands.

*

"That should do it," said Will, tightening the last bolt.

The hinge's screws had pulled out of the old wood and he replaced them with bolts that passed through the door. Nuts with over-sized washers on the inside held everything together. He climbed down the ladder leaning against the barn door.

"Thanks," said Barbara. "Are you ready for coffee?"

"Iced coffee," said Will. The sun already had sweat dribbling down his forehead. In the pasture the horse and goat stood in the shade of a rock maple tree. "How long can this hot weather last?"

"I try to get my chores done early, before I go to work," said Barbara, leading the way. "The garden could use some rain too." She looked nice, in shorts and a sleeveless jersey. Her hair was back and a big straw hat shaded her eyes.

Inside, she poured iced coffee and then gave a short tour of her old farm house. It looked well cared for and neat, with much of the furniture antiques. They stopped to sit on the screen porch that faced the backyard. He asked about her work as the part-time manager of a local insurance company office. The conversation drifted to family and mutual friends.

When the conversation lagged, Barbara feared Will might be about to leave. She said, "Let's have a picnic down by the falls."

"The falls?" said Will.

"You've never been there? It's at the edge of your own property, where the river doubles back. I can make us some sandwiches and there's a couple of beers in the refrigerator." She smiled, waiting for his response.

Will glanced at his watch.

She quickly added, "It will be cooler there, and we can go for a swim."

"I didn't bring a bathing suit," said Will, wishing he hadn't left Duchess at home with Ethan. The dog would have loved to go for a swim.

"You can swim in your shorts. It's too hot to do much else today."

"I'll help you make those sandwiches."

Forty-five minutes later, Barbara led Will out of the woods and onto the ledges, where the river tumbled into a natural basin and created a bubble filled pool.

*

Jimmy Deluga felt the phone in his pocket vibrate. By the time he stepped outside of Café d'Alsace and onto the Manhattan sidewalk, it had stopped ringing. The number said the call came from Robert Henderson. Jimmy called him back.

"What's up?"

"Have you ever been to New Hampshire?" said Henderson. "We need someone up there with your…expertise."

When outdoors, Jimmy didn't like walking on dirt. In his world, asphalt and concrete covered everything. New Hampshire sounded awful. "What's it pay?"

"Your usual, ten G a day."

"Nope. Going up there, I gotta get more. There's bears and dangerous shit out in the wild. Fifteen a day, but tell me what I'll be doing."

Fifteen thousand a day was more than Henderson wanted to pay. The cash had to come out of funds that the stock holders would never miss. And what if Deluga found nothing?

"I'll tell you what," said Henderson. "Ten grand a day, and then we'll pay you the other five when you get results."

"What will I be doing?"

"Finding a killer."

That confused Jimmy, because he was often hired as an assassin or hit man. "What do you need another killer for?"

"We don't need one," said Henderson, frustrated. "Someone killed a local up there and it might make my company look bad, like we did it or something. I want you to find out who the killer really was."

"Oh, that should be easy," said Jimmy. "I want a five day minimum, up front, just for driving that far." In Jimmy Deluga's shadowy world, most of the professional slime knew each other, and he figured a few questions asked in the right places would tune him into the underworld of rural America.

"Okay. We need to meet," said Henderson, "so I can give you the details and the money. Can you drive north tomorrow?"

"Yeah."

"Meet me at the scenic pullout on Rt. 3 in Lancaster, New Hampshire, by Mount Prospect. Be there at three in the afternoon and I'll have your money."

Jimmy glanced at his watch. It had to be a six hour drive, which meant getting going before nine. "Make it five and I'll be there."

"Okay."

15

Will opened a second beer and took a sip. Beside him sat Barbara against a smooth log they shared beneath a mammoth white pine, with soft pine needles under them and the tumbling swirling river in front. The enormous tree provided shade, the hurrying water cooled the air, and the narrow valley funneled the breeze. Everything worked in unison to create a piece of paradise.

Earlier, they had settled into the swirling water up to their chins. The tickling fizzy bubbles water made it almost impossible not to laugh, and they giggled like children. Afterward, they climbed onto a smooth ledge to dry off, before settling under the pine to eat lunch.

"I can't believe I've never been here," said Will.

"On the side we walked in on you have to cross my property to get here," said Barbara, "that's probably why you never came this far. On the other side, where most of your land is, a steep ledge blocks the way if you try to walk here along the river." She took a swallow of her beer. Their roast beef sandwiches were long gone.

"Do you come here often?"

"I usually ride Martha down to that little pasture in the woods. She likes to eat the grass there while I have a swim."

Barbara's damp sandy hair was back on her shoulders and she wore a small two-piece bathing suit. Will knew she was nearly his age, but she looked much younger. "I thought you said the other day it had been years since you wore a bathing suit."

Barbara laughed. "I did. Usually I go skinny dipping." A big smile covered her face.

"Ah!" teased Will, "I'll sneak down here for sure." Barbara's hazel eyes picked up the blue of the sky.

"There's no peeking," she laughed. "If I'm skinny dipping you have to too."

The suggestive bantering was new territory for Barbara, and she wanted to back up about three sentences, but she couldn't control the smile on her face. It was fun.

Will hadn't seen the impish side of Barbara before. "Oh God," he said, "I haven't been skinny dipping since…I don't know when."

It had been years since she had seen a man's face light up like Will's. "No wet clammy bathing suits," she said, continuing the banter. "Think about it."

"So why did we wear them?"

Barbara, feeling delightfully naughty, shrugged her shoulders. "It's a silly custom."

Will settled back against the tree, and said, "It's getting hot. Very hot."

"Almost hot enough for another swim," said Barbara, realizing she was nervously biting her lip.

Will grinned. "No silly suits this time?" He couldn't believe those words had come out of his mouth.

Barbara stood, grabbed her towel, and walked down across the ledge to the side of the pool. With her back to him, the bathing suit top came off. Nice shoulder, he thought. When she stepped out of the bottom and he noticed the lack of tan lines, and her firm ass. She slipped over the ledge's lip into the water.

Thinking he couldn't chicken out, Will followed. Barbara politely looked away as he shed his shorts and dropped into the water

"Whoa, that is nice," he said, settling down to his shoulders.

"It feels warmer than before," said Barbara. It was hard to hear over the grumble of the water.

"Do you ever fish in this pool?"

"I haven't fished since I was a child. My father used to take us."

They talked for a few minutes about their childhoods, but soon the river started to feel chilly.

"So who's getting out first?" asked Will.

Barbara found Will's polite shy manner cute. "Usually I lay on the smooth ledge to dry off. The warm rock feels good after the cold water." He actually looked nervous, which made her feel very in control.

Will rose up just enough to look at the rock shelf, then settled back down.

"Come on," she said, unabashedly standing to climb up out of the water.

Up on the smooth granite, she grabbed her towel, worked it into ball for a pillow, and stretched out on her stomach, pulling her wet hair around the right side of her head. Will scrambled up to lay on his stomach to her left.

"The warm rock does feel nice," he said. A puff of wind came up the river, evaporating the moisture on his back. The sensation of warm and cool felt delightful.

"This is my favorite spot on the whole planet," said Barbara.

"I can understand that. Thanks for sharing it with me."

She laughed and propped herself up on her elbows. "You own it. I still can't believe you've never been here."

"Burt and I were just upstream from here the other day," he said, still not believing he was actually lying naked beside Barbara on a rock.

She looked gorgeous.

*

"I got the mayor on board," said Senator Greggory Grogg.

Robert Henderson took a sip of his Jack Daniels, then said, "He's on the wrong side of the state. The power lines don't go anywhere near his damned city."

"His city has a lot of voters," said Grogg. "That's what counts. If he says it's good for jobs, then it'll count."

Henderson picked a French fry off his sandwich plate and pushed it into his mouth, wondering how the hell Grogg managed to get elected so many times. Did the asshole buy each individual vote? Or were his opponents really worse than him? It didn't seem possible.

Only a few patrons sat at tables in the dim red light inside of The Gold Club. Henderson liked the soft simulated-leather seats and the food was okay. It had been easy to talk Grogg into meeting him there.

An almost naked woman, illuminated by garish blue light, displayed tremendous agility around a polished brass pole in the center of the stage. Three men in work clothes sat along the edge of the platform, laughing and tossing money toward the dancer. She periodically bent to pick it up, always stopping with her cleavage inches from their faces and seductively licked her lips, before stuffing the cash into her G string.

After swallowing, Henderson said, "It will help some."

Grogg stuffed the last piece of his steak into his mouth, and while chewing said, "Did you see his statement in the paper?"

The woman's top dropped to the floor as she pirouetted around the pole.

"Yeah, I did. It was all blah, blah, blah, more jobs. How long are people going to fall for that bullshit?" His eyes never left the stage.

The music changed to a slow thumping bass beat. The woman bent over, placing her butt in front of the three men and twitched the cheeks like shivering balloons. The men roared and tossed more money.

"Look at that," said Henderson, mesmerized. "That woman's got talent."

The dancer pivoted around the pole with one of her very tall high-heels pointed straight upward over her head. Her nimbleness was amazing.

"There are going to be jobs, right?" said Grogg.

Henderson motioned to the waitress for another drink, and said, "Yeah, for a little while anyway."

With swaying hips and eyes locked on the three stage-side men, the woman teasingly toyed with the top of her G string.

Grogg asked, "Are you ready to leave?"

"Not for a while," said Henderson, pushing another French fry into his mouth. "I got more business to attend to."

16

Will followed Barbara up the narrow path. The air under the trees remained warm and humid, and perspiration tricked down his side. If they slowed the mosquitoes caught up to them, so they trudged on. The knapsack stuck against the bare skin of his back. At least his shorts had dried while they lay on the rock in the sun. He followed, noticing the sway of her hips.

He and Barbara had laid on that warm rock talking until the sun started to cook their skin, and then they slipped back into the water. Will had found her easy to talk with and time slipped away. When the water felt cold again they had wrapped in towels and snuck back to the shade of the giant pine.

Walking up the hill, Barbara wondered what Will was thinking. The day had turned out to be fun and she hoped he felt the same way. Never would she have imagined skinny dipping with him, but it all felt right at the time. She smiled, remembering his nervousness when she asked for some sunscreen on her bare back.

Soon, they stepped from the narrow path out into the field behind Barbara's home where Will could walk by her side. "That was the best picnic I have ever been on," he said.

"I had fun too."

"We'll have to do it again sometime."

As they came to the house, his hand reached for hers. She said, "I'd like that." The day was turning out perfectly.

"Tomorrow?"

Barbara stopped and smiled, things were moving pretty fast. Too fast?

Will wondered what she was thinking, so added, "It's supposed to be another hot day."

"I have to work," she said, "but I'll take the afternoon off. Meet me here at noontime."

Will put his arms around her and placed his mouth against hers.

*

Jimmy Deluga sat on a stool in the Eastern Mountain Sports store in Manhattan, trying on another pair of hiking boots. The clerk assured him that rattlesnakes were almost unheard of in New Hampshire, and snake proof boots or leggings were unnecessary. Over a dozen open boxes of boots already sat on the floor. Jimmy's outdoor experiences had been limited and rather gruesome, having once almost died from a bad case of poison ivy.

His shopping basket already contained a compass, a large Buck belt knife, Woodsman's Friend insect repellant, a Leatherman tool, the most expensive Garmin GPS the store carried, a Space Blanket, waterproof matches, a first aid kit, and a book called *Wilderness Survival*. Still on his list to buy were pants, shirts, hats, and gloves. He had no idea what the weather would be like that far north.

While he waited for the salesperson to return with another pair of boots, he pondered what to bring for weapons. His favorite concealed carry pistol was a stainless steel Walther PPK, but up there in the woods he thought its demure .380 bullet might prove too small in the chance encounter with a bear. Perhaps he would bring the much more lethal Kimber Model 1911 that he recently purchased, with its larger .45 caliber bullets.

"Perhaps these will fit better," said the clerk, handing him another boot. "These run a little narrower."

Jimmy noticed the box said Women's Size 9. Before trying it on, he looked the boot over to make sure nothing on the outside said "Women's".

*

"Where have you been all day?" asked Amy.

The screen door shut behind Will. "I helped Barbara fix the door on her barn."

Amy grinned. "All day?"

"I'm glad you missed me. What about you?"

"Ethan and I went swimming in the river," said Amy, noticing how he changed the subject. "Kim called looking for you about an hour ago.

She's got two tickets to the concert down at the Robertson's Center. It's a band from Montreal playing."

Will realized he had not thought of Kim all day. "I'll give her a call."

"So did you have fun with Barbara?"

"Yeah," he said, then dashed upstairs

*

Frank Atkins and his wife poked along Circuit Ave in the town of Oak Bluffs, holding hands like two teenagers in love. She had driven down by herself and taken the ferry across to the island of Martha's Vineyard. Frank had cleared an extra day off with his pain-in-the-ass boss, Robert Henderson, and they planned to enjoy their little getaway. It had been years since he and Angie had time away from their two teenage children.

Earlier, they had walked along the harbor, stopped to sit on the rocks of the breakwater, followed the beach down to the Steamship Authority's Oak Bluffs terminal, which they detoured around, and continued along the beach. Neither of them had put their feet in salt water in over a decade and they spoke little, instead watching the beachgoers and sea birds. At the south end of Ocean Park, they walked back toward town and headed north on Circuit Ave to where Frank's car sat not far from Nancy's Restaurant. They had planned to eat dinner there later and watch the boats on the harbor. Circuit Ave's sidewalks were filled with window shopping tourists and they too lingered at many of the storefronts to peer inside.

Cindy Hammond and John Johansson walked the opposite direction on Circuit Ave, mindlessly passing the time until she heard from the lawyer. Never had John seen so many people at once as on that street. Families were eating ice cream. Teenagers zipped along on skate boards. Automobiles inched along, hoping to find a precious place to park. A tall lanky kid sat on a planter outside the post office, strumming a guitar.

A face on the other side of the street caught John's eye. He grabbed Cindy's hand and ducked into The Royal Ice Cream and Chocolate Emporium.

"What is it?" she asked.

"Frank Atkins is across the street."

"Who?"

"Frank Atkins. The guy who's been buying up all the land for United Eastern Power. He's the guy that was at your parents' house."

She tried to look out the window, but John pulled her back. "Don't let him see you. He's with a woman. Maybe she's his wife or girlfriend."

"Why would he be here?"

"To frame your sons. Or else it's an awfully big coincidence."

"What are we going to do?"

"Let's follow them."

"Won't they see us?"

"We'll stay far back and blend in with the tourists. I'll get us some ice cream cones," said John. "Keep an eye on them. What kind do you want?"

"Chocolate chip."

He slipped into the line at the counter while she stood by the window. Frank and the woman sauntered along. Cindy stood well away from the shop's glass front and watched. Right after Frank and his lady friend passed by, John handed her a cone. They stepped out onto the sidewalk, licking their ice creams.

Frank and the woman held hands, ambling toward the end of the road. John and Cindy followed, hiding behind their ice cream cones.

At the end of the street, Frank led the woman to the left, then crossed over to the harbor side. They stopped for a few minutes to watch a sailboat attempting to back into a slip, before disappearing into the restaurant named Nancy's.

"What are we going to do?" asked Cindy.

John noticed Frank's silver Range Rover with its New Hampshire number plates parked curbside about halfway down the road that bent along the side of the harbor. "Follow me," he said.

Away from the bustle of Circuit Ave less people were on the sidewalk. Across the street from Frank's car was the Westerly Hotel, where Cindy had rented a room. John looked back toward Nancy's. The deck in the front was crowded with diners and drinkers. Anyone inside would have a hard time looking out past the throng. He led Cindy further down the road.

Approaching the Range Rover, John pulled a Buck knife from his pocket and opened its blade. The nearest people ahead of them were thirty feet away and going the same direction as they. Glancing back, everyone still watched the sailboat trying desperately to maneuver into the confines of a slip.

John ducked down and pushed the blade into the sidewall of the Rover's right front tire. Immediately, air started to hiss out.

"Let's go buy a bottle of wine and take it up to your room," he said, straightening up. "They won't be going anywhere for a while."

*

Jerome Toll scratched at his crotch. A cluster of empty beer cans and two spent whiskey bottles cluttered the coffee table. He picked his cigarette from the ashtray, took one long pull, snuffed it out, and lit another. Since he wife died he had hardly left the couch and the TV hadn't been shut off in days. In the hot weather he had stripped down to his boxer shorts.

A belch escaped his gut, and he reached for the only container within arm's length that still contained any liquid, a fifth of Canadian Mist. The beagle lay sad-eyed on the rug, patiently hoping for food.

"It weren't suicide," he said, to the dog. "Naw, she had it too good heyah ta wanna kill herself." He sniffled and wiped his sleeve across his nose. "Kathy..." Tears welled up in his eyes and he couldn't finish the sentence. "Awe Christ," he slobbered, "I gotta get a grip."

He took another swig from the bottle.

"Who da wanted to kill my honey?" he asked, looking at the dog. "It don't make no sense."

Sitting up straight, he asked, "Is Brian at home?" The dog made no response. "He's a useless fucking piece of crap." Jerome inhaled through the newly lit cigarette and said, "He's old enough to be workin' and payin' his fair share." He tried to remember when he had seen his son last. Was it before his wife died?

A vehicle came in the driveway and stopped. Standing felt risky, so Jerome just waited. A moment later footsteps came across the deck and the front door opened.

"What are you doing here?" said Jerome.

"Checking on you. We heard the news. How are you doing?"

"Okay I guess, considering," said Jerome, still sitting on the couch. "Want a drink?"

"No. Where's your son?"

"Brian? That useless piece of shit ain't around." Jerome wiped his nose against his sleeve again. "At least I don't think so."

"Brian!"

They both listened for a second, then Jerome said, "What the hell do you want him for?"

"I don't."

A huge handgun came up and pointed at Jerome's face, whose last cloudy thought was "Holly fuck. I must be drunk...I didn't see that coming."

From the barrel of the .410 Thompson Contender flew one hundred and fifty-five lead pellets, which weighed together slightly less than three quarters of an ounce. Traveling in a clump, they hit Jerome's chin at a velocity of over twelve hundred feet per second. Their combined energy shattered the jawbone and mashed most of his alcohol soaked brain out a fist-sized hole punched through the back of his skull.

17

The distance between homes along Route 3 surprised Jimmy Deluga. He had never been north of Boston before and rural northern New Hampshire intrigued him. It felt like a different planet.

Before leaving New York he had rented a shiny black Cadillac Escalade, hoping that driving a SUV would help him to blend in with locals. Piled in the back were two suitcases of clothes and three duffle bags of things bought at Eastern Mountain Sports.

Franconia Notch amazed him, with the steep mountains that climbed up on either side of the road. Only on television had he ever seen anything like that. The long stretch of wilderness north of the notch felt disconcerting, but soon he passed by a series of hotels in Twin Mountain and a few miles later the little town of Whitefield.

Fifteen minutes later, he slowed and pulled into the scenic outlook next to the Mt. Prospect State Park. Nobody else was there, but he could see a town in the valley ahead and far beyond the rolling hills of the next state. Using a phone recently bought under an assumed name, he called Robert Henderson, who assured him he was almost there.

Jimmy pulled the .45 caliber Kimber from his shoulder holster and checked the magazine, then slipped the gun back in before climbing out. The heat outside of the air conditioned Escalade surprised him, having expected it to be much cooler. And the air smelled far different than in New York. Reflexes brought on a cough.

A dark blue Chevy pickup truck pulled into the lot and Jimmy recognized Henderson driving. He parked next to Jimmy and stepped out.

*

Brian Toll watched the thin monofilament line and waited. Where the dark silky stream slipped beneath the roots of an old hemlock tree, he knew there would be brook trout. Seven fish, none longer than the width of his hand, already lay on the bank.

He had not been home since his learning of his mother's brutal death. Brain was not sure if she had killed herself, possibly because she couldn't stand his drunken father, or if his asshole father had murdered her. Either way, it had been the old man's fault and Brian hated the bastard.

To keep his mind occupied, Brain set up an elaborate campsite on the north side of Hawk Hill. It didn't matter to him who owned the land, only that it was difficult to approach due to steepness both above and below, and thick softwood trees sheltered him from any aerial view. The only reasonable approach came along a game trail from the east, and there he rigged fishing line to a prop that help up a dead fir tree the size of a man's thigh. If the line was accidentally kicked, the prop would be yanked out from under the tree and it would fall with a thud, alerting him of anyone approaching.

A small stream provided water and a stack of firewood sat by a ring of stones. The nearest home was over two miles away and down in a valley, so Brian believed that on clear nights it would be safe to light a fire.

Brian didn't own a tent, but he did have a portable hunting blind. It set up much like a tent and its camouflage fabric almost disappeared into the trees. The only problem was its short length, and when he lay down his head poked one end and feet the other.

While waiting for another fish, Brian started a mental list of things he would need for camp life. First would be a gun, preferable a few guns. A pistol would be handy to carry, but a .22 rifle could put meat in the pot and not make much noise. A shotgun would be handy for shooting rabbits and birds. Back at his parent's home were both, along with clothes that he would also need.

Most of his cooking had been done on a stick over the fire. He needed at least a frying pan and some sort of pot. An axe would be handy, and a bow saw too. Brian loved chainsaws, but they made too much noise and needed gasoline too.

Brian wound up the fishing line, gathered up his trout, and then started back up the hill to his campsite. In steep areas the climb required holding onto trees to keep from sliding back down on fallen spent needles from the spruce and fir trees. The softwoods gave way to hardwoods, which then became mixed with softwood trees again. Soon he climbed upward through thick spruce and fir trees that blotted out the sky. By the time he reached his new home, he heart pounded and he gasped for air.

He stowed his fishing things and started a Coleman stove. The trout would go directly onto a stick to cook over the flame. After savoring the last morsel, he headed for his parent's home.

The walk took almost an hour and he reached the place just before nightfall cloaked the woods. He found a comfortable place to sit and wait, watching to see if lights came on in the house. With luck his old man would be in town drinking.

The idea of a hot shower grew in his head. It had been days since he had washed, and then it was in a cold stream where his one cake of soap barely lathered. Maybe he would risk it. First, he would get the things he needed and pile them on the back step, that way, if he had to make a hasty exit it would be easy to grab the stuff and run.

Fireflies created white flecks that drifted in the darkness. Crickets rattled off their raspy song. Somewhere faraway a dog barked and an owl hooted. The house remained dark.

Brian sprinted for the back door.

*

"You're home early," said Amy, turning to look from the couch. "How was the concert?"

"Good," said Will. "Kim has to open the restaurant in the morning." Duchess stood to sniff Will's leg as he pulled a bottle of Glenmorangie out from beneath the kitchen counter.

"She'll be wearing you out."

"I'm not used to staying up late," said Will, sitting down beside her. The late local news played on the TV, something about a building inspector downstate taking a bribe.

"You don't have to get up at the crack of dawn," said Amy, grinning.

Will knew his daughter liked teasing him. "It's the best time of the day."

"I have a job interview at the hospital tomorrow at one. Can you watch Ethan for me?"

"A job interview? That's great. Of course."

He would have to call Barbara early to change plans. Maybe the three of them could do something together. The thought of Amy actually moving nearby caused a smile on his face that wouldn't go away.

"So, are you seeing both of them again tomorrow?" asked Amy, almost laughing.

Will swallowed a gulp of scotch, then took a deep breath. "I don't know what I'm doing."

"That's obvious," said Amy, giggling. "You had better be careful or you'll lose both of them."

"Are you seeing Shawn again?"

"Tomorrow night. We're taking Ethan down to Lancaster to see the new Disney movie."

Will wondered if Shawn really liked kids or if he was just acting the part to get into his daughter's pants. Then he wondered why he didn't trust anyone that approached his daughter. There are nice guys out there, he reminded himself, and his daughter was pretty smart.

"I'm going to bed," said Will. "I'll see you in the morning."

*

Brian shut off his flashlight. The things stacked on the back step created a dark pile. Only a few stars poked through the haze overhead, yet they provided enough light to make out shapes in the yard. Beyond, the forest appeared a black wall.

Using an old rucksack that he had found under his bed, he would be able to carry everything in one trip, but the pack weighed so much he could hardly lift it. An axe was strapped to its back, the cast iron frying pan hand poked out of the top, and the guns he would carry in his hands. Thinking he might never be at the house again, he decided to take one last walk through.

The place stunk. He had never noticed it before, but after living outdoors it smelled of beer and cigarettes and sweat. In his bedroom he turned on the light. It looked as it always did, with clothes scattered about and the bed a mess. Shutting off the light, he followed his flashlight's beam to the bathroom, stripped off his clothes, and slipped into the shower.

The warm water felt heavenly, but, naked with the water masking all other sounds, he felt vulnerable and hurried. After drying and dressing, he walked down the hall and turned into the living room.

The beam of his flashlight hit the clutter of bottles on the coffee table, and found a hand. Brian flicked a light switch.

His father's face was unrecognizable, but he knew it was him.

What looked like splattered dark spaghetti sauce covered on the wall behind the couch, and the cushions were soaked with dark blood and urine. A pistol that Brian had never seen before rested in his father's hand. Suicide? Maybe. Murder?

Brian's knees buckled and he landed on his hands as his stomach rolled to regurgitate its entire contents.

"Oh fuck," he said, gasping and dropping his face into his arms. He started to cry uncontrollably.

18

The hydraulically driven ram pushed the log into the splitter's steel wedge, triggering it to pop and groan in protest. When the wood fell to the ground, Will tossed it onto the growing pile.

"You got started early," said Amy, coming from the house.

Will shut off the motor. "I couldn't sleep, so I got up early."

Amy grinned. "Women troubles?"

"No. Just stuff." He rolled another log up onto the splitter.

Amy knew her father kept things bottled inside. Her mother used to complain about it. "Ethan wants you to cook flippers," she said.

Will smiled. Almost nobody called pancakes flippers, except him and Ethan. "Tiger too?" he asked.

"Yes, he wants flippers and tiger."

"Did I ever tell you I wanted to start a sugar bush? There's a good stand of sugar maples just across the river."

Amy smiled. "No. I bet Ethan would love to help you."

Will put his arm around Amy's shoulder and started walking toward the house. "Do you know where I got that phrase, flippers and tiger? It came from a book written by a guy named Bradford Angier."

"You told me that once, Dad."

"Just checking," he said, giving her a squeeze.

Inside he started bacon in a frying pan and then mixed the ingredients for pancakes. Ethan wanted to help, so Will had him set the table. Amy poured two mugs of coffee.

*

The State Police SUV blocked the driveway and wide yellow ribbon stretched across two of the home's three doors to prevent entry. A police van and three cruisers sat in the driveway, and four officers stood on the deck outside the front entrance.

Just before midnight, someone had dialed 911 from the Toll's home and then left. A local officer had been dispatched, who soon reported the horrific scene. The frantic call from the commander of State Police F Troop brought the homicide team up from downstate. Two possible murders at the same address was certainly an unusual event.

A short portly State cop said, "A local officer is keeping the press out by the road."

"Good. Has the daughter been contacted?" said the tall taller cop.

"We can't find her. Someone said she lives with a boyfriend, but that hasn't been confirmed."

"And the son?"

"Nobody has seen him for days."

"Maybe he's dead somewhere."

"Nothing would surprise me with this bunch."

The tall officer stepped further from the front door, and said, "I didn't really know them."

"They were always in trouble, the whole family. The father even did some jail time down in Concord."

A second State Police van came in the driveway and two men in street clothes climbed out to open up the vehicle's back.

"For once the people down state are paying attention to what's going on up here."

"It's all about money," said the shorter officer. "The people behind that proposed power line got money to burn and it's attracting a lot of attention."

"Could this have anything to do with that?"

"The power line was supposed to go right across this property."

*

John Johansson listened to the heron gulls squawking over the harbor and stared up at the ceiling. A boat motor grumbled in the distance and cars passed by on the street below. Beside him, Cindy Hammond slept silently while the world outside still woke.

The night before they sipped wine and watched the street from Cindy's rented room, until Frank Atkins and his wife came out of Nancy's Restaurant. Of course Atkins found his car with a flat tire, which gave John and Cindy ample time to go down to the hotel's lobby and watch. Atkins made at least two calls on his phone, and then a taxi picked them up.

John and Cindy dashed out to his Chevy Blazer to follow the taxi along the shore to Edgartown, where it deposited Atkins and his wife at the Harborview Hotel. There was no point on following them inside, so he and Cindy went back to Oak Bluffs and ate a late dinner of fried clams at a place called The Lookout Tavern.

He couldn't remember exactly how they ended up in bed together. Back at her room, they had been talking about her two sons and finishing off the last of the wine. She was distraught and he offered a consoling hug and then they started kissing.

John smiled. It had been a long time since he made love with someone he really cared about. His hand slid across the sheets to touch hers. Hopefully, she would remember it as fondly as he did.

The sound of a blue jay startled him…it was a text coming in on his phone.

When he first bought his phone, he set it up the alarms as bird calls. Slipping from the bed, he picked it up. The text came from a State cop that he was friendly with.

Jerome Toll dead, shot in head. Maybe suicide.

John stepped to the window. Atkins's silver Range Rover still sat on the road beside the harbor. He couldn't see the side with the flat tire, but doubted anything had been done to it.

"You're up."

He turned to see Cindy smiling. "Yes," he said. "I just got a text message. Are you ready for some breakfast?"

"Are we going to follow Frank Atkins again?" She stayed under the sheets with her head on the pillow.

"No. Let's get some breakfast and then talk to your lawyer again. Your sons are going to be arraigned this morning."

Cindy said, "It's early. Come back to bed and snuggle with me first."

*

The rumble of a logging truck passing on Route 3 rattled the windows of Jimmy Deluga's motel room. He stood in front of a steamy mirror, having stepped out of the shower only moments before, and with careful strokes sliced away his whiskers.

Dressing was always an important event to Jimmy, but dressing for the north woods would be a new experience. He chose pants that he had bought called Mountain Khakis and a cotton button shirt with epaulets. The hiking boots looked ugly, but he felt they were necessary.

Jimmy despised hot weather because concealing a weapon always turned out to be difficult. The Kimber Model 1911 was too large to hide beneath his shirt, so he opted to carry a small knapsack everywhere he went. Waterproof matches, Space blanket, energy bars, and other survival gear filled the pack.

Glancing at his new Rolex Adventurer II, he tried to remember the last time he had woken up before nine o'clock.

He drove the Escalade into town looking for a place to get breakfast. The amount of activity surprised him. Trucks hauling logs rolled through town and it seemed like every other vehicle was a pickup truck. Several cars had out of state number plates, and a few even had Canadian. Four motorcycles sat next to the gas pumps in front of a variety store. Jimmy parked between two pickup trucks in front of Big Bear's Restaurant.

Inside smelled of bacon and elderly patrons shared tables near the front windows. At the counter sat two men in dirty jeans and tattered short sleeved tee shirts. Beside them, two men wearing sports jackets looked like they might be insurance salesmen. Jimmy doubted the place would compare too well with his usual New York City breakfast haunts.

He slid onto a stool at the counter as far from the two dirty men as possible and set his knapsack on the floor between his feet.

An attractive young woman with wavy auburn hair stepped out of the kitchen and said, "Hi, I'm Kim. Can I get you a coffee?"

"Sure, black," answered Jimmy, wondering how hard it would be to seduce this backwoods beauty. "What's your favorite thing on the menu?"

"For breakfast? The crab omelet. It has sundried tomatoes and a chipotle sauce. You'll love it," she said, setting his coffee down.

"I'll have one," said Jimmy, flashing his best smile. "So what is there to do around this town?"

"Are you here for a while?"

Jimmy liked that question and guessed that she was already interested in this sophisticated man-from-out-of-town. "A few days," he answered. "I always wondered what was up in this part of New England and decided to do a little exploring. What do you like to do on your days off?"

"This area is known for hunting and fishing," said Kim. "And there is some great hiking."

The chance to kill something sounded like fun. "What can I hunt?" asked Jimmy.

"This time of the year there isn't much. Come back in the fall if you want to hunt."

Kim had noticed his brand new clothes and the ostentatious watch on his wrist, plus the fat gold ring with a glittering diamond on his finger. She figured Jimmy to be a city-slicker from down country that wanted desperately to do something outdoorsy and masculine.

"I'm going to have my guide's license soon," she said. "Look me up when you come next time and I'll take you fishing." She disappeared into the kitchen.

Jimmy wondered if that was a pickup line in the north woods. A local newspaper sat on the counter and he picked it up while waiting.

When he had met with Henderson at the Mt. Prospect overlook, Henderson had given him a stack of newspaper clippings on the events in the North Country, both surrounding United Eastern Power's plans and the deaths of Charlie and Agnes Hammond. The newspaper had an article on the front page about the death of Kathy Toll, and then articles on the next three pages rehashing information Jimmy already knew.

Kim reappeared with his omelet. Setting down the newspaper, he said, "There's been some excitement up here this summer."

"Yes," she said, noticing the front page story. "And someone this morning said that Kathy Toll's husband killed himself." She wondered if Jimmy might be a reporter from a news service. "I hope the news doesn't scare away the tourists."

"As long the tourists aren't the one getting knocked off, the news will attract them," said Jimmy. "People love this stuff.

"What time do you get through work?" he continued. "Why don't you show me one of your favorite hikes?"

Kim smiled. The last thing she wanted to do was go into the woods with a total stranger that dressed like wanna-be-explorer. Hell, the guy could be a psychopath. There had just been too many strange things going on lately. "I get through late," she said. "And besides, I've been seeing someone lately."

Jimmy understood her reluctance to go into the woods with a man she didn't know. He really didn't want to go into the woods either, unless he had to. "Is it serious?" he asked.

"I don't know."

"How about dinner someplace tonight?" asked Jimmy. "Where's the best meal around? It's easy to see you're the most beautiful woman in town."

Kim laughed and started to wipe the countertop. The guy was charming and might be fun for one night. No plans had been made with Will, and for some reason he had seemed distracted the night before. Maybe a little competition would sharpen his game.

And what was with this deal of Will's? At first it had been cute, but not spending an occasional night together was starting to feel odd.

She said, "That would be the restaurant at Big Spruce Lodge."

"And where shall I pick you up at nine?"

"Things move along a little different up here," she said, grinning. "They stop seating at eight-thirty."

"Okay. So where do I pick you up at eight?"

19

Will swallowed another spoonful of ice cream while watching Barbara explain the parts of a horse's saddle to Ethan. The boy listened intently, having already gobbled up his own ice cream.

Earlier, when he had called Barbara to explain the need for a change of plans, she offered to let Ethan ride her horse. Of course Ethan thought that was the greatest idea ever. Will had brought sandwiches and they ate lunch on the back deck first, while Ethan impatiently waited. While Will put away the lunch things, Ethan helped Barbara get Martha Washington ready to ride and asked a million questions. For almost an hour she let him sit on the saddle while she walked the horse around the paddock. It was easy to see the boy was smitten with her.

Afterward, Barbara offered homemade ice cream, which they ate in her screened porch.

"Can I feed Martha something?" asked Ethan.

"How about we go out to the garden to find a carrot," said Barbara. "She loves carrots."

"What about Ram?" asked Ethan.

"Rambunctious the Goat?" laughed Barbara. "He loves carrots too,"

Will loved the smile on Ethan's face and wondered how Amy was making out in the job interview. Life certainly took unexpected twists.

"I know what carrots look like," said Ethan.

"Well, go get a couple," said Barbara. "We'll want to wash them before we give them to Martha and Ram."

The boy dashed out the door.

"Would you like to have dinner with me tonight?" asked Will. He hadn't been planning to ask her out, but the words seemed to come out of his mouth on their own.

Barbara raised an eyebrow. "You don't have other plans?"

Will guessed she meant Kim. "I would love to take you someplace nice," he said, ignoring her query. "We could go up to Big Spruce Lodge."

"I haven't eaten there in years. I would love it."

"Ethan's mother will be home soon, so we'll get going after Ethan feeds Martha and Ram. I'll come by to pick you up tonight about seven."

"Can you make it eight?" she asked.

*

Jimmy Deluga sat at the bar inside The Fenton House Inn and sipped a Marker's Mark bourbon.

After breakfast at Big Bear's Restaurant, he had spent the morning wandering Main Street and trying to get a feel for the town. The small rural municipality felt as alien as a Martian landscape. Trucks seemed to outnumber automobiles and people were actually friendly.

When Jimmy stopped in the police station he introduced himself as a newspaper man. The officer at the front desk was very helpful, but didn't provide any new information. He had confirmed though that Jerome Toll had been found dead, but said no information could be released on the cause of death. It all felt surreal, because Jimmy never had met a police officer so friendly before.

Across from the police station were the offices of a local newspaper. Jimmy walked in and introduced himself as an insurance adjuster for the company covering the Hammond's home. The paper's staff had happily answered all his questions and one man even offered to buy Jimmy lunch, but he declined.

A small sporting goods store had caught Jimmy's eye. The inside was filled with fishing and hunting gear, and guns stood in a row against the back wall. He bought a lightweight camouflage jacket for no reason there than he liked the looks of it. Most of the guns were designed for hunting, and Jimmy preferred semi-automatic black rifles. He did buy a box of .45 ACP jacketed hollow points for his Kimber pistol.

At the north end of the business district stood he found a grand old building called The Fenton House Inn. Jimmy walked up the steps and into a recently refurbished bar and restaurant. Two business men ate at a table by the window and a busty woman wearing a short skirt sat at the rectangular shaped bar talking to the bartender. Long ago, Jimmy had learned that bartenders can be a great source of information, and loved cash.

Jimmy had slid onto a barstool opposite the woman and ordered a Maker's Mark. After the bartender placed it in front of him, the man went back to chatting with the woman. At a few minutes before one o'clock the woman left, and Jimmy guessed she headed back to a job somewhere.

"Are you new in town?" said the bartender, approaching while polishing a glass.

"I'm here for a while," said Jimmy.

"Business?"

"I'm a private investigator. A relative of Kathy Toll has asked me to look into her death."

"Really? I didn't know she had any relatives."

"I can't tell you much," said Jimmy, "but she had an estranged relationship with a wealthy relative that now wants to…see that justice is done." The bartender set the glass down. "We are willing to pay for information," continued Jimmy. "Do you know any idea why someone might have wanted her dead?"

"My name is Roy," said the bartender, offering a hand. "There has been a lot of talk around town that her husband did her in."

"What do you think? Could United Eastern Power have had a hand in it?"

"Is that what you think?" said Roy, glancing to see if anyone might be listening. During the previous six or eight months, some of the best tippers had been the lunchtime brass of United Eastern Power. Robert Henderson once tipped him a hundred bucks after a single beer and a steak sandwich. Of course, Roy had introduced Henderson to a slender young woman who had caught his eye. "They seem like pretty straight shooters to me," said Roy, setting down the glass.

Jimmy noticed the hesitation and smiled. "Most of the best hired killers are."

"No, I think it was her husband. That family was whacko. He's been thrown out of this bar more than once."

"Did he have a motive?"

"Just the money Eastern Power would have paid when the power line went through. He might not have wanted to share it with her."

"What about the rest of the family?"

"The son's trouble. I've seen his name in the paper, usually it's the Fish and Game Department arresting him for something. And there's a daughter. She's come in here with a boyfriend."

"What's he like?"

"I don't know much about him, but I think he's a lot older than her. She tried to buy a drink here once using a fake ID. I don't think she's the sharpest pencil in the drawer." Roy picked up another glass to polish, then said, "She's a looker though. Nice tits, and she knows how to flaunt 'em."

"What's the boyfriend's name?"

"Jake, that's all I know."

"Who killed the Hammonds?" asked Jimmy, pushing his empty glass forward for a refill.

Roy shrugged his shoulders and reached for the bourbon bottle. "The Tolls is my guess. Maybe old man Toll did it, and then killed the only one that could implicate him."

"He's dead now too," said Jimmy, watching Roy's reaction to the news.

"I heard that rumor too," he said, unfazed.

"It is true. The police won't give a cause of death yet."

"Someone told me once that Jerome and the son didn't get along, actually hated each other. Maybe it was the son."

Jimmy pulled out a money clip and peeled off a hundred dollar bill to set on the bar top. "Where does the son live?" he asked.

"Go ask at the outdoor store. The kid goes in there to buy stuff every once in a while. He used to live at home, but, from what I hear, he used to run away and live in the woods every time he had a blowout with his old man. I bet that's where he is now, living in a tent somewhere."

The thought of searching for an unpredictable teenage kid hiding in the spooky woods gave Jimmy a chill. There was no telling what could happen out there.

"Thanks," he said. "Here's a card with my phone number on it. If you hear anything, let me know. I'll make it worth your while." He placed a second hundred dollar bill beside the first and left.

A few minutes later, Jimmy walked into the sporting goods store for a second time. "Hi," he said to the proprietor, "I noticed a gun when I was in here before. Can I take a look at that one?" He pointed at a used Winchester Model 100.

The man handed Jimmy the rifle, mentioning what a rare gem it was. Jim worked the action and looked down the sights at a deer head on the wall. It was easy to imagine blowing the critter away.

"It's .358 Winchester," said the store owner. "It's a hell of a bear or moose gun. There's lots of stopping power there."

Jimmy liked the sounds of that. "I hadn't planned on buying a gun," he said, "but it is tempting."

Jimmy did not legally own any weapons. Each of the guns in his possession were either stolen or bought using an alias. Buying that gun would run the risk of a background check, and he chose at that time not to take it. Handing the gun back, he said, "I'll be in the area for a few days. I'll think about it."

They talked about other rifles in the rack. Finally, Jimmy said, "I'm here investigating the death of Kathy Toll for a relative of hers. Do you know where her son is?"

The proprietor looked puzzled. "No. I don't know. He comes in here once in a while to buy fishing stuff."

"If he should come in, I'd like to ask him some questions," said Jimmy, handing the man a card. "Give me a call. I'll make it worth your time."

*

John Johansson slowed for the toll booth and promised himself to look into a Speed Pass, as he did every time he approached a toll booth. The late day after-work traffic on Route 93 moved slowly.

Cindy Hammond sat beside him. They had left her car for her sons to drive up to New Hampshire so they could attend their grandparents' funeral, which was scheduled for the next day. In the two hours since driving off the ferry they hadn't spoken much, but often she reached for his hand. It was nice to be wanted.

The Massachusetts prosecutor had dropped the drug charges. The heroin had been traced to a large shipment that recently arrived via private aircraft to Teterboro Airport. How it arrived at Martha's Vineyard was anybody's guess, because the entire shipment had been confiscated by the New Jersey authorities. The Massachusetts prosecutor asked only that the sons keep in contact with their whereabouts, but gave them permission to travel to New Hampshire for the funeral. Their car was still impounded at the Massachusetts State Police lab and wouldn't be released for a few more days.

The city of New York no longer had an interest in the boys either, because both of Cindy's sons had solid alibies when the dual murders happened there. Cindy had written the lawyer a check, thanked him, and then made plans to go north with John, who was glad to be away from the hectic insanity of the Martha's Vineyard summer crowd.

"There's a state liquor store at the next rest area," said John. "Shall we buy some wine?"

Cindy's dark eyes lit up. "Yes, a case. And champagne too. We'll celebrate tonight."

20

Brian Toll steadied the .22 caliber rifle on a log and found the biggest turkey's head through the 4X scope. There were four other turkeys in the grassy opening, pecking at the ground, and several more moved among the shadows of the woods beyond. Aware of his heart's pounding, he took a deep breath to steady his hands. Centering the cross hairs in the middle of the old gobbler's pale blue head, he gently squeezed the trigger.

The big bird flopped down dead.

Brian glanced about and then dashed to the bird. It looked enormous and its weight surprised him. Hurrying, he carried the turkey into the woods and followed the edge of the river downstream.

Where a flat rock poked out into the stream, he skinned the bird and filleted the meat off the breast. The legs would be sinewy and tough, but he saved them to make soup. The heart and liver were set aside and saved too. Other than fish, he had eaten little meat for almost a week.

He tossed the stripped carcass and skin into the river and cleaned up his hands. Potatoes, he really wanted potatoes. Even carrots and broccoli sounded exotic and desirable. Bread too. For too long he had been living on fish and junk food he had brought when he ran away. It was time to look for something besides fish and game.

Brian started diagonally up the hill.

After finding his father dead, he had dialed 911, and then disappeared into the woods. Far from the house, he had dropped the things he carried and tumbled to the ground crying. There was no going back. Life would never be the same. He had no family and nobody cared about him. He fell asleep there and didn't wake until the mosquitoes started chewing on exposed flesh around daybreak.

Since waking that morning he had not thought about his former life. With serious determination he had been planning a life alone in the woods.

A more permanent shelter had to be made before the arrival of cold weather. The winters that far north were vicious. It had to be a real building of wood and insulated, with a small woodstove for heat. A tiny structure would be easiest to keep warm.

First, he needed to find the right place, somewhere that nobody would find it.

He intersected a game trail and followed it north along the side of the hill. Soon the thick boughs of evergreens blotted out the sky and he stepped into his campsite.

On a blunt stub poking out from the side of a fir tree, Brian hung the turkey meat, and then went about starting a small fire. He dropped the plump breast in a frying pan. In the hot weather none of it would keep, so he cooked it all. After gorging himself, he put the legs in a pot with water and set them over the fire to simmer.

Next to the hunting blind that he slept in each night, he settled against a large log and opened a second can of beer. Beer was something else he would have to find. When he left his folks home he grabbed what was left of his father's supply. Each night he would allow himself only one can, but soon it would be gone.

A mosquito whined and bounced against his head. He swatted at it and then climbed into his shelter. The next day he would start collecting the needed things. He would build the camp right there.

*

"You look beautiful," said Will, holding the door open.

"Thank you," said Barbara, stepping out of her home. "What a lovely evening." Her eyes picked up the blue of her dress.

"On a night like this I wish we had a convertible," he said, reaching for her hand.

"It would mess up my hair," she laughed.

Will's nerves surprised him. He hadn't felt that rattled when he took Kim out for the first time. It felt more like his first real date, back during his sophomore year of high school. He struggled with small talk and opened his truck's door for her.

Barbara found his nervousness cute. And the dress made her feel sexy. She hadn't worn a dress in ages, and that one stopped at mid-thigh, which made her feel like a young person again. After he shifted the truck into drive, she reached to hold his hand.

*

Jimmy Deluga strolled down the boardwalk to Big Spruce Lodge with Kim on his arm. He hadn't asked her last name and seldom did when he met a woman. That would only be necessary if he planned on a relationship lasting more than one night.

She looked delightful in a short skirt and sleeveless jersey. Her hair was pulled back and she never stopped smiling. More than once he wondered if she was laughing at him, but decided that was unlikely.

The animal heads on the pine paneled walls of the inn's lobby made him grin. It would have been nice to make trophies of some of the people he had killed. Paintings of fish or birds covered the walls and a thick rug muffled their steps.

An attractive hostess met them just as Jimmy noticed a sign that said Wanigan Pub. She offered to seat them either in there or the dining room, assuring them that the menu was the same in both. Jimmy asked for the Pub.

They sat next to a window that looked out over the lake. About a dozen small tables filled the room and along the longest wall stretched a bar of thick pine. Above the bar stood a full size stuffed bear that watched all the patrons at tables. Jimmy wondered how many rounds from his Kimber .45 it would take to drop one of those critters.

Kim noticed the way Jimmy looked apprehensively at the bear. He obviously was out of his element. Her arm had been inside his when they walked into the lobby and she felt him flinch when he noticed the stuffed bobcat on the ledge over the front desk.

She also doubted anyone else at Big Spruce Lodge would be wearing patent leather loafers like his, with little gold balls attached to tiny chains on the front. He wore black pants with a black open-collar shirt, and an off-white sports jacket. A thick gold chain around his neck matched the one on his right wrist, and a gold Rolex, rather than the silver one he wore earlier, adorned his left wrist. She wondered what his annual clothing budget was…probably more than she had spent on clothes in her lifetime.

He was charming, in a practiced sort of way, always asking the right questions and listening patiently, or at least appearing to. Yet she only learned tidbits about him, with Jimmy always turning the conversation back to her or the north woods.

He ordered the most expensive cabernet on the wine list and they started the meal sharing a crab stuffed ravioli appetizer. Kim was very aware of his foot resting against the side of hers beneath the table, but he was going to have to do a lot better than he had done so far if she was going to sleep with him.

Through the doorway where they had entered, she glimpsed Will walk by.

*

Will wanted the evening to go perfectly. The hostess had sat Barbara and him next to the fireplace in the main dining room. Of course the night was much too warm for a fire, but they sat and shared a bottle of Three Blind Moose cabernet and talked without even looking at their menus. He loved how easily she smiled and listened attentively to her stories. It was easy to see Barbara rolled with life's punches and always came up seeing the glass half full, never half empty.

After they finally ordered, Will excused himself to go to the men's room. The night was turning out to be the best one in years. He walked past the entrance of the Wanigan Pub and down a pine-paneled hall to the men's room. On the way he hummed a song, something that he hadn't done in years.

Coming out of the men's room, he stepped directly into Kim's arms. Her mouth landed against his and she pinned him against the wall. The kiss wouldn't stop.

When it finally broke off, he gasped for air with his back still against the wall, and sputtered out, "Well, hi there."

"I thought you'd miss me tonight," said Kim. Her eyes darted about his face.

"What are you doing here?"

"The same thing you are," she said.

"A date?"

Kim nodded and smiled, then asked, "Are you going to sleep with yours? I haven't decided yet."

She kissed him again, pressing her hips against his.

When it ended, she said, "We can compare notes tomorrow."

Turning, Kim disappeared into the bar.

When Will returned to the table, Barbara asked, "Are you all right?"

Reflexes brought the back of Will's hand up to wipe his mouth. "I'm fine," he said. Lipstick? He hoped not.

"When will Amy find out if she got the job?" asked Barbara.

*

Brian Toll silently slipped down the row of lettuce in Barbara Hawkins garden, picking a leaf here and one there. Too many taken in one spot would be noticed. The house remained dark and an owl hooted in the woods. Brian pulled a few carrots and pressed the disturbed soil back into place. The string beans were small, but he picked a large handful. His bare feet did not disturb the garden's soft soil.

21

Jimmy Deluga strolled into Pricilla's Northwoods Emporium and slid onto a stool at the bar. Four men crowded around a pool table at one end of the dimly lit room and two others played darts in the corner near the sign that advertised rest rooms. Booths lined one wall and most contained couples. For a week night the place was busy, yet probably it was the air conditioning rather than the food that had inspired everyone to come in.

A television over the bar played the weather channel and a second one a baseball game. The bartender, a woman with lines on her pasty face that reminded him of wrinkled cellophane and lemon-yellow hair, asked with an emotionless face what he wanted. Wondering if she was Pricilla, he ordered a Bushmills neat.

The men sitting at the bar wore soiled jeans and tee shirts and Jimmy guessed most did some sort of physical work. He had worn a button shirt untucked to hide a Walther PPK in a holster stuck to his left hip.

The bartender set the whiskey down and with a detached look said, "You on vacation up here?"

If she was working on tips, she needed to improve her technique or she would starve to death, and her best tip making years were certainly long gone. "Business," he answered.

She attempted a smile, but her eyes remained lifeless. "What kinda business? Real estate?"

"I can't say. It's for a private client." Jimmy turned to watch the TV and she took the hint.

He sipped the whiskey and wondered what had happened with Kim. It was the weirdest date he had in years. Things started out okay, even if she was rather quiet, but then went to hell after she returned from the restroom. What changed? It was like a switch flipped and she became the bitch from hell. When they got back to town she gave him a peck of a kiss and then bolted from the car. Maybe these backwoods babes were as wild as the country up there.

Jimmy turned on the barstool to look at the patrons, trying to decide if anyone in the bar might be the hired killer type. The crowd looked so different from the ones in his usual New York hangouts that he might as well have been looking at extra-terrestrials. Most of the men at the bar looked rugged enough to pick up Jimmy with one hand, but nobody had the cold isolated look of a professional killer, which was what Jimmy was looking for.

He was about to douse his drink and leave when a man and young woman walked in and took the two empty stools to his left. The woman smiled and said, "Hi, I'm Suzy, and this is my boyfriend Jake."

Jimmy offered a hand and she shook it. It was easy to see she wore nothing beneath the skimpy halter top. "Nice to meet you," he said. "Are you from around here?"

"Oh yeah, born and raised," she said. "Jake too, from over in Vermont."

Jimmy reached to shake Jake's hand too, and then asked, "What do you two do?"

"I'm looking for work at the moment," said Jake, looking Jimmy in the eye. "I do whatever needs to be done."

The guy was cocky and Jimmy could relate to that. The faded tattoos on his muscular arms were unintelligible and looked like enormous black amoebas. Below the left sleeve of his tee shirt a ragged scar marred his shoulder.

"Let me buy you two a drink," said Jimmy, motioning to the bartender. "How'd you get that scar?"

"A chainsaw. The fucking thing kicked back. I was lucky it didn't hit my face."

"You a lumberjack?"

"Naw. Not anymore. I been doing freelance stuff, you know…doing things for people, stuff that needs to be done."

The bartender came and asked what they wanted. As they ordered beers, she gave Suzy a look over, but didn't ask for an I. D.

"What do you do?" asked Jimmy, looking at Suzy.

"Jake takes care of me," she said. "I let him worry about the money." Her arm slipped inside Jake's and she leaned to give him a quick kiss. Turing back, she asked, "What about you? Where are you from?"

"I'm from New York," said Jimmy, leaning in as if to share a secret. "I work for a large private investigating firm." He noticed their eyes grow big. "I'm looking for information on the Hammonds, the couple that were killed in the fire."

Jake sat up straight on his barstool. "What kinda information?"

"We have a client that thinks they might have been murdered, and wants us to find out who did it." Jimmy took a sip of his whiskey, letting the information sink in. "We pay handsomely for anything useful."

"I might know some stuff," said Jake, turning to look about the room. "Let's go sit in that booth over there." Before leaving the barstool he signaled to the bartender for two more beers.

They no sooner slid into the booth when Jimmy felt Suzy's toes sliding along his calf and then working up under the cuff of his pants. When he looked at her, she smiled. Jake seemed oblivious.

"Listen," said Jake. "The Hammonds were in the way of that big power line. Thems people got money and don't let nothin' get in their way. It had to be them."

Jimmy sipped his drink, as if thinking deep thoughts, then said, "It's too obvious. They would know it looked like they did it." Jake looked excited, as if he could smell money.

"Well, they musta got someone to do it for 'em. There's lots a people that would do it for that kinda serious money."

They talked about the various neighbors. Jimmy learned that Suzy's parents were the recently dead Tolls, and that she was basically glad to be rid of them. Jake seemed to know most of the land owners along the proposed power line route, or at least pretended he did. Beer bottles started to collect on the table in front of Jake and his speech slurred. Suzy's flirting became more and more blatant, to the point that her toes lightly traced the fly of his pants. Jimmy still sipped his first drink. Jake's alcohol enhanced stories became quite farfetched.

The bartender announced last call.

"Do you like scotch?" asked Jimmy. "I bought a bottle of 15 year old Dalwhinnie on the way up. It's back at my motel room. We could go have a nightcap?"

"Yeah," said Suzy, beaming. "That's my favorite."

Jimmy doubted she had ever tasted good scotch, but went along with her game. "You'll love it," he said. "You two can follow me back to my room."

Outside, Jake's red Dodge pickup truck was parked next to Jimmy's Escalade, and he climbed up into the driver's seat. Suzy opened the passenger door, but instead of climbing in, said, "I want to ride with Jimmy." She slammed the door and trotted around to climb into the Escalade.

"Wow, this is nice," she said, looking around and touching the dashboard.

"Jake isn't going to mind?" said Jimmy, backing up.

"He's about three breaths from falling asleep," said Suzy, running her hand over the leather seat. "I love the smell of a new car." She straightened up and faced Jimmy. "Jake passes out on me all the time, right when I need a man, if you know what I mean." She leaned over so her fingers could toy with his hair. "So, do you really have scotch back at your room, or were you just trying to get me back there?"

This was too easy, thought Jimmy. The joker following in the red pickup truck might be an issue, but a minor one.

22

Will woke savoring the soft bed and silky sheets. Pale light filtered in from the east facing windows. The leaves of the trees outside were motionless and not a breath of air stirred the lace curtains inside the open windows. He could smell the faint sweet aroma of apples and vanilla. Sliding his hand across the sheet, he found Barbara's bare thigh.

After their dinner the previous night, he drove her home slowly, not wanting the evening to end and listening to her stories about Martha Washington. Will knew little about horses, but it was obvious that Barbara was passionate about them and her excitement was infectious.

Reaching her home, he had walked her to the door and they stopped on the porch, and, because it felt right, he had kissed her. It wasn't a fireworks kind of kiss, more like a northern lights kind of kiss, with a warm flow that waxed and waned and then waxed still stronger. When it finally broke off, she had squeezed his hand and invited him in.

Barbara rolled over and snuggled against his side. "Are you awake?" she whispered.

"Yes." He rolled to face her and slipped an arm across her waist. "Last night was lovely."

She smiled. "Yes."

He kissed her, and then said, "What time do you have to get up?" Her sandy blonde hair lay splayed on the pillow and the sheets were pulled up over her breasts.

"About fifteen minutes ago," she laughed. "There's things I need to do before work."

"I forgot you had to go to work," said Will. "I guess there's no lingering with a chance for a replay."

Barbara gave him a kiss and said, "I want to keep you wanting, so you'll come back for more."

Will laughed. "Can I help you with anything?"

"Can you make breakfast while I take care of Martha? Everything is in the fridge and coffee is on the counter."

"Of course."

Barbara slipped from the bed and pulled out the top drawer of a dresser. With her back to him, she stepped into underwear.

"Has anyone told you lately how beautiful you are?" he asked, his head propped up on an elbow and watching.

"I can't remember anyone telling me that this week," she joked, turning to face him.

"Nice breasts," he said, smiling.

"They're the only ones I have, so I hope you like them." She leaned over the bed and kissed him, but as he reached to touch, she stood up and with a coy grin said, "I've got to get going."

Will slipped from the bed to find his clothes. "How do you like your eggs?" he asked.

*

"I'm surprised he's still asleep," said Jimmy, looking over at Jake passed out on the other queen-size bed.

"He crashes hard when he's drunk," said Suzy, shaking her head. "This happens all the time."

"You fucking some other guy while your boyfriend is passed out?"

She curled against Jimmy's side. "I didn't say that."

Jimmy guessed it true. She certainly didn't appear to be the wholesome type. The night before, as soon as they got back, Jake passed out on the second bed of his motel room. Suzy practically tackled Jimmy and they tumbled onto the empty one. He certainly had experienced more talented partners in his life, but few as enthusiastic.

She asked, "What are we going to do today?"

Jimmy thought...we? She obviously was attracted to his money, and Jake definitely didn't have the self-discipline to be the professional killer he was looking for, but Jimmy felt he might be able to use them both.

"Why don't you go get onto the bed with your boyfriend, so when he wakes up it isn't obvious that we slept together," said Jimmy.

"He'll know."

"How? You done this before?"

Suzy laughed and slid from his bed and onto Jake's.

A few minutes later, when Jimmy shut off the shower, he could hear the grunts and moans of sex coming from the bedroom. At least Suzy was taking care of her man. Jimmy took his time shaving. When the sounds in the bedroom stopped, Jimmy entered. Giggling, Suzy darted naked into the bathroom and the shower started again.

Jake dressed with his back to Jimmy.

Jimmy asked, "Did you like that scotch?"

"Yeah, it was good stuff."

None of them had tasted a single drop. Jimmy was just seeing what Jake remembered. Evidentially not much. The man smelled sour and he wondered when Jake had showered last.

"Ask around, see what you can learn," said Jimmy. "Try to be discreet. You live here so it should be easy. People will trust you while they won't trust me." It was easy to see Jake was eating it up. "I'll give you a couple hundred spending money. You get me the name of the Hammonds' killer and proof, it'll bring you a grand."

For the look on Jake's face, Jimmy could have said a million dollars.

Jake scratched at his stomach and asked, "How will I get in touch with you?"

"I'll be at Pricilla's Emporium having a drink at eleven. If you got news, you can find me there."

*

Frank Atkins walked into Grandma's Restaurant and slid into a booth across from Robert Henderson. A plate of half eaten eggs, bacon, sausage, home fries, baked beans, and English muffins sat in front of the rotund man. Henderson always ate when he was nervous, and that looked like a giant plate of food.

"How was your little Martha's Vineyard honeymoon?" asked Henderson, scooping up a piece of egg.

"Nice. Not long enough." Frank didn't like Henderson's tone on the phone and it wasn't much better in person. "What's up?"

Henderson sipped his coffee, made a face, and then tore open three sugars and dumped them into the cup. Frank waited, wishing he still sold automobiles for a living.

"The investors are getting nervous. There's some talk that the power line will never get built." He noisily sipped the coffee. "There's a bottleneck up there by the Hammond's place. We must find a way around it." He stabbed at a home fry and stuffed it into his mouth. Chewing, he said, "The property owners south of there have sold us their land."

Frank already knew that information and motioned to the waitress for a coffee. "I thought your guy on the Vineyard there was going to fix things?"

"Ah, the fucking police. They figured out where the heroin came from and the kids had solid alibis when the murders happened. The Hammond's daughter isn't going to sell."

Frank didn't know the particulars, nor did he want to know. Heroin? Murders? What the hell had he gotten himself into?

"Some of the investors have been nervously asking who killed the Hammonds, like we might have done it," continued Henderson, "and a couple of the newspapers are saying it was to our advantage. One investor pulled out yesterday." Henderson spread butter on a blueberry muffin.

"What do you want me to do?"

"Go find out what it will take to get that Hawkins woman or the Northrop guy to sell. Everyone has a price. Either property will connect our corridor through to the timber company land."

"What about the timber company?"

"They have to do what generates the most profit for their stockholders, and our power line will make them more money than fucking trees."

Frank could still see problems ahead. There was the National Forest to go through and dozens of hostile towns. The Appalachian Mountain Club would fight the power line in court. It was going to be a long time before they had electricity flowing south.

"You got help," said Henderson. "That guy you met on the Vineyard does some private investigator work, and we have him up here looking for whoever murdered the Hammond's. We would like to clear that up." He laughed, and added, "And thank the guy."

Some joke, thought Frank. Their deaths hadn't paved the way for their project because the daughter was just as stubborn as the parents were. "Do I have to get in touch with him?" asked Frank, not really wanting to ever see Jimmy Deluga again.

"Naw. He prefers to work alone," said Henderson, stuffing the last piece of bacon into his mouth. "Just go talk to Hawkins and Northrop. You once said she was kind of sweet on you. Sleep with her if you got to." Henderson laughed. "Take one for the team." He wiped his sleeve across his mouth.

"I'll see what I can do," said Frank, looking out the window. A logging truck roared down the hill.

"Listen, it's been a while since we gave you a raise," said Henderson. "If you get either of those properties for under five mil, there's two hundred grand bonus going into your checking account."

Frank guessed Henderson could see his lack of enthusiasm. Two hundred thousand dollars would be incredibly helpful. His wife would be very excited and, better yet, he could even quit working for this asshole.

"I'll see what I can do," promised Frank.

"I got to meet with our good buddy Senator Grogg," said Henderson, looking quite excited. "He's trying to revive the eminent domain bill again. Tell that to those land owners. If they don't take our offer they might lose the land and only get pennies on the dollar."

Frank remembered the bitter feelings the eminent domain bill had brought out of the locals when the legislature fought over it the year before. Nobody in the North Country wanted a private enterprise to be making money off of land stolen by the government. But, if the legislation might be revived, maybe it could persuade reluctant land owners.

"That's good news," said Frank, feeling like he had just sold out to the Devil.

*

Jimmy Deluga sat in the Coos County Registry of Deeds in Lancaster, New Hampshire, searching for information. A series of maps indicated land owners, but he also searched out next of kin, what the owners did for a living, who they owed money to, and if they had ever been in trouble. Information was power, and he wanted to rule the north. An open laptop computer and multiple search engines answered questions that the registry could not.

He noticed Cynthia Hammond had no siblings, and only two sons. Jimmy guessed all young men were much like he was at that age, wise-ass-punks ready to grab what they could.

Jimmy wondered where Cynthia Hammond was.

23

John Johansson opened a beer and walked out onto the deck behind his home. Upstairs, Cindy Hammond changed out of the clothes she had worn to her parent's funeral. He could hear one of her sons coming down the stairs.

Justin walked out onto the porch.

"Want a beer?" asked John.

"I'm not twenty-one," he answered.

"Would your mother let you have one?"

He nodded, "Yes."

"Then go help yourself. Just don't drive anywhere tonight,"

The door opened again and the older brother Warren stepped out. Justin promised to bring him a beer.

"Your mother is taking it pretty well," said John.

"Better than I am," admitted Warren. "I should have spent more time with my grandparents."

Cindy's two sons had been incredibly polite and presented themselves well. Very early that morning they had left Martha's Vineyard to drive north in time for the funeral. "You both can stay as long as you like," said John.

"Thanks. We don't have to be back to work until next Monday," said Warren. "We may stay a day or two.

Justin came out with the beer. "I'd like to stay as long as we can," he said. "But we don't want to freeload. Let us buy the groceries while we're here."

John smiled. "Do what you want."

The door opened again and he turned to see Cindy barefoot in shorts and a tee shirt. In her hand she carried a glass of red wine. They settled into chairs and talked about the day. Relatives and town folk that they had not seen in years had attended the funeral. After the service, everyone gathered at a neighbor's farm house to reminisce.

"Tomorrow I would like to get started on the conservation easement on my folk's property," said Cindy.

"What's that?" asked Justin.

She explained how it would restrict what could be done with the land. Never would the property be used for anything other than farming or timber, with a small portion set aside for a home. It was a large tract, and she was undecided about limiting subdivision.

"Keep it," said John, "and allow it to be divided one day between your two sons."

"Yeah," said Justin. "I would love a place up here."

"This corner of the state is tough place to make a living," said John.

"Oh, I wouldn't want to live up here," said Justin. "It would be a place to go, a second home."

Cindy smiled. "Things change as you get older, you might want to live up here someday."

She had turned to John as she said that.

The conversation drifted to the winters. Both of the boys had been up there to visit during the snowy months and loved the snowmobiling. Warren asked about deer hunting and conversation wandered from the deer herd to the declining moose population.

When Cindy's sons went into the house for a second beer and then disappeared upstairs, she moved to sit next to John.

"They're good kids," he said.

She smiled. "I know."

He slipped an arm across her shoulders and pulled her close. "Are you ready to call it a night?"

"Yes, I'm exhausted."

"Are we being New England proper with the boys here and sleeping in separate bedrooms?"

Cindy smiled. "I hope not."

*

Jimmy Deluga strolled into Big Bear's Restaurant and slid onto a stool at the counter, just as Kim walked out of the kitchen.

"Hi," said Jimmy, setting his knapsack on the floor. She looked surprised to see him. "I had fun the other night."

Kim had not expected to see Jimmy ever again. By the time their date ended, she was in a sour mood. The sight of Will out with Barbara Hawkins affected her in a way she had not expected. And then to make the evening even worse, Jimmy turned out to be more of an arrogant ass than she had ever thought possible.

"Hi," she said, believing him to be lying and looking for something. "What can I get you?"

Jimmy smiled. "That isn't a very warm greeting. I'd like coffee and that breakfast special again."

"Coming right up," she said, filling a mug with coffee before disappearing into the kitchen.

Things weren't going as Jimmy had hoped. He turned and looked around the room. At a table by the corner window he recognized Jack, a man from the newspaper office. Jimmy picked up his coffee and wandered over.

"Hi," he said. "We met the other day at the newspaper office."

"Oh, yes. Care to join me?" There was a hint of an English accent.

"Sure," said Jimmy, sliding onto a seat. "Anything new in the local news?"

"Not really, other than the State Police finally coming out with an official cause of death for the Hammonds. Now we're waiting for one on the Tolls."

They drifted into small talk about the local police department. Jimmy was surprised to learn that some of the small towns didn't even have a police department, but instead relied on the State Police. Jack obviously enjoyed talking to somebody new for a change and went on about the local fire departments. Kim reappeared from the kitchen and brought his breakfast to the table.

"The Hammonds funeral was yesterday," said Jimmy. "Was there a large turnout?"

"Oh yes. They were well loved and heroes to many in the community, the way they turned down the money to stop the power line from coming through"

"They have a daughter," said Jimmy. "Is she still up here or has she gone home?" The breakfast didn't taste quite the same as the previous time he had ordered it, and he wondered what Kim had done to it. Soap?

"I'm not certain. She's friendly with John Johansson, the Fish and Game officer."

"Is he local?"

"Oh yes. Lives right here in town over on Pleasant Street."

They talked about the Fish and Game Department and then somehow the subject changed to a local fundraiser for the high school football team. Jimmy wanted to ask what the Fish and Game Department did to control the bears around there, but decided Jack looked more bookish than the outdoorsy type.

Five minutes before the hour, Jack left for work. A few minutes later, Jimmy stood and counted out the exact change for the meal, leaving nothing for a tip and most of the food on his plate.

Pleasant Street was easy to find. About two thirds of the way down, on the left hand side, a car with Connecticut number plates sat in a driveway beside a Chevy Blazer. Behind the Blazer a Fish and Game Department truck almost stuck out to the sidewalk. Jimmy drove slowly by and then turned around at the end of the road. Parking in the shade of a Norway maple, he settled back in the driver's seat to wait.

24

Agnes Bartholomew looked out the picture window of her living room and noticed the strange black Cadillac Escalade parked in front of her home. She walked into the kitchen to get her Nikon Monarch binoculars that she kept by the window over the kitchen sink, a window that looked out at multiple bird feeders in the back yard.

Back in the living room, she adjusted the focusing knob. A Maine coon cat brushed against her leg below the hem of her dress.

"He's not up to any good," she said, fine-tuning the focus. "There's New York plates on the car. What's he doing here?"

The cat didn't answer, but jumped up on the window sill to look out too.

Jimmy Deluga hadn't realized that it is easier to hide in a city of eight million than in a town of three thousand.

Agnes went into the kitchen again and from a drawer retrieved a small camera. Back in the living room, she took several pictures of the black SUV.

"I should call Dennis," she said.

The cat turned to look at her, as if to say that was a good idea.

"He'll want to know about this," she said, picking up the phone.

Dennis Bartholomew was her only child and a member of the local police department, a fact that she was quite proud of.

"Dennis?"

"Yes?"

"There's a suspicious car parked in front of the house."

"Really?" He had heard this, or something similar, at least once a week.

"It has New York number plates. I wrote down the number, do you want it?"

"Sure," he answered.

Dutifully, he wrote down the number, then said, "I'll run the number and then drive by,"

"Good," said Agnes. "Did you go out with Carol's daughter last Saturday?"

Dennis hated his mother's constant meddling in his life, and was so disappointed when he didn't get the job downstate that he had applied for, which was over a hundred miles and two hours away. "No."

"You are going to die alone," she said. "She's a perfectly nice young woman."

Dennis didn't want to break his mother's heart, but he wasn't interested in any woman. "I'll be fine," he said.

The number came back from a leasing company in New York. He decided to drive by for no reason other than to appease his mother.

*

Seeing the Fish and Game truck back out of the driveway, Jimmy sat up straight in the driver's seat. A woman sat on the passenger side of the truck. He guessed it was Cynthia Hammond.

Agnes had noticed Jimmy sit up, and also the truck driving out of John Johansson's driveway. How many nights had that woman been staying there? Not that Agnes would judge anyone. Far down the street came a police car from the local department. It had to be Dennis. She smiled, what a great son she had.

Jimmy noticed the oncoming police car and wrote it off as a coincidence. He started the Escalade and shifted into drive. As the Fish and Game truck started down the street, he followed. It drove by the approaching police car.

Dennis's cell phone rang. It was his mother. "Hello."

"The man in the Escalade is following John Johansson in the Fish and Game truck. Johansson's got some hussy riding with him."

"Yes mother." He shut off the phone. Some days he just felt like run away to the West Coast.

*

"The conservation people are meeting us here," said John, stopping in front of a nicely kept old Victorian building on Main Street. A sign in the front advertised law offices. "They are anxious to talk to you."

"Should I have a lawyer present?" asked Cindy.

"Do you remember Nick Dudley from high school? He's a lawyer. We're meeting in his office and he's agreed to look after your interests. He's a straight shooter."

Cindy remembered him as a quiet young man that went to Boston University after high school, but she had lost touch with him after graduating. "That's good. I'll want to send any agreement to a lawyer friend of mine in Connecticut too."

"That's fine."

For the next hour Cindy talked with two members of the state's largest conservation organization, The Trustees of New Hampshire Wild Lands. She found them easy to talk with and full of ideas. They all agreed to meet up at her parent's property at one o'clock.

Agnes Bartholomew wondered where her police officer son had disappeared to. When his cruiser reached the end of Pleasant Street, rather than turn around, it made a left and disappeared. She hoped Dennis had zipped down the side streets to head off the black Escalade, but he didn't sound much more interested in catching that car than catching a woman. What was wrong with that boy?

Dennis had indeed made a second left and hurried down a second road parallel with Pleasant Street, reaching Main seconds after the Escalade. He followed the black vehicle until it parked in front of a bakery, about a hundred feet behind Johansson's Fish and Game truck, which was in front of Nick Dudley's law office.

Dennis took a left to circle behind the hardware store and stopped before reaching Main Street again. Stepping out of the cruiser, he walked to the corner.

The man in the Escalade did something on his phone, maybe wrote a text or played a game. Every few seconds he glanced down the street toward Johansson's truck. Dennis hated to admit it, but his mother was right…the man was following Johansson.

The Escalade looked brand new and Dennis wondered for what reason he could ask to see the driver's license. He decided he needed none. Judge Morris was his mother's second cousin and would back him up if anything made it to the courthouse. He turned and walked back to his police car.

A moment later Jimmy Deluga looked up into the rear view mirror to see a police cruiser, with bright flashing lights, park behind him. The officer climbed out and sauntered up beside his SUV.

"Could I see your license and registration?" said the officer.

"Sure," said Jimmy, digging out his wallet. "Can I ask what this is about?"

"Yes." The officer waited for the license. When Jimmy handed it and the registration to the cop, he walked back to the cruiser.

The registration showed the lease company's name, as Dennis knew it would. The license belonged to James Hannicka, with an address of Katonah, New York, and the check came back as good with no record.

He walked back and handed the license and registration to the driver. "There you go," he said.

"What was this about?"

"There's been a report of a stolen black Escalade," said Dennis, forcing a smile. "I was just checking to make certain it wasn't this one." On the front seat of the vehicle a stack papers sat next to a laptop computer. "Are you up here on business or pleasure?"

"Both," said Jimmy, thinking there wasn't much pleasurable about small town America.

The driver didn't offer more information, so Dennis said, "Have a good day."

Watching the officer climb back into the cruiser, Jimmy wondered what that had been all about. He climbed down from the Escalade and walked nonchalantly across the street to the hardware store. The cop drove down the street and made a right beside a Cumberland Farms variety store.

Jimmy dallied around the front of the store, peeking out frequently to see if anyone came out of building with the lawyer's office. Eventually, he bought a small LED flashlight and then walked back to his vehicle. He had just climbed back inside the Escalade when Cindy Hammond and a man, in what Jimmy guessed was a Fish and Game Department Uniform, came out. They crossed the street and disappeared into the little restaurant beside Pricilla's Emporium.

Jimmy glanced at his watch and then started his SUV. During a lapse in the traffic, he made a U turn and drove back to the sporting goods store he had visited earlier. Inside, in the long gun rack against the back wall, the Winchester Model 100 still stood. He asked to see it again.

An older Leupold 4X scope was mounted on the top. Jimmy looked through the scope and out the window at the front of the store, aiming at the top of the building across the street. The price tag said $1450.

"Will you take thirteen hundred for it?" asked Jimmy, handing the rifle back to the store's owner.

"Oh, I got to do better than that. That gun is a classic. Not many Model 100's were made in .358. It's a late sixties gun."

"How about thirteen fifty and you throw in a box of shells?"

The store owner wiped the gun with a soft cloth, and then said, "I'll let it go with two boxes of shells for fourteen hundred, and that's as good as I can do. It comes with two extra magazines."

Jimmy looked at the other guns in the rack. Not many were semi-automatics, and only a few had a hole in the end of their barrels as large as the one in that Model 100. "I'll take it," said Jimmy. He had always liked guns that punched big holes.

They filled out the necessary paperwork, then the store owner asked for identification and called the FBI for the required background check.

The name on the driver's license that Jimmy had handed the owner said James Jewel. The name would clear the background check easily, as James Jewel had no police record and had never been in any sort of trouble, because the real James Jewel died three months after his birth.

Jimmy looked around the store while he waited, and picked up solvent, gun oil, and bore brushes for .35 caliber. From a rack at the end of an aisle he found a canvas gun case that looked long enough for the rifle. He picked up a camouflage ball cap from a collection of hats atop a display of turkey calls. Camo shirts hanging on a rack caught his eye and he found one his size in Mossy Oak. Most of the matching pants were too large, but he found one pair with his waist size and decided he could always cut three inches off them if need be.

"You're all set," said the store owner, setting down the phone.

Jimmy set the things he had collected on the counter and dug the cash out of his wallet. "Is there someplace I can go sight this in?" asked Jimmy, thinking that there might be a gun club locally.

"Sure. At the south end of town take Hill Road. Up there about two miles is a sandpit on the right. Nobody will bother you. Lots of the local boys shoot up there on the weekends."

Jimmy didn't say anything, but it seemed strange that a person could shoot in a sandpit without someone calling the cops. Back where he came from it was shoot at the gun clubs or not at all. Maybe there were some good things about living out there in the sticks. He thanked the man and walked out of the store.

Five minutes later he was parked on Main Street again and watching John Johansson's green Fish and Game Department truck. While he waited he toyed with one of the .358 Winchester cartridges, admiring the reddish copper bullet with the exposed lead tip. It felt heavy and enormous compared to the ones he put in his pistols.

25

John Johansson and Cindy Hammond crossed the street and climbed into the Fish and Game Department truck. The drive up to her parent's property took little more than ten minutes and they parked well away from the burned rubble of what once had been her parent's home. A few minutes later, the people from the conservation group drove up in a white Ford Explorer.

The group started across the field on foot towards the woods beyond. One of the men from the conservation group had brought a map of the property. When Cindy was young, she had walked most of the land with her father and the forest had grown considerably since then.

Jimmy Deluga had followed from town, but stopped when he noticed the parked Fish and Game truck. In town it had dawned on him that Cadillac Escalades were not common up in that neck of the woods and he feared Cindy Hammond or the Game officer would notice it if he drove by. He had just decided to back up when a white SUV approached and he waited for it to pass. On the door of the vehicle he read "The Trustees of New Hampshire Wild Lands".

Was Cindy Hammond going to donate her land to a conservation group?

Jimmy backed down the road and pulled into a weed filled old logging road. It led into a dark stand of large softwood trees and then petered out, but had taken him far enough from the street to hide the SUV. He shut off the engine and opened the door. The air smelled of Christmas trees.

He stepped out into the alien world where sound seemed to be absorbed by everything around him. Beneath his feet the ground felt soft as a mattress, very unlike the familiar concrete and asphalt of back home. The rapping of a pileated woodpecker on a nearby tree caused Jimmy to duck. What had he gotten himself into?

Opening the vehicle's back door, he pulled out the camouflage clothes that he had bought in town. The thought of removing his clothes to change made him feel vulnerable.

Jimmy set his Kimber pistol within easy reach and slid the newly acquired rifle out of its case. It took a minute of fiddling to figure it out, but he removed the magazine and filled it with the fat Winchester .358 shells and then snapped it back into the gun. Pulling back the slide and releasing it chambered a round, with the metallic slamming of the bolt making him feel much better. After setting the rifle next to the pistol, he started to unbutton his shirt.

*

Amy stepped in the door and said, "I got the job!"

"That's great," said Will. "When do you start?"

"In two weeks," she said. "I have to tell Ethan."

"He's outside with Duchess."

She dashed through the house and out the front door while Will went back to his lunch. Ethan's empty plate sat on the far side of the table.

The morning had been spent marking the property line between his land and Barbara Hawkins's. It was hard work, blazing trees and running compass lines. In some places the steep land made for slow going. Many big hardwood trees stood on her property and he thought she could probably use the money they would bring if harvested. The best way to get it out was to haul it downhill and across his property, which was fine with him.

Ethan came barreling in the door with Duchess. "We're going to live up here," he yelled. "Grandpa, we're going to live near you."

"That's what I heard," he said, putting an arm around his grandson. "We'll have lots of time together."

Ethan bounced about. "Are you going to take me hunting in the fall?"

"We'll see what your mother says," answered Will.

The door opened again and Amy came in. They talked about the new job and Will could hardly contain his excitement. Amy wanted to look for a small house in town, something that would be easy to maintain. He promised to help.

"What are you doing this afternoon?" she asked.

"I want to walk the bounds along the Hammond's property," he said. "I own a chunk of land on that side of the road too."

Amy grinned. "You're a regular land baron."

Will rose from the table to set his plate in the dishwasher. "I'm just a simple woodsman," he teased, grinning.

"Can I go with you?" asked Ethan.

"It's a tough walk," said Will, knowing it really wasn't. "Duchess will come with me."

"I can do it," insisted Ethan.

Will looked at Amy, who answered, "It's up to you."

He asked, "What are you going to do?"

"I'm going to look at real estate listing online, and then call some realtors."

Will ruffled the hair on Ethan's head. "Get your hiking boots on. And we'd better bring some water."

*

Jimmy Deluga walked parallel with the road, but stayed hidden inside the woods, periodically making sure he could still see the asphalt. There was no sense in risking getting lost. When the woods ended and the enormous field opened up from the side of the road, he stayed amongst the trees and followed its edge. Cindy and the group were no longer in sight.

The fabric of the camouflage clothing was soft and a tag had advertised it as being quiet in the woods. Jimmy never would have considered some clothing quieter than others, but it hardly made a sound when it rubbed against twigs or brush. The fabric felt soft like pajamas, which he found a bit disconcerting. Something rigid like new blue yeans might have been to his liking.

He carried the Winchester rifle and the two extra magazines were in pouches on his belt. The Kimber Model 1911 hung in a holster on his hip, opposite a large belt knife on his other side. When he had left the Escalade, he stuffed his GPS into a pocket, fully confident that it would lead him home later.

He hurried along. The softwood trees gave way to birch and poplar, but he only recognized them as trees with leaves as opposed to trees with needles. The field he paralleled came to an end and he followed the woods around it. Where an old cart path entered the trees he stopped and listened, but heard no one. Walking down the old road, he stopped often to listen.

Voices. He heard them off to his right. Stopping to hear better, they seemed to be getting closer.

He darted into the trees on the road's opposite side and stood among a cluster of striped maple. The voices were laughing about something, but he still couldn't see anyone. Then they sounded like they grew further away, moving back toward the fields.

Jimmy cautiously followed. Stopping at the edge of the field, he could see the group walking back toward the road. It had to be over half a mile to the parked vehicles, which gave him plenty of time.

The trunk of a large fallen poplar lay where the grass met the woods. Jimmy dropped behind it to rest the forend of his rifle on the log. It took a moment to find Cindy Hammond in the scope, but then he settled the cross hairs on the middle of her back. His index finger clicked the safety off.

The Game officer stepped behind Cindy to talk to one of the others in the group. Jimmy waited. The group grew further away. The officer moved beside Cindy again, and that time held her hand.

Jimmy took a deep breath, placed his finger across the trigger, and started to squeeze.

*

Ethan was tired, Will could easily see it.

They had walked most of the way to the furthest corner of his property, following a moss covered stonewall through a stand of maples and hoping to find the corner marker. Duchess had tagged along, sniffing and exploring as dogs always do. To give Ethan a break, Will decided to shorten their hike and take a shortcut back home. Leading Ethan up through a stand of smaller maple and poplar trees, they would soon intersect the big fields behind what was left of the Hammond's home.

The boy had said little along the way, but Will stopped often to point out a large mushroom or peculiar tree. At the base of a lone dead fir tree, they found the rectangular hole created by a foraging pileated woodpecker. In another spot near the stone wall, a rusted hay rake, deserted by a farmer decades before, poked up from accumulated leaves.

"We're almost to the field," promised Will.

*

Jimmy knew that one of the secrets to good marksmanship was a good trigger. With a couple of pounds of pressure, the trigger should move crisply, like breaking a small piece of glass. And Jimmy also knew that after you buy a gun you should always sight it in, but there hadn't been time.

With the woman out of the way, before any papers could be signed deeding the property to a conservation organization, her sons would inherit the land. Jimmy knew what young men were like, and drugs, alcohol, and women could persuade them to do almost anything. At least that was the way he saw the world.

Henderson hadn't authorized the hit, but Jimmy also knew the man well enough to know that with his company's problems solved, he would be ecstatic. And Jimmy wasn't above extorting an extra chunk of cash from Henderson. Of course, it would all be done over friendly drinks, probably at a strip club downstate somewhere.

Jimmy squeezed the trigger, trying desperately to keep the crosshairs centered between Cindy Hammond's shoulders. Pressing harder, the trigger creeped. He held it there and took another breath, then steadied the gun's sights on the woman's shoulders.

What Jimmy didn't know was that Winchester Model 100s were notorious for lousy triggers. They pulled hard, crept, and fired when you didn't expect it.

Behind Jimmy a twig snapped. He flinched. The gun roared. The people in the field dropped to the dirt. Jimmy jumped up to see what was behind him.

A wolf! A wolf with a Devil's beard. And a man and boy beyond stared his direction. The man yelled something and the Devil turned away and then they all ran like hell to the left. Jimmy bolted to the right, holding the rifle tightly.

The irregular ground made it difficult and he felt his heart racing. Several times he tripped and almost fell.

26

"I want to get Ethan home," said Will. The boy waited patiently by his side.

"Go ahead," said the State Police officer.

"We're going home," said Will, turning to John Johansson. "Stop over for a beer."

He smiled. "I could use one, be along in a bit."

"Let me drive you," offered the officer.

A second State Police car and a local cruiser had parked next to John's Fish and Game truck and the white Ford Explorer.

After the gunshot, John and the group had raced across the field to their vehicles. Hiding safely behind them, he called the State Police on his truck's two-way radio. There wasn't any sign of whoever had fired the shot, but the group stayed hidden until the police arrived.

John had clearly heard the bullet pass over their heads. Someone had definitely shot at them, and he suspected Cindy was the target. Three minutes after he had placed the call, the first State Police car showed up, it had been stationed at the remains of the Hammond home. Eight minutes later the local police arrived.

Not long after that Will, Ethan, and Duchess came across the corner of the field. The two police cruisers had driven to the edge of the woods and the officers peered into the trees. Soon they came back and for almost an hour Will answered questions from the police. A man from the local newspaper showed up just before Will and Ethan climbed into the police car.

"Someone may want to talk to you again tomorrow," said the officer, as they started down the road, leaving the newspaper man behind.

"I'll be around," said Will.

Ethan stared wide-eyed at the inside of the police cruiser. Will couldn't tell what half the things along the dash board did.

"I think everyone was lucky today," said the cop, as he dropped them off.

Will led Ethan inside and recounted the events for Amy. She sat in a chair wearing an expression of disbelief.

*

After ten minutes of running, Jimmy slowed to catch his breath. His clothes stuck from perspiration and the gun felt slippery in his sweaty hands. Where the hell was he? Scratches from tree branches stung his skin.

What was that animal? A wolf? And who was that man with the boy? And what were they doing out there?

He dug the GPS out of a pocket and turned the thing on. The night after he bought it he made it do the basic functions, but out there in the wilderness it felt like it took forever just to start up. He brought up a topographical map on its tiny screen and a small triangle marked his location.

Something just above the treetops made a raspy pterodactyl-like sound. Jimmy would never know it was a raven, but it caused him to stop and look up, with the hair on the back of his neck standing like bristles on a brush. The rifle in his hand provided a sense of security.

Looking at the map, a road was not far away to the north. He had no reference for direction, so he tried bringing up the GPS's compass function.

Jimmy heard a car wiz up the road and it wasn't too far away. He stuffed the GPS back into a pocket and walked toward the street. Ten minutes later he found his Escalade.

After driving back out to the pavement, he sped down the hill and headed for town. He wanted to get back to his motel room and out of those camouflage clothes. A hot shower would feel heavenly.

*

"You don't think you could recognize him?" said John, opening another beer.

Will shook his head. "No. He was too far away. He wasn't a big guy, maybe five six, maybe less. I couldn't really see his face."

John sipped his beer, then said, "The camouflage part is what worries me, and shooting prone. That spells pro, like paid assassin. I can't help but think he shot at Cindy, to kill her before she put the conservation easement on her property."

"How many knew she was going to do that?"

"Not many," said John, staring at the beer bottle between his fingers.

Will looked through the windows in the front of the house. The women were sitting on the porch and talking. Barbara Hawkins had come over right after she had heard of the events. Her home was close enough to the Hammond's place that she had even heard the gunshot.

Will said, "The property would just go to her sons then. Wouldn't they do the same thing?" Tall thunderheads piled up over the trees beyond the far end of the field.

"Maybe somebody gambled they wouldn't." John wondered if paranoia was setting in. Cindy being in danger rattled him like nothing had in years. He swallowed a mouthful of beer.

The door opened and Shawn Ash walked in, still dressed in the clothes he wore logging. "I heard about the shooting," he said.

"You did?" said Will. "How?"

"One of the truckers heard in town and told me when he came back to our jobsite."

"Small town," said John.

"Is everybody all right?" asked Shawn, looking out a window at Amy on the porch.

"Yes," said Will, motioning toward the refrigerator. "Have a beer." He liked that the man cared enough about his daughter to drop what he was doing and come right over.

"Any idea who would take a shot like that?"

"It was a man in camouflage with a rifle," said Will. "Ethan and I had been out running my property lines when we came upon him."

Shawn popped the top off a beer bottle with his Leatherman tool and took a sip. "You're lucky he didn't shoot you."

"I think we all were lucky today," said John.

The phone rang and Will answered it.

A voice said, "Will? It's Kim. Is everything all right? I heard about the shooting."

Of course she would, working in the restaurant. "Yes, we're all fine," he said.

"What happened?"

He ran through an abbreviated version of the events, while Shawn and John wandered out to the porch.

"I'm glad you are all okay," she said, and then asked about Ethan.

Will smiled. Usually she said nothing about his grandson and he was glad she had asked. He told her how Ethan had looked concerned during the event, but never cried.

After a pause Kim added, "I haven't heard from you."

Will hesitated, not knowing what to say, then said, "I've been busy."

"Let's go fishing again," said Kim. "We had fun."

Will remembered how at home she was on the river. "That was fun, wasn't it," he said, turning to look out the front of the house. The women on the porch laughed about something. "It's been rather hot for fishing," he said, looking for a way to back out. Barbara sat somewhere out of sight.

"I've got a spot that I guarantee will have fish," she said. "Let's go tomorrow evening. We can meet me at the bridge at eight and fish the last hour of daylight. Okay?"

"Yeah, sure. I'll see you at eight." He hung up the phone and walked out on the porch.

"Who was that?" asked Amy.

"A concerned neighbor," said Will, wanting to change the subject. "I left my beer in the kitchen." He walked back into the house.

Amy guessed who had called, as did Barbara who had overheard the question. She picked up her wine glass and followed Will inside.

"Are you all right?" asked Barbara. He had stopped by the sink and looked out the window. Thunder grumbled and pulses of blue light lit the outside. She stopped beside him and set her hand on his.

"I'm fine," he answered, glancing at her hand, "just tired."

"The thunder storm will take away some of the heat," she said. "We'll all feel better when the hot weather leaves."

"I know."

"Can I make you dinner tomorrow night?" she asked.

Will turned his hand to clasp hers. "I'd like to stay home with my family tomorrow night," he said. "It's been a tough stretch." Barbara looked hurt, so he added, "How about the next night?"

Barbara thought he might be seeing Kim, which caused the quiver of panic. She squeezed his fingers. "I worry about you."

Will put his arms around her and she tucked her head against his chest. It felt good to have somebody to hold.

*

Robert Henderson said, "Did you fucking try to shoot Cynthia Hammond?"

Jimmy guessed Henderson had heard from someone in the State Police. "I didn't know anything about it until you called," he lied. The phone call had come not long after Jimmy returned to his motel room. "Why would I try to shoot her?"

"It's looking bad for us," snapped Henderson. "There's been four people killed, and now an attempted murder too. The press will be trying to tie it all to United Eastern Power. Find out who the fuck did it."

"But what would happen if she got killed?" said Jimmy. "Think about it. Her punk kids would probably want money rather than the land."

"Listen, you scum bag, if I find out you took it upon yourself to try and knock her off, I'll turn you inside out and let the crows pick your guts."

Jimmy was unfazed, no hick from New England could ever hurt him. "It wasn't me," he lied again, "but I'll find the asshole that did."

"You're fucking right you will."

The call went dead. Jimmy tossed his phone on the bed and walked out of the room.

When he returned to the room earlier, he had taken off the camouflage outfit and showered. No sooner had he dressed and his cell phone rang.

Driving slowly down Main Street, he recognized faces. Another week in that town and it would start to feel like home, and that thought had worried him. Jimmy sorely missed the hustle and bustle and anonymity of the big city.

He parked across from The Fenton House Inn and crossed the street. A man also entering the restaurant opened the door and waited to let Jimmy to enter first. That would never have happened in New York, thought Jimmy.

The bar was almost empty and nobody was in the dining room at that hour. Jimmy noticed a man and woman that had been there before. The bartender was a slender woman with long bleached blonde hair, which she had pulled back behind her head. Long earrings brought his eyes to her long slender neck. The short skirt might have made her a fortune in tips if she were fifteen years younger, but she still looked attractive. Sliding onto a bar stool, he asked for a Glenfiddich neat.

"You're new around here," she said setting the glass down. "Here on business?"

"Something like that," said Jimmy. "This place is kind of quiet." He noticed the top four buttons of her Oxford shirt teasingly undone.

"It'll pick up around five, when people get out of work," she said. "Of course I get out at four-thirty and will miss it."

That was a half hour away.

"How about I take you out for dinner," said Jimmy, wondering if she were taller than he. "Someplace nice," he added, offering a hand, "My name is Jimmy Deluga."

"Brenda," she said, shaking the hand. Then smiling coyly, "There's been a lot of crazy things happening around here lately. How do I know you're not a serial killer?"

"Do I look like a killer? I work as an independent news agent, and I'm here covering all that has been going on."

"You must have heard about the shooting today?" said Brenda, leaning in as if sharing a secret. "I heard it was fully automatic weapons, like machine guns."

She smelled nice and it was easy to imagine her in his bed. The story certainly had grown, from one single shot to a barrage of fire. "Really?"

"Yes. It's lucky they all weren't killed."

"Who was there?"

A new patron sat two stools down from Jimmy, interrupting their conversation. Brenda left to ask the new arrival what he wanted.

27

Will sat on the porch and sipped 23 year old Pappy Van Winkle from a heavy tumbler. The bourbon was a favorite and usually reserved for special occasions. Amy shared the couch in the living room, where she read to Ethan. Duchess lay by Will's feet.

The guests had left just before dinner time, so he cooked up pork chops on the grill while Amy prepared spinach and baked potatoes. The three of them ate on the porch as thunder rolled through the hills. By the time they finished eating, the rain poured down, yet before the dishes were washed it had stopped.

Outside in the dark, crickets hesitantly chirped. Headlights turned in the drive, followed by a second set. Will stood and walked through the house to the back door. Before anyone could knock, he opened it. John Johansson stood there with a State Police officer.

"Can we come in?" asked John.

"Of course," said Will. "What brings you out?'

"Well," said John, looking uncomfortable, "this is Bill Hopkins from the State Police lab. He would like to swap your hands for gunshot residue."

"Gunshot residue?" said Will.

John half-heartedly shrugged a shoulder. "I told these guys you were a good guy, but someone pointed out that you came out of the woods not long after the gunshot, so maybe you did the shooting."

"That's nuts," said Will.

"I know. Do you mind?"

"It will rule you out as a suspect," said the officer. "Nobody thinks you did it."

Will held his hands forward. "Be quick about it."

The officer took a moistened cotton swab and wiped the palms and backs of Will's hands.

"That's all there is to it," said the officer.

Trying to be gracious, Will said, "Can I get either of you a drink?"

"I'm on duty," said the officer. "I'll be going."

"I'm off," said John, smiling. "Is that bourbon you're drinking?"

The officer went out the door as Will poured from a bottle on the counter.

"They found a casing," said John. "A .358 Winchester. It's not all that common."

"The shooter left the casing?"

"It makes me think it was an automatic," said John. "It's hard to catch the casing when it spits out of the gun. The only common .358 guns are lever actions, like Winchester Model 88s and Browning BLRs."

"Savage made the Model 99 in .358 for a while," said Will.

"That was a damned good rifle," said John, "and that's damned good bourbon. Anyway, the State Police are looking for recent transactions involving 358 Winchesters."

"Let's sit on the porch," said Will. "The air feels better after the rain."

"So who did it, took the shot at Cindy?" said Will, settling back in a chair. "Assuming they were shooting at Cindy."

"I think they were," said John. "Someone wanted her out of the way before she could put a conservation easement on the property."

"Who? Not many people knew her plans."

"Someone did and I bet they're connected with United Eastern Power."

"I find it hard to believe that a large corporation would be involved with murder, or attempted murder."

"Maybe it was some lowlife wanna-be that thought they could impress their boss." John took a swallow of his drink. "Do you have a better idea?"

Will looked out at the darkness behind his home. The crickets sang a longer note and fireflies silently glowed among the weeds. Even the insects seemed to appreciate the change in the weather. "I don't," he said. "Where's Cindy now?"

"She's at my house, with her two sons. The State Police are watching the house tonight." John glanced at his watch and stood. "I should be going."

Will stood too. "She's nice, Cindy."

"I know," said John.

"How long is she staying?"

"If I had my way," said John, "forever."

*

Jimmy Deluga ignored the knocking, wondering who the hell could be at his motel room's door. Beneath him, naked Brenda approached an orgasm and he desperately didn't want to start the process over. Always take care of the woman first was his motto.

"Jimmy!" yelled the woman on the other side of the door. "He'll kill me." It sounded like someone pounded on the door with a sledge hammer.

"Oh…myyyy God," squealed Brenda, squeezing his arms.

About time, thought Jimmy.

It sounded like mammoth woodpecker attacking the paneled door.

Jimmy slid off the bed and grabbed a pair of pants. "Wait a second," he yelled.

Brenda, gasping like a grounded guppy, pulled the sheets up to her chin.

Opening the door, Suzy Toll stumbled in, holding a shoe with a six inch spike heel as if it were a hammer.

"What the fuck?" said Jimmy.

"Jake's gone crazy," said Suzy, grabbing Jimmy's arm. "He went looking for you at Pricilla's bar. He wants money." A bruise by her left eye said she had been hit.

"Are you all right?" He slammed the door shut and locked it.

"Yeah." Suzy straightened up when she noticed Brenda in the bed. "What's Brenda doing here?"

"You two know each other?" Brenda had to be almost twice Suzy's age, maybe older.

"I know her," said Suzy, looking unpleased. Turning to Jimmy, she touched his bare chest. "I thought we might spend the night together."

"I can be going," said Brenda, appearing unfazed.

"No," said Jimmy. "Suzy doesn't have to stay."

"Yes I do, Jake'll kill me. He figured out we fucked last night and he's pissed."

Jimmy had picked up Brenda at her place, so the only way she might get home was if he gave her a ride, which meant either Suzy coming along or leaving her in the motel room alone. Jimmy had guns and money hidden in the room and wasn't about to leave anyone there alone.

"I'm not leaving either of you here by yourself," he said.

"I don't want to go back outside," said Suzy, seductively running her fingers down Jimmy's chest. "We can have some fun." Her hand stopped on his belt buckle.

"It's a big bed," laughed Brenda, sliding to one side. "There's room for all of us."

"Get on the bed," said Jimmy, grabbing Suzy's hand.

She smiled. "What are we going to do?"

"Whatever you two do, don't keep me awake," said Brenda, grinning.

"Get in," said Jimmy.

His Kimber pistol was in the side table between the two beds and he wanted easy access to it. "We're going to sleep. I'm taking the other bed."

"Sleep?" Suzy knew she would convince him otherwise and started undoing the tie on her halter top.

"Yeah," he answered.

Her breasts popped free.

Brenda noticed his gaze. "Yeah, right."

Jimmy grabbed a bottle of scotch and poured an inch in a cup. "Either of you want some?" he asked.

"I'll have a taste," said Brenda.

He passed her the bottle and she took a swig. "That's good. You want some?" she said, offering it to Suzy, who slid naked into the bed.

She took a swallow too and set the bottle on the side table. Grinning, she patted the sheets and said, "Come on." Turning to Brenda, she added, "This should be fun, I've never done a threesome before."

"Don't get your hopes up," said Brenda. "Do what you want, but I'm going to sleep." She slid down under the sheet and pulled it up to her chin.

"Come on," said Suzy, smiling at Jimmy and again patted the sheet.

"I'm using the other bed," said Jimmy.

Suzy swatted Brenda's hip. "Don't be a party pooper, this could be fun."

"I've had my fun," said Brenda, turning her back was to Suzy.

Suzy slipped from the bed and onto the other. "Come," she said to Jimmy.

He swallowed the last of his scotch and set the tumbler down. Thinking, what the hell, he started to undo his pants and said, "Slide over."

Jimmy wanted to be next to the side table and handy to the gun.

28

The crash against the door woke Jimmy.

"It's Jake," said Suzy, pulling the sheets up.

Jimmy slipped from the bed to yank on pants. He already had the Kimber 45 from the side table. Brenda hadn't said a word, but even in the dark he could see the whites of her wide-open eyes.

Someone or something crashed against the door again.

Jimmy picked up the pistol and pulled back the slide to chamber a round, then calmly set it down while he put on a shirt. About the third button up something smashed into the door again. As he did the last button on his right cuff, the door burst open and Jake stumbled into the room.

Jimmy picked up the .45 caliber pistol and aimed it at the young man's forehead. "Is there something you want?"

Jake, being seriously drunk, almost fell. Straightening up, he said, "My girl, I wanna take my girl home." Using the back of a sleeve, he wiped drool from his mouth.

"Ask her nicely if she wants to go with you," said Jimmy.

"Honey," he said, turning to Suzy. "Come home with me."

"I'm not going anywhere with you," said Suzy. "You're a drunk and a nobody."

"We're going to be rich someday," he pleaded. "Just you wait and see."

It looked like Jake might cry.

Jimmy said, "You're pathetic."

Jake straightened up, which made him several inches taller than Jimmy. His hands clenched in fists and the muscles along the sides of his neck tightened. Anger hardened his bloodshot eyes.

In a blur, Jimmy kicked him in the nuts, which caused Jake to buckle over, and then brought the butt of his pistol down hard on the back of Jake's head. The man lay splayed on the floor like a rug.

"Kill him," said Suzy. "Kill him and put him in the river. Nobody will find him for days, and by then he'll be miles downstream."

Jimmy eased the gun's hammer and set it on the bed. Suzy wasn't the first woman he had met that was turned on by the thought of killing. Usually they were the crazy ones who would try anything, which also made them the most fun in bed. But killing always complicated things and usually turned out messy. Jake might be an asshole, but he didn't deserve to die.

"I'm not going to kill him," said Jimmy. "Why don't you take him home?"

"I don't want to," said Suzy. "I want to stay with you."

"Take him home. Here's some money," he said, pulling out his wallet. "In the morning take him out for breakfast somewhere. Remind him he's supposed to be looking for information on the Hammonds."

She looked at the cash, there were six one hundred dollar bills. "What about us?"

"Oh come on," said Brenda. "You're not that naïve. This man isn't settling down with you."

"Suzy, get you clothes," said Jimmy. "Do you have a car? I'll help you get him into it."

"He's got a truck," she said, sounding defeated.

Five minutes later Jimmy returned and locked the door.

"What took you so long?" asked Brenda.

"Suzy is a pain in the ass," he said, undressing.

"What time is it?"

"A little after one."

Brenda lifted up the corner of the sheet and said, "Slide in."

"I was hoping you'd said that."

*

"I'm glad you are all right," said Amy, finding her father still sitting in the porch.

"Me too," he said, as she sat on the seat beside him. "Is Ethan asleep?" A tumbler containing an inch of bourbon sat on the arm of his chair.

"Yes, hours ago. All the excitement wore him out."

"Did you have any luck with the realtors?"

"There's a house in town we're going to look at tomorrow. If I like it, I'd like you to look at it too."

Thunder grumbled over the distant hills.

"There's enough land here you could build a house," said Will. "There's a little knoll that overlooks the river that I always thought would make a great spot for a home. I could deed you ten or twelve acres."

Amy smiled. "I'll think about it. Building a house would take time and be a big project."

"You can stay here until it is done, and we'd be neighbors. Ethan could visit as often as he wanted. Think about it."

Lightning skipped about towering thunderheads.

"You're seeing Kim tomorrow night, aren't you?" said Amy.

Will nodded. "We're going fishing."

"She wants to hook you, and not catch and release either," said Amy. "I think Barbara guessed that was Amy who called you. She likes you a lot."

Will smiled and patted his daughter's knee. "Are you taking sides?"

"No. But I like Barbara. Kim I hardly know."

"I'm not getting serious with either," said Will. "Isn't it time for bed?"

"Yeah, and I don't mean to pry into your life," said Amy, standing to give her father a hug. "I'll see you in the morning."

*

Barbara Hawkins stepped from the barn and recognized the silver Range Rover coming up her driveway. She didn't have a watch, but guessed it to be only a little after seven. Frank Atkins had certainly gotten up early. He spotted her and walked across the back lawn as she led Martha Washington to the paddock.

She used to enjoy his visits, even if he was trying to buy the land out from under her, but a long time had passed since his last visit. Barbara really didn't want him to start showing up again on a regular basis.

"Good morning," he said, as she took the bridal off the horse.

"Good morning," she replied. "What can I do for you?"

"I was just passing by and saw you outside." He leaned against the gate.

Barbara made no move to open it, but stayed inside. He was lying, because there was no way he could have seen her from the road. "I have to go to work," she said, coldly, "and there's things I need to get done."

"I'll cut to the chase," said Frank, wearing his best salesmanship smile, "I've been authorized to offer much more for your land. Enough so you can buy another piece somewhere and hire someone to do your chores."

"It's not for sale."

"Think about it, four million dollars."

Barbara didn't want to be tempted. "Get off my land."

"All right," said Frank, still smiling. "Here's another card, in case you lost the one I left before. Think about it."

As he walked back toward the driveway Barbara headed toward the barn. The air smelled sweet and felt drier after the previous night's rain. And the garden even looked greener, as if thankful for the precipitation.

A footprint in the rain softened soil caught her eye.

*

Frank drove down the road and around the bend, then turned up Wilson Northrop's driveway. Besides Will's truck was a Camry and an old International Scout in the drive. He wondered what could be going on.

A knock brought Will to the door, who said, "My answer is still the same."

"I've been authorized to offer much more," injected Frank, hoping the door didn't slam in his face. "Four million."

Will realized his daughter stood behind him. "This is my daughter," said Will, opening the door wider. "And you probably know Burt."

"No, I don't," said Frank, wondering if Will was possibly coming around. "I might even be able to get a little more." He had been authorized to spend five million.

"Would you like a cup of coffee?" asked Will.

"That would be great," said Frank, stepping inside. He noticed the flask sitting next to Burt's coffee mug. It smelled like breakfast cooking. Burt ignored him and kept his face in a newspaper.

As Will poured the coffee, he said, "Tell my daughter what you are offering."

Frank slid onto a seat at the table and started his spiel, telling of the advantages to New England and the United States if the power line ran though. Will set a coffee in front of him, while he talked about future generations and the cost of colleges. Frank ended by saying how happy he was to be able to offer four million dollars to Will for his property.

"Won't the power lines be ugly?" asked Amy. "Why can't you bury them?"

"It would be cost prohibitive," said Frank, still wearing the same practiced smile.

"But I read power lines are being buried in Maine and Vermont."

The smile wavered. "The country is different there, not so mountainous."

"Well, why don't you skip our state and run your power through those areas."

Frank needed a change of tactics, so asked, "How do you plan to pay for your son's college?"

Will heard his daughter say, "What good is college if his home is turned into an industrial park?" He never felt more proud of her.

"It's something to think about," said Frank, still forcing the grin. "I recently talked to Barbara Hawkins. She sounds interested. Of course, if she sells us her land we wouldn't need this property."

"Bullshit," said Burt, without looking up from the newspaper. "The way Will's land jogs, down by the river, you'll still have to go across the corner of it."

"I don't think so," said Frank, but his smile wavered a bit.

"The hills on both sides are too steep," continued Burt, finally looking Frank in the eye. "You've got to come down the valley."

"We'll see," said Frank, looking a bit less cocky.

Turning to Will, Burt said, "I say we run some more property lines today."

29

Barbara Hawkins stopped to look at the footprint in the rain softened soil of her garden. It wasn't hers. The morning suddenly felt cold.

More prints led down the row of peas, and the pea pods were missing. Many of the young carrots had been pulled. And there was less red fruit in her hard earned strawberry patch than there should have been.

She walked the perimeter of the lawn, looking for tracks that might indicate where the thief had come from or gone, but found none. She followed the gravel driveway to the street, but learned nothing.

Who would do such a thing?

She walked back inside, thinking that maybe it was time to buy a dog. Later, she would go into town to the sporting goods store to buy a trail cam, like the hunters use to find where the deer are going. If the thief returned, she would at least get a picture of him and see what he looked like.

Inside her home, Barbara picked up the phone and dialed Will to tell him of the footprints in her garden and the missing vegetables, and suggested he keep an eye on his garden too. He thanked her and mentioned his plans to mark the property line between his and her property that day, adding that the old woodsman Burt Bertram would be helping him.

"Can I come along?" she asked. "I can help."

Will chided himself for not thinking to ask her. "Of course," he said. "We'd actually like to walk in from you place."

"I can go anytime," she said. "I just need to call the office and tell them I'm not coming in today."

*

Jimmy Deluga sat in his black Cadillac Escalade and fiddled with the still confusing GPS. Climbing out, he stuffed the thing in the cargo pocket of his newly acquired camouflage pants, swung his knapsack over his shoulders, and headed across the big field toward the river. Occasionally logging trucks zipped by on the highway and every few minutes a car or pickup passed, but it was far from a busy road. Overhead a big black bird made a hoarse raspy call and soon he could hear the grumble of the river. The dew on the grass dampened his boots and he was glad that he had bought the expensive Gor-tex lined ones. Tall trees edged where the field met the hurrying water.

There he stopped to look at the GPS again. A shaky red line indicated his path across the field. With new confidence, Jimmy walked along the river toward the woods to the east. He even ventured into the woods to try the GPS out of sight of his vehicle.

Swallowed up inside the forest, where the river rumbled over smooth boulders and blotted out all other sound, he stopped to take the powerful Kimber Model 1911 out of his knapsack. The heft of the gun in his hand brought a feeling of safety. It still looked brand new, and he hoped it always would. It was the prettiest pistol he had ever owned. After clipping a leather holster onto his belt, he slipped the pistol into it. If he were to stumble onto a bear, it would be nice to have the weapon handy.

Once on TV he had seen pictures of a bear feeding on fish in a river and the memory brought a momentary chill. Little did he know that bear and river were thousands of miles away, and the bear was of a variety far different from the local black bears.

A path led along the river, but whoever maintained it did a lousy job. In places he detoured around fallen trees or ducked under low tree limbs. Little did Jimmy know that traveling deer, moose, and bear were the only ones keeping that trail open. Several times he stopped to check the GPS. With his pistol on his hip and the GPS in hand, Jimmy's confidence grew. Soon, he started back toward his SUV.

*

Frank Atkins pulled his silver Range Rover to the side of the road and stopped. The morning had been a long one, and it wasn't even ten o'clock. The old guy, what was his name...Burt something? He had been pretty animate that the power line couldn't go through without crossing both Will Northrop's and Barbara Hawkins's land. Could he be right?

Frank took a tablet out of a briefcase and brought up a topographical map on the screen. The valley was tight where the river cut through the two properties. The image didn't show the property lines, so he brought another map onto the screen. It was tough to tell without imposing one map over the other, and his software wouldn't do that.

The surveying team hired by United Eastern Power was supposed to sort all that out, but Will Northrop had kicked them off his land. Frank couldn't blame him, he might have done the same thing if he found surveyors hacking out lines on property he owned. More than once Frank suggested to his boss Henderson that maybe they should ask permissions first. That was not Henderson's way. The man was an ass.

From the briefcase Frank dug out a compass. It still worked. He also pulled out a paper map, which he folded small enough to slip into a back pocket. Stepping out of the vehicle, he took a deep breath. The morning air still felt cool and smelled of freshly moistened vegetation.

He locked up the Ranger and started into the woods. Years earlier, when he was much younger, he used to hunt and loved to spend time in the woods. Frank missed those days.

*

Jimmy Deluga drove slowly by the burnt remains of the Hammond's home. The yellow police ribbon still circled the pile of rubble, but no one was around. He stopped and backed up, parking next to the building's remains. Putting down the window, the air smelled of wet charred wood.

He tried to imagine how someone might approach the house unseen. Enormous fields ran off in every direction. The closest woods grew across the street, and even that was more than the length of a football field away. The cover of darkness would help, even be necessary. But the police report indicated the fire started late in the day, while the summer sun still lit the sky. It looked like a tote road might come out of the trees where the woods met the field. He wondered where it might go.

Could the killer have been someone the Hammond's knew? If he could figure that out, Robert Henderson owed him a pile of money. Jimmy put the window up and drove down the road to the end of the fields. He parked beside an old rock maple and stepped out of the Escalade.

With the gun still on his hip and the GPS in hand, he walked into the woods, intending to stay in the trees and follow the edge of the field back to the old woods road across from the Hammond's place. Maybe it would lead him to the killer.

*

Brian Toll settled back against a log and surveyed his campsite, which was slowly becoming a little homestead.

A few days earlier, on one of his forays to raid neighboring vegetable gardens, he spotted several sheets of plywood behind an old barn. It took four trips, but he carried four sheets back to the campsite, along with an old window that someone had stored against the back of the building. The day before, using only an axe and a bow saw, he dropped enough fir trees to make the walls of a cabin large enough to sleep in. The entire morning had been spent fitting the bottom two tiers together, but he was optimistic things would start to go faster. The plywood would make an easy roof, but it was clear that a few boards would make framing the window and doors easier. He tried to remember where he had seen some.

Pillaging neighboring vegetable gardens had provided easy food. Fish were easy to catch in the river and small game was abundant. The biggest challenge was planning for the cold months and, of course, the home site had to be kept secret. That morning, long before the sun came up, he had been careless and worn his boots while stealing Barbara Hawkins's peas, and he reminded himself not to do that again. One mistake could cause the authorities to find his home, which would get him booted off the land and possibly sent to jail.

Brian remembered Will Northrop did a lot of work on his home and barn the previous year, and probably had saved leftover material in his barn. It wasn't much further to his place than Barbara Hawkins's. He decided to take a look there that night.

He went back to work, carefully cutting logs to length and then notching the ends. Once he had read about packing mud mixed with straw between the logs, to make them air tight, and he wondered what type of mud might be best. Where the Mooslikamoosuc River cut into some of the steep banks, a half mile before reaching the highway, it exposed yellow clay. He decided to try that and wondered where he might find some five gallon buckets. It would take many trips, because the clay would be heavy.

The roof would not have much pitch, but stout spruce purlins would make it strong. By the time the sun climbed to its highest point, he hoped to have the four walls up to head height.

30

Will wore a woven pack basket and carried a small axe. Ahead of him, Barbara followed Burt's shuffling gait. The path led down the hill behind her place, passing rough barked maples and gnarly yellow birches, with an occasional tall fir or spruce tree mixed in. Striped maple crowded the path where sunlight snuck through the forest's crown, and in one area a dense stand of young spruce grew head-high, like a crowd at a bus station.

Coming to an ancient lichen-covered stonewall that had almost disappeared into the leaf covered ground, Burt turned to the left to follow its course. Some sections of the wall were many times wider than tall, where homesteading farmers, over a century before, had tossed the abundant rocks out of newly cleared fields. Since then Mother Nature had worked hard to reclaim what was hers.

Fifteen minutes later they came to a tree marked with a blaze painted red, signifying Barbara's property line. While Barbara and Will waited, Burt waddled off looking for another. Several times he looked back to see where they stood and get his bearings. Finally, he found another.

Using axes, they swamped out an alleyway through the underbrush to see from one blaze to the next, and then hacked several new blazes on trees along the property line. Fresh paint was applied to both the old and the new marks. Will wished he had bought gloves to keep the red liquid off of his hands.

Whenever they lost track of the blazes, either Will or Barbara or both would stand by the last one they had found until Burt yelled back that he had found another. It was going to be a long day, and it would take several days to do both his and Barbara's property lines.

*

Frank Atkins could hear the distant slap of the axe. He trudged through the woods with the land sloping to his left. Every few minutes he looked at his compass to check his course. Eventually, the land started to drop away in front of him. The strike of the axe sounded closer and he thought he could hear voices.

Stopping to listen, he realized just how hard his heart pounded. Maybe he should exercise, like his wife always nagged him to.

But being out in the woods was fun, something he hadn't experienced in ages. For the last half hour he hadn't thought of Robert Henderson or Untied Eastern Power, or any of life's other problems. Instead birds caught his eye and their songs filled his ears. He tried to remember the names of the trees. Deer and moose tracks caught his attention. Maybe he would deer hunt the coming fall.

The voices…there were several. And one sounded like a woman, maybe even Barbara Hawkins. What would she be doing out there? Frank slowly walked toward the sounds.

*

Jimmy Deluga followed the old tote road. Soft green moss grew where rotting leaves didn't cover the soil. Occasional bulbous mushrooms poked from the ground like swelling balloons. Knee-high ferns covered much of the forest floor. The leaves overhead whispered as a breeze filtered through the tree tops. Soon the trail crested a rounded hill and started downward. The soft ground silenced his steps.

The pounding of a woodpecker caused him to jump, but when he realized it was only a bird he re-holstered his pistol.

Where the soil was soft, clusters of animal tracks made him wonder what creatures lived in the woods. Some hoof prints looked big enough to have come from a cow. Were there wild cows? He had never heard of such a thing, but he had never paid much attention to wildlife, other than the pigeons that picked up crumbs on the sidewalks of New York.

Frequently he stopped to check the GPS. The dashed red track across its tiny screen brought confidence. Jimmy marched on.

*

"How far have we done?" asked Barbara.

"Not far," said Will. "It will take us a few days to do both of our properties. Burt at least wants to do where the power line would cross."

"Do you see him?"

Will looked ahead. The blazes had run out again and Burt had wandered ahead, looking for another. A cluster of striped maple, not half again as tall as a man, made it difficult to see where Burt had disappeared to. "No I don't," answered Will. Usually Burt let out a yell when he found a blaze.

"Do you like strawberry shortcake?" asked Barbara.

"I love it," said Will, still looking for Burt.

"I have lots of strawberries, or at least I did before the thief robbed my garden."

"Here comes Burt," said Will.

"I wonder if he found the next blaze."

"I'm sure he did," said Will, trying to understand the look on Burt's face.

When close, Burt said, "We have company."

"Company?"

"There's someone on the hill above us," he said. "I just got a glimpse of him." He shifted the hold of the axe in his hand.

"Who could be here?" said Barbara.

"I don't know," said Will. "Let's hope it isn't the shooter from yesterday."

"Follow me," said Burt, starting off down the hill.

Will walked last, wishing he had brought a pistol or rifle. An axe at a gun fight was a severe handicap. Barbara said nothing, but stayed right behind Burt. They walked directly down the slope until the ground fell precipitously away. There, they turned to the left to angle downhill.

Where an enormous chunk of ledge poked out of the hillside to form a nub Burt led them around its base and up through thick fir trees on the back side. Stopping amongst thick green boughs at the top, he motioned to stay quiet. They could easily see the slope they had just walked down. Below them, at the base of the valley, the river rumbled.

Frank followed, but only because the people who had been making the noise had headed in the direction he wanted to go. Softwood trees became more prevalent and the ground sloped downward. Where it dropped quickly he turned to the left to find a way less steep. The people ahead of him had disappeared and he wondered if they had detoured to the right. The river hissed and he no longer heard the slap of the axe.

The land grew steep, more than he imagined from looking at the topographical maps. Perhaps that old fart Burt was right and the power lines would have to follow the river's course, which meant crossing both Will Northrop's and Barbara Hawkins's properties. That meant it would take more than the five million that Robert Henderson wanted to spend to get one of their properties.

The spent spruce and fir needles on the ground were slippery, so he walked slowly, often holding onto tree trunks to keep from sliding down the hill. He had been listening to the river for quite a while, yet it didn't sound much closer. Frank wondered how far away it was.

"There," whispered Burt, pointing.

Will could see nothing, but then a movement caught his eye. It was Frank Atkins, the land buyer from United Eastern Power. What the hell was he doing out there in the woods? The man wore the same city clothes that he had worn when he appeared at Will's house. His shoes were made for walking on sidewalks, not the forest floor.

Will realized Barbara's hand held his. She watched Frank and looked concerned, but not scared. It didn't appear the man was armed. Soon he disappeared down the slope.

Will turned to Barbara, glanced at their coupled hands and then her eyes. She smiled. He gave her hand a squeeze.

"He's on your property," said Burt, looking at Barbara. "Do you want to ask him to leave?"

She shook her head, "No."

"Let's call it a day," said Will, releasing Barbara's hand. "We can work on the property lines another day. There's no hurry."

Burt scratched at his chin and pulled his flask from a hip pocket, offering it to both Will and Barbara. When they both declined, he took a swig, and then said, "The easiest way back is along the river, but that's where our friend is heading. Let's go back uphill a ways and see if we can cut across the slope."

*

Brian Toll slipped through the woods, not following any path or trail, but picking a course through open hardwoods. He planned to cut across the hill and drop down into town. In his back pocket were the few remaining dollar bills that he owned.

Crows cawing to the east caused him to slow and look. It might be they were harassing a red tailed hawk, or maybe it was people that had them riled up. He could see nothing but trees, but nonetheless he quickened his pace and walked diagonally away from their commotion.

It was unlikely that anyone would be out in the woods, but he did not want to take a chance.

He intercepted a long abandoned logging road, which made walking easier, and turned to the left, even though it brought him closer to the disturbed crows. The soft damp soil muffled his steps and he moved without a sound. Deer and moose tracks were abundant.

And then a blue jay squawked off to his left.

Brian stopped to peer down the hillside through the trees. After a moment, he spotted a movement. He slinked off the road to behind a waist-high rock. Down the hill, something moved again.

There were people, three…one a woman. It was Barbara Hawkins. Could they have figured out he was the one that raided her garden? How? Were they really looking for him? He recognized Burt Bertram, the old woodsman who had been around forever. The other man looked familiar, and Brian thought it might be Will Northrop, the man he hoped to steal some wood from that night.

What were they doing out there? He could not believe they were looking for him…but maybe they were. Looking at the direction that they came from, they had to have been less than a half mile from his camp. Maybe the woods around there wasn't big enough for him to hide out in indefinitely.

When they disappeared into the trees, Brian walked straight up the hill.

31

Jimmy Deluga slowed. He had never been that far from asphalt in his entire life and the woods was a spooky alien world. For the third time in less than ten minutes, he pulled the GPS out of his pocket to make sure it still worked.

The old road he walked was easy enough to follow. In places it had grown in to the width of a doorway, but most of it was still wide enough to drive on, if only the ground had been harder. It turned gradually to the west and sloped slowly downhill, in some places becoming soft and muddy. Occasionally, the breeze rattled the leaves overhead, but most of the time he heard nothing. Once, an unseen bird with a deep raspy call reminded him of his mother. As a child he didn't know it, but the whiskey and cigarettes had created her voice.

Glancing at his watch, it surprised him that he had only been in the woods twenty minutes. It felt like hours. He decided to walk on for twenty more minutes, and if he found nothing, he would turn around and trace his steps back to his SUV. Mumbling the words to the song from the old Gilligan's Island TV show calmed his nerves. The dankest neighborhoods of New York City did not make him as uncomfortable as the green living forest.

Where the trail dipped a small silent stream flowed through ferns and moss covered rocks. He stopped to watch the water and noticed a large dead tree trunk in the woods downstream. A small gray bird with a white belly hopped along its bark, obviously looking for something to catch with its pointy bill.

Jimmy slithered the pistol from its holster, took a wide stance, chambered a round, carefully aimed at the little bird, and squeezed the trigger. At the roar of the gun the bird flew away.

"Lucky bird," said Jimmy, slipping the weapon back in the holster. Looking at his watch, he still had ten minutes before turning around.

*

Two hundred yards away, Brian Troll dropped to the ground at the roar of the pistol. Were they shooting at him? And where were they? His heart pounded like a hammer.

Lifting his head up, he could see no one. It didn't seem possible that Barbara Hawkins and the two men could have headed him off. Who could be there? The woods felt deathly quiet.

He tried to remember how far it was to his sister's boyfriend's house. Brian didn't know much about Jake, other than he was way older than his sister, but had never liked the man. He guessed Jake liked playing with his sister's tits and he could understand that, but what she saw in him was a mystery. Jake wasn't ever going to turn into anything more than the same sort of disaster that was Suzy's dad.

Jake's house couldn't be far. Could he be doing the shooting? Maybe it was target practice. Brian could not think of any reason for Jake to be shooting at him.

Brian stood and nervously looked around. Seeing no one, he took off trotting toward Jake's ramshackle home.

*

The old cart path took a hard left in front of Jimmy Deluga. He decided to round the corner, just to see what was there, and then strike back toward his Escalade.

When Brian crossed the old logging road, he spotted a man walking in the direction of Jake's house, which he knew to be only a short distance ahead around a bend in the road. Brian crossed unseen to take a shortcut through the trees. As he reached the edge of the weeds that Jake would call his lawn, he noticed the man step out of the woods.

The man pulled a large pistol from a holster, held it aimed skyward, and then walked toward the back door of the house. Brain waited in the trees, wondering if his sister or Jake were at home. The man walked up on the deck and knocked on the back door.

The door opened and Brian's sister stepped out, then threw her arms around the man like a long lost friend. The guy laughed and holstered the gun, then gave Suzy's ass a squeeze through her tiny cutoff shorts. Obviously they knew each other. Brian wondered how the hell that was possible as the two disappeared inside.

"How did you find us?" asked Suzy, dropping down on a couch.

"It's a long story," said Jimmy, sitting at the opposite end. Beer cans cluttered the coffee table and a soap opera played on the TV. "Where's Jake?" he asked.

"He's been gone all day," said Suzy. "He says he'll have some answers for you by tonight." She slid to his end of the sofa. "Do you want something to eat?" Where the front of her tee shirt stretched across her chest, it said "Feel the Mountains".

"I'm fine," said Jimmy, doubting Jake would find anything other than trouble. "I shouldn't stay."

"It's gotta be a long walk back," said Suzy, cozying against his side. "We could have a little fun first." Her index finger hooked the front of his pants.

If she had offered a ride back to his vehicle, Jimmy would have taken her up on it. At the moment, sex with a bimbo had little appeal. Standing, he said, "Later. I'll see you in town tonight." He knew then it had been a mistake showing her and Jake where his motel room was and wondered if there was somewhere else he could move to so they wouldn't find him.

"Let me put a smile on that face," she said, cocking her head.

Jimmy figured what-the-hell and dropped back into the couch. Fifteen minutes later he left out the back door, leaving Suzy smiling like a cat that had just caught a mouse. At least she was still an ally.

The slamming screen door snapped Brian Toll back from a dream about a hamburger with a side of fries and a very dill pickle. The man had just stepped out onto the deck, tucking in his shirt and adjusting his holster, and stopped to scan the yard before disappearing into the woods in the direction he had come from. Brian waited a few minutes, and then dashed down to the back door.

He knocked and Suzy inside yelled, "Come on in."

"It's me, Brian," he said, opening the door.

"Oh shit," she said, turning her backside to him and pulling on a little tee shirt. "I thought you were Jimmy."

"Who's Jimmy?" he asked. At least she had on panties.

Turning to Brian, she said, "A friend. Jimmy Deluga. Jake and I are doing some work for him, undercover kind-a-stuff."

She made no move to put her shorts back on. Brian asked, "Does Jake know you're fucking him?" Her nipples pressed against the inside of the thin fabric like missiles ready to launch.

"Jake don't care."

Brian wondered if that were true. His experience with women and relationships was almost nonexistent. "Where's Jake?"

"Working," she said, defiantly, and then looking friendlier, asked, "Do you want a beer?"

Other than water, Brian hadn't had anything to drink for two days. "Sure." At fifteen years of age, his beer drinking experience had been mostly limited to a few six packs shared with buddies and a couple he'd stolen from his father.

He followed her to the kitchen. The tiny panties hardly covered her swaying butt and his swirling emotions made him uncomfortable. Clutter and crumbs covered the countertops, just as it had at his parent's home. She pulled two Budweisers from the refrigerator and handed him one.

"We ain't got much to eat in the house," she said. "There might be some hot dogs."

"That'll do," he said. "When's Jake getting home?"

"Not til late probably. Where have you been?"

Brian gave his sister an abbreviated account of his recent life, being particularly vague about where his new home was. When she hadn't moved toward the refrigerator, he said again that a hot dog sounded great.

She pulled an open package from the refrigerator and set a cast iron frying pan on the stove. Fishing one out, she said, "You must get lonely."

"I like it," he said. "There's nobody to bother me."

"I get lonely," she said. "And I live with Jake." The dog landed in the pan with a sizzle.

"What do you see in that guy?"

"He's good to me." She looked defensive.

"Yeah, he fucks you and buys you beer," said Brian. "Do you think he loves you? The guy is never going to amount to nothing." It was easy to imagine her ending up just like his mother had.

"I'll worry about me and you worry about you," she said, using a fork to roll the hot dogs over.

Brian swallowed another mouthful of beer. It tasted good. Very good. Suzy looked better than he remembered, having lost some of the pudginess that she used to carry. He thought she could be a model if she lived in the city.

"So when was the last time you had sex?" she asked, looking at him out of the corners of her eyes.

He wondered where that came from, and said, "It's been a while."

"Have you ever?"

Suzy pushed the end of an uncooked hot dog slowly into her mouth. Brian had never seen that sultry look in her eyes. "Of course," he lied, watching the way her lips wrapped around the disappearing meat. She eased it back out and then her tongue traced her lips.

She shut off the stove and stepped closer to her brother. "Jake says I'm the best he's ever had." Her hand reached for his.

Brian's brain screamed for everything to stop, but he couldn't speak or move. Her hand brought his up to her chest and pressed it against a soft warm mound. He could feel the hard nipple against his palm. Her mouth met his. His mind shrieked that it was wrong, yet his hand found its way up under her tee shirt with a will of its own.

Twenty minutes later, lying naked together on the couch, Brian said, "What did we just do?" He felt the best of his entire life, physically. Emotionally, he was a mess.

"We had some fun," said Suzy, holding him tight against her side.

"It was wrong, we shouldn't do that."

"Says who?" Her head nestled against his shoulder.

"We'll make a baby with two heads," said Brian.

"I take the pill."

"I should leave," he said, pulling away from her. Sitting up, he looked for his clothes.

"Take me with you," she said. "I want to get out of here."

Pulling on his pants, Brian said, "I thought you had found your soul mate."

"I think Jake might have killed Mom and Dad."

Brian flinched involuntarily, as if someone had thrown ice water on him. "Why?"

Suzy started to slip into her clothes. "I think he wanted me to inherit their property, and then sell it to the people putting the power line in. They would have paid millions."

"I would have inherited it too," said Brian.

"He might have killed you too."

Brian said, "Grab your things."

32

John Johansson pulled into his driveway and parked beside Cindy Hammond's car. Stepping from his truck, he found himself hoping that she never would leave. Her younger son, Justin, met him at the door.

"John, would it be possible for me to rent my bedroom for the rest of the summer?" he said.

"What's up?" asked John.

Justin said, "I took a job at Wilk's Hardware Store"

John laughed. "Now why in the hell did you go and do a thing like that?" Something good smelled to be cooking in the kitchen and he wondered what Cindy was up to.

"I want to stay up here a while. There's great hiking and I'd love to learn to fly fish."

"You can stay as long as you like," said John. "Mow the lawn and that is rent enough."

"Great, thank you," said Justin, before dashing upstairs.

In the kitchen John found Cindy peeling potatoes. He learned that earlier in the day she found a local farmer's market on Colby Street, where she bought ground lamb, potatoes, and a pile of vegetables. A shepherd's pie was planned for that night.

"I love having you around here," he said, stopping close enough that his shoulder touched hers.

Cindy smiled. "I love being up here," she said. "Do you know how much produce is grown locally up here? Lots." He could tell she was excited about something. "There could be a lot more too, but they have trouble marketing it all. I've been trying to think of a way to sell it over the Internet."

"What are you going to do, quit nursing?"

"I might," she said. "If I sold the house in Westchester County I'd get almost three million for it. I could buy a place up here and start a business."

John so wanted that to happen. "I'd help," he offered.

"Think about it," Cindy said. She went on about marketing things grown in the north woods, on small farms, where the streams are clean enough to drink from…the spiel made it all sound so appetizing he found himself getting hungrier. "I've got friends that work in advertising that would help," she said. "And some of the restaurants I know in the city would kill to get this produce."

"Let's do it," said John.

"I just might," said Cindy, dropping the last potato into the pot. "Is there anything new?"

John knew she meant on her parents death. "No. The State Police haven't said anything." He went on to tell her about Justin's request. She already knew he was going to ask and hoped John didn't mind.

"Of course I don't mind," said John. "Both of them are great kids."

"Warren loves it up here too, but I think he's got a girl that he's interested in on Martha's Vineyard."

John laughed. "Tell him to bring her up here."

*

Burt had left, but Barbara lingered on Will's porch. It felt awkward. In a few hours he was supposed to meet Kim to go fishing. Amy was upstairs with Ethan, and he guessed she was laughing at the predicament that her dad had gotten himself into.

"I could make us some dinner," said Barbara.

"I have some things I need to do tonight," said Will, wishing he hadn't promised to see Kim later. Life suddenly seemed incredibly complicated.

Barbara had already guessed what was making him appear so uncomfortable. Not about to throw in the towel, she said, "How about tomorrow night?"

"I would love that," he said, relieved.

Not long after the she left and the door had closed, Amy came down the stairs. "My dad is playing with fire," she said, not looking at her father and walking to the refrigerator.

"I know," said Will. "Can you grab me a beer?"

"I might," she said. "You know, you're going to have to pick." She handed him the beer without letting her eyes meet his.

"Yeah, yeah, yeah." The last thing he wanted was advice, particularly from his daughter.

"I guarantee you that whichever one decides you are a jerk and dumps you first will be the one that you want." She opened a bottle of water. "That's the way it works."

He smiled. "Is it?"

"Yup. I know from experience."

"What's Shawn up to?"

"He'll be here soon," she said. "He's taking Ethan and me to the races in Groveton."

Loud cars and loud people, thought Will. The beer tasted good. "What's Ethan been up to all day?"

"I took him and Duchess down to the river. He loves that dog."

Shawn's truck came in the driveway and Amy ran to make sure Ethan was ready. A few minutes later, Will found himself alone. He poured a half inch of Oban in a tumbler and sat at his computer.

With the images enlarged, Google Earth showed his and Barbara's property with the river weaving a jagged line through his land and then along the side of hers. He wished topographical elevation lines could be superimposed on the pictures. Magnified, it was possible to even see her horse standing in its paddock.

Zooming back out, he noticed the distance from the Hammond's home to where Suzy Toll lived with her boyfriend. It wasn't all that far through the woods, possibly a forty minute walk. And then the distance to the Toll's home wasn't much further. Could they be the killers of all four? Money could be the motive, if they thought Suzy would inherit her parent's land. On the computer screen it looked too obvious. Could her brother be next? Where was that kid?

Will thought about calling John Johansson to ask his opinion, but noticed the time. In less than an hour he was supposed to meet Kim down by the river. He swallowed the last of the scotch and went upstairs to shower.

*

Jimmy Deluga's phone vibrated. "Excuse me," he said to the owner of Rumbling Stream Cabins. "I got to take this." He pulled out the cell phone and turned his back. "Hello."

It was Robert Henderson, asking, "Are we gaining?" He sounded in a good mood.

"Nothing solid," said Jimmy. "I've got some locals working on it." He didn't mention that the reason he was moving from the motel at the edge of town to one of the Rumbling Stream Cabins was to avoid them.

"Listen, some of the investors are going to be up that way tomorrow, staying at The Fenton House Inn, and I'm going to be joining them, just to show them around and explain what we can do for the community. It would be great if we had a definite right-of-way sorted out."

Jimmy wondered why that was so important, thinking Henderson could tell them anything because all the fucking woods looked alike. "Have you got other people working on this?"

"Yeah. Frank Atkins, you met him on the Vineyard." It sounded like Henderson was eating something. He was always eating something. "I'd love it if you could find out what happened to those people that got killed. I'm sure it will make the investors feel better. I might even squeeze out an extra bonus for you."

Not very likely, thought Jimmy, but said, "I'll see what we can do."

He stuffed the phone back into his pocket and walked to one of the little log buildings. The owner of Rumbling Stream Cabins was standing by the door and led Jimmy inside. The cabin even had a tiny kitchen, not that Jimmy would cook anything. The hiss of a tumbling stream along the far edge of the lawn sounded much like a freeway and he liked that. After a few minutes of chit chat, the owner left and Jimmy hauled the remainder of his belongings inside. The evening had cooled enough that he could wear a sports jacket.

An hour later he walked into the bar at The Fenton House Inn. Brenda tended bar and smiled when she saw him. "What'll you have?" she asked.

"Give me your best bourbon," he said, sliding onto a stool.

One other man sat on the far side of the bar, eating a sandwich with a beer, and two women sat at a small table against the paneled wall. Jimmy wondered if the place ever was busy. When Brenda reached for the bottle, he noticed her long legs below the short skirt.

"I had fun the other night," said Brenda, setting the drink in front of him. "Have you seen those two whack jobs again?"

He shook his head and sipped the bourbon. "Listen, I need you to do me a favor. Some bigwigs connected with the power line are going to be staying here. One of them, a fat guy named Henderson, is entertaining the investors. See if you can hear anything interesting." He noticed the skeptical look on her face. "I'll make it worth your while."

"Cash?"

He smiled, she was talking the universal language. "Yeah, cash."

She laughed and patted his arm. "I mean you're good in bed, but I like cash better. So what's this Henderson guy like?"

"Rather full of himself, likes good food, lots of it, and expensive hookers. He'll be trying to impress the investors. Some of them are getting antsy."

"Business groups often rent the top floor, where the rooms are bigger. Out the back you can see the river and in the front you're looking down Main Street. It's nice."

"It sounds like you've stayed there."

"Let's say I've visited."

33

Will watched Kim flick the fly line off the water, pause as the line straightened out behind her, and then snap it forward to drop the fly an inch from a fern that leaned out from the river's far bank. The water dimpled and the fly disappeared. Her wrist snapped back and the fish was hooked. She made it look easy.

The muscles in her shoulders flexed as she held the rod high. Kim wore a little tank top, which Will guessed was more for his benefit than anything else. It certainly wasn't as warm as it had been the last few evenings and mosquitos were always an issue at that time of the day. Whatever she wore for insect repellant seemed to be working, and she sure smelled nice.

The fish sliced upstream and then bolted down.

Kim's eyes were locked on the trout.

They had fished for over an hour and Kim had easily caught three for every one that he had, maybe more. Things had slowed down and they had decided to stop, setting their rods against his truck and peeling off their waders. That was when Kim spotted that last trout rising, which surprised Will because it was getting too dark to see. Not able to resist, she waded barefoot into calf deep water to cast. He guessed the little shorts she wore were for his benefit too, because the waders must have felt clammy against the bare skin of her legs.

She bent to release a fat nineteen inch brown trout. Will didn't know there were any fish that big in the river.

Grinning, Kim sauntered back up, leaned her rod beside his, and wrapped her arms around Will's neck to place her mouth against his.

"That gets me hot," she said, giggling.

Will laughed. She felt nice in his arms. "It does?"

She kissed him again, putting her hands behind his head so he couldn't break away. Finally, she said, "Yeah."

"Shall we go get something to eat?" Her hips pressed against his.

"You could take advantage of me first."

He could see it in her eyes, she really was aroused. Her mouth came to his again and their groins ground together. A hand was tugging on his belt buckle.

Will never gave the mosquitos a thought.

Twenty minutes later, driving across the field toward the road, he laughed and said, "I think a mosquito bit my ass."

Kim squeezed his hand. "Maybe you should shower in insect repellant whenever we go fishing, in case I catch another big one."

"Does that happen with every big fish?"

"Often."

"I should take you fishing in the ocean," he laughed.

In town, they parked in front of The Fenton House Inn and went inside. A short man in nice clothes chatted with the barmaid, and three other people sat on the far side of the rectangular bar. A waitress said to sit anywhere so they picked a small round table in a dimly lit corner. A few seconds later she came by to ask what they wanted.

Afterward, Will asked Kim if she knew who the man was talking to the bartender.

Even though she had seen him in the restaurant, she said, "No. He must be from out of town. That sports jacket looks like it's tailored."

Will didn't mention it, but he noticed a bulge under the man's left armpit, which could have been a cancerous growth, or more likely a concealed pistol. "I wonder what he's doing in town."

"He's alone, so I bet he's a business man and it has something to do with the power line."

The conversation drifted to fishing and then fly tying. Their drinks came and then food. When they got up to leave the man still sat at the bar and chatted with the bartender whenever she wasn't busy.

*

"Have you been back to the house?" said Brian, meaning their parents' home.

"No," said Suzy, "have you?"

They sat on a log beside a small campfire, sharing a bottle of cheap wine that Jake had taken from his parent's home and saved for a special occasion.

"No," said Brian. "The place freaks me out."

"Me too," said Suzy. "It's nothing but bad memories." She took a swallow of the wine. "What do you suppose is going to happen to the place?"

"I don't know. We should inherit it, and then we could sell it."

"The power company would pay big bucks, if they could get the Hammond's place."

Brian scowled, "Do you really want that power line coming through here?"

"I just want to leave this place, go somewhere that winter never comes."

He took a swig of wine and said, "I'm not sure we can inherit the place, with us both being minors." Poking at the fire with a stick, sparks swirled up into the sky.

"I'll be eighteen soon," said Suzy.

An owl hooted off in the distance. In the still of the night they could hear the whisper of the river in the valley below.

"Do you suppose Jake misses you yet?"

"I don't know, he may not be home yet." Suzy took another sip of wine, then said, "Sometimes he doesn't come home until late."

Brian reached for the nearly empty bottle. "How pissed is he going to be?"

"Pretty pissed, but he'll be so drunk he'll be harmless. Tomorrow is what I worry about. He's pretty used to waking up beside me."

"He won't find us here," said Brian. "We're safe." He offered her the last of the wine, but she shook her head. He swallowed the last drop, then said, "The bed ain't much, it's made of fir boughs, but you take it. I'll sleep under the stars."

"No, you can sleep with me," she said.

Brian shook his head. "What we did…I don't want to do it again."

"We don't have to. I just want you there. You're all I've got."

In the warm light of the fire her she looked both sad and beautiful. Suzy was right. Each other was all they had.

"I'm leaving my clothes on," he said.

34

Robert Henderson wheeled the shiny dark blue Chevy Silverado into town. Fenton looked exactly like the last time he left it and, for the life of him, he couldn't understand why people loved that town.

He stopped in front of Big Bear's Restaurant and walked inside. A cute young waitress stood behind the lunch counter so he ambled up and slid onto a stool. "Hi there," he said.

Kim had seen him in there before and long ago decided he was a ball of slime. The man obviously over indulged in everything and thought very highly of himself, both of which turned her off. "Hi," she said, not even forcing a smile. "What can I get you?"

Undaunted by her cold demeanor, Henderson said, "What's an attractive young woman like you do on your evenings off?"

"We have an omelet special today," she said, motioning toward a sign beside the kitchen door. "Let me know when you decide what you want."

"Hey, get me two eggs over easy with bacon and sausage, and extra home fries," he said, thinking *she's a bitch*. "What's the latest with the murders in town?"

Who *is* this guy, she wondered, then said, "Read the papers."

"Awe, come on, you must hear stuff."

He's an asshole connected with United Eastern Power, Kim guessed. What was he fishing for? She leaned close, as if sharing a secret, and said, "I heard someone from the power company killed the Hammonds and the Tolls, all four of them. The State Police have proof."

He laughed and said, "That's ridiculous. United Eastern Power has too much to lose."

Kim wasn't listening, but instead disappeared into the kitchen.

Henderson scratched at his belly. Was she toying with him? She hadn't even poured him a coffee. The last time he had visited that restaurant he tipped her a fifty on a ten dollar meal, and then pinched her ass on his way out the door. The memory brought a smile. Could she still be pissed about that? His next meal would be over at The Fenton House where the bartender was a bit friendlier, or at least knew how to play the game.

He read the paper and the cook brought out his breakfast. It wasn't until he turned to look back on leaving that he saw the waitress again.

Wiping down the counter, Kim went over again the previous evening with Will. He had seemed distant or distracted. Was she losing him? Did she ever have him?

After their meal, they went back to his place for a drink on his porch. When it became obvious that he wasn't inviting her to stay, she left. Was it Barbara Hawkins? She had to be how old…almost Will's age. Could he *really* be interested in her?

Climbing back into his truck, Henderson glanced at his gold Cartier watch. There was time to kill before meeting the investors, so he drove out of town and turned right toward the remains of the Hammond's home. He hadn't seen it since right after the place burned. Slowing as he passed, nothing had changed.

Continuing on down the far side of the hill, he noticed a mailbox with the name Hawkins on it. Wasn't that the name of one of the properties that United Eastern Power needed? He was sure of it, and it was owned by a woman that Frank Atkins used to visit regularly. Henderson laughed. Atkins had said he would sweet talk her into selling, but that never happened, which didn't surprise Henderson. Atkins had the charm of a slug and wasn't much of a lady's man. Henderson though maybe he would stop and see her later.

*

Jake woke with a head that complained bitterly about the quantity of alcohol consumed the previous night. With his eyes still shut, he hand slid across the sheets, expecting to find Suzy Toll's warm flesh. She wasn't there, so he thought she must be in the kitchen making breakfast.

In spite of his best attempts, he couldn't remember getting into bed, or even coming home. The last thing he recalled was going to Pricilla's Northwoods Emporium, looking for the private investigator. He couldn't recall Jimmy Deluga's name, and wasn't even sure if he ever knew it.

The face he would never forget though because the guy had promised money.

While waiting at the bar, he had doused a couple of drinks and then started to play pool with some buddies. That was the last thing he remembered.

Slipping from the bed, he realized he was still dressed…at least that made starting the morning easier. A belch rolled up from his gut and he wandered toward the kitchen, wondering why he couldn't smell coffee.

Suzy wasn't there.

Jake stepped outside to the edge of the back deck and peed on the weeds he called a lawn. Where the fuck could she have gone? His truck was in the driveway, so she didn't drive away. Did she walk somewhere? He went back inside and into the bedroom.

He yanked out the second drawer down from the dresser and it fell to the floor. It was empty. Suzy's clothes were gone. The few things that she used to hang in the closet were missing too. The bitch had left him.

Jake walked out of the front door to the gravel drive. The only tire marks were from his own truck. Did she really walk? It was a long way to anywhere from his place. And how did she carry everything? A helper? Could it have been that fucking private investigator…Jimmy? That was his name!

That was the man's first name…what was his last? Enough alcohol had seeped from Jake's brain for him to remember Suzy calling that city-slicker-asshole Jimmy.

He stomped inside and grabbed a beer from the refrigerator. Eggs and coffee would have been nice, but a beer was certainly easier.

What the hell does she see in that jerk, he wondered. Money? Did she think she could fuck her way to his wallet? He took a long swallow. That schmuck will drop her like a stone. Guys like him want classy broads, not some bimbo.

He set the empty beer can down with thud and opened a drawer under the counter. There he kept an old Ruger single action pistol that he won years before in a card game. The 45 caliber bullets had punched huge holes in paper targets the few times that he had shot it. Twice, when big snowshoe rabbits had wandered into the back yard, it turned them nearly inside out. Maybe it was time to punch big holes in something else.

He stuffed the pistol in his belt and stepped out the back door. For no reason that he would ever remember, the old tote road that entered the woods at the far edge of his weedy lawn caught his eye. Did they go that way? Other than just wading into the surrounding forest or the driveway, it was the only way in or out from his property.

Like everyone in that part of the country, Jake had hunted deer. He walked to the old grown-in road and looked for tracks.

Leaves in various stages of decay covered the ground, but some had been disturbed. It might have been a deer or a moose, but they would have left footprints on the soft lawn. He decided it had to have been human feet that moved through those leaves.

Staring down the old road, Jake mumbled, "Dumb mother fuckers."

*

The wood splitter sputtered and then abruptly stopped. Will straightened up and looked at the pile of firewood. It would easily heat his house for the coming winter, and possibly most of the next. The mindless busywork suited his mood and he walked toward the barn to find the gas can.

"Grandpa, grandpa." It was Ethan running from the house. "Mom says to come in, she has breakfast for you."

Will grabbed Ethan's shoulders and tossed him up in the air to catch him on the way down, and then set him gently on the ground. "She does?"

"Yup, your favorite. Pancakes and bacon." Ethan started to climb up the woodpile as if it were a small mountain.

"Be careful," said Will. "Are you going to have breakfast with me?"

Ethan ran down the firewood pile to the ground again. "Yeah. What are we going to do today? Do you have to work?"

Will smiled...sometimes he had to remind himself. "I can do whatever I want today. What do you want to do?"

"Can we go see the horse again?"

They started toward the house. "Barbara Hawkins's horse?"

"Yeah. The nice lady with the horse."

"Do you remember the horse's name?"

"Martha Washington."

"When we get to the house, why don't you call Barbara Hawkins and ask if we can visit Martha. I bet she'll let us."

"Do you think I can ride Martha again?"

"You'll have to ask her."

Ethan ran on ahead and yelled back over his shoulder, "I will."

"Remember to be polite and ask nicely." Will knew the boy would. Amy had done a great job of raising him.

The air smelled of grass and a light breeze wafted in from the northwest. It was hard to imagine a nicer day, or a pleasanter place to be than on his own property. Far overhead a red tailed hawk made lazy circles in the sky. Maybe he would spend some time in the vegetable garden later.

As Will reached the house a dark blue pickup truck turned into the end of his driveway, as if to turn around. That wasn't an unusual event, as his place was the last on the road. The driver must have spotted Will though, because it proceeded up the drive. Will noticed the out of state number plate.

"What a beautiful spot," said the driver, stepping out.

Will didn't like the guy. He wasn't sure why, but it was a first impression sort-of-thing, so he tried to brush that aside because it was based on nothing. "I think so too," he said. "What can I do for you?"

"My name's Bob Hanson," said Robert Henderson. "I'm thinking of retiring up this way. I'd love to find a place like this."

The man looked familiar, like Will had seen him on TV or in the newspaper. Not offering a handshake or his name, he said, "That's what I did."

"What's a place like this cost?"

Will felt a red flag. "Oh, I don't know. You'd be better off talking to a realtor." The guy smiled like a car salesman. Was his name really Hanson?

Hanson asked, "How long have you owned this place?"

"Not long," said Will. "There's a couple of realtors in town, both are good." He turned and started up the stairs to the house.

The man, whatever his real name was, took the hint and climbed back into his truck.

*

Jimmy Deluga pulled the blankets up to his chin and listened to the stream. It did sound like the cars on FDR Drive, which runs along the East River next to Manhattan. Only the honking of horns was missing. The cabin smelled of wood and a large truck rumbled by out on the highway. The bed wasn't bad, but he would be glad to get back to his luxurious Manhattan apartment. The time up in the sticks was just one of the things that he had to do to pay for it.

In spite of the closed shades, the room was quite bright. Turning on his side, he settled into the pillow and shut his eyes. He couldn't think of any reason to get up before noon.

35

"Can I make us some lunch?" asked Barbara Hawkins, holding Martha Washington's bridle.

"How about I take us all out to lunch?" said Will. The look on Ethan's face said the boy didn't want to stop riding, but he was too polite to protest verbally.

For over an hour Ethan and Will had been visiting Barbara. She had patiently showed Ethan how to saddle Martha, not that he was big or strong enough to do it, but he watched intently. Will balanced his grandson up on the saddle and then Barbara led the horse around the yard and paddock. Ethan grinned the entire time.

"I'd like that," said Barbara. "I can't remember the last time I ate lunch out."

After they turned Martha back out into the pasture, they drove to town in Will's truck with Ethan in the middle of the front seat. Not wanting to bump into Kim at Big Bear's Restaurant, he parked in front of The Fenton House Inn. Two identical shiny new Chevy Suburbans were parked in the front also.

"This is a pretty fancy place for lunch," said Barbara, stepping out of the truck. "I've only come here for dinner." She silently knew Kim might be working at Big Bear's and why Will had chosen The Fenton House.

Ethan dashed ahead to hold the door open for Barbara and his grandfather. They took a table at the far end of the tavern. When a waitress appeared, Will and Barbara ordered iced tea and Ethan a lemonade.

"The place is busy," said Barbara, opening a menu.

A group of men wearing jackets with ties sat around a large table, obviously together. The heavy man who had stopped at Will's house earlier in the morning was with them, but he hadn't noticed him walk in.

"They must be business men," said Will.

"From United Eastern Power?" asked Barbara.

"It wouldn't surprise me." Will handed Ethan a pen to draw with on his paper placemat.

A man walked in that Will recognized from when he visited the bar the night before with Kim. He wore a blue windbreaker this time, rather than the sports jacket that hid his pistol the previous time. Will wondered if a gun hid under the windbreaker too.

Stopping inside the door, the man surveyed the room, paying particular attention to the group of businessmen, and then took a seat at the bar where he could see both of the room's entrances. Will decided the man must be a pro. But what kind? Private detective? Or a maybe Fed?

The woman bartender that had been so friendly with that man the night before wasn't there, but the guy tending bar seemed to know him. The man's head never turned directly toward the businessmen, but his eyes frequently glanced their way.

The heavy guy that had visited Will's place earlier happened to look at the bar and did a double take when he noticed the new arrival. After a momentary glare, he ignored the man. They obviously knew each other and the heavy man didn't want the new arrival there.

"Are you all right?" asked Barbara, touching his hand.

Will clasped her fingers. "Yes." Ethan looked to be engrossed in whatever he was drawing, so Will explained to Barbara what he had noticed.

They ordered food and talked about the weather. Another unsettled hot sticky air mass approached from the west. Barbara said swimming in the river would be the only relief.

"You'll have to take me to that special spot again," said Will, with a big smile.

"Look," said Barbara, nodding toward the front entry.

A wiry muscular man about Will's height had just entered, wearing dirty work clothes with a pistol stuck in his belt. He looked around, as if searching for somebody. Nobody else in the bar noticed him.

The bartender glanced the man's way, and said, "Sit anywhere." Then he went back to polishing a glass.

Will couldn't believe it. Didn't the bartender notice the pistol? Were things up there really that different from the suburbs where he had come from? Apparently.

The man in the blue windbreaker pulled the left side of his jacket back. Was he exposing a gun? His face looked cold as stone.

Will put his hand on Ethan's shoulder, ready to push him to the floor.

The new arrival smiled, and then the man in the blue windbreaker did too, motioning him over. The two sat together at the bar and the man in the windbreaker bought them both drinks.

"I wonder what they are talking about?" said Barbara.

The two men laughed like old buddies.

"I'll be back in a minute," said Will.

He walked to the men's room, which brought him by the table with the business men at it. Hanson, or whatever the man's name was, never looked at Will as he passed. On the table were maps, photographs, and brochures. The "United Eastern Power" logo was on several papers, plus embossed on two briefcases.

Returning to the seat beside Barbara, Will said, "That group is definitely with the power company."

Barbara said, "I wonder what they are talking about."

"Maybe they are the investors," said Will. The two men at the bar still appeared to be friendly.

"Look at this," said Ethan, holding up a picture of a horse. "It's Martha Washington."

They complimented his drawing as their meals arrived.

"Look, there's Frank," said Barbara. "Frank Atkins, the man who was buying land for United Eastern Power."

The last time Will had seen Frank was out in the woods, the time before that he had shut his door in the man's face. Of course he had visited Barbara too. Several of the men at the United Eastern Power table stood when he arrived and seemed to know him. Amid handshakes and laughter, they all sat again.

"He must be late," said Will, before taking a bite out of his hamburger.

"I liked the man," said Barbara, "but not the company he works for."

The twinge of jealousy surprised Will.

*

Jimmy Deluga's heart had skipped a beat when he noticed Jake stride in the bar's door. That's when reflexes caused him to push his jacket back for easier access to his concealed pistol. On noticing the pistol tucked into Jake's belt, Jimmy started to reach for his gun.

But the smile that spread across Jake's face when he spotted Jimmy defused any anguish.

"Hey, man," said Jake, as he approached. "I've been looking for you."

"I was going to go to Pricilla's Emporium later to see if you'd be around," said Jimmy, not really sure if he meant it or not. "Let me buy you a drink. What'll you have?"

"A Bud."

Jimmy nodded to the bartender, who had obviously overheard, and said, "I'll have another too."

"That's quite a weapon you got there," said Jimmy.

"Oh that, I won it in a card game, years ago. I forgot I was carrying it."

Jimmy wondered how that was possible, it had to weigh a couple of pounds and couldn't have been comfortable stuck in his belt like it was. When the bartender set their drinks down, Jimmy gave the man a scowl. The man took the hint and wandered to the other end of the bar.

"Have you heard anything?"

"Yeah," said Jake. "Them Hammonds was killed by old man Toll. Everybody in town is saying that."

"You got any proof?"

"Not yet, but I'm onto something. I can't tell you what it is. Not yet."

Jimmy guessed it was all bullshit, just a lie hoping to earn some cash. "What about the Tolls?"

"Well, that's a tough one." Jake looked uncomfortable. "Nobody knew them well."

Jimmy sipped his bourbon while Jake babbled on, only half listening. It all made sense. Jake was shacking up with the Toll's daughter. With the vast sums of money involved, he had much to gain if she inherited her parent's property, particularly if he married her. After the Hammonds had turned down the power company's offer, old man Toll could have killed the Hammonds, hoping that whoever ended up with the land would take their deal. Then Jake took things a step further.

But Henderson would want proof before he paid Jimmy another cent. How could he get it?

"Bartender," said Jimmy, "bring Jake here another beer."

*

Brian and Suzy Toll walked down to where the river slowed and snaked through the valley. The only scattered houses were up nearer the highway, out of the way when the stream flooded its banks during the spring runoffs.

It was easy for Brian and Suzy to stay undetected. In places the moose had worn muddy paths, but most of the way they tread on firm soil crowned with knee-high ferns. Near town, they walked out of the woods to follow the streets.

Suzy led Brian into the second biggest store in town, the hardware store. The grocery store might have been larger, but it didn't have the possibilities they were looking for. A lone young man worked the cash register island in the front section, surrounded by battery displays, maple products, and a display case of Schrade pocket knives. The only other staff member stocked shelves in the home plumbing isle.

Brian stopped to look at electrical fixtures, while Suzy wandered over to talk with the man at the register. She learned his name was Justin and that he had only worked there a short while. Her breasts swelled above her skimpy tank top, distracting the young man terribly. When she asked about frying pans, he gladly led her to the kitchen department. While the register was unattended, Brian scooped the large bills out from under the cash drawer and then slipped out the side door. Wearing a big smile, Suzy thanked Justin and then followed after Brian.

Ten minutes later they were tracing their earlier path along the river, both a bit giddy from their success. About a mile from town a combination variety store and gas station stood beside a small motel on the highway. They walked up and bought a bag full of groceries and, on a whim, Suzy set a twelve pack of beer and four bottles of wine next to the register. The woman at the cash register never asked for any identification and happily took their money.

They ducked back into the woods to walk under the silver maples and elms along the river. The day had become hot and humid, so a half mile from the store they decided to stop for a swim where the river made a hairpin turn. A sandbar poked out from the inside of the bend, creating a peninsula and their own private beach.

"Don't you get bored?" asked Suzy, popping up from the river and squeezing the water from her hair.

"No," said Brian, sitting on the sandy bottom beside her, with the water up to his shoulders. "Finding food keeps me busy. And I like just being out in the woods."

They both wore their underwear, planning to dry in the sun before dressing again.

"Let's have a beer," said Suzy, standing to walk out of the water. Her wet underwear had become transparent, which made Brian very uncomfortable. She asked, "How much money do you got?"

He shrugged his shoulders. "Whatever we got today, plus about twenty bucks."

Suzy laughed. "You were broke. What were you going to do?"

Brian had been trying not to think about it. Stealing money wasn't the same as stealing vegetables from someone's garden, at least in his mind. It was something he preferred not to do, but Suzy made it look so easy

"I took some cash from Jake's," said Suzy, opening a beer with a pop. "He had it hid and's going to be pissed." She held the beer out for Brian to take.

Reluctantly, he stood from the river. "Much?"

"Just a couple a hundred." In the wet underwear, she might as well been naked. He fought to keep his eyes away from the two dark orbs on her chest.

Brian dropped to sit on the sand against a washed up log, facing the river. The beer tasted good, so he guzzled half of the can. Suzy sat beside him. Together they counted the hardware store's money. Eight hundred and thirteen dollars, after buying the groceries.

"We'll split it," said Suzy.

Brian had been thinking of it as "theirs", not half for each of them. "What are you going to do with yours?" he asked.

"I'm going south, to someplace where it's warm all year." His face must have showed hurt or surprise, because she added, "I can't stay here. You can come too."

"I don't want to go anywhere else," he said, then took a large swallow of beer.

"What are you going to do in the winter?"

"My cabin will be done and I'll be fine." He polished off the last of his beer and crinkled the can into a ball with one hand.

"What if someone finds your place? Somebody owns that land. Someday the landowner will want to cut those trees."

Brian knew she was right. It was something he tried hard to ignore. She opened another beer and handed it to him without a word. He took another large drink. "I might go west," he said. "There's work in North Dakota I heard, where a man can make lots of money."

Suzy sipped her beer and smiled. "I thought about that too. There's lots of men there working the shale oil. It's like the old gold rush days. The winters are brutal there though." The lost look on his face made her say, "You're only fifteen."

He took a long slug, the beer buzz glowed. "I'll be sixteen next summer."

Suzy downed the last of her first beer, and said, "It's hot, I'm going for a swim again."

"Our underwear will never dry," said Brian.

"Ha, I'm not going to wear mine," she said, standing and slipping hers off. Sand stuck to her legs and rear.

He watched the sway of her hips and the bounce of her hair. "You look fucking hot," said Brian, surprising himself.

Looking back over her shoulder, Suzy said, "I know."

36

Burt Bertram followed the edge of the softwoods down toward the river. The hellishly steep land made walking difficult. Dropped spruce and fir needles covered the ground and made it slippery, so he constantly reached for tree trunks to maintain his footing.

The property belonged to Barbara Hawkins, but was far from her home. Burt had spotted the large softwood trees from Will's land a few days earlier and made a mental note to walk in and see what harvesting them would involve. Some of the white spruce were so big two men together could not put their arms around the trunks. Burt hadn't seen any spruce like that in decades.

It would be tough land to log, but a chainsaw crew with skidders could do it. Burt hoped to find an area at the bottom of the hill where the wood could be yarded, and then a way to build a road in to truck the wood out.

White wood, where a small branch had been snapped off a fir tree, caught his eye. He stopped, wondering what had broken it, and noticed a path traveling along the contour of the hill. A game trail? Probably. Game animals often knew the easiest way to travel, so Burt decided to follow it a way and see where it went. Perhaps there was an easier way down the hill.

He felt something brush his leg and then a log dropped next to him with a thud.

Burt froze.

Against his leg a strand of monofilament fishing line ran between a stake in the ground and a prop that had kept the log two feet above the ground. A human had to have done it. Was it a primitive attempt at a trap? There didn't appear to be any bait near the fallen log. Could it be an alarm to alert someone of intruders?

A red squirrel chattered nearby, and then another answered further away. Far below in the valley the river whispered one long never ending song. Burt could hear his own heart beating. Someplace above the hill a raven rattled its raspy call.

Burt backed up and turned around. Too many strange things had been happening lately and he did not want to encounter somebody who needed an alarm. The Game Warden, John Johansson, was paid to deal with that sort of thing.

*

"How much further is it?" asked Suzy.

"We're almost there," said Brian, understanding her anxiousness. The groceries and wine were heavy. The softwood trees muffled their footsteps and blotted out the sky, but they were not far from his hidden cabin.

The afternoon had been spent swimming and drinking beer by the river. It was the longest time he had ever spent talking with his sister. Between the beer and the warm sun loosening inhibitions, they shared secrets that had never been told.

Brian learned their father had often made lewd suggestive remarks to Suzy, and had even snuck up behind her once to slide a hand up under her shirt to caress a breast. She both hated and feared the man, which inspired her to become the brat that she had always been. Even she wasn't sure how many times she had run away from home. The last time, which was with Jake, happened just after her sixteenth birthday. That time her father didn't even try to bring her back.

Suzy knew their father had hit Brian multiple times, and once, when he came home drunk, beat Brian to the point he stayed out of school for several days while his blackened eye returned to normal. Brian said that only thing that kept him from running away, like his sister had done, was he wanted to protect their mother from their father.

At some point in the middle of the afternoon they both had noticed how pink the other was becoming from the sun. The sight, combined with the effects of the beer, brought a round of laughter like Brian hadn't experienced in years, and for the first time he felt like he had a relationship of sorts with his sibling. By then the day's heat had waned and their clothes had dried long before, so they dressed and started back.

"Stop," whispered Brian, holding up a hand. "Someone tripped the alarm." Beside him, the once propped up log rested on the ground. Listening, they could hear nothing inside the thick stand of softwood trees, except the taunt of the river down in the valley. The air felt heavy and smelled of fir.

"It probably was a deer," whispered Suzy.

He knew she was probably right because the path originally had been a game trail. Brian motioned for her to be quiet, and slowly led the way along the path. Nearing the camp, he indicated for her to stay put while he crept ahead.

A few minutes later he returned. "Nobody is there," he said.

"I told you it was probably a deer," said Suzy.

"You go on ahead," said Brian. "I'm going to reset the alarm."

Balancing the log on the prop had not been easy the first time and proved just as difficult the second time. After three attempts, he finally got it to stay in place. Before walking back to the camp, he searched the ground for deer tracks, but found none on the needle covered ground. It seemed as though a startled animal would have made some sort of mark.

Hurrying to catch up with Suzy in camp, he wondered how many beers were left.

*

Jimmy Deluga drove past the two shiny Chevy Suburban's parked next to a vast field. The same group that had been at the restaurant now stood beside the vehicles, with all eyes looking to where Robert Henderson pointed at a far-off hill. Frank Atkins listened with his hands stuffed inside his pockets, looking like he would rather be someplace else. The rest of the group listened patiently to Henderson's spiel. Jimmy wondered if any of them asked about the charred remains of the Hammond's home, which they had passed only a half mile before they had parked.

Inside Jimmy's Escalade, Jake babbled on about who owned each of the properties they had passed, complete with their ages, who they were related to, what each did for a living, and the marital prospects of any young female family members. Jimmy hardly listened to any of it, but used his peripheral vision to keep an eye on Jake's big revolver, which sat on the console between them.

When the group of business men had stood up to leave the Fenton House Inn after lunch, Jake still lingered on a barstool next to Jimmy. Hoping to follow Henderson, if for no reason other than to make the man nervous, Jimmy dropped a hundred dollar bill on the bar top to cover their tab and asked Jake if he wanted to go for a ride. Fear flashed across Jake's face, possibly he thought Jimmy was going to kill him.

Jake's terrified expression brought a warm feeling to Jimmy, who then explained that he wanted someone with local knowledge to tell him who owned the properties along the proposed power line route.

Jake offered, "I'm your man."

Driving away from the cluster of men standing at the roadside, Jimmy wondered if either Henderson or Atkins had noticed him drive by.

"The next place belongs to Barbara Hawkins," said Jake.

The name Barbara caught Jimmy's attention. It was a name he always liked, probably due to memories of Barbara Kolinsky, one of his first childhood crushes. He asked, "What's she like?"

"Another fucking fruit cake," said Jake. "She turned down a barrel full of money from the power company."

A large white farmhouse came into view, set way back from the road on the left side. The place looked neat, with flowers growing along the front and black shutters beside the windows. Out back, a horse stood in a paddock beside a weathered red barn. A farmer's porch stretched around the front of the main house and up one side, and flowering plants dangled from hanging pots. The lawn looked recently mowed and very green.

"She keeps a neat place," said Jimmy, noticing a vegetable garden in the back too. "What does she look like?"

Neatness was a concept that eluded Jake…he just saw a place owned by a woman who had lucked into money. "She's a looker, for her age anyway. I guess she's about fifty."

A Rav4 sat next to the house. "How much land does she have?"

"A shitload."

Going down the hill the country became wooded with several long driveways that disappeared into the trees. Jake babbled on about each of the unseen homes. Some of the lots were small and the owners had never been approached by United Eastern Power, but most of the larger ones had been visited by them. Jake seemed to know all the details.

At the bottom of the hill the woods opened into large flat fields and the road turned abruptly to the left.

"The last house belongs to a flatlander named Wilson Northrop. Everybody just calls him Will. He's rich."

"Rich?"

"Yeah. Retired up here and bought this place. There's hundreds of acres here. He doesn't have a real job."

Jimmy wondered how rich. From the ads he'd seen in the newspapers, property up there was cheap. For what a large home sold for near New York City, you could buy half the town.

"He don't need United Power's money, that's my guess," said Jake. "They approached him too, but he turned them down."

Where the road petered out the driveway to Will's place went off to the left. The house looked like a big Cape sheltered beneath a handful of enormous white pines. A screened-in porch stretched across the side that faced the distant mountains across the road. Behind the house a big barn stood before a large field that stretched off for hundreds of yards.

"That's the Game Warden's truck up there," said Jake. "I wonder what he's doing there."

Also beside the house, an old International Scout sat behind a silver Ford pickup and a Camry. To Jake that many vehicles meant a party.

Jimmy wondered what the hell Game Wardens actually did.

He turned into the driveway to turn around. Starting back the direction they had come, a Rav4 approached.

"That's Barbara Hawkins," said Jake. "She must be going to the party too."

Jimmy wondered what the hell Jake was talking about.

When the vehicles passed, Jimmy caught a glimpse of her and thought she looked very attractive. And also wondered what the hell was going on in the house she was obviously headed for. A moment later a large dark green pickup truck with a young man driving went by.

Was he going there too? Maybe it was a party.

37

"Tomorrow morning then, at seven," said Johansson. "We'll meet right here."

"I'm sorry that I have to work," said Barbara.

Ethan balanced on Shawn's knee, imagining himself on Martha Washington's back. Amy stood beside the two with her hand on Shawn's thick shoulder. Burt sat at the table and alternated between sips on a bottle of beer and his flask.

Earlier, Burt had walked out of the woods beyond Will's house and told him about the trip line he had encountered. Using Will's phone, he called John Johansson and they agreed to meet there. Because the trip line was on Barbara's land, Will called to ask her to come over too. By coincidence, Shawn Ash dropped in to visit with Amy and listened to Burt's story as he told it to John and Barbara. The description of the large spruce trees caught his attention.

"I'll go with you," said Shawn. "If you don't mind. I'd like to see the wood."

Will liked the idea of the big strapping young man coming along, and said, "That's a good idea." There was no telling what they might find, which was why it suited him fine that Barbara wouldn't be coming with them.

"Of course you can come along," said Johansson, glancing at his watch. "I have to get going. I promised Cindy I'd go to a meeting with her."

Barbara smiled and said, "You two are becoming quite the couple."

"She's talking about moving up here," he said, grinning. "She wants to start a business selling local farm products on the Internet."

*

"They're gone," said Jake, as they approached where Henderson and his group had been beside the road.

"Probably playing golf," said Jimmy. "With business men, you can almost bet on it."

"There's only one course, just east of town."

They rode there and, sure enough, the two shiny Suburbans were parked by the club house. Jake had yakked the whole way and Jimmy tried to filter out what sounded like bullshit, which was most of it, from what might be real.

"I have things I need to do," said Jimmy. "How about I drop you in town and we meet at Pricilla's about eleven? Maybe you can find out more about that guy at the end of the road, Wilson Northrop." Giving Jake a task would make him feel needed and trusted.

Jimmy went back to his rented cabin and opened the window to hear the rumble of the nearby stream, and then turned on the television to create noise. He really missed the constant stimulation of the city. Dropping onto the bed, he opened up his laptop computer. In the modern era, more could be learned via the World Wide Web than working the streets.

He found several news pieces about Will Northrop. One told about the accident that killed his wife. Another mentioned his involvement in a Trout Unlimited stream conservation project. There appeared to be no dirt…the man had never been arrested or involved in anything shady. Leverage, that's what Jimmy wanted, something he could pry a man away from his morals with.

A copy of Will's wife's obituary mentioned a daughter, Amy, and a grandson, Ethan. There was possible leverage there. Jimmy wondered where they lived. A simple search turned up Duxbury, Massachusetts.

Jimmy typed in Robert Henderson's name and came up with 72,312,567 hits. There certainly were a lot of people named Robert Henderson. He added United Eastern Power to the search and whittled it down to 984,781.

Several pictures showed him shaking hands with politicians. In several, an attractive blonde woman stood smiling by his side, which Jimmy guessed to be his wife. For an hour Jimmy sifted through the information, but learned nothing new.

He typed in Frank Atkins.

The man led a putridly boring life, selling automobiles and real estate, until he fell into the job at United Eastern Power. For the last two years he had been trying to buy up land along the power line's route. He was married with kids, but Jimmy could find nothing about other interests. At least Henderson had smiled in his pictures and played golf. When Jimmy found pictures of Atkins his smile always looked forced, like he really wanted to be somewhere else.

He didn't know Jake's last name, but used Google to search local police records. A Jake Parquett came up often, and finally a mug shot picture that cinched the identity. He had been arrested multiple times for drunkenness, fighting, driving under the influence. There was no record of him even entering high school, let alone graduating. His life appeared to be a road to nowhere.

Jimmy showered and shaved, then put on clean pressed clothes. If he stayed up there much longer his clothes would need laundering and ironing. Jimmy always dressed to impress and the clothing he had brought along was limited.

Twenty minutes later he walked into the bar at The Fenton House where that night Brenda tended bar. He chose a seat away from other patrons so he could talk to her without being heard.

"What'll you have?" she said, approaching with a smile.

"Old Forester bourbon," said Jimmy. "Where's all the business boys?"

"They left a few minutes ago, heading north. I bet they're having dinner up at Big Spruce Lodge."

"Skip the bourbon," said Jimmy, dropping a fifty dollar tip on the bar top.

Thirty minutes later he walked into the pine paneled lobby of Big Spruce Lodge. A stuffed bobcat, perched on a shelf over the front desk, glared at all who entered. The attractive woman behind the counter didn't look up as he passed. A younger woman with a big smile and straight blonde hair met him at the hostess podium. Jimmy tried to remember if there had been any other women in dresses since he had left Manhattan. When asked, Jimmy admitted he had no reservation and said he planned to eat in the Wanigan Pub. A painting of a majestic moose hung on the wall behind her.

"There's a private party in there tonight," she said. "The tables are all taken, but you can sit at the bar."

"That's fine," he said, noticing her six inch heels. She was a tiny little thing with perky breasts that pressed against the front of her dress. "Maybe we could have a drink together later."

She smiled. "I have a boyfriend."

"I hope he knows how lucky he is," said Jimmy.

The tables inside were filled with the same men that had eaten lunch earlier at The Fenton House. Some stood to talk, but most sat, all drank and appeared to be having fun. A large moose head hung on the wall over a muted TV that played a Red Sox game. A larger one to his left had a fishing show on. Frank Atkins was back to Jimmy, but even back-to looked bored. Robert Henderson faced the TV under the moose.

Jimmy slid onto a stool at the bar beside an attractive woman whose perfect hair, eye liner, and mascara looked out of place with her jeans and hiking boots. Long earrings flashed beside her neck and he looked to see if there was a ring on her finger. There was none.

"Hi," he said, offering a hand, "Jim Frank." His peripheral vision watched Henderson.

"Betsy," she said, shaking his hand.

Boston accent, he thought, asking, "Up here fishing?"

"Yes, with my boyfriend."

Jimmy guessed she would rather be shopping. He knew he would. "Have you been catching anything?"

"Probably a cold," she laughed. "My boyfriend is into this, not me. Here he comes now."

While Jimmy ordered a bourbon a man about fortyish slid onto the barstool the other side of Betsy and introduced himself as Charles Cabot. Typical WASP with old Boston money, thought Jimmy—button collar, blue eyes, and not an ounce of fat.

Betsy said, "I was just telling Jimmy how good a fisherman you are."

"Not really," he said. "In the evening the fish have been hitting blue winged olives with abandon. It has almost been too easy."

As easy as going to the fish market? Jimmy failed to see any fun in fishing.

Charles Cabot asked, "Are you fishing too?"

Jimmy said he worked as a consultant for the state tourism board and was on an information gathering trip. Henderson had turned, but still had not noticed Jimmy at the bar. The look in his eyes indicated a blood alcohol level of at least point one point zero.

"Too bad about that proposed power line," said Charles. "It would take a lot of the charm out of this area."

Jimmy couldn't imagine that "charm" Charles was talking about, the area was nothing but a wasteland of trees and mountains, but said, "I know what you mean."

Henderson noticed Jimmy on the barstool. His eyes flashed hate.

Then he sauntered over, wearing a forced smile, to set his hand on Jimmy's shoulder. "What a surprise to see you here," he said.

Jimmy loved to make people squirm, so took a moment to sip his drink. He noticed a bead of sweat swell on Henderson's temple. Setting down his glass, Jimmy said, "It is nice to see you too."

"Can I talk to you a minute?" said Henderson. "Outside."

Jimmy made no move to get off his stool. "What's up?"

Henderson shot a nasty glance at the couple beside Jimmy. The woman then turned her back and leaned closer to her man.

"You got any news?" said Henderson.

"Nothing concrete," answered Jimmy, again sipping his bourbon. Henderson's discomfort was fun to watch.

"I'd rather not see you again until you have something to tell me," said Henderson.

The man's size might have normally been mildly intimidating, but, with his alcohol inspired unsteadiness, the guy was a joke. "You'll see me whenever I want to see you," said Jimmy. "Let's step outside."

On the plank walkway, between the lobby and the docks on the lake, Jimmy stopped to light up a cigarette, offering one to Henderson, who refused.

"I only smoke one or two a month," said Jimmy, exhaling the smoke. "It's such a shame they are bad for us."

He went on to tell Henderson how Jerome Toll had killed the Hammonds, hoping that whoever inherited their land would sell to United Eastern Power.

"You got proof?" said Henderson.

"Close. It's true though."

"I need proof."

"You'll get it. Right now you can appease your money men with the story."

"So what happened to the Tolls?"

"Someone wanted their land."

"Their land too? Who?"

"I got it figured out, but it's going to be tough to prove."

Behind them, the screen door slammed as a patron left the lobby. The footsteps sounded loud on the wooden planks, but faded toward the parking lot. Far across the lake a loon made a mournful call.

"I've got to get going," said Jimmy, tossing the cigarette into the water.

Thirty five minutes later he walked into Pricilla's and slid onto a barstool next to Jake, who appeared hammered. Obviously, he wasn't going to learn much from him, but asked anyway, "Anything new?"

"Ya, da dumb lil' bitch run off en I miss her."

Jimmy wondered just how much alcohol Jake had consumed.

"Ta my tinkin'," mumbled Jake, "she run off with you." His face showed more drowsiness than defiance.

The bartender approached and Jimmy motioned her away, then said, "I haven't seen her."

Jake worked at focusing on Jimmy's eyes. "I believe ya," he said. "You're too big a pussy to a taken her through da woods. I tink she's wid her brother."

Jimmy ignored the remark. "Where's he?"

"He's livin' out in da woods somewheres."

"Where?"

Jake's head bobbled a bit, as if fighting to think, then he said, "Fucked if I know."

38

The wicker loveseat squeaked when Will shifted his weight, sipping coffee inside the screened porch. Outside, a gray glow lit the eastern sky. The trees across the far side of the field created a jagged black edge against the pale light. One lonely star still refused to fade. In the motionless morning air, the whisper of the river carried all the way across the fields to the house.

Sleep had been elusive. The simple life he sought in a rural setting had slipped away. While he lay in bed, thoughts of Amy and Ethan, Barbara and Kim, and the mysteries surrounding the Hammonds and Tolls bounced through his head. Finally, he got up to make coffee.

"What are you doing up?" said Amy, stepping into the porch still wearing her pajamas and carrying a steaming mug.

"I couldn't sleep," said Will. "My brain wouldn't stop thinking."

Amy smiled. "Can't decide?"

He knew she meant between Barbara and Kim. "That's part of it."

She settled onto the seat beside him. "Are Ethan and I…crowding your space?"

"No. You being up here is a dream come true. It's the power line company and what happened to the Hammonds, and the Tolls too. That sort of thing isn't supposed to happen up here."

Amy blew on her coffee to cool it. "Did you see Barbara last night?"

"Yes," he nodded, adding, "She's nice."

Amy warily sipped from the mug, then said, "The coffee is good. I could smell it upstairs." She took another swallow, then added, "I like her. She's good to Ethan. What about Kim? Are you seeing her again?"

Will shrugged a shoulder. "Maybe. There's no plans at the moment."

Amy mentioned that she planned to take Ethan to a playground in town later, hoping he would meet kids his own age, and then had another meeting with the realtor.

*

Brian Toll woke nestled against his sister's backside. Inside the little shelter, tucked beneath the thick softwood trees, no light entered through the one window. She smelled heavenly and her warmth permeated the thin tee shirt she wore. The soft hair on the back of her head rested beside Brian's face.

His arousal pressed against the front of his jeans.

He didn't dare move, enjoying the feeling…so alive and strong and invincible…he ached to caress a breast and press his mouth into hers…the tension needed to be released.

Silently, he took a deep breath, and then rolled away from her to climb from the bed.

Outside, tiny patches of sooty sky poked between the dark branches overhead. An owl hooted from somewhere down the hill and the river continued its constant crackle. Brian gathered up a few sticks and arranged them in his stone lined fire pit, atop a shred of stringy birch bark. A single match started the blaze and the burning twigs snapped and popped. He settled back on a log to watch. The fire wasn't as warm as Suzy.

It was lonely out there, he hated to admit it. And Suzy…the pleasures she had introduced. Brian wondered about girls he had known in school. What they were doing? And were they as warm and soft and sweet as his sister? Memories of one in particular, Nancy Bilideau, a brown-eyed girl with a shiny black ponytail, brought a smile to his face.

He tossed another fistful of small wood on the fire. Sparks spiraled upward. The fire was a risk, because someone might smell the smoke, but Brian needed the warmth. A small fire was almost like having company.

Suzy would leave someday and he would be alone again. And cold. He didn't want to think about it.

For a moment Brian contemplated sliding into bed with Suzy again. She wouldn't refuse him, of that he was sure. They both were lonely. Desperate.

He set three logs on the fire, enough to burn until the sun filtered through the tree limbs overhead, and then pulled a woolen blanket onto the ground between the flames and the log he had been sitting on. Stretching out and facing the warmth, he tried to imagine Nancy Bilideau there with him.

*

Burt led the way, followed by John Johansson. Will and Shawn followed in the rear. The group had crossed the dew covered fields behind Will's home and then started up the hill and away from the river. Leaves in the tree tops twitched from a light southwesterly breeze. No air moved down among the trees and a bead of sweat trickled down Will's temple. It would be a warm day and Duchess, who had stayed back at the house, would go swimming with Ethan and Amy.

Johansson wore the standard Fish and Game Department issued Glock pistol in a holster and Will had dropped an old Colt Woodsman pistol into a fanny pack before they had left. Not that he thought they would need it, but just in case.

Shawn carried a small axe along with a roll of orange flagging tape, the type surveyors and loggers use for marking property. Will thought the axe made the muscular young man look like a Viking. Twice Burt stopped to get his bearings, and each time took a sip from his flask. A gray jay had been shadowing them for the last quarter of a mile, swooping about tree limbs only feet above their heads.

Soon softwoods trees mixed with the hardwoods, their numbers increasing until the maples and yellow birch disappeared, leaving only the tall straight trunks of spruce and fir trees. Shawn often slowed, admiring the wood, and dropped behind as they passed a cluster of giant old hemlocks.

Burt found the game trail and signaled for quiet, even though nobody had said a word during the last mile.

*

"Let's go," said Brian.

"What's the hurry," protested Suzy, pulling the sheet back up to her chin.

"Come on, it's going to be hot. We'll spend the day down by the river." He stuffed two towels and their last remaining six pack of beer into a knapsack.

"It's early."

"You know the log alarm that was tripped? What if it was somebody, and they went for help, and then it was too late to come back, with dark coming and all? They could be coming this morning."

"It was a deer," said Suzy, still not moving from the bed.

"Why take the chance? If someone comes, we'll end up in jail." He jammed a couple of boxes of .22 long rifle shells into one of the pack's pockets. "This afternoon we'll sneak back to see if anybody found our camp."

She propped herself up on an elbow. "What would they be putting us in jail for?"

"The money. We stole it from the hardware store?"

Suzy dropped back into the bed. "Let's wait a while. Go make some coffee."

"I'm going. You can do what you want."

"Oh, I'll come," she said, sliding from the bed.

Her skimpy wrinkled tee shirt didn't hide much. Brian looked away, and said, "Hurry up."

While she brushed the knots from her hair he filled a second backpack with jackets, food, and a bottle of wine, trying hard not to look at his nearly naked sister.

*

"The fire is still warm," said Will, holding his hand over the ashes.

"There was a woman here," said Shawn, pointing at a pale pink halter top hanging from a fir tree stub.

Burt shuffled around the perimeter of the campsite, looking at the ground. "John, look at this," he said.

John Johansson strode over. Someone had scuffed the fallen evergreen needles as they slid straight down the hill.

*

Jimmy Deluga drove north and away from town, wondering where Suzy Toll had disappeared to. The night before, at The Fenton House, Jake had mentioned she was missing, but hadn't seem all that concerned. Was it just because he was so drunk? Or perhaps she had run off before? Jake wouldn't have hurt her. She was his meal ticket.

Jake had mentioned Suzy's brother living out in the woods somewhere and Jimmy wished he knew more about the kid. Where the highway crossed over the Mooslikamoosuc River, he slowed to look upstream. How hard could it be to keep from getting lost if he just followed the river?

Jimmy parked on a gravel pullout frequented by fishermen and climbed out of his black Escalade. The loud rumble of the river surprised him and drowned out all other sound. A logging truck suddenly roared by, its tires whining, and then disappeared toward town. Its unheard approach had startled Jimmy.

He hefted the big .45 ACP semi-automatic pistol, enjoying its weight. Fearing that he might be approached by a bear, he tucked the weapon into a holster against the small of his back. There he could grab it in a flash if needed. A loose fitting Hawaiian-style shirt, which he had bought in Manhattan, more or less hid the big gun beneath a pattern of bright green leaves and yellow flowers. The shirt's colors were bright compared to the camouflaged clothes Jimmy had bought, but he hoped it would still blend in somewhat with the summer foliage.

Mossy Oak Break-Up camouflage pants with large billow cargo pockets covered his legs and sturdy hiking boots protected his feet. On his head he wore a rumpled military-spec Boonie hat and dark aviator-style glasses hid his eyes.

From the Escalade's back seat he pulled a small black knapsack and stuffed a coffee-filled thermos, a Power Bar, and a foil wrapped breakfast sandwich that he bought before leaving town. Already in the pack were matches, a compass, his recently acquired GPS, a map of the area, an all-black survival knife, and a plastic poncho in case it rained. Should he take along the sleeping bag? He decided not to.

Taking a deep breath, he pushed the clicker, locking the Escalade's doors, and then strode into the forest beside the river.

The river cooled the air and walking beside it proved to be easy. He would never know it, but the path he followed was worn by fishermen, moose, and deer. Several times he looked back, to be certain nobody followed him. With the river's constant rumble filling his ears, it was like being deaf and he could hear nothing else. A blue jay dropped from a limb in front of him and flew out over the river.

Where could Suzy and her brother be? If they were camped someplace, they would need water. Maybe he would get lucky and find them beside the river.

But the further he went into the woods the less certain he was of his plan. Perspiration trickled down his forehead.

39

Suzy loved the roar of the river. It reminded her of her childhood, when hot afternoons were spent playing in the clear water, and always with her mother watching over. Large smooth rocks lined the banks and the water tumbled over and between big boulders that divided the flow. The sun hadn't climbed high enough to reach down between the trees, so shadows still blanketed river.

Brian, carrying a knapsack and a .22 caliber rifle, picked their course downstream, stepping or jumping from boulder to boulder. Suzy followed, wearing the second pack and wishing for the sun to climb higher. Talking was impossible over the river's growl.

Where a series of hippo-sized rocks divided up the stream, they leapt from one to the other, crossing to the far side. A short distance downstream a tall rounded granite knob poked out into the river, forcing the stream into a hairpin bend. A majestic white pine crowned the ledge, leaning out over the river.

They climbed up to the top, where the morning sun had found the soft needles under the tree. A faint breeze funneled up the river, moving the air just enough to keep any flying insects away.

Brian stopped and said, "We'll stay here for a while."

Looking back upstream, Suzy could see where they had crossed. "Okay," she said, not sure what his plan was. Sitting beside the river would get boring, but for a while she could work on her tan. "What are we going to do?"

"I'm going to catch some fish," said Brian. "If anyone comes looking for us, the only place they can cross without getting wet is over those boulders." He pointed back up to where they had just crossed. "We'll keep an eye out for them."

"Nobody is coming," said Suzy, shaking her head and dropping the backpack to the ground. "You're paranoid."

"I'd rather be safe," he answered.

She peeled her jersey off over her head and unclasped her bra, letting both fall on the pack. With a teasing laugh, she said, "Did you bring the sun lotion?" She shook her hair back and with both hands pulled it into a ponytail.

Brian turned toward the river, so not to look. "No. Don't let those things get burned."

With his back to her, he dug out a six piece pack rod and a small reel and started to assemble them. Stringing the rod, he twice dropped the line to have it slide back through the guides. Even when facing away from his sister, she was a major distraction.

From a small plastic box containing dozens of crudely tied flies he picked a number 14 nymph made of rabbit fur wound with soft grouse hackles. Poking the fine leader through the hook's eye wasn't easy, but he finally tied it on.

Leaving the ledge, and not able to stop himself, Brian glanced back. Suzy looked beautiful.

Just downstream from the knob, where the water dove over a ledge into a blue fizzling pool, he stopped and stripped out his fly line. Upstream, he could see the boulders they had crossed the river on, and downstream the river eventually disappeared around a bend. He couldn't see his sister, but he remembered exactly what she looked like.

Using his teeth, he squeezed a piece of split shot onto the leader six inches above the fly, and then cast it to where the water tumbled into the pool. It landed with a plop.

Concentrate on the fishing....

*

Jimmy Deluga hated the river's noise. Fearing that someone or something could approach unheard, he frequently looked back over his shoulder. Following the game trail under the shelter of the trees, little air moved and mosquitos swarmed around his head. Occasionally, one would fly near his ear and he could hear it whine over river's grumble. More than once he cursed himself for not remembering insect repellant.

Where the river looked wide, he walked out onto the stones and grass along its shore. There a faint breeze cooled his skin. Both upstream and down there was nothing but trees, rocks, and water. Some of the trees leaned out over the stream, and in places logs had been pushed up against the shore. He would never imagine how high that water rose and its ragging force during the spring runoffs.

The clear water didn't look over waist deep, but felt cold when he bent to touch it. Sticking his hands into the cold water felt good.

A voice gave him a start, and he stepped back into the trees. Did he imagine it? Waiting, the mosquitos swarmed. Reaching behind his back, touching the large pistol gave him comfort. He clasped its grip, squeezed it, but then released it, leaving it holstered.

Deciding he had imagined the voice, he decided to follow the river to the next bend.

*

The line hesitated and Brian flicked the rod tip up. A tug, and then nothing.

"Shit," he snapped. Another miss.

A roll cast flopped the weighted fly back upstream to drift through the pool again.

Periodically, he glanced upstream at the boulders where they had crossed earlier, but his mind kept drifting back to his sister sunning on the knoll.

When she left for someplace where winter never comes, he was going to miss her, desperately. Building his camp and finding food had kept his thoughts from the loneliness. Having her around reminded him of all he was missing.

He rolled the fly upstream again.

*

"Which way?" asked Will.

Beside him, Burt and Johansson stood on the riverbank, looking upstream and down. Pale gray rocks shouldered the river, all polished bare by the multiple millenniums of springs torrents. Shawn was still up in the woods, trying to find a way to build a road in to harvest the softwood trees they had just walked down through.

"Upstream goes back by your place," said Burt, pulling out his flask. "But it's a couple of miles. I'm guessing they went downstream, toward the highway."

"We could split up," said Will.

"No," said John. "The kid has a gun with him. I doubt he would shoot at anybody, but I don't want to be responsible for anyone getting hurt."

Will knew they had found .22 caliber ammunition and no .22 caliber gun at Brian's camp, so they assumed the kid had it with him, but the idea of him shooting at someone had never crossed his mind. "We could flip a coin," he said.

"I think they went downstream," said John.

"There's a place downstream that you can cross to the other side when the water is this low," said Burt. "It's a bunch of big boulders you leap between."

*

The movement caught Jimmy's eye.

A kid flicked a fishing rod, lifting its line back into the air, paused, and then snapped it forward to lay the line the water upstream. And then the kid waited, watching the line intently.

Hidden among the trees, Jimmy watched the end of the yellow line drift back again. Could that be Suzy's brother? It had to be. A rifle leaned against a tree on the far side of the river.

The young man stood on the smooth rocks along the shore. The water looked too fast and deep to wade through, and Jimmy remembered how cold it had felt. Mosquitos hummed about his head, but he ignored them. How could he get to her brother? And was she with him and out of sight somewhere?

Slinking further back into the woods, he decided to walk further upstream to look for a place to cross.

A short distance later, he snuck to the river again for another look. On the far side a large rocky knoll poked out into the river, forcing the water into a tumultuous abrupt turn. Downstream, the kid still fished, focused only on his fishing line. Upstream he noticed the large boulders that created the stepping stones over the river. He slunk back into the trees.

A hundred yards upstream, Burt, leading the way through the trees, said, "We're almost to the crossing place."

"Are we going to cross?" said Will.

John Johansson said, "We'll see what it looks like."

Will wondered where Shawn had disappeared to. He had last seen him tying an orange ribbon to a tree and then marching over a small rise to the southwest. The young man was certainly determined to find a way to build a logging road into that valley.

"Look," said Burt, pointing out through the trees and toward the river.

A man in a flowery tropical print shirt leapt from rock to rock across the river.

"I've seen him before," said Will.

Jumping to the next rock, his shirt's back slid up, offering a glimpse of the hidden pistol.

40

Suzy, with eyes shut, savored the warmth of the sun and dreamt of faraway places. Below the knoll, the river sang on long melody and occasionally a soft breeze wafted up the valley, almost tickling her naked skin. Brian was nearby, fishing in the river, and she felt quite safe.

"Well, hello there," a voice said.

Suzy sat up, bringing her arms across her bare chest. Jimmy Deluga stood next to the giant pine tree. "Where did you come from?" she asked, glancing toward the river. She couldn't see her brother.

"He's all right," said Jimmy. "He's behind the ledge."

She knew Brian would never hear them, even if she screamed, not over the rumble of the river. "What do you want?"

"I've missed your company," said Jimmy, squatting down beside her. "Your boyfriend is looking for you."

"Jake? I never want to see him again." She grabbed her jersey to yank it on over her head. As her head cleared the neck hole, she noticed three men crossing the river upstream behind Jimmy's back.

The look on her face caused Jimmy look back over his shoulder. "What the fuck?" he said.

In a flash a pistol was in his hand. "Come on, put some clothes on. I'll get you out of here."

"I don't want to go, not without my brother."

Jimmy pointed the gun at her head. "Dress, quickly. Or your brother won't live to see another day."

*

The trout were there, unseen, down deep in the swirling pool. Three times he had felt a tug, but each time the fly failed to hook. It had been several minutes since the last hit and the cool water running around his knees had started to feel cold.

Water dropping over the ledge aerated the pool, causing clouds of fizz, much like in a glass of ginger ale. Brian flipped the fly into the froth for what felt like the thousandth time, and stared at the line. Nothing.

He repeated the act. With attention focused by fear of hunger, he never noticed the men leaping from one boulder to the next and crossing the river upstream of him.

Again the fly disappeared beneath the surface again, but a flash indicated a fish. Reflexes snapped the rod back and the weighted fly, which missed hooking the trout's lips, popped out of the water directly at Brian's head.

"Shit," he said, slamming his eyes shut and turning his head as the fly slapped into the left side of his temple, impaling the hook past its barb. The weight of the falling line, combined with the heft of the split shot, yanked the hook down through his flesh until the barb was firmly planted under his skin.

"Oh fuck." His hands grabbed at the line to stop the river from pulling it downstream.

It hurt like hell, but forcing the left eye shut eased the pain.

Walking to dry ground, he held the line and dropped his rod on the stones. Using his teeth, he bit the leader off, leaving an eight inch tail on the hook that protruded from his brow. "Suzy!" he called, holding his hand over his left eye.

A movement among the trees caught his one uncovered eye. It was Suzy's white jersey, and a man behind her carried a very big gun. Together they ran into the woods.

Brian forgot about his wound, grabbed his .22 rifle, and started after them. Who could the guy be? He hadn't seen him well, but it wasn't Jake. The man's brightly-flowered shirt looked like it belonged in Hawaii. Was it the guy that he'd seen at Jake's house? Already they had disappeared.

Brian broke into a trot.

*

Johansson crossed the river first, followed by Burt and Will. Shawn still was up in the woods somewhere and they certainly weren't going to wait for him.

"It's the Toll's daughter," said Burt, stopping on a boulder.

Johansson glanced ahead. "Where?"

"I just saw her up on that knob," said Burt, pointing to the base of the giant white pine. "That guy who crossed the river was with her. I think they went down the back side."

"Come on," said Johansson, pushing into the young alders along the bank. The going got easier as the forest turned to larger fir trees.

Around the backside of the knoll the forest opened up, becoming predominately maple and yellow birch. Ferns grew knee high and the land sloped gently upward.

"There they go," said Shawn, looking ahead.

Will grabbed his arm and pointed ahead to the left. Through the trees they could see a young man running in a crouched position.

"That's Brian Toll," he said. "He must be after them too."

The young man slipped through the forest, squatting low and obviously hurrying after his sister, and had not yet seen them. They all noticed the rifle in his hand.

"They're heading parallel with the river," said Burt, shuffling along.

*

Frank Atkins wound in his fly line and then sat on the riverbank next to a rock maple. Scattered along the stream were five of the investors who had risen before the sun for the morning fishing expedition. Three additional investors were still back at The Fenton House and far too hung over to leave their beds at that early hour. Frank's own head felt rather foggy and he wasn't sure what time they all had finally called it a night.

Robert Henderson, wearing baggy waders, a floppy wide-brimmed hat, and in intensely serious look, stood in the river and cast a tiny woolybugger into slack water behind a dark boulder. Two of the investors appeared to be experienced fly fishermen and possibly enjoying themselves. The other three struggled, snaring branches or themselves with stunning regularity, and spent a great deal of time untying knots in their lines.

Frank wished he still smoked. Smoke would have kept the annoying mosquitos away. A handful of black flies swarmed around his face too, but those he could ignore. The insect repellent seemed to be working for everyone else, but the mosquitos loved to land on the back of his neck to push their tiny proboscises into his flesh.

Henderson let out a whoop as he set the hook and a fifteen inch rainbow trout danced across the surface.

Frank guessed it was the man's thirtieth fish. Unbeknownst to everyone but he and Henderson, a hatchery truck had dumped almost two thousand trout in that stretch of the river during the dark of the night. Private parties stocking the river was totally illegal, but for three thousand bucks the hatchery owner willingly took the chance. Every third or fourth cast another hungry and not-yet-street-wise trout latched onto somebody's fly. Henderson appeared to be having a ball, and the two experienced guests appeared mystified. One of them asked if the fishing was always that good.

After only a few minutes, Frank had found it all too predictable and boring. Adjusted his collar against his neck, he settled back on a tree. Shutting his eyes, he wondered why Jimmy Deluga's Escalade was abandoned near the bridge where they had parked.

*

Brian waited behind a boulder, the dangling monofilament from the embedded trout fly totally forgotten. Early in the chase it became obvious that the man who had kidnapped his sister was traveling parallel with the river. Being woods-wise and young, he darted up the hill and cut around ahead of them, and he was certain that in a few moments they would come into view. The river, further down the slope, sounded out one long hushed clatter.

Breathing deeply to calm his pounding heart, he scanned the trees and waited.

*

The slap in the left shoulder startled Jimmy, followed by the crack of the little rifle, which made him realize he had been shot. Grabbing at his sleeve, he found blood.

He yanked out his pistol and fired toward the gunshot, not really aiming, but trying to buy time while he dashed cover.

His .45 sounded like a cannon.

Brian ducked behind the boulder, not believing he had missed. The man's head was easily ten times as big as a turkey's, and he had killed dozens of them with headshots.

"A gunshot," said Johansson, stopping to peer into the forest ahead. The sound of Brian's little .22 had been lost in the rumble of the river, but not the blast of the .45. Johansson hurried on.

Will dug his Colt Woodsman pistol out of his pack and tucked it into his belt, and then followed. Burt, because of his age, had dropped behind and was out of sight, and it had been a long time since they had seen Shawn.

"Do we have a plan?" asked Will.

"Not getting shot," answered Johansson.

Frank Atkins, Robert Henderson, and the investors, standing in the rumble of the river, heard none of the gunfire.

41

The instant flow of blood startled Suzy, first soaking through Jimmy's shirt, and then turning his hand red after he grabbed at the wound. Her mouth opened to scream, but she froze and no sound came out.

The roar of Jimmy's gun snapped her back to reality and she dashed up the hill at the same moment he dove behind a fat fallen poplar tree. She hadn't seen her brother, but knew he had to be the one who shot Jimmy. The cavalry had arrived.

Brian peeked around the side of the boulder, but could see only trees. With heart racing, his hands shook. What was wrong with him? Buck fever? He had never felt that way before.

Where did the guy go? And where was Suzy. A bead of sweat trickled down his temple.

If Brian had peered just a little further around the boulder, he would have seen Suzy running wildly up through the woods.

The man had to show himself eventually, so Brian took a deep breath, brought the rifle up, and steadied it on his knee ready to shoot. Time dragged.

Blood had ruined Jimmy's shirt, which pissed him off immensely. The bullet had only grazed his arm, but it ached and the blood was sticky. Hiding safely behind the moss covered log, he wished Suzy was still there to tie something around the wound and possibly slow the blood's flow. Where the hell did she go?

He poked his head up to peak and something splatted against the log, followed a split second later by the crack of the rifle up the hill. The shooter was still there and waiting.

Jimmy knew from the sound it was only a .22 caliber rifle, but even a small gun like that was more than enough to kill a man. Whoever was doing the shooting had to be a lousy shot, or Jimmy would have been dead. He guessed it was Suzy's brother.

Hardwood trees stood around him, widely spaced with little brush to offer cover beneath. If he ran, it would be in the wide open. Down the hill, less than the length of a football field away, a stand of thick softwood trees provided shelter all the way down toward the river.

Brian waited, the gun's sights set on the top of the log where he had last glimpsed Jimmy Deluga. The river continued to growl. In the distance a raven cawed and another answered. He tried hard to control his breathing and calm his hands.

Jimmy popped up at the far end of the log with the .45 pointed back up the hill at Brian, who fired a quick poorly aimed shot just as the big pistol bellowed. Brian rolled back behind the rock, shaking.

Taking a deep breath, he peeked around the rock, expecting to see Jimmy charging up the hill. Instead, Jimmy ran downhill toward the softwood trees.

*

Frank Atkins dozed in a sunny spot along the river, slipping through a vague dream about summer thunderstorms. Henderson and the rest of the group still stood in the rattling river fly fishing, only hearing the sound of the water or the hoots and hollers every time one of the group hooked another fish. Their chatter was nearly constant.

The dream took Frank and his wife to a beach, maybe it was on Martha's Vineyard somewhere. Another rumble of thunder brought him back to reality, but it wasn't thunder...he realized the sun was warm and the sky was much too clear for thunder. Sitting up and blinking his eyes open, he wondered if he had heard anything at all, or if it had all been a dream.

Then he remembered the sound as a gunshot. It had come from the woods...and hunting season was still months away. What it could be?

*

Jimmy stepped out of the softwood trees into the bright blue sky that stretched over the river, causing him to squint. Upstream, men stood in the water and fished, and he recognized a heavy one as Robert Henderson. What the hell was he doing there?

Jimmy didn't stop to ponder, but started downstream along the bank, wading through patches of waist-high grass and stepping from smooth worn boulder to smooth worn boulder. Glancing back, every single one of the men still fished and intently faced upstream.

The river grew wider and shallow, its bottom covered with rounded boulders, the sound more of a whisper than a roar. On his side of the water, three boulders, each the size of a van, blocked the way, unless he climbed up a steep banking to get back up into the woods. Glancing back, he didn't see anyone following. Was Suzy's brother still up in the trees? Maybe he went after his sister?

Jimmy opted to wade across the river.

The current felt cold and tugged at his legs. He walked with his arms out to steady himself, as if walking a tightrope. In the moving water, it was impossible to see clearly the rocks on the bottom, and his feet often slipped into holes between them. Midstream, with the water up over his thighs, it was all he could do to keep his balance. Fearful that he might slip and lose his pistol, he tucked it into the back of his belt.

Frank watched from the shadows of the trees, noticing the gun in Jimmy's hand and recognizing the red on his shirt as blood, and he certainly didn't want to get involved. Why had his boss hired that troublemaker?

42

The sound of gunshots caused Shawn to stop on the shoulder of the hill. It sounded like they had come from across the valley.

A precipitous slope along the side of the river had forced him to look for an alternate route for the logging road he hoped to build. He found a way up a gentle slope, which took him well up above the river, and the far side looked like a long gradual decline back to the flat land beside the river. His plan had been to flag it with the ribbon he carried.

But he wondered if Will, Burt, and Johansson had heard the gunshots too. How far behind him were they? Did they stay right along the river? At least the shooting was off on the far side.

Shawn decided he could flag the proposed road another day and started back down toward the river, hoping to find his friends.

Two more shots echoed off the hills. He recognized them as coming from different guns, one the crack of small caliber and the other the roar of something bigger. Were people shooting at each other? The river grew louder as he dropped down the slope.

*

Brian raced down to where Jimmy had been hiding, hoping to find his sister still there. But the far side of the log was empty. The only direction he hadn't been able to see from his hiding place behind the boulder was up the hill, so he guessed she had run that way. Sure enough, ferns had been trampled and leaves disturbed.

He pulled up a large fern and hung it from a twig, then sprinted up the hill, where he stopped to look for tracks or maybe some other sign that his sister had passed there. Moss on a rock had been broken off by someone's step. Marking the spot again with a second fern, he trotted further up the hill in the same direction.

When he stopped a third time he couldn't find any indication that his sister had passed that way, and twice he had to look down the hill at the hanging fern to get his bearings. Finally, he noticed ruffled leaves on the ground. Suzy's course had changed, heading south and back into the woods rather than toward the highway, which was where Jimmy had originally led her.

Brian hung another marker in a tree and took off after her.

*

In spite of the cold river water up over his thighs, the precarious footing beneath Jimmy Deluga's feet caused him to perspire profusely. Yet in two or three more steps he would reach the far bank. He took a deep breath, slid one foot ahead, and then the other.

Out of the trees stepped a tall broad-shouldered man carrying an axe.

Jimmy's lips mumbled, "Thor." He had recently seen the movie on cable.

Thor smiled.

Jimmy slipped and fell back into the river.

The water rushed him downstream and he fought to get his footing.

*

Hiding in the shade of the forest, Frank Atkins had been watching Jimmy slowly wade across the river. The way he angled downstream, away from the group fishing, made it obvious he wasn't headed their direction. Frank wanted nothing more to do with Jimmy Deluga. Ever.

The man stepping out of the forest with an axe in his hand startled Frank almost as much as it had Jimmy. When Jimmy fell over backward Frank actually laughed, and kept laughing as Jimmy floated downstream. The man on the shore followed and yelled something that the river's sound swallowed up. Jimmy managed to stand and said something back, then slipped and floated downstream again.

Twice Jimmy regained his footing to only loose it again. The man on the shore appeared to be laughing. The current carried Jimmy around a bend in the river and the two disappeared.

"Who was that?" asked Robert Henderson, stepping out of the river.

"Must be tourists," said Frank. "It's a wonder more of them don't drown while they're trying to fish this river."

*

When Jimmy bobbed to the surface the first time, Shawn noticed the large pistol tucked against the small of his back.

"Let me help you," yelled Shawn, offering a hand without getting his feet wet.

"I don't need anyone's help," answered Jimmy, taking one shaky step before slipping back under.

When he popped up the pistol was gone. As he fought to regain his footing, re-submerging several times, Shawn dropped the roll of fluorescent flagging tape on the ground to mark the spot. Jimmy dunked completely under again to come up twenty feet further downstream.

"Jesus fucking Christ," screamed Jimmy, fighting to get the pack off his back.

"Don't panic," said Shawn.

The pack floated away. "I ain't fucking panicking."

Shawn, with the axe still in his hand, started to wade in to retrieve him.

Jimmy freaked and reached for the gun.

It was gone.

His feet found a rock on the bottom and he pushed off to swim like an Olympic swimmer toward the fastest current in the center of the river.

"Well I'll be," said Shawn, following along the shore.

When Jimmy flashed him the middle finger of his left hand, Shawn stopped. "Let the motherfucker drown," he said to no one.

It had been years since Jimmy had swum anywhere. Oblivious to the water's temperature, the current shot him downstream and he never looked to see if "Thor" still followed. Soon the water slowed and felt warmer. Little did he know that it was backed up and mixing with the water of the Connecticut River. Looking up he could see a large bridge. Could it be where he'd left his Escalade?

He headed for the shore, looking to see if he had been followed. Nobody was around.

Thankfully he had put the car's keys in his pocket, rather than the backpack he had abandoned in the river. The doors unlocked with a reassuring click.

43

Will peered out from behind the wall of alders. Frank Atkins sat on the river's far bank, and he also recognized the fat man standing in the river fishing. The others he guessed were part of the group he had seen in The Fenton House Pub the day before. The heavy man snapped his fly rod back, setting the hook into a fish.

"That's about the eighth trout we've seen someone catch in less than five minutes," said John Johansson. "You think these guys are the investors that United Eastern Power was trying to impress?"

"Yes," said Will. "They must have fished upstream from the highway."

"I bet they dumped a load of fish in here last night. It's only a hundred yards, maybe two, to the bridge."

Burt pulled out his flask to take a sip. "Look," he said, pointing down the river.

"It's Shawn," said Will.

The tall woodsman sauntered up the far shore, carrying his axe in his right hand. Still well downstream from the men fishing, he disappeared back up into the trees.

"Where did the Toll kid go?" asked Will.

"Up the hill I think," said John. "He's chasing after his sister."

"And the guy with the gun?"

Johansson scratched at his chin. "Damned if I know."

"Let's go back to your house," said Burt. "I'm getting hungry."

*

The knock on the door startled Amy. Opening it, she found Barbara Hawkins outside.

"Can I come in?" she asked.

After the usual pleasantries, iced tea was poured and they moved to sit on the porch.

"Where's Ethan?" asked Barbara, looking nervous.

"He's over at a friend's house for the afternoon," said Amy. "So what brings you here?" It was obvious something had.

Barbara sat on the couch and looked down at the floor, and then squarely into Amy's eyes. "I'm worried about your father."

Amy smiled. "He's a big boy and can take care of himself."

Tears welled up in Barbara's eyes and she looked out at the pasture beyond the house. "I know." For a moment she could not speak. "I'm sure you have guessed that I like your father. I like him a lot. He's a nice man."

"I know," said Amy.

Barbara's fingers nervously intertwined. "Maybe I shouldn't have come," she said.

Amy moved to sit closer, touching Barbara's hand, and said, "He likes you."

Looking down at her lap, she asked, "What about Kim?"

Amy gave Barbara's hand a squeeze. "My father is a grown man, and can do as he wants. I know he likes you and loves all you've done for Ethan. We both do."

"I'm making a fool of myself," said Barbara, wiping an errant tear from her cheek.

"I think Kim is too young for him," said Amy, sitting up straight and hoping to lighten the mood.

Barbara smiled for the first time. "You do?"

"She's close to my age."

"I know. It's hard to compete with someone like that."

"You're attractive," said Amy. "You can blow that woman away."

Barbara smile feebly. "I don't know where to begin."

Amy stood and said, "I'll help you. Let's go up to your house and see what's in your closets for outfits."

*

Brian searched the ground for some sort of sign. Where had Suzy gone? There wasn't a disturbed leaf or broken twig anywhere. Occasionally he looked back from where he had come, but nobody followed. More than a dozen times he made a wide circle around the last sign he had seen, a clear footprint in a rare patch of soft soil.

He flopped down onto the ground and set his back against a young rock maple. The sound of the river had vanished far down the hill and not a sound could be heard except the leaves rattling overhead in the faint southwest breeze.

Where could she have gone? Would he ever see her again? She might keep on going and not stop until she reached the Dakotas. Or Florida. Or wherever she might be heading.

Loneliness washed over Brain. He had let his sister down. At least he saved her from that creep who had her in the woods. But would he ever see her again?

Hunger gnawed at his stomach. His fishing rod lay back by the river somewhere, along with his knapsack. He wondered if anyone had found his campsite.

Things looked bleak.

*

Duchess greeted Will when he entered his home. On the counter, a note from Amy that said she would be back in time for dinner. Outside, Johansson's truck started and followed Burt's rig out the driveway.

"It's been a long day," he said, patting the dog before going upstairs to shower.

When he came back downstairs Ethan rushed to meet him. He snatched the boy up in his arms, to carry him into the kitchen where Amy put away groceries. Duchess stood by his dinner bowl, patiently waiting.

Will asked Ethan what he had done all day, and then suggested feeding the dog. Ethan loved to feed Duchess.

"So how was my favorite daughter's day?" he asked, stopping to sort groceries with Amy.

She filled him in, leaving out the part about Barbara Hawkins visiting. He ran through the details of his day. When the groceries were put away he took out a bottle of Cotes du Rhone and poured his daughter a glass.

"Thanks," she said. "So you don't know who the guy was that ran off with the Toll daughter?"

"I'm pretty sure I've seen him in the bar at The Fenton House." Will poured a dab of Dalwhinnie into a tumbler. "He was there when a bunch from United Eastern Power was having drinks."

"With all the drama it sounds like a TV show." Amy sipped the wine. "Where's Shawn? I see his truck still in the driveway."

"He's all right," said Will. "He got to looking for a way to build a road in to get some big softwood off the back of Hawk Hill. We saw him go back into the woods on the far side of the river, after all the excitement was over."

At knocking on the back door, Will said, "I bet that's him now."

Shawn entered and gave Amy a hug. Will noticed how happy his daughter was to see him. "Can I get you something to drink?"

"I'll have one of those," said Shawn, motioning toward the tumbler.

Pouring the scotch, Will saw Shawn's pants were damp and a large pistol protruded from his belt. "What do you have there?"

Shawn pulled the gun from his belt to set it on the counter, and then told of arriving at the river as Jimmy Deluga was about to wade out and how Deluga lost the pistol out of the back of his belt when he slipped and fell back in. "That crazy bastard actually gave me the finger before swimming away," said Shawn, chuckling. "I dropped my roll of ribbon to mark the spot when he lost the gun, and then went back to find it after he'd disappeared downstream," he said.

Will laughed. "He really gave you the finger?"

"Yeah, he's nuts," said Shawn.

"Was the gun hard to find," asked Amy, imagining him wading into the river.

"Not really," said Shawn. "I took off my shoes and felt among the rocks with my toes. The water was clear enough that I could actually see it once I found it."

Will asked, "What are you going to do with it?"

"I'll talk to Johansson, but I'd like to keep it," said Shawn. "It's a Kimber and probably worth a thousand bucks."

44

The sound of Duchess moving woke Will. She sat up, then let out a low growl. Listening, he could hear vehicles come up the driveway and continuing across the fields behind his barn, headed toward the woods beyond. It sounded like three trucks or SUVs.

It had to be John Johansson and the State Police. Only the palest of morning light trickled in the windows. When they had reached the house the day before, John mentioned going back to the young Toll's campsite first thing in the morning. Both Will and Burt offered to accompany him, but John said he preferred to bring along the State Police.

Will tried to remember Amy coming home. He had watched Ethan while she had gone out with Shawn.

Duchess trotted down the stairs, so he slipped from the bed to put on his jeans and follow. Downstairs, he found Amy's bag on the dining table, so he knew she'd come home. He opened the back door to let Duchess out.

Mindlessly, he started coffee and then made the dog's breakfast. A scratch at the door said she wanted to come in.

"Let's go fishing," he said, as Duchess entered. "Just you and me."

His rod sat in its tube, leaning against wall inside the back closet. By the time Duchess finished eating, he had gathered up his things and finished his first cup of coffee.

"I'll leave Amy a note," he said, searching for a pad of Post-It notes in a drawer.

Will looked across the back field, but it was still too dark to see the vehicles that had passed earlier. They had to be parked next to the trees, but that was over three hundred yards away. With Duchess on the truck seat beside him, he followed the old road across the field down the where the river snaked along the side of the pasture and there he parked next to the timber bridge.

The pool above the bridge looked like ink. The sky's gray glow illuminated shapes around the truck, but colors had yet to blossom. He threaded the line up the rod, then pulled on a pair of camouflage hip boots that he used to wear duck hunting. A breath of air pressed against his face from the direction of the field.

"What do you think girl?" he said to Duchess. "What fly should I use?"

She sat patiently waiting, obviously remembering the routine.

Will tied on a #12 green and black wooly-bugger, his favorite fly when suffering indecision, and stepped down to the river. Duchess lay down and placed her head on her paws as he worked out the line. Will's first cast sent the fly to the middle of the pool, where it landed with a plop.

After a dozen casts that covered most of the pool, he sat on the grass beside Duchess, leaving the fly dragging in the current.

"Things sure change as you get older," said Will, rubbing the dog's ear. "Years ago I'd have been out here fishing every morning. Now I'd just as soon stay in bed most days."

Duchess moaned, and Will wondered what it was about.

"But we got it pretty good," he continued. "Particularly now that Amy and Ethan are here."

A kingfisher cackled as it flew across the river.

"Where do you suppose this guy Jake is? He's got to be the one killed the Hammonds, and I bet the Tolls too."

Duchess put her head back down on her paws and Will ran his hand along her back.

"It's all the power company's fault. They made people greedy and crazy. Money corrupts everything."

Will stood up and worked out his fly line again, then let the fly drop into the slick tongue of water at the head of the pool. He mended line as it drifted downstream, raising the rod's tip to keep slack from the line, then lowered it as the fly passed downstream. At the end of the drift he started to raise the rod and felt the tug of a fish.

*

Jake woke needing to piss. He stumbled out the back door to stand at the edge of the deck, wearing only his boxer shorts. As the pressure flowed away, he stared at where the old tote road left his backyard.

"Where the fuck could she be?" he said, to no one.

Scratching at his stomach, he walked back inside and took a beer from the refrigerator. After the first sip he belched, then wiped his mouth with the back of his arm. The big Ruger pistol lay on the kitchen table. He picked it up and turned the cylinder, listening to the clicks.

"It's got to be that asshole brother of hers," he said. "He's talked her into leaving me. Dumb bitch. She don't know when she's got it good."

He pulled the guns hammer back and put his finger on the trigger, aiming it out the window. Laughing, he stepped to the back door and pushed it open, then aimed at a tree across the yard.

The gun's roar startled him. He laughed again at the spot of white splintered wood on the tree's trunk.

"That's what I want to do to that kid brother of hers, and maybe her too, if she don't smarten up."

*

Brian listened to the forest around him. Birds chirped and chattered in the trees. A cricket or something clicked not too far away. It wouldn't be light enough to track his sister for another half hour, so he waited, curled against the side of a moss covered boulder. At least the night hadn't been too cold.

He had followed her trail all afternoon the day before. Her course surprised him, going in an almost straight line. Her trail had led him south of Hawk Hill and much closer to town. Brian wondered if she knew where she was going.

Suzy had slept in a shed behind a camp. Late the previous afternoon, she intersected an old dirt road and followed it west. A few small neatly-kept camps were along the way. Two or three had cars or trucks parked next to them, but several more appeared to have no one around. With nightfall coming, she snuck up beside one that appeared empty to peer inside. The couch was covered with a sheet, and she guessed no one would be back around for a while. Testing the door, it was locked, but not the door to the shed out back.

By then it was quite dark, and a folded up lounge chair caught her eyes. She opened it up and stretched out on it, then abruptly fell asleep. Once during the night she woke because she was chilly, but she pulled a tarp across her shoulders and fell back asleep.

Hunger woke her.

Suzy looked in the windows of the camp again, and then tried the doors once more. Both the front and back doors were locked. She tried to open the windows too, but none would budge. For a moment she contemplated breaking one, but they all were high enough off the ground that she could barely look in, let alone climb in. Discouraged, she wondered how far it was to town.

Walking west on the road again, she heard an ATV coming up behind her. About to duck into the woods to hide, she glanced back and saw the rider already smiling at her.

He slowed and stopped. "You're up early."

"Hi," she said, "yes."

"Where did you come from?"

"I got lost yesterday," she said, panicking. "I've been out overnight."

He looked concerned, and said, "My name's Chris," offering a hand. "I've got food back at my camp. After you get something to eat I can drive you out to town."

Suzy hesitated. Lately her luck with men had sucked. But then she decided to take a chance and said, "That would be nice."

He had her climb on the back and they turned around, going back the way they both had come. In front of a small red house they stopped. On the far side of the lawn the land sloped down and she could see the entire Mooslikamoosuc River valley.

"I don't have cell phone coverage out here," apologized Chris, climbing off. "And land lines stop about two miles from here. Is there anyone worried about you?"

"I don't think so," she said.

"Where did you come from?" he asked again.

"Route 3. I started following the river, but then went up the hill."

"Alone?" he asked, heading toward the door.

"Yes." She wondered how much he believed.

A tail wagging Labrador retriever met them at the door. Dark knotty pine paneling covered the inside of the cabin. Next to the dining table, a big picture window faced the valley. A stone fireplace stood in the middle of the house, with stuffed chairs surrounding an oriental rug in front of it. The place looked cozy.

"I can make you eggs," said Chris, reaching for a frying pan. "Bacon too."

"Whatever is easy," she said, settling onto a chair. "Are you here alone?"

"I usually come here alone," he said, opening the refrigerator. "It's just me and the dog. Her name's Jet."

"Like Joan Jet?"

"Like Jet black," he laughed

She wondered if he was married.

*

Brian had followed his sister's trail for only an hour when he came upon the old tote road. The hard packed gravel showed only the faintest of deer or moose tracks, where the hard hoofs had compressed the soil. His sister's feet hadn't left any impressions at all. Discouraged, he followed the old road, walking past the little red house and still hoping to find a footprint somewhere.

*

"What did you find?" asked Will, opening the door for John Johansson.

"An empty campsite."

"Come on in and have a cup of coffee," said Will, swinging the door open wide. Amy sat reading the newspaper, but looked up when he entered.

Johansson sat at the table and went on to describe the campsite in detail.

"Do you think they were planning on coming back?" asked Amy.

"It's hard to tell. There wasn't any money there, at least that we could find." Turning to Will, he said, "You saw the camp, it looked like they planned to stay forever, but if they had money they took it all with them. Maybe they knew we were onto them."

Will poured coffee, and asked, "So who was there?"

"Brian Toll and his sister is our best guess. He's been hiding in the woods off and on for years. We think his sister joined him."

"So what happens now?"

"We dismantled the camp, knocked it down anyway. Finding Brian and his sister isn't a real high priority, unless the State Police can tie them to the murder of either their parents or the Hammonds."

"So, what's up for the rest of the day?" asked Will, hoping to lighten the subject.

"I'm going down to the fish hatchery, so see if anyone knows anything about an illegal stocking of the Mooslikamoosuc."

45

"We got big trouble," said Henderson. "About half of the investors are talking about pulling out."

Frank sipped his coffee. "What do you want me to do?"

"Talk to them. Tell them about our media blitz and the public relations campaign. We're going to turn this thing around." Eggs, sausage, bacon, pancakes, home fries, baked beans, toast, and a side of English muffins all sat in front of Henderson.

The previous night hadn't gone as planned. After dinner out, Henderson had arranged for a long limousine to pick up the group and take them back to The Fenton House. The ride cost a bundle, mainly because Henderson arranged for three very attractive, talented, and skimpily clad women from downstate to be waiting inside.

Some of the men chuckled and slid in next to the women, but one turned out to be some sort of holy roller who wanted nothing to do with the "women of the devil", so flatly refused to get into the limo. Frank ended up driving the man back to The Fenton House, where the guy locked himself in his rented room.

The other men stayed up and bantered with the women, and a fair amount of liquor was consumed up there on the third floor, but only one partook of what the women offered, and he was the investor with the least cash on the table.

Not long after midnight, Charles Hanson, a wealthy man from Iowa, pulled Henderson aside to say he and two other investors were reconsidering their interest in the project. Hanson then abruptly left and went to his room, not giving Henderson a chance to speak.

Henderson then grabbed a bottle of bourbon and the hand of one of the young ladies, and led her to his room. Not more than a minute later, she came out, slamming the door behind her. Whatever had happened in that room hadn't dampened Henderson's appetite for breakfast.

"It's going to be in today's paper," continued Henderson, stabbing at an errant piece of egg. "We're playing up the good-for-the-country aspect, making it look patriotic to put those power lines through here."

Frank's mind drifted, wondering what his wife was doing. She always disliked Henderson and never missed an opportunity to let Frank know it. The few times the two of them had met he stared at her breasts. Frank smiled. His wife was attractive, and more so every year. It was time to start thinking about another line of work.

"So are they still here?" asked Frank.

"I think so," said Henderson. "The only vehicle that's not in the parking lot is that holly roller's crappy car. What a chump." He jabbed a home fry then swirled it in ketchup.

*

Will picked up the phone and called Barbara, but of course she had gone to work. He then tried her work number.

"Good morning," he said. "Are you free for lunch?"

"It has to be quick," she said. "I only get a half hour."

"Can I bring you lunch?" he asked.

"That would be nice. We can eat on the park bench across the street."

He hung up the phone, feeling the best he had in ages. Maybe he had made the choice.

Stepping outside, he started toward the barn with Duchess racing ahead of him. Beside the wood splitter an enormous pile of tossed wood needed to be stacked in the woodshed. If he did some each day it would be done in a week or two.

A distant crack of a 22 rifle carried from the woods far across the field. Will stopped and looked, but saw no one. It had to have come from up in the woods.

"I bet it's that Toll boy," he said to Duchess, whose ears were perked up because she had heard it too.

*

Brian Toll broke off the driest branches that he could find among a stand of fir trees. Dry wood made little smoke, and he was desperately hungry, but not hungry enough to eat raw the ruffed grouse he had just killed.

He carried the branches up a long slope into open hardwoods, where he could see a long way in every direction, and there broke the wood into shorter pieces, then, using a Bic lighter, he lit a fire. While it grew he plucked the grouse.

Suzy was gone. After she turned onto the old gravel road, Brain could no longer follow her. Finally giving up, he hiked back down into the familiar valley, not really sure what to do next. Following the edge between the softwood trees and the northern hardwoods, he accidentally flushed a family of grouse, one of which landed in a nearby tree. The head shot was easy.

Using a green stick as a skewer, he roasted the carcass over the fire.

An hour and a half later he slipped across the bridge at the far side of the field from Will Northrop's home and then disappeared into the trees along the river. Before mid-morning he had climbed straight up through the softwoods to his old campsite.

The logs of his shelter had been pulled apart and the plywood that had been the roof lay on the ground. His fire pit had been knocked apart and none of his personal belongings remained. He wondered if Suzy had taken her money with her, or if the police had confiscated it. He hoped it was in her little knapsack.

He continued up the hill, clutching trees to keep from sliding on the slippery fir and spruce needles that covered the ground.

Where the softwoods mixed with hardwoods and the ground started to flatten out, he stopped to sit against a boulder.

More food. That was apriority. The closest and easiest pickings were in Barbara Hawkins vegetable garden. He might luck into game along the way, but, if his fishing things were still down by the river where he left them, he could easily catch some trout.

And then he would have to find a new campsite, one nearer town. Brian wanted to find that asshole that had tried to kidnap his sister.

*

Jimmy Deluga rolled over and looked out the cabin's window. The day before had been one big disaster, and he loathed getting out of bed. He feared the wilderness would be the death of him yet.

But after every survived brush with death comes a certain rush or high, a strong feeling of invincibility. Jimmy took a deep breath. Maybe he was as rugged as this country around him.

He slid up on the pillows and dragged his laptop from a side table. On *Google Earth* he could see the river he had walked along and then swam in the day before. With a little imagination, he guessed where the properties were that the power company wanted. The Hammond's home still stood in the images, and he even guessed correctly which house belonged to the Tolls. It really wasn't that far away through the woods.

A rectangular house on the far side of the hill had to be Jake's. There was even a faint line through the trees that had to be the trail Jimmy had walked to his house.

Jimmy googled "firearms dealers". Before he went back into the woods for any reason, he needed another large caliber handgun. He couldn't go back to the local store, because buying a handgun out of state would require identification from that state, and the driver's license he used there was for New York. He was sure he had another fake driver's license with a fictitious background attached for someone downstate.

A large firearms dealer was only twenty minutes away.

After he dressed, he would go buy another handgun, and then he would see what he could find at the Toll's house. Maybe the police had missed something.

*

Jake stepped out onto the back deck to piss again. The third beer had put him over the top, yet as the pressure poured away his mind felt sharper.

The Tolls house…that was a place to start. Suzy might even be there.

He walked back inside and stuffed the big Ruger pistol inside his belt, then grabbed another beer from the fridge.

46

Will turned on his directional and slowed, approaching the Tolls driveway. Before making the turn, he hit the brakes to stop. Someone had turned in the drive fast, leaving a crescent shaped mark of turned up gravel.

Will backed up and made a Y turn, then drove down the road a quarter mile to park his truck in the beginning of a grassy grown in logging road. Checking his cell phone, there was no service, so calling John Johansson would be impossible. After stuffing the phone into the glove compartment, he climbed out.

His original plan had been to drive in, maybe peek into the house if it was open, and then bring lunch to Barbara Hawkins. Part of that was curiosity, and maybe he hoped to see something that others had missed.

Glancing at his watch, he had plenty of time to slip through the woods to see who, if anybody, was at the house, and then go for lunch with Barbara.

He slipped through the woods, traveling parallel with the road, until he intersected the driveway. Still staying amongst the trees, he followed it toward the house, where a beat up red Dodge pickup sat at the edge of a cluttered front lawn.

Will stayed hidden in the trees, memorizing the truck's number plate. The front door of the house hung open and broken yellow police tape swayed in the breeze. Will wished he had brought his phone to take pictures.

A movement beyond the far end of the house caught his eye. Waiting, Will tried to make out shapes among the trees.

Finally, a man wearing camouflage pants and a tropical print shirt slipped from the woods toward the house. In his hand, a large handgun pointed toward the sky. Stopping next to the house, he crouched beneath a window.

Will recognized the man as the patron with the gun hidden under his windbreaker at the bar inside The Fenton House. What was he doing?

The man looked at the red truck, smiled, and then stuck his gun in a holster hanging on his right hip. He yelled, "Jake."

A skinny scruffy man peaked out the front door, holding a large revolver in his hand. "Who's there?"

"Jake, it's me, Jimmy." he said, walking toward the door.

"Jimmy?"

"Yeah, Jimmy Deluga."

"What the fuck are you doin' here?" asked Jake.

"I could ask you the same thing," said Jimmy, grinning.

"I'm looking for clues."

"Great minds think alike," laughed Jimmy, slapping Jake on the shoulder. "I didn't dare drive in here like you did. You've got bigger balls than me."

"I don't give a shit," said Jake, turning to go back inside. "You want a beer?"

"Fuck yea," said Jimmy, following Jake inside.

Will crept through the woods along the side of the weed filled lawn. Neither of the men could be seen through any of the windows. Where he could see along the back of the house, he stopped. Inside, the voices had raised. Will dashed to the side of the house to listen.

"I thought the dumb cunt was with you." It was Jake yelling.

"I ain't seen her."

"You're a lying piece a shit."

"She run off with her brother," said Jimmy. "When I found them she run off into the woods."

After a pause, Jake asked, "Where was that?"

"Up near the Mooslikamoosuc River."

It sounded like someone dropped into a chair.

"Want another beer?" asked Jimmy.

Cans rattled, and then Jimmy asked, "So, did you find anything?"

Will glanced at his watch. Soon he would have to leave, or else be late.

"No," said Jake. "There's nothing here."

"You were hoping to find Suzy," said Jimmy, "Weren't you?" A few seconds later, he added, "You already know what happened to the Tolls. It's the same thing that happened to the Hammonds. You killed them."

"Now why are you saying that?"

"It makes sense. Suzy would have become rich, and you were right in line to marry her."

"You're talking fuckin' crazy."

Silence. Then a chair or table crashed against the floor. Something smashed against the wall, shaking the whole house.

Will ran for the woods.

47

"So what did John Johansson say?" asked Barbara.

"He was going to call the State police and head up there," said Will, as they undid the wrappers of the sandwiches he had brought. Earlier, crossing the street from her office, he had told her about the events of the previous hour.

"There was an article in the newspaper this morning about burying the power line," said Barbara. "People might go along with that."

"It's too bad the Hammond's had to die because someone was greedy."

"The whole mess pitted neighbors against each other."

Will swallowed a bite of his sandwich. "Lives have been wrecked for no reason."

Barbara asked about Ethan, lightening the conversation, and talk turned to her horse and then his dog and then her goat. Before long she had to go back to work. As Will walked back toward his truck, his cell phone rang.

"Hey." It was John. "The place was a mess. It looked like a fight happened, and blood was on the floor, but nobody was around. The State cop is still there, but I told him a call had come in for me. I'll be in town in ten minutes. Meet me at my house."

Will arrived at John's home first and Cindy let him in. She had been working at the dining table and paperwork was piled in front of her chair. He explained why he was there, then asked what she was doing.

"I'm trying to get an Internet retail site set up to sell locally grown food," she said, sitting at the table again. "The state government has so many restrictions."

"It seems to get worse every year, like the government doesn't trust people to think for themselves." A truck door slammed outside, and Will said, "John's home."

"Will," said John, stepping inside, "let's step out back, so we don't bother Cindy."

"I'm coming too," she said. "I want to hear what's going on."

They sat in chairs on the back deck. "So what exactly did you hear?" asked John.

Will went through the events at the Toll's home, then asked, "Are the State police going to want to talk to me?"

"I kept your name out of it," said John. "Those guys are stretched so thin up in this neck of the woods that I doubt much will come out of this. The detectives downstate are going to see what they can find out about somebody named Jimmy Deluga though. It may turn out to be just an alias."

"So who's this Jimmy Deluga guy?" asked Cindy.

"I've seen him at the bar in The Fenton House," said Will. "He bought Jake a beer there. The bartender seemed to know him."

"Let's go pay the bartender a visit," said John.

*

Brian Toll stepped out of Valle's Department Store and sauntered down Main Street, wearing dark aviator glasses, clean khaki pants, a button oxford shirt, and a crimson ball cap that said "Harvard" on the front, all brand new and bought with his share of the money stolen from the hardware store. His own mother, if she had been still alive, would not have recognized him. Nervously, he chewed gum.

Slowing to peek into store windows, he also glanced up and down the road, figuring his best chance to find his sister was to find the man who had kidnapped her. Without any idea of where to start looking, he hoped to find him in town somewhere.

*

Suzy turned to give Chris a hug, and then climbed aboard the bus. Through the window she watched him walk back toward his SUV. She had never met a man like him, an honest gentleman who hadn't tried to get into her pants. Back at his house, when she stepped from the shower wearing only a towel around her torso, she had hoped to catch his attention, but he turned away and disappeared into another room, rather than leering, which was what every other man in her life had ever done.

At one point she had made a comment about him being a good looking man, and he came back with a compliment for her, and then added, "If you weren't so young I'd be chasing you around."

The remark stung, because she thought of herself as a woman, and also because it was true. She wasn't even yet eighteen.

So Suzy abandoned any idea of seducing him, instead deciding to find someone just like him that was closer to her age.

The bus started south.

*

It was time to ditch the Escalade. Jimmy had been driving it too long and someone somewhere must have noticed it, like at the turnout where he had parked it next to the river. Back when he had climbed up from the river he found the two shiny SUVs that the United Eastern Power big wigs had rented to shuttle the investors around in. Some of them would remember his Escalade there. As Jimmy shifted into four wheel drive, he wondered where the nearest place to rent another SUV was.

The road deteriorated to two tracks interrupted by large rocks and washed out holes. Brush on either side reached out to touch the vehicle's sides. Something was missing, and then Jimmy realized it was telephone poles, which, to him, meant it was *real* wilderness.

The Escalade jerked to the left, and Jimmy heard Jake moan in the back. He was tied up with duct tape and hidden under a plastic tarp, and at least the asshole was still alive. It had to be hotter than hell under that tarp, and that thought brought a smile to Jimmy's face.

Tumbled down stonewalls and weeds shouldered the road. Across a green field to the left, Jimmy could see a farm on a distant hillside. Where a logging road led into the woods on the right, he turned in. The forest immediately opened up into a small grassy field, which he drove across to an old tote road that continued beneath dark green softwood trees. He followed it down into the forest and where the road widened he pulled off into knee-high grass.

"I'm going to leave you here," said Jimmy, stepping out. He walked around the back to open the rear door. "You're going to stay out here in the woods until you sign a confession."

Jake said nothing when Jimmy grabbed his ankle to drag him out of the vehicle. He hit the ground with a thud and moaned. The duct tape made it impossible to say more. His sweat soaked clothes smelled sour and stuck to his skin.

Jimmy bent down to cut the duct tape that kept Jake's feet together, then yanked the tape off that covered his mouth. The binds on his hands and arms were left intact. "Get up," said Jimmy, un-holstering his gun.

"I can't," said Jake.

"I'll shoot your fucking nuts off if you don't," said Jimmy. When Jake still didn't move, Jimmy worked the slide on his newly acquired Ruger Model SR1911 to chamber a round, then added, "Your girlfriend won't be too interested if you got no nuts."

Jake got up on his knees, then stood. "What are you going to do?"

"I'm going to hitch you around a tree," said Jimmy. "Every day I'll come by to see if you're ready to write a confession. When you do that I'll set you free."

"I ain't gonna confess. They'll send me to Concord."

"That where the prison is?"

"Yup. I ain't going there."

"Walk that way," said Jimmy, motioning with his gun.

They walked a hundred yards through a stand of hardwood trees the diameter of telephone poles. The air felt thick from humidity and, even though the sunlight couldn't find a way through the foliage overhead, it was terribly hot. Tiny flies swarmed around their heads.

"Are you gonna leave me water?" asked Jake.

"You don't need water," said Jimmy. "Stop next to that tree."

"I'll die without water."

"Not if you write that confession first."

"I won't confess," said Jake, sounding panicky.

"Put your back against the tree."

"No."

The hammer of the Model SR1911 made an audible click as Jimmy pulled it back.

Jake backed against the tree.

Jimmy wrapped tape around Jake's ankles and the tree's trunk, then wrapped upward around the tree and Jake to his waist.

"What's the matter Jake? You got to piss?" laughed Jimmy. "Go ahead, piss your pants."

"You're tying me up too tight," said Jake. "I can't feel my legs."

"You'll be alright, if you don't wait too long."

Jimmy taped Jakes arms against the trunk. "You want a beer Jake? Wouldn't that taste good?" He continued wrapping around his chest and up to his neck. Tears tumbled from Jakes eyes and dripped from his cheeks.

"A nice cold frosty one?" asked Jimmy. "If you write a confession, I'll buy you a whole case of cold frosty ones."

Jake sobbed. "I can't go to Concord."

48

Walking into the bar of The Fenton House, Will's heart sank. It wasn't the same bartender, but a woman instead. He slid onto a bar stool. Except for one man reading a newspaper at a table near a window, the place was empty.

"What can I get you?" asked the bartender, looking away from the TV. She glanced questioningly at John Johansson in his Conservation Officer uniform, standing beside Will.

"Hi," started Will, then introduced themselves.

"I'm Brenda," she said, flashing her best smile.

"We're looking for a man," said John, "about five six, dark hair, from out of town. We know he's been in here during the past week."

"That would be Jimmy Deluga," she smiled. "I knew he was up to something. What did he do?"

"That's him. Do you have any idea where we could find him?" asked Will.

"No. He said he worked for an independent news agency. Always was flashing money. Drove a big black Caddie SUV. And he had a gun, maybe more than one. I know that." Grinning, she added, "Can't you tell me what he did?"

"Was there anyone with him?"

"He had something going on with that bimbo Suzy Toll and her boyfriend Jake. Jimmy was porkin' her and Jake didn't seem to notice. That guy is trouble."

"Which guy?"

"Both of them. Jake is a crazy drunk and Jimmy is probably some kind of killer."

John's eyebrows went up. "Some kind of killer?"

Brenda glanced back at the TV. "Like a paid killer, you know, a hit man."

"What makes you say that?" asked John.

"You should have seen the way he handled Jake…cool as a cucumber."

"What did he do?" asked Will.

"I've said too much already." Brenda turned to face the TV.

"We'd like to find him," said John. "Jake too."

"It's got something to do with the Hammonds," said Brenda, without turning to face them, "doesn't it?"

"Why do you say that?" asked John.

"Because everybody in town thinks the Tolls had something to do with their death."

"So where should we start looking?"

"There's only so many places in town to stay. I can tell you that Jimmy Deluga isn't the camping type. He's a flashy dresser and probably has to blow dry his hair every morning." Brenda laughed at her own joke. "He was staying at the far end of town, but he moved. I think to hide from Suzy. She was hot for him and he wasn't all that interested."

"Thanks for your time," said John.

*

Jimmy Deluga drove into town, heading toward a Ford dealer forty-five minutes to the south who, during a phone conversation, had promised to rent him a car. In the back seat sat his suitcases, with all of the paraphernalia he had brought north. He glanced in the mirror, chiding himself for not ditching the Escalade earlier. Passing The Fenton House, he noticed the Fish and Game Department's truck parked in front.

Smiling, he wondered if the mosquitos had sucked a pint of blood out of Jake yet. When he had left him wrapped to the tree, Jake was crying like a baby. That asshole would be writing a confession before the next day's sun had set, Jimmy was sure of it.

Driving by Pricilla's Northwoods Emporium, he noticed the young tourist in khaki pants and aviator glasses, but never gave him a second thought. It was time to wrap the job up and get back to civilization.

*

The shiny black Escalade caught Brian Toll's eye and, as it passed, he recognized the driver as the man who stole his sister. She didn't appear to be in the vehicle and he panicked. What he had done with her?

Brian stepped off the curb and glanced into the cab of a Chevy pickup. No keys in the ignition. He looked into a Toyota Rav4, a Dodge Durango, a Dodge pickup truck, and a Ford Ranger. Times were changing and it wasn't like when Brian was young and almost nobody took their keys out of the vehicles. And then in a red Jeep Wrangler he hit pay dirt.

He walked around the front, glanced about, and climbed into the driver's seat. The engine started right up. He backed up and then took off to catch up with the Escalade, planning on staying back far enough that the driver wouldn't notice him following.

At fifteen years of age, Brian's driving experience was limited. Three times, when his father had drank to the point of not being able to drive, he was asked to go for cigarettes. The last time he almost didn't come back, but he feared what his old man would do if he ever caught him. Brian could feel his pulse racing.

Thankfully the Jeep had an automatic transmission.

*

"What the heck," said John, swerving to miss a red Jeep that backed onto the road without looking.

"Probably from downstate," said Will. "Do you still see the Escalade?"

"Yeah, but I don't dare get too close."

"Can we get the State Police to help?"

"Let's just see where he's going," said John. "The State Police are stretched pretty thin at the moment."

When they stepped out of The Fenton House, Will spotted the black Escalade driving through town and Will recognized the driver. They jumped in John's Fish and Game Department truck and started to follow.

Soon they were outside of the town's business district and headed south. The Connecticut River wound through the valley on their right and green craggy mountains rose to the left. Old pastures hugged the road, some stretching down to the trees along the river, and a train track hugged the slope between the road and the river.

"How far are we going to follow?" asked Will.

"Until he gets on the interstate," said John, glancing at the rearview mirror. A red Jeep had been following them for quite a while, but that wasn't too unusual, considering there were few side roads to turn off onto.

On the truck's Fish and Game Department's two-way radio a dispatcher said to be on the lookout for a stolen red Jeep Wrangler, and then rattled off the license plate number.

"We got a stolen Jeep following us," said John, glancing in the rearview mirror again. "It looks like one person, a young male, driving it."

Will tried to see it in the side mirror. "Now what do we do?"

"Let's keep going and keep an eye on both of them," said John. "I'll call the Groveton police and see if they can intercept the Jeep."

Where the highway took a turn to the left they passed by an old railroad station in a town that consisted of little more than a post office.

"Shit!" said John, looking in the rearview mirror. "He took a right across the bridge."

*

Brian didn't like following the Fish and Game Department truck. Someone would miss the Jeep, if they hadn't already, and a call would go out over law enforcement radios. The extra antenna on the department's truck made him nervous.

After crossing the bridge, he turned left onto Vermont Route 102 and pushed the gas pedal to the floor, traveling parallel to the New Hampshire highway.

He figured the Escalade had to be heading for Lancaster, maybe even continuing south all the way to wherever he came from. The thought of following it to Boston or New York both terrified and excited Brian. Could Suzy have been in the Escalade out of sight? It seemed unlikely, but what else could he do?

The Vermont road twisted through long curves and the Jeep's tires squealed around one tight bend, and then where the road straightened he accelerated again. Corn grew in a wide flat field that stretched back to the river and cows fed in a muddy pasture on the right. He slowed into another turn and then pushed the throttle to the floor. Adrenalin pumped through his veins.

Traveling at those speeds, he would easily get ahead of the black Escalade, and then he would cut back into New Hampshire to wait for it as it came into Lancaster. Hopefully, the Fish and Game Department truck would have gone elsewhere.

Or could they have been following the Escalade too?

The road sloped down a hill and bent sharply to the left. Brian touched the brakes and then pushed the throttle to the floor again.

A moose sauntered out onto the asphalt.

49

"So what do you think?" asked Barbara.

Will, who sat beside her, said, "Jimmy Deluga is a lucky guy."

"Is the Toll kid going to be all right?" asked Cindy, sitting beside John.

"He's pretty lucky too," added John.

Earlier, immediately after John and Will passed through Groveton, a call came in over the Fish and Game Department's radio that a red Jeep had rolled over on Vermont Route 102, and asked for assistance. They were several minutes closer than any police vehicles, so they crossed into Vermont on Groveton's Bridge Street and made a left in Guildhall. A couple of miles down the road they found Brian Toll standing beside the rolled-over Jeep. The moose was nowhere to be seen, having continued down to the river.

The seatbelt had saved Brain's life and, though shook-up, he was fine. An ambulance arrived about five minutes later, along with both New Hampshire and Vermont police, and they insisted on Brian making the trip to the hospital back in Fenton. There he was arrested.

With the lost time, John and Will abandoned the following of the black Escalade, but instead trailed the ambulance back to Fenton where John sat in on the questioning of Brian. When Brian was led to a cell for the night, John drove back home to see Cindy, and then called Will to come over for a beer. Barbara had just stopped by his house with fresh lettuce when John called, so Will asked if she could come along, much to her delight.

"Yes," said John. "He's been spilling his story, as if he wants to put it all behind him."

"Maybe he does," said Will. "He's lost his entire family and doesn't seem to have much for friends."

"Poor boy," said Barbara.

"So where's Deluga and that Escalade?" asked Cindy.

John shrugged his shoulders. "I'd like to know who's paying him to be here. He's obviously been hired for something by someone."

"United Eastern Power has all the money," said Will. "Maybe he's on their tab."

"I don't think so," said Cindy. "They use lawyers to do all their dirty work."

"Maybe they have a bad egg in management who brought him in," said Will.

"I have friends in the State Police that owe me a favor," said John. "I asked them to see if they could find out anything about this guy." He took a sip of his beer, then said, "From what Brian Toll said, the guy's a pro and from New York."

"So where's Brian's sister?" asked Barbara. "And her boyfriend Jake?"

"Brian said she wanted to leave the area, so maybe she has," said John. "Tomorrow I'll ask the bus driver if he remembers her. Other than hitchhiking, that's the only way she could have left town."

*

As a professional hit man for hire, Jimmy Deluga had noticed the green Fish and Game Department truck following him. Their tailing effort was far too amateurish to go undetected.

In his profession, nobody lasted long without constantly being aware of everything in the environment around them. The green truck had stayed back a safe distance, never getting closer, even when Jimmy slowed going through Stratford. Obviously, the driver had hoped not to be noticed and was new at the art of tailing.

Several scenarios played out in Jimmy's mind...out running the truck, losing it by turning abruptly onto a side road, or just pulling over and killing the truck's occupants. That sounded the easiest.

But before they reached Lancaster the truck turned off. Maybe it wasn't following him. Or possibly they had called ahead and the police had the road blocked somewhere. But wouldn't the truck have stayed behind to block a retreat?

Jimmy pulled over and stopped. It was so much easier to hide in the city of a million people.

He turned the Escalade around and headed north, then took Route 110 east. The road wound along a wide shallow river with mountains beyond. Passing through a small town with a white covered bridge and a white church, he never noticed the perfect calendar scene. Large flat fields, broken up by picturesque old farm buildings, stretched back to green hills that rose abruptly. To Jimmy the country looked empty and barren. Cresting a hill, he looked down onto the small city of Berlin, and suddenly felt more at ease.

Two hours later he headed north in a used blue Ford pickup truck he had purchased at one of the car dealers on the Berlin-Gorham Road, using a Conway, New Hampshire alias.

50

Jake slept, sagging like a bag of potatoes, yet supported by dozens of wraps of duct tape around the trunk of a maple tree. Mosquitos swarmed around his head and flies landed to walk about his clothes.

"Hey Jake."

In a dream his father called his name. His face contorted, anticipating a blow to the head, but it never came.

"Jake."

It wasn't his father, he knew the voice, it was…he tried hard to think through the fog.

"Jake. It's me, Jimmy."

Jake's eyes blinked open, then settled into a squint. His swollen blotchy face looked like a giant strawberry.

"Wha, wha, whar you been?" he mumbled.

"You pissed your pants," laughed Jimmy. "You ready to write that confession?"

Jakes head shook. "Na, na, I ain't gonna." He swallowed hard. "I need water. Can I have some water?" The hum of the mosquitos sounded like a distant jet. Flies darted about Jake's damp jeans and swollen face.

Jimmy took his gun from its holster and sat on a fallen log. "You can have water, or even a cold beer, if you write that confession." He dropped the magazine out of the pistol and opened the slide, then pushed the magazine back in. When the slide closed, it chambered a round.

Jake's eyes stretched open wide, staring at the gun. "Uh-ah, I canna go to jail."

"If I shoot you in the leg," said Jimmy, "say the kneecap, the blood will attract all sorts of insects. I wonder how long it would be before maggots would appear. What do you think? A couple of days?" He sighted along the top of the gun, aiming at Jake's knee, then put the gun down. "The smell of the blood would probably attract animals too. Are there wolves around here?"

Jimmy re-holstered the gun, then took a bottle of insect repellant from a shirt pocket. While applying it liberally to his forehead, neck, and arms, he said, "Well, I'm going to leave you now. In the morning I'll be back, to see if you've changed your mind." He stuffed the bottle back into his pocket.

Jake started to sob. "Don't leave me. Please don't leave me. Not all night."

"I don't think the animals will bother you," said Jimmy, standing.

As he walked back to his newly purchased truck, Jimmy smiled. Jake's pleas and sobs sounded desperate. He wasn't sure if a bear or something might actually eat Jake during the night, but he was certain that if Jake was still alive in the morning he would be willing to write a confession.

Twenty minutes later, driving through town, he passed the Fish and Game Department truck going the opposite direction. It was time to find a new place to stay for the night.

*

Robert Henderson looked at the letter. Another investor had pulled out, which meant a full third of their financiers were gone. Money spent on the new advertising campaign had been in vain, and the weekend of wining and dining had actually chased some of the moneymen away. The assholes had actually thought the wining and dining a senseless waste of cash. Henderson shook his head in disbelief. The continued stubbornness of the local land owners, combined with the murders of the Hammonds, had given the shareholders the jitters from the beginning. And now things were rapidly sliding down hill. What the hell was Deluga up to? Why hadn't he found the Hammond's killer?

He motioned to the bartender for another Maker's Mark, then swallowed the last of the one in front of him.

Henderson dialed Frank Atkins, but didn't leave a voice mail when Frank didn't answer. He had left three messages earlier, and still the asshole hadn't called back. Could that piece of shit be avoiding him?

As the bartender set down another drink, he punched in Jimmy Deluga's number.

"Hey, what you got?" he snarled, when Jimmy answered.

"Tomorrow. I'll have a confession tomorrow."

"For real?" It was the first good news Henderson had heard in days. He took another swallow of whiskey.

Jimmy laughed. "Yeah. For real. You got the rest of my money?"

"I'll have it," said Henderson, wondering from where the hell he would get it. "Where are you?"

"You don't need to know. Just make sure you have the money," said Jimmy, "and have it up here. I'm not driving halfway across the countryside to pick it up." The phone went dead.

"Hey," said Henderson, motioning to the bartender. "Give me another. And I'd like to buy a drink for the two young ladies at the table over there."

*

Jimmy unpacked his things in a small rented cabin at a place called Snowy Owl Camps. The main lodge sat on an elbow of the Magalloway River, but his cabin was further down along the river's bank, where the property's shaggy lawn blended into the forest. Jimmy doubted anyone from Fenton would look for him that far away, it had to be almost an hour drive.

The silence outside unnerved him. When he checked in at the main lodge earlier, a distant cry, which sounded like a crazy person, went unnoticed by the place's staff, so Jimmy never asked about the loon. Stepping from his cabin, he heard the noise again. Involuntarily, his muscles stiffened. The 9mm pistol stuck in the back of his pants and hidden under his shirt made him feel safe.

Distant rapping, which his reflexes cause him to duck, he later guessed correctly came from a woodpecker.

*

Ethan came running up the back steps into the screened porch, and said, "Grandpa, we're going to the lake to go fishing."

Amy and Shawn followed up the steps.

"You are?" said Will, sitting on the wicker couch.

"That'll be fun," said Barbara, who sat beside him.

"Hi Dad," said Amy. "We're going fishing for horned pout." Shawn stood beside her smiling like a man who had won the lottery.

"Bring plenty of insect repellant," said Will.

After they had left, Will poured more wine into his and Barbara's glasses. "It's going to be a sticky night. The humidity is awful."

"I bet we'll see heat lightning later," said Barbara. "Nature's light show."

They talked about the events of the last couple of days, wondering where Suzy Toll and the man in the Escalade had disappeared to. Conversation drifted to Barbara's garden and then Martha Washington. When Barbara mentioned that the horse needed new shoes, Will laughed, saying that all females seemed to need new shoes. As dark settled in, flashes of light lit the sky over the hills across the far side of the field.

"Want to go for a swim?" asked Will.

"Now? It's dark."

"There's a big pool below the bridge, it's just on the far side of the field. The bottom is all fine pebbles and it's like a big swimming pool. It'll cool us right off."

Barbara smiled coyly, "You know I don't have a bathing suit with me."

Will laughed. "I'm counting on that. Let me grab some towels."

An hour later they sat wrapped in towels on a smooth washed-up log and watched a campfire dance by the side of the river. Above the bridge the river rattled, but below it flowed peacefully into the darkness. Fireflies glowed and then faded amongst the weeds along its banks, and once they glimpsed an owl's silhouette gliding across the river against the night sky.

"We don't get many nights this warm," said Barbara. "And the mosquitos aren't even out."

"There's enough air moving to keep them away," said Will. "Would you like more wine?"

Barbara held her glass out for him to fill. "Do you think this guy you're looking for would kill Suzy's boyfriend Jake?"

"I don't know, what would he gain?"

"Revenge? For the murders of the Hammonds."

"Who would have hired him? He's a professional from down country. I don't think he would do it for Suzy. Someone with money brought him up here, so I don't think it was for revenge."

"Do you think he's still around?"

"Maybe. I'm hoping he left the area. But I'd like to know what happened to Jake."

51

The faintest of morning light woke Will. He pulled on jeans and a shirt, then went downstairs to start coffee. Duchess stood by the door as she always did, her tail wagging, so he let her out first. He knew Amy had come home safely the night before, because her bag was on the table. He smiled, still mildly disbelieving that his daughter and grandson would soon be living nearby. How lucky was that?

Turning on his computer, he brought up the downstate newspaper. As the coffee brewed he read the headlines, stopping at one about the proposed power lines. Political pressure was building to bury them, and the governor of a neighboring state had even offered to bury them down the center strip of a major highway there.

Duchess scratching at the door got Will up, and then he poured a mug of coffee before feeding the dog her breakfast. Sitting in the screened in porch, he wondered if Barbara was up.

Probably. She rose early most mornings to do the chores around her little farm. Will smiled, thinking of Barbara on her horse…she looked beautiful in her riding outfit. The night before had been fun and he really had enjoyed her company. It was a little before midnight when she had left for home.

Duchess stopped by Will's knee and he scratched at the dog's ear. "We should split a little more firewood," he said.

He hadn't more than started the splitter when John Johansson drove in the driveway. Shutting off the machine, Will walked toward the Fish and Game Department's truck.

"What's up?" he asked.

"I got a call from the owner of Snowy Owl Camps," said John. "Last night I sent an email out to all of the motel and lodge owners in the area, hoping someone might recognize Jimmy Deluga or his Escalade. Someone fitting the description is in one of their cabins, but has a different vehicle."

"Did you call the State Police?"

"There's no warrant on him, so they're not going to do anything. It is so frustrating that they don't pay more attention to this corner of the state. Let's go over there and see if we can follow him again."

"I'm up for that," said Will.

"Can we take your truck? It's less conspicuous than the Fish and Game rig."

Ten minutes later they started toward Snowy Owl Camps with Duchess riding on the small back seat of Will's F-150.

*

Whatever that crazy sounding thing was out on the lake, it woke Jimmy long before daylight. For almost an hour he lay there, listening to the cries, sometimes close and others further away. Why didn't someone shoot the things?

Unable to sleep, he slipped from the bed to pull on canvas cargo pants, a khaki shirt with epaulets, and heavy hiking boots. He stuffed his pistol into a holster against his left hip, hidden inside his pants and beneath the shirt.

Outside, fog shrouded the river and mist hung in the air. Tree trunks stood as dark poles against the gray wall. Water dripped from the thick branches overhead, some of it landing in the river with abrupt plops.

At the cry of a loon Jimmy's reflexes reached for his pistol, but stopped just short of grabbing it.

Laughing nervously at himself, he climbed into the safety of his truck. "I got to get back to civilization," he said to no one.

A half hour later he parked in front of the Errol Restaurant.

*

Robert Henderson reached for the TV's remote. Beside him still slept the hooker he'd hired the night before, her platinum blonde hair spread over the pillow. Empty glasses and a half full bottle of vodka sat on the table beside the bed, and clothes were scattered about the hotel room.

What was her name...Stacy or Tracy? Whatever, the woman was a looker and, at twenty-four hundred bucks for a night, supposedly one of the most talented, but nothing had happened. Erectile dysfunction...it had first reared its ugly head when the investors began bailing on the power line project and grew worse as the financial future of the project became a concern. It was a mental thing, he knew that, but stress had never bothered him before. The idea that excessive eating and drinking might affect his performance never entered his mind.

He reached for the vodka bottle and took a swig. Maybe it was time to pay attention to those commercials for E.D. on TV.

Soft fingers ran lightly along his thigh. "Hey baby," said the woman. "Want to give it one more try?" Her head still rested on the pillow, but she had pushed the sheets down to expose her well-rounded artificially enhanced breasts.

"I have a meeting this morning," lied Henderson, not wanting to humiliate himself any further. "I should take a shower and get going." The breasts looked tempting, with their nipples pointed skyward like little missiles ready for launch, but he knew frustration would follow.

She smiled, probably relieved. "Okay. Lock the door on your way out. I'm going to sleep in for a bit longer."

*

Kim sat at the front of the counter in Big Bear Restaurant, reading the local paper and waiting for a customer. The click of the door opening caused her to look up. The man entering as Frank something-or-other, who had been trying to buy up land for United Eastern Power. Stepping around behind the counter, she asked, "Welcome back. Coffee?"

"Sure," said Frank.

As she poured, "What would you like?"

He laughed. "To be back home."

Kim smiled. "You homesick?"

"Yeah," said Frank, reaching for the coffee. "But I'm heading home this morning."

"A long weekend?"

"Yes, a real long weekend. I quit my job," he said, and then smiled. "And I haven't even told my boss yet. He's going to go berserk."

Kim leaned on the counter. "You didn't like your job?"

"I used to. But then I spent a little time out in the woods and so much came back to me. My boss, Henderson, he's such an ass, always just looking for money, screwing everybody along the way. The people up here deserve better than what they've been dealt."

He ordered breakfast and Kim passed his requests on to the kitchen, then snuck out the back door. Behind the restaurant the shallow Abenaki River rumbled over a rocky bottom, drowning out all the other sounds of the town. She stared at the moving water, wondering why rivers drew her to them like they did. Farther upstream she had fished, and Kim wondered if trout might be there right behind the restaurant. The water looked clear and cool and tempting.

And she wondered why she hadn't heard from Will.

52

"That's his truck there," said John, motioning toward the blue Ford pickup.

"What's the plan?" asked Will, lightly touching the brakes and slowing.

"Let's park across the street and wait until he comes out."

Will drove past, turned around in front of a red brick building with a big sign that advertised Husqvarna chainsaws, and then came back. In the nearly full parking lot of a large sporting goods store, Will backed into a parking slot to face the restaurant across the street.

*

Longevity in the hired-muscle business came with paying attention to details. Jimmy fervently believed that. Dumb people were dead people.

Inside the restaurant, Jimmy sat at the lunch counter, waiting for his omelet and glancing at a day old newspaper. He had already noticed a back door on the far side of the restaurant's kitchen, an emergency exit into the parking lot, eight patrons that all looked to be locals, and, through the large windows in the front, a silver F-150 that drove by only to come back and park across the street.

And the way the pickup backed into a space to face the restaurant spelled amateurs.

Nobody got out of the truck. The waitress set Jimmy's omelet on the counter and he stayed to eat it, even asking for a second cup of coffee. The omelet tasted particularly good.

*

"There he is," said John.

Jimmy Deluga had just walked out the restaurant's front door. He passed by his truck and crossed the street.

"Where's he going?" asked Will.

John said nothing.

Deluga walked by a rack of kayaks in front of the sporting goods store and through the glass front door to enter.

"What are we going to do?" asked Will.

"You go in and keep an eye on him," said John. "I'll wait here, because he'll spot me in this uniform."

Will stepped out of his truck and crossed the parking lot. Looking through the store's glass doors, he couldn't see Deluga.

Racks of clothes and tables of sale items greeted him inside, along with a stuffed full-size moose. A ruffed grouse sat on one of its antlers and beside the moose stood an albino beaver. Deluga had disappeared.

Will walked through the store, glancing down a wide isle at the hardware section, then stepped into the home goods department. After making a circle back toward the front of the store, he trotted up the stairs to the firearms department.

Across the room Deluga stood at the counter with his back to Will, chatting with the man behind the register. Two boxes of ammunition sat on the counter, obviously being bought. Will drifted toward the racks of rifles and shotguns to his left, trying to appear like a prospective buyer.

Poking along the rows of standing long guns, Will repeatedly glanced at the counter. Deluga stuffed his change into a wallet, laughed about something with the sales clerk, picked up the boxes, and then went to his right.

Will started to follow.

Deluga disappeared down stairs that led to the fishing department.

Will dashed to the stairway, Deluga wasn't in sight, so he hurried down. The only person downstairs was a man sorting trout flies near the cash register.

It was only twenty feet to a large doorway that led to the store's main lobby. Will hurried, only to find a family with young kids looking at the stuffed moose and two sales people standing near the register. Where had Deluga gone?

Back inside the fishing department, on the far side of the stairs he had just come down, was a closed door. Will returned across the room, looked back at the sales person who still sorted trout flies on the counter, and then opened the door. The bright sunlight caused him to squint. He stepped outside onto a gravel driveway that ran behind the building.

Several boats sat on trailers and canoes were stored in a rack. A large box truck had parked backed against a loading dock. A tall long covered framework held various types of lumber.

Where did Deluga go?

*

Around the east end of the building sat several vehicles, which Jimmy guessed belonged to people employed inside the store. He glanced through the windows of each, until he found an old Chevy Blazer with the keys piled in a cup holder on the center console. The way people trusted others always amazed him.

He opened the driver's door and climbed in. The vehicle smelled of musty cigarettes and ashes were piled high in the ash tray. Two empty beer cans lay on the floor. Jimmy took a moment to dump the ashes out, but then decided to toss the entire tray, and then pitched the cans too.

"Oh shit."

It was a standard transmission. Jimmy had never driven one of those, but he understood the principle. He pressed in the clutch, turned the key, and the engine started right up. After putting the transmission into reverse, he gently released the clutch. The engine stalled.

On the second attempt, the rig started to move and he backed out to the right, but when he hit the brakes the engine stalled again.

He pushed in the clutch, twisted the key, and the motor grumbled to life.

Around the corner of the building he noticed a man standing outside the door he had come out of only a minute earlier. He jammed the shifter into first and then let out the clutch. The engine stalled.

Shit!

Feeling vulnerable, he pushed in the clutch and turned the key again. The engine started right back up. Revving the engine and popping the clutch, the tires chirped and the Blazer jumped ahead.

He didn't slow turning onto the street.

The silver Ford F-150 was still parked in front of the store, and the man inside watched the front door of the store.

It was almost too easy.

Heading back toward Fenton, he pulled into a large field where logs had been spread out into small piles for sorting. At the back side, beyond a parked truck-mounted knuckle-boom loader, he stopped behind a cluster of young fir trees and climbed out of the vehicle, leaving the door open wide. Jimmy feared the stale cigarette smell inside the vehicle would permeate his clothes.

He pulled his pistol from its holster, chambered a round, and then set it on the Blazer's hood. Who were those men following him? Could United Eastern Power have hired them? Maybe Henderson wanted him dead. If those assholes had hired this bunch, they'd hired amateurs.

Four minutes later the silver Ford went by heading for Fenton.

Jimmy stuffed the pistol back in his holster. It was time to find a different ride.

*

"You're sure it was him?" asked John.

"Yeah," answered Will, glancing down at the speedometer. It read eighty-five.

"He might have gone down 16, towards Berlin."

Will nodded and said nothing. They could only guess which route Deluga had taken.

They rounded a long turn to see a mile of empty road ahead of them. If Deluga had gone that way he was flying. On the other side of the notch there were several side roads he could slip away on.

Will pushed the gas pedal to the floor.

53

"Let me buy you lunch," said John, as they approached Big Bear's Restaurant. "We can get my truck afterward."

"I'm not really hungry," said Will, not wanting to bump into Kim if she was working.

"Well I'm starved," said John. "Let's get something."

Will pulled into a parking place and then followed John inside. Kim was wiping down the lunch counter. The place was empty but for two older couples that sat at tables. John walked directly to the counter and slid onto a stool.

As Will sat beside him, Kim smiled and said, "It's nice to see you."

"Nice to see you too," said Will.

Her hand slid across to touch his. "We should go fishing again."

"That would be fun," said Will. Turning to John, he added, "Do you know Kim?"

"Of course," he smiled.

They talked about the water level in the river and then ordered food. Kim disappeared into the kitchen.

"That woman has her eye on you," said John, laughing.

"We went out a couple of times," admitted Will.

"She's a looker."

"I know. And a hell of a fisherman. She wants to get her guide's license."

"She's talked to me about it once," said John. "Kim would do well at it. Her enthusiasm for the sport in contagious."

Remembering Kim's reaction to landing a large fish, Will smiled and said, "I've experienced it."

Laughing, John asked, "Does Barbara know she's got competition?"

Shaking his head, Will said, "I can only guess."

Kim popped back out of the kitchen, wearing a big grin and a sparkle in her eye.

*

Shawn Ash noticed the tracks. Someone in a hurry had turned onto the asphalt, spinning their tires and leaving upturned gravel on the old tote road. Probably teenagers, he thought, either partying or parking.

He followed the road past scattered camps hidden in the woods and then sprawling fields behind tumbled down stone walls. Tall old maples arched over the road and brush crowded the edges. He turned to the right onto an old logging road that had been used for over a decade as a snowmobile trail. Thick softwood trees blocked out the sky and moss covered the ground.

Soon the softwood petered out and the forest turned to second growth maple and poplar, perfectly sized for his mechanical tree harvesting operation. A few weeks before a forester had contacted him for the property's owner to ask if Shawn would be interested in harvesting the wood. He had promised to look at it.

The gentle slope of the land would be easy to work and the firm ground meant it could be done summer or winter. He pulled into a spot between the trees and stopped. Stepping out of his truck he noticed vehicle tracks beside his truck's front tire. Someone else had recently parked in that same spot.

From the tool box behind the cab, Shawn grabbed a roll of florescent orange flagging tape and from behind the seat a small axe. A blue jay cawed a warning up in the treetops.

Shawn looked back up the brushy road, wondering what alarmed the jay, and then started into the woods. The air smelled sweet, of green leaves and summer scents. It felt good to be out walking in the woods.

He stopped, thinking his eyes played tricks on him. A hundred feet ahead a man sagged against a tree.

Hurrying closer, the man appeared unconscious, possibly even dead. Shawn reached the man's neck, hoping to find a pulse.

The man's head jerked upright, startling Shawn.

Red blotches covered the man's puffy skin, caused by thousands of mosquito bites, and flies danced about his soiled clothes. In spite of the mottled swollen face, Shawn recognized Jake. Everyone around Fenton new Jake as a trouble maker and tried to avoid him. For a moment Shawn thought about leaving him there.

A feeble "help" escaped Jakes lips.

"Are you all right?"

Jake gurgled something unintelligible and his chin sagged against his chest again. Then he said, "No…no, I can't. Go, fuckin' go."

"You can't what?" said Shawn, dragging the sharp edge of his axe across the tape that held Jake against the tree.

As the tape parted, Jake sagged to the ground.

"Water," whispered Jake. "Daddy, I need water. Please Daddy, I gotta have water…."

In the fetal position, Jake whimpered.

*

"Fuck," said Jimmy, looking at the tape still stuck to the tree's bark. "Who the fuck freed the asshole?" he said to no one.

He turned to look about the forest with his hand held his pistol ready and aimed skyward. It didn't seem possible.

Jake couldn't have cut the tape. But what were the odds on someone finding him out there? The chances had to be miniscule. Bad luck…it had to be bad luck. Jimmy believed in luck, it came and went in clusters, and the thought of a string of bad luck scared him.

He walked about the tree, looking at the ground. The leaves had been disturbed, but nothing hinted at what had happened. Jake's foul odor still hung in the air, so he couldn't have been gone too long.

Could the cops have found Jake out there? Jimmy didn't see how that was possible. How would he get the confession that he had promised Henderson? Maybe it was time to cut his losses and just go back to New York. Fuck Henderson, fuck the whole north woods.

Jimmy started back toward the five year old pale-green GMC pickup that he had bought from a man down in Gorham earlier that day. It was a cash deal, outside a trailer in Gateway Trailer Park. Jimmy had swapped the plates and driven the rig away.

As his feet shuffled through fallen leaves, a black-backed woodpecker rapped on a dead poplar tree. Jimmy stopped, then, using two hands to aim the pistol at the bird's head, squeezed the trigger. At the blast the bird flew away.

"Fucking sucky luck," said Jimmy, jamming the gun into its holster and heading for the truck again. Bad luck was continuing, which wasn't a good sign. "Nothing is going right. I should just go pop that asshole Henderson and be done with this mess."

But Jimmy wouldn't do that. It would have been bad for business in the long run, because nobody would ever hire him again if he killed his employer. Even though he really liked the thought of it, Jimmy forced the idea from his mind.

Satisfied customers led to future good jobs. How the hell could he prove that Jake had killed the Hammonds and the Tolls?

54

As Will and John stepped out of Big Bear Restaurant, Shawn Ash's truck stopped in the street and the side window went down.

"Hey," he said, pointing with his thumb at the bed of his truck. "I got something for you to see." Shawn backed up and parked next to Will's truck.

"What the hell?" said John, stepping to look into the truck.

Jake lay on his side, his hands and ankles still bound by tape. Tears had created streaks below his eyes, but he said nothing.

"I couldn't put him inside," said Shawn, stepping out, "not the way he smells."

The truck had only been stopped seconds when flies started to swarm around Jake.

"I found him up on South Hill. Someone had left him there overnight, taped to a tree. It was the damnedest thing. I was taking him to the hospital, and then going to call the police."

"I'll call the police for you," said John, digging out his cell phone. "You best get him up there. I'll be along in a minute."

Will dropped John off at his truck and then started for home. Duchess jumped from the back seat into the front seat to sit to watch the world go by through the windshield. Almost immediately Will's cell phone rang. It was Kim.

"Hello," he answered.

"It was nice to see you," she said.

After a pause, he said, "It was nice to see you too."

"There's been a caddis hatch the last few nights and there's been some big browns hitting right after the sun goes down. I'd like to share it with you tonight."

She sounded excited, and his smile came involuntarily. It was easy to imagine her standing in the river and casting a fly. "Where shall we meet?"

"Let's meet in the turnout next to the bridge where the Mooslikamoosuc flows into the Connecticut River, about seven."

"I'll see you there," said Will.

Shaking his head, he stuffed the phone back into his pocket. Did he really want to see Kim again? Or did he just like getting his ego stroked? Duchess looked at him questioningly, or was that his imagination?

He tried to think about what flies to bring. There weren't many caddis imitations in his boxes.

*

Jimmy sat in his truck, parked at the far end of the hospital parking lot, and watched the two State and one Fenton Police cars parked near the hospital entrance. A Fish and Game Department truck had parked a few spaces further down. The air conditioner worked so poorly in the truck that Jimmy had shut off the engine and opened the windows, hoping for a breeze. Warm humid air barely drifted through the truck and perspiration trickled down Jimmy's ribs inside of his shirt.

It was easy to imagine the cops inside trying to get Jake to talk. Maybe he would, but Jake doubted they'd have any better luck than he had. Jake was scared shitless of going to jail.

The Fish and Game officer didn't stay long and soon drove off.

Jimmy wondered what shape Jake was in. There hadn't been any blood where he had been taped to the tree, so wild animals hadn't ripped him up during the night. The thought brought a smile to his lips. Were there wolves up there? Jimmy didn't have a clue, but to him it seemed likely.

Jake must have been a mess, between insect bites and pissing and shitting all over himself. The guy had been delirious the last time he'd seen him. Could a man die in one night from not having water? It seemed doubtful, but Jake hadn't turned out to be too tough.

Jimmy's cell phone rang. It was Henderson again, and for the third time Jimmy hit the mute button so not to hear the ring. That asshole had to learn to be patient.

Two women dressed in nurses clothes came out of a door halfway down the building and started toward Jimmy's truck. Their leather soles clicked on the asphalt, but then they stopped at a Toyota Corolla and climbed in. Soon the car left around the far end of the hospital.

The parking lot was a quiet as a cemetery.

Almost a half hour went by without anything happening, but then a pickup truck entered the lot and parked against the far side, across from the police cars. A young man, dressed in a police officer's uniform, stepped out and went into the hospital. A few minutes later two State Police officers came out, each got into one of the two cruisers, and then left.

Jimmy guessed the police were going to keep Jake under guard while he recovered in the hospital. Soon a Fenton police officer came out and left in his police car.

That left the one young officer inside to guard Jake.

*

Robert Henderson stuffed his phone back into a pocket. Neither Jimmy Deluga nor Frank Atkins would answer his calls. And corporate headquarters had called, wanting to know if the mess surrounding the Hammonds deaths had been cleared up yet, and of course he had nothing new to offer. His boss sounded about to lose it and started yelling over the phone. Henderson felt very alone.

Early that morning he drove north and checked into a room at The Fenton House. Since then he sat on the bed with the TV on and ate Doritos while he placed calls that no one would answer. A briefcase beside the bed contained a little more than two-thirds of the money he had promised Jimmy Deluga.

Henderson hoped Deluga wouldn't stop to count the cash. How could he? It was bundles of twenties, fifties, and hundreds, all in mixed stacks. He planned for it to be difficult to count.

The money had come from Henderson's own personal savings account and a major cash advance on a credit card. Later, when the mess between the local land owners and United Eastern Power cleared up, he would find a way to reimburse himself from company funds. He knew stiffing a known killer was a dumb idea, but there didn't seem to be a better plan.

Glancing at his watch, Henderson decided it was time for a drink, so he left the room, carrying the briefcase, and headed downstairs for the bar. The woman polishing a glass behind the bar looked familiar and he tried to remember her name. Two men sat at a table near the windows and a couple with two small children were at a table near the door.

"Hey," he said, sliding onto a barstool. "How have you been?"

Brenda recognized Henderson right away as the pompous overbearing businessman from down country. But he had money, apparently lots of it, so she flashed a smile. "Fine. It's nice to see you."

"I'd love a bourbon," he said. "Give me your best."

As she reached for a bottle, she said, "So what brings you to town?"

"Business. It's been a rough day."

Brenda wondered if the man knew what rough was. He probably had a new car parked outside, he always appeared wearing expensive clothes, even if they did fit terribly, and, judging by his enormous girth, he had plenty to eat. The asshole wasn't nearly prostituting himself for tips.

"Do you want to talk about it?" she asked, trying hard to appear interested.

Slurping his drink, Henderson started to babble on about the shitheads who populated the world around him. Occasionally, Brenda would interject a "that's awful" or "how can they do that", and always with a practiced caring look. When Henderson's drink neared empty she poured him another.

His sad story started to repeat itself and, with the lack of details, Brenda's mind started to wander. The guy was obviously desperate, but she could only guess what his real problems were. It had to be something to do with the United Eastern Power Company's project. All the bigwig business men that had passed through town during the previous year were connected with it somehow.

"What time do you get off tonight?" asked Henderson.

Brenda forced a smile. "What do you have in mind?"

*

After cresting Hawk Hill, Will noticed Barbara standing next to her mailbox and reading something. He slowed his truck and stopped. "Hi," he said, smiling. "Is that the letter announcing you've won the Publisher's Clearing House prize?" Duchess insisted on sticking her head out the window and her hind end wagged.

Barbara shook her head and patted the dog. "No, just more rubbish. Would you like some lemonade? Or a beer?" With her hair pulled back and in shorts she looked nice.

Will said lemonade sounded good and pulled off the road onto her driveway. Barbara climbed into the truck and he started toward the house, telling of the day's events.

"I got a call from my cousin," said Barbara. "Brian Toll has been released into his uncle's care down in Grafton. That should keep him out of trouble. Nobody has seen his sister anywhere."

Martha Washington stood in the paddock watching the truck come up the driveway. When they climbed out of the truck, Duchess dashed over to the fence, stopping just short of going under it.

"I think Duchess likes Martha's company," said Barbara, shaking her head. "I'm not so sure how Martha feels." The horse stared warily at the dog, but didn't move off.

They sat on the back porch to sip lemonade and speculated on whether the power line company would abandon their project. Duchess trotted back to sit with them and Martha Washington moved to the shade of a maple tree where the goat waited.

"Would you like to come over for dinner tonight?" asked Barbara. "We could cook on the grill."

Will felt a tinge of anxiety, and it must have showed on his face, because Barbara continued with, "Maybe you have other plans?" Her smile appeared frozen.

"Can I take a rain check?" said Will.

"Of course." Barbara looked away.

55

Jimmy slipped from the truck and walked across the parking lot toward the nearest door of the hospital. The engine of a large truck rumbled in the distance, probably another load of logs coming down the hill into town.

Stepping inside the hospital, the air conditioner had cooled the air a tad. The place looked like most hospitals, with white walls and worn tile floors. Beside a door marked "Maintenance" a mop leaned against the wall next to a plastic bucket. Jimmy walked down the short hallway to where a large corridor ran both left and right.

Peaking to the left he saw the officer down at the far end, talking to the woman behind the receptionist's desk. Both of them laughed about something. Three doors lined either side of the corridor, and a chair sat outside the closest one. Looking down to the right, there were four more doors and no one in sight.

The sound of footsteps caused him to look back toward the front desk. A nurse stopped next to the police officer and set her hand on his shoulder. With the smiles, everyone appeared to be old friends. The nurse took a folder from the receptionist and walked down a hallway beyond the front desk.

Jimmy walked back outside, got into his truck, and drove to the hardware store. A few minutes later he came back outside and went to the local Radio Shack. After that he stopped at the gas station.

Twenty minutes after his departure, he returned to the hospital and parked in the same spot he had been in earlier. From the back of his truck he took a one gallon can of gasoline, two candles, a plastic cup, and a toy helicopter designed to be flown by remote control. He walked down the parking lot and stopped behind the pickup truck that the police officer had arrived in earlier.

Jimmy carefully filled the plastic cup with gasoline, then set it under the truck along with the almost full gas can. About a foot away, he placed the two candles upright, and, using a wooden match, he cautiously lit both candles. Three inches from the cup of gasoline, he placed the toy helicopter.

Carrying the toy's remote control, he walked back toward his truck, which he then drove around the back of the building to park against the loading dock. In front of him, across the far side of a large expanse of lawn, another road led from a housing development to a main street. It looked like an easy escape route.

Jimmy entered through a small door next to the loading dock. Silently, he walked down a short hall to peak around the corner. It was the same corridor he had stopped at before and the police officer still flirted with the young woman at the front desk.

The anticipation made Jimmy tingle. Hopefully, at least one of the candles still burned. He took a deep breath, turned on the remote, and then pushed the button marked TAKE OFF.

Jimmy would never know it, but both of the candles still burned. The helicopter's rotating blades whacked the cup of gasoline, flipping the copter over, but also hitting the flammable liquid with enough velocity to spread the propellant around both candles and onto the gas can.

Inside the hospital, Jimmy couldn't hear the muffled *whumph* of the fuel igniting. Flames danced beneath the truck.

The gasoline in the can started to heat, pressurizing the container and pushing fumes out the vent.

Jimmy heard the explosion.

The cop dashed out the hospital's front door, followed by the receptionist. Soon others appeared and all rushed out the front door.

The bursting container had spread gasoline around the underside of the truck. Flames licked the vehicle's sides.

Jimmy ran down the hall and into the room with the chair outside the door. There, Jake lay unconscious and attached to various machines. A wheel chair sat in the corner of the room. Jimmy pushed it to beside the bed, ripped the tubes and wires from Jake's arms, and then dragged him onto the chair.

Jimmy looked down the hall again. A nurse standing by the front desk talked frantically to someone on the phone.

A loud WHOMP outside shook the building's windows, which meant the truck's gas tank had exploded. The nurse tossed down the phone and dashed back outside.

Jimmy pushed the wheel chair, with Jake more laying on it rather than in it, down the corridor and to the door of the loading dock. There, he pushed the button to raise the door. With a clackity-clack, the door took forever to roll upward and open.

When it was just over head-high, Jimmy pushed the wheel chair, with Jake still unconscious on top of it, into the back of his truck, where the chair landed on its side and Jake splayed out beside it.

Jimmy, feeling the high that comes from pulling off something quite daring, jumped down, climbed into the driver's seat, and took off across the back lawn.

*

"What's up?" asked Will, seeing it was John Johansson calling his phone.

"Jake's out," said Johansson, "about twenty minutes ago." He ran through an abbreviated account of what had happened at the hospital, ending with, "A pale green pickup truck was seen driving across the lawn behind the hospital a few minutes after the biggest explosion."

"Who do you think did it?"

"I don't have a clue. The police hadn't got a thing out of Jake. They were hoping he would be more talkative after a night's rest."

"Where are you now?" asked Will.

"I'm on Route 3, north of town. The police are hoping to find the truck somewhere. It couldn't have gone far. The State Police have the roads covered south of Fenton."

Will glanced at the clock on his stove. If was over two hours until he was supposed to meet Kim at the river. "Can I help?" he asked.

"Yeah, the police are stretched pretty thin and can't cover every road out of town. Go park someplace inconspicuous on Hollow Farm Road," said Johansson, "and keep an eye out for that green truck. The witness thought it was a GMC. If you see it, give me a call."

Stuffing his phone back into a pocket, Will turned to Duchess and said, "Do you want to go for a ride?"

*

Jimmy guessed Henderson would be in The Fenton House, or at least nearby. Long ago he had learned that it is sometimes easier to hide out in the open than to sneak about in the shadows. The police would be watching all the roads out of town, looking for a faded green truck, so Jimmy planned to stay right in town until he could arrange another ride.

Driving in along the side of the building he recognized Henderson's shiny new pickup truck parked near the back door. Jimmy drove past to the back of the lot and parked facing the building.

He climbed out of the truck and walked back back to drop the tailgate. Jake was conscious, but still groggy from whatever the hospital had given him.

"Are you ready to talk?" asked Jimmy, grabbing Jake's ankle and dragging him to the back of the truck's bed. "I got another roll of duct tape here."

The tearing sound, as he pulled a length of tape from the roll, caused Jake's eyes to bulge, which made Jimmy grin.

"I'm not leaving you out in the woods again," laughed Jimmy, binding Jakes ankles with the tape. "You're going to sing a song for Mr. Robert Henderson, and tell him all about killing the Hammonds and the Tolls." Jimmy pulled off another length of tape and chuckled.

Jakes eyes had swelled at the sound of the tape.

*

Henderson felt his phone vibrate. Pulling it from his shirt's pocket he saw Jimmy Deluga's name. "Excuse me," he said, turning away from Brenda and slipping from his barstool.

She rolled her eyes and shook her head when he wasn't looking, and went back to polishing a glass. A man walked in wearing heavy jeans, a snug tee shirt, and thick soled boots. Brenda liked loggers and smiled honestly. "What can I get you?" she asked.

Carrying his drink into the empty dining room, Henderson said, "What's up?"

"Where are you?" asked Deluga.

"At the bar in The Fenton House. Do you have the killer's confession?"

"Go out the exit at the back of the building," said Deluga. "Get in your truck and drive it to the back of the parking lot. I'll meet you there."

"We can't meet like that," said Henderson, panicking. "Someone might see us together."

"Do it, now." The phone went dead.

Henderson looked back at the bar, and the sight of his briefcase on the bar top gave him a jolt. Brenda gave him a little wave and mouthed the words "you forgot this", and then went back to polishing a glass. The logger had left.

How could he have forgotten it? Was the alcohol affecting him?

Henderson marched into the bar and grabbed the briefcase. Brenda ignored him, setting the clean glass down and picking up another. He barely noticed her and headed for the back door.

56

"You like Barbara, don't you?" said Will, rubbing Duchess's ear. "She likes animals, and her horse is your buddy." The dog lay across the truck's front seat with her head resting on Will's thigh. He ended with, "I like her too."

They sat in his F-150, which Will had parked against the woods on the far side of a field that looked down on Hollow Farm Road. Every ten or fifteen minutes a vehicle went by, but none of them ever noticed Will's truck tucked against the distant trees. On the hump in the truck's floor, between the two front seats, lay Will's old Colt Woodsman pistol.

Only a half dozen roads led out of Fenton. The State Police had come from both the south and the east, effectively watching those roads. To the west, across the river in Vermont, there were even fewer roads, with only two leading away from Fenton, and the Vermont State Police had those covered. Twice John Johansson called Will to let him know what was going on, but nobody had seen the pale green pickup truck.

"She's a good cook too," continued Will. Duchess shifted her position on the seat. Grinning, Will added, "And she's fun in bed."

Duchess lifted her head, as if shocked at the remark, which made Will laugh.

Glancing at his watch, it was almost time to meet Kim. Will wished he hadn't let himself get talked into fishing with her, but couldn't just stand her up. Something about the young woman pulled at him. What was it? Her age? She was attractive, but they had such differences. He felt like a moth drawn to a flame.

Will pulled his phone from his pocket and punched Johansson's number.

"Hey, I got to get going," said Will. "Has anybody seen anything?"

"No. I'm on the highway north of town and haven't seen him. Everybody has drawn a blank. Maybe he stole a different vehicle and slipped away."

"Wait...." said Will.

"What you got?" asked Johansson.

Will recognized the nearly brand new dark-blue Chevy pickup passing on Hollow Farm Road. "That big wig Henderson, from United Eastern Power, is going by, and he's got someone with him." Duchess sat up to look out the windshield too.

"Are you sure it's him?"

"Yeah. He pulled into my driveway once, and I've seen his picture in the newspaper since then. It's his truck."

"I can be over there in ten minutes," said Johansson.

"He'll be long gone," said Will. "I'll follow him."

He started the truck and slipped it into drive. Henderson's truck had already disappeared around a bend in the road. Will's Ford bounced across the field.

At the next straight section of the road Will glimpsed the Chevy just before it rounded a sharp bend. When he came around that turn the road ahead was empty. Cobble Hill Road bent off to the right. It had to be where the Chevy had gone.

Turning up the road, Will dug out his cell phone and punched Johansson's number. The symbol in the corner of the phone's face meant no signal. He dropped the phone into a cup holder and sped up.

*

Cold perspiration soaked the sides of Henderson's Brooks Brothers shirt. On the passenger side, Jimmy Deluga sat with his semiautomatic pistol resting in his lap, having removed it from its holster when he climbed into the truck. Cobble Hill Road kept on climbing, as if it were headed for the heavens, and Henderson doubted anyone there would be welcoming them.

Henderson had walked out the back door of The Fenton House, as Jimmy had asked, then moved his truck to the back of the parking lot, where Jimmy directed him to back it in next to his own.

There, Jimmy had dropped the tailgate of Henderson's truck, yanked Jake to the back of his own truck, and then slung the putrid-smelling taped-up young man over his shoulders to deposit him in the back of Henderson's shiny pickup truck with a thud. Other than a sorry moan, not a sound escaped Jake's taped-up mouth.

But Henderson had protested, not wanting to soil the back of his unblemished new Chevy. Jimmy ignored his objections and, just once, flashed his firearm to quiet the man down. It was obvious that Henderson had been drinking and was near panicking.

Jimmy had ended their conversation in the parking lot with, "Shut the fuck up and let's get out of here."

Where the asphalt ran out on Cobble Hill Road the tires started to rumble over stones in the packed gravel. Henderson flinched, expecting a rough ride, but the road had recently been graded. A few small camps hugged the hill to the left and on the right the land fell away to a tumbling stream in a gully. It felt like the road to nowhere.

"Where are we going?" asked Henderson.

Jimmy said, "Just drive."

The woods opened up to fields and a cluster of houses. Jimmy had Henderson turn through a couple of intersections and then continue uphill past a stately old farm. Majestic rock maples lined the road and a sugar shack sat in a field against the woods.

"Go left up there," said Jimmy, as they approached an old log camp.

The road leveled, but became rougher. A clearcut on the right looked to Henderson to be a vast wasteland. Where the road dipped, they entered the woods again and soon passed three camps with nicely mowed lawns. Jimmy held his pistol firmly so it wouldn't fall from his lap. Henderson's mouth felt very dry.

Ledge poked up through the gravel, making for large bumps, and Henderson slowed. The road grew narrower and started down a hill.

"Take the next left," said Jimmy, pointing ahead with the gun.

Henderson's stomach felt about to revolt and he hoped the junk he'd eaten earlier would stay down. Where the heck were they going? It seemed like the middle of nowhere.

And he needed to piss so bad that it hurt, but he didn't want to ask permission to stop. As long as they kept moving he figured Jimmy wouldn't shoot him.

A brown bird that looked like a chicken paraded into the tote road ahead of them and stopped. Reflexes cause Henderson to hit the brakes.

"It's a fucking bird," said Jimmy. "Keep going."

Dark feathers around the bird's neck flared up and the bird started to strut. Neither of them would ever know it was a ruffed grouse.

"Get moving," snarled Jimmy.

Henderson didn't want to run the bird over, so he inched his truck ahead slowly.

With its right wing flailing as if broken, the bird ran off the road toward a wild apple tree, attempting to lead the danger away from her hidden brood.

*

Will hit the brakes. Ahead, around a gentle bend in the narrow old road, glared the brake lights of Henderson's blue truck.

"Yeah, I can see the truck," he said, into his phone.

"Don't crowd them," said Johansson. "I'm turning onto Cobble Hill Road now."

The brake lights went dim and the back of the truck disappeared. Duchess stood on the seat, hoping to see better.

"Sit," said Will.

"What?" asked Johansson.

"I was talking to the dog."

"Stay back, don't let them…." The call was dropped. Will stuffed the phone into his shirt pocket.

"Duchess, sit," said Will. "Keep your nose off the windshield." They started ahead again.

Slowly rounding the bend, the road created a tunnel through the trees. At the far end bright light indicated an opening, probably a field. Henderson's truck had disappeared ahead. Nearing the open land, Will slowed and pulled into the beginning of a logging road that climbed steeply to the left.

Grabbing the Woodsman pistol and slipping from the truck, he left Duchess inside and snuck to the edge of the trees.

The big field sloped precipitously to the east. A sign with a picture of a snowmobile on it said "Stay on the Trail or Stay Home". Distant gray mountains to the east rose in faraway haze and two ravens flapped their wings, heading south. Far across the valley to the north rose Hawk Hill, with the open pastures near its top and on its lower eastern flank, which was where Will's home stood.

Henderson's pickup had stopped in the middle of the field, facing away. The tailgate was down and Will could see someone laying in the truck's bed, but the distance was too great to tell who. Maybe a corpse?

He easily recognized Henderson by the man's girth, but couldn't be certain other man's identity remained a mystery...possibly it was Deluga.

Will dug out his phone again and punched Johansson's number. Surprisingly, the call went through.

"I'm at a big field," he said, then explained what he could see.

"Stay put," said Johansson. "I'll be there in two minutes."

The other man dragged whoever it was in the back of the truck to the tailgate's edge and ripped tape from the man's mouth.

Will felt pretty certain the second man was Jimmy Deluga, the same guy he had seen in the bar at The Fenton House and at the Toll's house. And he had been armed both times, so it was a safe bet that he still was.

Henderson and the other man talked to the guy laying in the truck. Their voices started to raise, but Will couldn't make out words. The smaller man pulled out a pistol and aimed it at the man lying in the truck.

*

"Are you ready to ready to sign that confession," said Deluga, poking Jake with his gun. "I got it already for you. Just put your name at the bottom."

Henderson's knees felt weak. "Did he do it?"

"Yeah. He offed the Hammonds and then the Tolls too, hoping his sweet girlfriend would inherit everything," said Deluga.

Jake, stretched out on his side with tape around his hands and wrists, didn't say a thing.

Henderson asked, "Where is she now?"

Deluga laughed. "Run off somewhere, probably with some meal ticket rich boy." Jabbing Jake again with the gun's muzzle, he asked, "Shall I cut your hands free so you can write your name?"

Henderson started to panic. Since they got out of the truck, he still hadn't turned his back on Deluga to pee, and he fought desperately for control. He swallowed hard, scared shitless and trying not to whimper.

Jake nodded his head.

Jimmy tucked the gun in his belt and dug a small knife out of his pocket. It easily sliced the tape, freeing Jake's hands.

"Sit up," said Deluga, unfolding a piece of paper from his pocket.

Jake, looking like a cornered animal, rubbed his wrists and gingerly propped himself up on an elbow. Deluga handed him a pen.

Turning to Henderson, Deluga said, "Now you got your confession, get me the money."

Henderson grabbed the briefcase from behind the truck's seat and set it on the tailgate. A cold bead of sweat trickled down his ribs as he undid the clasps. Deluga wouldn't actually count it...would he?

He opened the top.

Stacks of napkins imprinted with "The Fenton House" filled the inside.

"You're a dead man," said Deluga.

Warm liquid ran down Henderson's thighs.

Deluga turned back toward the woods and said, "What the...?"

*

Will heard it too, a loud metallic thud. Johansson must be coming too fast and gone over a bump hard, probably a piece of ledge somewhere.

The man turned back toward Henderson and raised his pistol. Will could see him say something, then he pointed the gun at Jake. The weapon barked and Jake slumped.

Will snatched up his pistol and, steadying his hand against a tree trunk, aimed at Deluga.

As Deluga's gun swung toward Henderson, Will pulled the trigger.

Deluga heard the pop of the 22 that same instant that Henderson swatted something on his own left shoulder.

Will had missed, hitting Henderson.

Deluga fired two shots towards the woods, which caused Will to duck down behind a boulder.

Johansson's truck pulled out into the field and Deluga fired three shots. The windshield crumbled and the truck spun sideways and stopped. Johansson rolled out the driver's door to dash behind the truck's rear fender.

"You all right?" he yelled up at Will.

"Yeah."

"Is it just the two of them?"

"They got someone tied up in the back of the truck," shouted Will. "I think they killed him."

The thud of a car door caused them both to look. Henderson still stood in the field, clasping his left shoulder, but his pickup truck bounced across the pasture towards the woods. The man who had been in the back of the pickup lay by Henderson's feet.

"Shit," said Johansson, starting back toward the driver's door. "You get Henderson. I'll try to keep up with the other guy."

"You've got fluid running out of your radiator," said Will. "You're not going far."

"Damn it," said Johansson, watching the trees on the far side of the field swallow up Henderson's truck. "That asshole will be gone in no time."

He climbed into his truck to call the State Police on the two-way radio. Will walked out into the field toward Henderson.

"My truck got hijacked," said Henderson, his right hand still clutching his blood soaked left arm. "He took my truck." The man looked about to cry.

"How's your arm?" asked Will. Jake lay in a heap on the ground beside an open briefcase. The Fenton House napkins fluttered in the breeze like autumn leaves.

"It's just a nick," said Henderson, flexing the fingers of his left hand. Blood dribbled down and dripped from his wrist.

Will could find no pulse on Jake's neck.

"We got an ambulance coming," said Johansson, as he approached, "and the State Police and a wrecker."

"It's too late for Jake," said Will.

"Aren't you going after my truck?" pleaded Henderson.

Johansson shook his head. "No. Who's the guy who stole it?"

Henderson's face turned a pasty gray. "That truck cost me a lot of money?"

"Who's driving it?" asked Johansson.

"I don't know his name. He hijacked me right behind The Fenton House."

"You're lying. I think that man works for you," said Will. "You brought him in to kill the Hammonds. His name is Jimmy Deluga."

Henderson's complexion faded to white. "That's not true. I've never seen that man before today."

57

Will opened the door of his truck to let Duchess out and glanced at his watch. Kim probably was madder than hell and had already gone home. The State Police and Johansson were still out in the field and the sun had slipped behind the hill almost an hour before. An ambulance had come and then left with Henderson inside, accompanied by another State Police vehicle. A hearse still waited to retrieve Jake's body.

"Come on," said Will. "Get in."

Duchess jumped back into the truck and he followed.

"You must be hungry," said Will, backing out onto the old road. "I am. What have we got in the house to eat?" As they started to leave, he glanced in the rear view mirror and said, "I haven't seen this many State cops up here, ever."

In the dark shadows of the trees, he turned on the headlights. "Kim is probably pissed. I don't blame her."

Pulling his cell phone from his pocket, he checked to see if it received a signal, which it did, but a weak one. Maybe once they got around the other side of the hill he would call her.

The local police had covered the only road to the north, which was the direction Jimmy Deluga was heading in Henderson's truck. The trail dropped down into the valley to come out on the side of Hawk Hill about a half mile from his home.

Will wondered if they would have any luck finding the truck or Deluga. Maybe they'd find the truck, but that guy was a pro. If it hadn't been such a hot dry summer, that woods road, which was a snowmobile trail in the winter, would have been muddy and impassible.

*

A large knot formed in Jimmy Deluga's stomach. The thought of getting lost terrified him. The late hour, combined and with unknown wilderness ahead, didn't bode well. Entering the worst neighborhood of any North American city would not have caused such concern.

Deep ruts gouged the road, first tilting the truck to the right and then snapping it to the left. He drove as fast as he dared, not knowing if anyone gave chase. After a violent dip, where his head bounced off the truck's headliner, Jimmy buckled his seatbelt and cinched it up tight.

The woods opened where recent logging had taken place. A few spindly trees poked up from green weeds and abandoned tree tops. A few beat-up shattered logs lay in the road, but the truck easily bounded over them. Soon the grassy road dropped down into eerily dark forest again.

There didn't seem to be anybody following, but Jimmy still drove fast. The end of a stick whipped up to whack the underside of the vehicle, which startled him, and at first he thought someone had shot at the truck. He hurried on.

The thick trees blotted out the sky. Tall ferns crowded the forest floor only a few feet from the trail, thick enough to swallow up a man, or even a bear. The road had turned from grass to hard dried mud, with deep ruts and occasional white rocks poking through.

A metal pipe gate blocked the road.

A sign had a picture of an ATV on it with a slash through it, and a chain around a fat wood post kept the gate closed. Beyond it, the woods looked different, with younger trees and more sunlight getting through to the ground. Jimmy would never realize it, but the area on the other side of the property line was early successional forest, having been logged fifteen years before.

Jimmy pushed the gas pedal to the floor and the truck plowed into the gate. The frame swung and the chain yanked the post out of the ground. The truck's right tires clawed up over the mess.

The road went down a steep slope and at the bottom a deep gully crossed. Jimmy stopped and shut off the truck. Stepping out, water gurgled through the ditch, but at least no vehicles could be heard. The air felt the coolest it had in days.

The trench looked about knee deep, with a stream of water tumbling through it. Jimmy stepped into the chasm. The bottom was hard, but the edges were steep. Could he get through in four wheel drive?

He climbed back into the truck, started it up, clicked the transmission into drive, and then eased the front wheels into the ditch.

The truck's front end dropped and the front bumper hit the far side with a crunch. Jimmy pushed the gas pedal.

Both front and hind wheels spun.

He slipped the transmission into reverse. The same thing.

Rocking the vehicle fore and aft moved it inches, but the front end stayed down in the trench.

"Fuck," he said to no one.

He stepped from the truck, leaving the door open, and continued on foot. About thirty feet from the front bumper, he stopped, turned back toward the truck, drew his pistol, and then fired a shot through the windshield. If Henderson had been still driving, he would have been killed.

"I should have done that a long time ago," he said, stuffing his weapon back into its holster.

The shot echoed off the hillsides and Jimmy realized he had done something irrational. It wasn't at all like to him act unprofessional. Had anyone heard it?

"What the fuck is wrong with me?" he mumbled.

The road rose up a long slope and then traversed the side of a hill. Animals had left tracks where the soil was soft and Jimmy wondered what wolf tracks looked like. Were there mountain lions? Bears?

In the distance he could hear an airplane. Were the authorities searching for him by plane? Soon it would be too dark for that. The flute-like sound of a wood thrush spooked him, and he found himself wondering about elves and dwarfs. Could there really be such things? All those fairy tales had to originate somewhere.

"Snap out of it," he said, shaking his head.

Jimmy had never been one to talk to himself, and he wondered if all the time in the north woods was making him loose his mind. He touched his gun, which gave him a feeling of security.

Maybe.

58

Will dialed his home number. Amy answered. He ran through a brief discourse of what had happened, ending with, "I'm still on Cobble Hill Road, but I'll be home soon. Lock the doors and keep Ethan inside."

"Do you think he'll come here?"

"I doubt it," he said, not wanting to scare her, but added, "Is Shawn nearby? Call him and have him come over."

"He's working I think. The phones don't work up where they're cutting."

"I'll be home soon," promised Will, ending the call.

After making the sharp turn by the old log cabin, he punched Kim's number using the thumb of his right hand. When she didn't pick up he guessed she was either in the river still fishing or madder than hell and ignoring him, probably the latter. He left no voice mail.

Will pushed Barbara's phone number.

*

Jimmy walked out into a large field circled with dark spooky woods. Stars hadn't started to poke through the waning daylight, but he knew it wouldn't be long. Following wheel ruts across the grass, the place felt like the middle of nowhere. Jimmy, ever the city boy, wondered how many people were eaten each year by wild animals.

A dog barking somewhere ahead brought him back to reality. Or was it a wolf? Jimmy felt pretty certain it was a dog. Still, he pulled his gun from its holster and carried it in his hand, ready for instant use.

At the far end of the field the wheel ruts led to a gate. He walked around one end and onto a gravel road. The dog barked again and someone yelled at it. Jimmy laughed...it wasn't a wolf. He stuffed the pistol back in its holster. Soon, lights up the hill to the left poked through the trees.

A short distance ahead a driveway led up a steep slope to that house. Jimmy stayed in the shadows and the dog remained silent. Soon he walked by a trailer with all its windows dark, and then another home perched on the left above an expansive green lawn. Ahead, he could see where the gravel road intersected an asphalt one.

Jimmy slipped along the edge of the lawn. Through a large picture window he could see an older couple watching TV. Around the uphill side of the house a SUV and a pickup truck sat in the driveway. Starting either would alert the people inside, so he kept on walking, and headed out the driveway.

Approaching the street, he slowed and looked up the hill to his left. It was a long way to the crest and looked sort of familiar. He guessed correctly that the burned Hammond house hid up near the hill's top. And he guessed incorrectly that the road going down the hill to the right had to go through to somewhere.

The hour had grown late enough that any vehicles coming would have headlights on and hiding in the shadows would be easy. He started down the hill.

*

Barbara Hawkins looked out the front window into the night. Out beyond the end of the driveway, headlights drove past. Earlier, she had seen the Fenton police car drive by, twice, which was extremely unusual, and she wondered if the vehicle passing by was again the police. What could they be looking for? Could someone be lost?

She walked back into the kitchen where a small plastic container of strawberries waited to be picked through. It was probably the last batch of the summer, and she wanted to wash them and put them in the refrigerator to save for one last strawberry shortcake, which she hoped to share with Will Northrop. A smile spread across her face.

But then she frowned. So that young hussy from the restaurant had talked him into going fishing. What did that young woman have that she didn't, except youth? That was a pretty big something, at least to most men she guessed. Will didn't seem like the kind of man that needed his ego stroked, but maybe all men did a little.

The phone interrupted and hearing Will's voice brought back her smile.

He quickly ran through the late afternoon's events and asked her to lock the doors, ending by saying he would stop by in about ten minutes.

Walking to the front door, Barbara smiled, appreciating Will's concern, but feeling his fears were probably groundless. After locking the back door too, she went to the hall closet and took out an old side-by-side shotgun that her husband had used for bird hunting. Why not? It is always better to be prepared, she told herself. On a shelf over the hanging coats she found an old box of Remington low brass number eights, which she guessed would discourage anyone from bothering her.

After leaning the gun against the kitchen counter and setting the box of shells next to it, she went to the back door and looked out through the glass, then flicked on the outside light.

A man stepped behind the corner of the barn.

Barbara gasped and turned to snatch up the shotgun. With trembling hands she managed to open the breech and insert two shells. Then she picked up the phone.

There was no dial tone. And nobody's cell phone ever worked on that side of Hawk Hill.

*

Inside the barn it was as dark as a cave. Jimmy felt certain he had slipped behind the corner of the barn before anyone could have seen him, but he wasn't going to linger. Taking chances would be stupid.

The air smelled of hay and animals, not cars or machinery. He had hoped to find a vehicle parked inside.

Something moved, causing the hair to prickle up on the back of Jimmy's neck. Without thought his hand reached for his pistol. He guessed there were horses in there, maybe one, maybe a bunch. Horses didn't worry him. He had seen enough of them on TV to believe they were friendly docile animals.

His eyes adjusted enough to make out the walls and windows at the far end. Letting his fingers slide along the right wall, he walked further in. A horse snorted and Jimmy stopped. Something moved over on the left side too. There had to be at least two horses. The hoofs of the one on the right clacked against the floor.

Jimmy took one more step.

The dark shape of a head that looked the size of a tyrannosaurus rex's came out of the wall to Jimmy's right and nipped his right arm. He leapt back, landing against the left wall. His left hand found a wooden latch and opened a small door to step through it.

The startled goat lowered its head and slammed into Jimmy's hip, knocking him over.

*

The gunshot caused Barbara to pick up the phone again, but there still was no dial tone. At the second gunshot she started toward the door.

59

The flash of the first shot sent the bullet into a stout spruce post on the far side of the barn, but burst of light also gave Jimmy a glimpse of the demon goat. Still on his side, he rolled and aimed into the darkness and pulled the trigger. But the goat, Ram, ever the opportunist, had realigned with Jimmy's forehead and, living up to his name, slammed his craggy horns into it. That bullet plowed through the pine planks overhead and borrowed into the hay in the loft.

Reflexes brought Jimmy's hands up over his face to find warm blood. Not certain if he could remain conscious through another contact with the goat, he rolled onto his feet and staggered out of the stall's doorway and across the barn.

Martha Washington bit his shoulder.

"What the fuck!" he screamed, yanking away and stumbling toward the barn's back door.

The air outside smelled clean. His hand found little new blood on his face, but his head hurt like hell. A crick in his neck prevented him from straightening up or turning his head.

Turning to the right, with his head cocked to the right, he hurried into the night.

Behind him, the lights came on in the barn.

*

The lights had caught Will's attention. He pulled into the long driveway and climbed out of his truck near the house, stopping to glance at the door. Duchess jumped from the truck and bounded toward the barn. With long strides, Will followed.

"Barbara?" he called.

"Will." She stepped from the barn. "Will, someone was shooting inside the barn."

Reaching for her, he asked, "Is everything all right?"

With the shotgun dangling from her right hand, Barbara folded into his arms. "I think so," she said, with the side of her face against his chest. "Martha and Ram are both fine."

"Let's lock up the barn," said Will. "I want to get home and check on Amy and Ethan."

"I already locked up the far end," she said. "We have to get Ram back in her stall."

"How are we going to do that?" said Will. The large goat nibbled at hay on the barn's floor. The critter looked both strong and stubborn.

"I'll run in the house and get a carrot."

"You're not going anywhere without me," said Will. "Let me carry the gun."

When they returned to the barn, Ram proved wary and ignored the offered carrot.

*

The headache felt the worst of Jimmy's life. Following the edge of the woods, he crept along the side of Barbara's property, his pistol ready in his hand.

Fireflies glowed and then faded among the murky shapes around hm. Voices caused him to stop and peer toward the house. In the glow of the back door's light a dog pranced toward the house, soon followed by a woman and a man carrying a gun.

Jimmy hurried on, searching for the road. But when he walked fast, pain shot up his neck with every footfall. The loud gunfire inside the barn had caused his ears to start ringing.

The stars shared enough light to illuminate shapes, but shadows swallowed up everything else. He walked cautiously, so as not to trip and possibly jar his neck. Crickets ratcheted and a screech owl shrilled its descending call.

Beyond the black shape of a spruce tree he found the road.

Turning to the left, he followed the edge of it down the hill. It seemed appropriate, because lately his whole life had been going downhill. He longed for the noise and smells of the city. Insects and frogs shrieked their summer songs, but Jimmy missed the clatter of vehicles, the honking of their horns, and the raised voices of irritated people.

He stuffed his gun back into its holster and walked fast along the edge of the asphalt. Frequently he turned to look back, twisting at the waist because moving his neck was so painful. After a few minutes the road started to level out. The edge of the moon peeked over a hill to the east, bringing a pale white light and casting long shadows. Jimmy found himself almost running. Only the pain in his neck prevented it.

"Calm down," he said to himself. "You're losing it."

He turned to look back up the hill. There wasn't a manmade light in sight anywhere. A coyote yipped on a faraway hillside. Jimmy pulled out his pistol to carry it in his hand again.

"There has to be a vehicle to steal somewhere," he mumbled, continuing on. "And then it's back home, I'm out of here."

*

"Would you like a glass of wine?" asked Amy.

"I would love one," answered Barbara.

Amy looked into the living room where Ethan sat on the floor with Shawn sorting out a set of Lincoln Logs that he had just brought over. "Shawn, a beer?"

"Yes please," he said, getting up. The thick soled logging boots made him look exceptionally tall.

Will headed through the house to check the lock on the front door. It had never been used since he had bought the house. Content that it was secure, he took an Ithaca pump shotgun out of the gun cabinet and a box of OO buckshot from a drawer.

After he and Barbara had finally tricked Ram into entering his stall, they secured the barn, locked up her house, and then drove down to his place. Amy had locked the doors as he had asked, and it felt good to be back there with her. Shawn had arrived not long after with the set of Lincoln Logs for Ethan, and they quickly filled him in on the day's events.

Walking back into the kitchen and stuffing shells into the gun, Will said to Amy, "Did you take the keys out of your car?"

"Yes. Do you really think you are going to need that?" asked Amy, her eyebrows going up.

"You never know if you're going to need a fire extinguisher until you do," said Will, leaning the weapon against an inside door casing. "So you always want it to be ready."

"Scotch?" asked Barbara.

"No thanks," said Will.

The phone rang and Amy picked it up. Will's stomach tightened…could it be Kim calling?

"Dad, it's John Johansson," said Amy, offering him the phone.

"What's up?"

"Henderson was sticking to his story," said Johansson "said he had no idea who that other guy was. Now he's demanding to see his lawyer.

"The State Police have found his truck abandoned about half way through the woods to your place" continued Johansson. "They brought in dogs to pick up the trail and are patrolling the roads up your way. They really want that guy. Keep your doors locked."

Will ran through what had transpired at Barbara's home, and Johansson said he would head over there with one of the State Police officers.

60

Kim wasn't sure what she felt.

After arriving at their meeting spot, she readied her fly rod and then slipped into stocking foot waders. When Will didn't show on time, she waded into the river next to the road to fish while waiting.

He could have had truck trouble, or maybe something happened at home. There were dozens of reasons he could be late. She checked her cell phone and the signal was strong. Mindlessly, she changed flies, taking off the hair wing caddis and tying on a Copper John. The heavy nymph landed with a plop.

An hour later she waded from the water and sat on the bank, deciding either the fish weren't biting or her mind was distracted. Caddis flies had been skipping over the river's surface and she hadn't seen a single fish rise, but, then again, Kim knew she hadn't really been paying attention.

Did she really like him? Or was it she couldn't take losing? Kim's competitiveness had often been a problem. She couldn't fish beside someone else with *having* to catch more fish than them. Playing cards, softball, tennis, it had always been the same. Every time she had to be number one.

What was it Will had told her once…fishing was supposed to be a contemplative past time, not a competitive sport. How could anyone not want to catch more than everyone else? Weren't we all supposed to be the best at whatever we were doing?

Kim tossed a stone out into the river.

Could Will really have feelings for Barbara? Kim didn't know her well, but knew Barbara had to be close to fifty. How could Will want to curl up with her when she was so much younger? Wasn't that what all men wanted?

The cooler night air had settled in and few caddis flies still danced on the river. A bat fluttered its erratic flight over the rumbling water, dipping down to catch errant insects and then twisting up toward the sky before diving down again. A mosquito landed on Kim's cheek and she brushed it away.

Maybe it was time to head for Colorado or Idaho, someplace new, where there were trout and maybe less confusing men.

She nipped the fly off the end of her line and then walked up toward her car, cranking in the line.

*

Turning, to look back behind him, Jimmy noticed the glow of headlights in the tops of trees far back up the road behind him. He slipped into the woods and remained motionless. The vehicle passed by.

Was it the police? Jimmy couldn't tell, but thought it might be. When he could no longer hear the tires on the asphalt, he walked back to the edge of the road. If only the blazing headache and the crick in his neck would go away life might not seem so desperate.

He continued down the road, his footsteps scrunching sand on the road.

Headlights appeared far down the road ahead of him. Jimmy slithered into the trees again to let them pass. It felt like forever before it drove by. Was it the same vehicle? He couldn't tell, but maybe.

Again he waited for silence before creeping back out to the road and continuing down the hill. Soon the woods on the left stopped and enormous fields looked to run off forever. Far ahead black mountains rose against the stars of the night sky. The lights from one distant house off to the north brought a sense of relief, at least he wasn't alone on the planet. Soon the road bent toward that house.

*

"Shawn, did you leave your keys in your truck?" asked Will.

"Yeah, I did," said Shawn. "I never take them out." He rose from the floor, where he had helped Ethan build a log house the size of a shoe box. "I'll get 'em. I'm the last one in the driveway."

"I'd hate to see someone steal it," said Will, watching Shawn head for the door.

"Me too," laughed Shawn.

After the lights inside, the night seemed dark as ink. Shawn opened the door of his truck and reached for the far side of the steering wheel.

Something hard poked him in the ribs.

"Don't say a thing," said a voice in the darkness. "And don't turn around."

"What do you want?" asked Shawn, glancing down at the knob of his axe handle, which poked out from behind the truck's seat. He guessed it was a gun barrel against his ribcage. The Kimber Model 1911, which used to belong to Jimmy Deluga, was under the front edge of the truck's seat.

"Your truck."

"Now why would you want that?" said Shawn, seeking a diversion. "Aren't you the guy that was hired to kill the Hammonds? Why don't you just turn yourself in?"

The pistol moved away and the voice said, "That asshole Jake killed the Hammonds. Henderson hired me to figure it out."

"Well, take the truck," said Shawn. "The key's in it. I'm not going to argue with you."

"Get away from the truck and lay on the ground."

As Shawn stepped back he snatched up the axe handle and yanked the weapon clear of the seat and spun in a blur with the axe held head high. A hollow point .380 bullet ripped into his left shoulder, but his massive muscular spinning body was already in motion.

The axe cleared the top Jimmy's head by an inch and plowed into the corner of Shawn's truck's cab. For the first time in his sorry life, Jimmy was glad he was short.

The second bullet missed Shawn completely as he crumbled to the ground. Deluga scrambled over him and up into the truck.

The key wasn't in the ignition.

The back door of the house flew open and Will stepped out holding the pump shotgun. Jimmy stuck his hand out the cab and fired. Will dove off the back of the steps into the darkness. A hand grabbed Jimmy's ankle. Shawn had rolled upward into a sitting position beside the truck.

Jimmy jammed the muzzle of his gun against Shawn's temple. "Give me the keys."

"On the floor," said Shawn, frozen motionless.

Jimmy slammed the butt of his gun against Shawn's temple. Feeling around, he snatched up the keys, just as Shawn's large hand again grabbed his leg and yanked. Jimmy swung the gun and fired wildly, but Shawn's burly arm propelled him out onto the ground.

Jimmy rolled over to look up at a Kimber Model 1911 aimed at his face.

"I think this once belonged to you," said Shawn.

"Are you all right?" It was Will beside the house.

When Shawn's head turned to answer, Jimmy rolled and fired three quick shots.

Shawn staggered back and stumbled behind Amy's Camry. Jimmy clambered up into the truck as Shawn aimed. The forty-five roared.

The truck's engine started.

A shotgun blast took out its windshield.

Shawn's truck bolted out the driveway with Jimmy at the wheel. Buckshot and forty-five caliber slugs ripped through the truck.

61

"The EMTs said Shawn's going to be fine," said Will, sitting on the couch beside Barbara. Outside the screened porch a cricket rattled out one long note. "None of the bullets hit anything vital."

"He must hurt," said Barbara, taking the wine glass he offered.

Faraway, on the far side of the field near the river, the blinking blue lights of three State Police vehicles continued to flash. Duchess slept soundly on the rug in front of the couch and outside the screens the summer insects crooned.

"I'm sure he does, but he's pretty tough. Amy's keeping him company at the hospital and I'm sure that makes him feel better."

"Do you suppose Ethan is asleep?"

"I don't know. He was worried about his mother and Shawn, but it has to have been an exhausting night for him."

None of the police cars had moved in almost two hours, and they guessed the officers were searching up in the woods across the river. Fireflies glowed and then faded over the dark lawn surrounding Will's home. About ten minutes earlier, the State Police detective had finally left after asking what seemed like a million questions.

"This is going to make front page news," said Barbara, "even in the papers downstate."

"I think this is the last nail in the coffin for United Easter Power," said Will, setting down his tumbler of Glenmorangie and then slipping an arm behind Barbara's shoulder. "All the dirt with Henderson and this hired gun is going to give them an awful lot of bad press."

He leaned in to kiss Barbara.

"I really enjoy your company," he said, taking her hand in his.

"Me too, I mean your company," said Barbara, a bit flustered.

He laughed. "Dinner tomorrow night?"

She smiled. "Yes."

"And the night after that?" said Will. "And the night after that?"

Barbara grinned. "Maybe."

"Look," said Will, motioning toward the field. One set of headlights bounced back toward the house.

The phone rang and he excused himself to answer it.

"That was Amy," he said, returning. "Shawn is doing fine. He's very lucky, all the bullets just tore flesh, and nothing serious was damaged. The hospital is releasing him and Amy's going to spend the night at his house."

The headlights turned into the driveway and Duchess's head came up off the floor. Will went to the door to find John Johansson coming up the back steps.

"Come on in," he said. "Are the police having any luck?" Duchess sniffed John's leg.

John shook his head, reaching down to touch the dog's head. "No. The guy drove Shawn's truck right into the river. The truck is totaled and stuck up to its hood in that pool next to the bridge. There's a wrecker on the way to pull it up onto dry land. There's blood inside, so maybe he was hurt or passed out and couldn't drive, we don't know. The door was open and nobody's found a body."

"Want a beer?"

"No, I should go home and get some sleep. Cindy must be worried about me."

"We should have you two over," said Will. "How's she doing?"

"Great. She's really settling into life up here," said John, beaming.

"Hi John." It was Barbara coming in from the porch. "I've noticed a spring in your step since Cindy has been around," she said, teasing.

He laughed. "That may be.

"The State Police are starting a search in the morning at daybreak," he continued, "and the Fish and Game Department is coming out in force to help. Have you heard anything about Shawn?"

Will filled him in, then asked, "Do you think the guy's alive or a body floating downstream somewhere?"

"I don't know," said John, shaking his head. "Maybe he jumped out of the truck long before it went into the river, just to throw us off. We couldn't tell if the cruise control had been left on. I keep thinking he jumped out halfway across the field and let the truck drive on into the river. Everyone would have chased his taillights while he dashed off into the woods somewhere."

"We'll keep the doors locked," said Will.

"Yes, do that," said John. "I'll let you know if we find him."

Will shut the door and locked it, and then took Barbara's hand and walked back into the screened porch where their drinks waited.

"So that settles it," he said, with a grin. "They haven't caught the man yet, so you have to stay here tonight."

Feigning disappointment, Barbara said, "That's too bad."

The End

Epilogue

The next morning Jimmy Deluga stole a car, which a fisherman had conveniently left parked where the Mooslikamoosuc River went under the highway, and headed south. By the time the fisherman walked out of the woods, hoping to drive to town for lunch at Big Bear Restaurant, Jimmy was two states away.

*

A week after the stitches were removed from his wounds, Shawn asked Amy to marry him and she readily agreed. The large size of the engagement ring's diamond surprised her and she insisted he had spent too much of his hard earned money. Shawn just smiled.

*

Kim packed up her things and drove to Idaho, where she met a man a year younger than her while fishing on the St. Maries River. He rapidly learned to let her catch all the big fish and by the next spring they had bought a small home together in Sandpoint.

*

After a series of viciously critical newspaper articles, United Eastern Power announced the burying of their power lines and fired Robert Henderson, all in the same day.

Frank Atkins purchased a small coffee shop downstate near his home, bought a dog, and took up bird hunting, all of which made his wife very happy.

*

Cindy Hammond stayed in Fenton and started a company that shipped fresh locally grown produce to New York City and Boston. A year later she and John Johansson married and moved to a small home on the outskirts of town. There she learned to grow her own vegetables and even raised a few chickens.

*

Suzy Toll never returned to Fenton, but went to beautician school in south Florida and eventually married a man who owned a liquor store in Ft. Lauderdale. Brian Toll lived with his uncle until he finished high school, then, after a stint in the Army, went back to school to earn a degree in Wildlife Biology, eventually becoming a Fish and Game officer in Wyoming.

*

The following fall, Will and Barbara married in a simple ceremony atop the wooden bridge over the river beyond his home. Their combined properties created the largest farm in Fenton.

*

Ethan got a pony.

Jerry Allen grew up west of Boston as the landscape changed from rural to suburban, so to escape he moved to northern New England and worked as a logger for the now defunct Brown Company. Spending all his time in the woods, he developed a love for bird hunting and gun dogs.

Eventually Jerry moved back to his hometown, where he planned to help run a family business, but the bustling community felt so different from the sleepy one he remembered that he felt like a fish out of water. To fill free time he took up sailing, and in the late eighties sailed to the Caribbean and called it home for ten years, working as a yacht carpenter and starting to write.

But Jerry's strong New England roots called him back again, so he threw out the anchor and he built a cabinetmaking and boat carpentry shop. Since then he's have been traipsing his old grouse and woodcock haunts throughout the Northeast every chance that he gets, accompanied with two German Wirehaired Pointers.

Made in the USA
Middletown, DE
13 November 2020